I0603866

I RAN AWAY TO EVIL

BOOK 1

Mystic Neptune

All rights reserved. No part of this publication may be reproduced, stored in a retrieval system, or transmitted in any form or by any means electronic, mechanical, photocopying, recording, or otherwise without prior written permission from Podium Publishing.

This is a work of fiction. Names, characters, places, and incidents are either products of the author's imagination or used fictitiously. Any resemblance to actual events, locales, or persons, living, dead, or undead, is entirely coincidental.

Copyright © 2024 by Jessica Marie McIntosh

Cover design by MsArtsy
Interior illustrations by Leah Zink and Arturo Gómez Martínez

ISBN: 978-1-0394-5422-4

Published in 2024 by Podium Publishing
www.podiumaudio.com

To cozy fantasy and found family.
And my tea goblets; for these things bring me joy.

The
Empire of Sands
Hollow
Nilh
Peldeep
Gren's
Keep

The Untamed Ice Fields
Depths of Despair
North Sumbria
Thistlecrick
Servalt
oria
Kith Bog
Sumbria

I RAN AWAY
TO EVIL

Welcome to Dungeon Delves and Debutantes

Buzz.

New notification.

[Season Two: Dungeon Delves and Debutantes]
[*Welcome back to the World of Valaria, an Open-World Battle Otome RPG for the ages.*]
[In Season One, our Heroine Henrietta has worked hard to kill the Dark Overlord, King Monfort, and defeat his minions.]
[After overcoming her traumatic past with the help of her love interests, she finally picked a partner for Grand Duchess Calisto's Spring Ball . . . but is she ready to take the next step?]
[Season Two features three new ikemen love interests, new dungeons, and new crafting material. But beware the threat of revenge from the Dark Enchanted Forest!]
[Come back to your favorite Heroine with even more Dungeons, Dragons, and Debutantes!]

"Ooh! It's finally out. I've been waiting so long. Time to hurry home and—"
Screeeeech.
Bang!
"Oh my God! Did that truck just hit someone?"

CHAPTER 1

Gosh-Darned Isn't Very Vicious

Henrietta

"How can you be so naive, Henri?" my father, King Simon Doryn of Drendil, nearly spat at me in frustration. Not an uncommon occurrence. "If I've told you once, I've told you a thousand times:

"People are tools, and you're a fool for trusting them."

"People are tools, and I'm a fool for trusting them," I quoted him under my breath as he spoke, resisting the urge to roll my eyes. Not proper behavior for a warrior crown princess and all that.

He continued. "That is why you can't show mercy to the lesser folk, Henri. They will simply walk all over you."

So said my father, crushing the hand of a maid under his boot. She'd had the misfortune of spilling tea on the breakfast table. Thank goodness she wasn't screaming or making a fuss; that would have set father off. Nothing I said was going to save her, but I still tried. I even took a different approach this time!

"Father, you are absolutely right. This gosh-darned maid is keeping you from your morning audience and needs to be punished for insulting the royal family." I was never the best at being vicious; who said *gosh-darned*? Oh well. I continued. "Let me show you what I'm capable of and leave her punishment to me."

[You have attempted to use the Skill: **Bureaucracy**. You have succeeded.]

And against all odds, it worked. My father stopped stepping on the poor woman and looked me up and down. "Are you finally going to stop being useless and take your duties seriously? How much did we sacrifice to raise you as the heir, and you only understand now? You . . ."

I bit my lip and thought of other things as father continued a long-repeated diatribe of my faults.

They didn't really have a *choice* but to make me the heir. I was their only child, and my cousin Francis couldn't add two numbers together. He was twenty-seven, nine years older than me, and they'd given up on him long before I was even born . . . and so, I had been trained as the son my father could never have.

If you counted being locked in a closet when I didn't sit still *training*.

Granted, sword lessons were pretty princely, and after a decade of intensive study by the best of the best, I could honestly say that my skills were first class. I also had some royal treasures that gave neat bonus modifiers.

I was still a disappointment for not unlocking the [Magic] skill, but I just couldn't focus long enough for spellcasting. It was easier to get thrown into a dungeon and fight until I passed out. Memorizing complex formulae wasn't my cup of tea . . .

"Do you understand, Henri?"

I had gotten distracted and not followed along at all, so I simply said, "Yes, Father. I'll deal with this bug, and you'll never see her again. I promise."

"See that you do," he said. And I was suddenly left alone with a crying maid bleeding on the carpet. She looked up at me with terror.

"So." I tried to smile naturally, but probably looked like I was sucking on lemons. I mentally counted the coins in my pocket and wondered whether it would make for a good severance package. "Want me to let you out the West Gate or the south one?"

"Henri!" Queen Thalia screeched with a voice like a particularly obnoxious tea kettle. "Henri, get down here *this instant!*"

My mother was kinder than my father. She would ruin your life but still leave you with it.

You suffered more that way.

I jumped the second-floor banister unceremoniously and landed gently in the mezzanine of the Royal Suite. The maid sent to fetch me was still only half-way up the grand stair.

My mother was in the Tulip Parlor. I entered just in time to cut off a third loud summons.

"Yes, Mother, I'm here."

"Your lapel is crooked." She frowned, glaring me up and down. "If you can't be beautiful, you can at least be tidy."

"Sorry, Mother."

"Honestly, dear, you will need to look the part when you leave. We can't have anyone speaking ill of the royal family because you can't keep up appearances."

One word stood out. When Mother summoned me, it was always important to listen carefully to discover the exact reason. Sometimes, it got lost in between all of the helpful recommendations she gave me on how I could be a better version of, well, *me*.

"Leave?"

"Your father just announced it on the King's Crystal." Queen Thalia's eyes smiled a moment of genuine happiness, and my heart hurt. Not for the first time, I wished I'd been born with her gorgeous raven-black hair or blue eyes. She had high cheekbones and a cut beauty that made anyone look twice.

Not to say I was ugly, mind. I liked to think my fluffy brown hair and soft brown eyes made me perfectly respectable.

Mother snapped open her fanciest fan and hid her smile. "Our kingdom is still struggling with the Dark Magician King. His evil golems have been spotted patrolling our borders closer than ever, and something must be done."

The Dark Magician King, also known as Evil Overlord, Dark Overlord, His Royal Viciousness, or Arcane Sage Keith Monfort of Nilheim, had ruled the Dark Enchanted Forest for as long as I could remember. He'd actually come to my tenth birthday party and cursed one of the palace fountains to pour blood instead of water. I'd thought that was really something, but Mother had fainted.

Apparently, Keith hadn't liked the assassins my father had sent him.

"So, what must be done?"

"Your chance to redeem yourself," Mother said. "The court astrologer [Divined] that *you* will be our hero to vanquish the Dark Lord."

"I have to kill King Keith?" This was madness. "But what if I fail? I'm barely a level sixty Sword Master, and nowhere near a Sword Saint! Isn't he a level eighty Arcane Sage?"

"If you fail, then you wasted all the benefits we gave you growing up." Mother sniffed. "Your cousin married last year, and we've received good news. Even if Francis proved too dumb to train, I'm sure his son won't fail us."

Ah. I guess that was that, then. Time to pack my bags. I had a feeling if I fought this, I'd find poison in my food or a bag on my head as they physically threw me into enemy lines.

I chose to walk out of there on my own two feet. I'd take my chances with any number of Dark Lords over my mother.

CHAPTER 2

So You're Here to Kill Me?

Keith

Keith Monfort, level eighty-three Arcane Sage, also known as the Shadow Magician, Evil Overlord, Dark Lord, His Royal Viciousness, and the ruler of the Dark Enchanted Forest of Nilheim, had *not* been expecting to be interrupted.

The magic circle [Animate Large Construct: Golem] that he'd been working on for *six hours* rebounded in a wave of energy as his skill backfired. He staggered back from the force of the mana explosion as it ripped at the edges of his consciousness, hitting him with an unreasonable amount of damage. He was lucky the construct hadn't outright exploded into a thousand pieces and finished him off. He was doubly thankful for the extra protective properties imbued in his desk.

Keith ripped off his glasses, massaging his temple and the roaring headache now beating against his skull. He turned his attention to his notifications window.

[Error! Skill: ++**Construct Creation: Large** requirement Perk: **Pure Concentration** has failed. You take base mana cost x3 modifier damage to Health and cannot attempt another Skill: **Construct Creation** until Well Rested.]
[Warning! Your Health has dropped below 10%]
[Warning! You have **Mana Burn**. You will continue to burn mana until you Rest. Mana burned at 1/3 base rate due to Arcane Sage Perk: **Slow Burn**.]
[You have 01:28:10 until Death by **Mana Burn**.]
[You have 01:28:09 until Death by **Mana Burn**.]
[You have 01:28:08 until Death by **Mana Burn**.]

Keith closed his notifications tab.

Nothing he did was going to get rid of the [Mana Burn] headache until he crawled into bed and slept until he was [Well Rested] . . . but he could certainly get rid of the person making that infernal knocking!

Keith tore open the door and found a petite woman with fluffy brown hair standing there. She was dressed in expensive adventuring attire, and she was holding a sheathed sword awkwardly by the body, strap dangling.

"Um." She blushed lightly and looked over his disheveled form. Keith wasn't one to button all his buttons—it got hot making golems—and tight-fitting clothes were useless when [Crafting]. He leaned on the door and looked down at the woman expectantly.

She coughed. "Greetings, King Keith. I'm the hero." She lifted up her sword as if to prove it. "And I've been sent to kill you."

"I don't understand." Keith looked past the woman and found none of his automatons patrolling the hallway. His lizardkin minions weren't allowed in the inner sanctum, but he couldn't see how they would have let her over the moat, through the dark fortress, and down the only hallway into his personal domain without any bloodshed. Had she sneaked past them? Or had they been summoned away and disposed of? Keith would need to summon his necromancer back from holidays early.

"I'm sorry. I've been sent—"

"No. I don't understand how *you*"—he waved a hand at her clothes, dusty from travel but without the telltale sign of blood or guts. He also noticed that she smelled absolutely delicious; like freshly baked cinnamon cookies—"defeated my constructs and killed my—"

"Oh, I haven't killed anyone!" The hero shook her head vigorously, looking downright appalled at the idea. "No, I just had lunch with your guards before they decided to let me fight you. They were wonderful company."

"What?"

"Oh, I'm sorry, are you hard of hearing? I HAVEN'T KILLED ANYONE!"

"I heard you just fine!" He flinched as her loud voice set off waves of pain through his body. Keith rubbed the bridge of his nose again and waved a hand for her to please stop. He hurriedly asked, "So you're here to kill me? Alone?"

Maybe it was the headache, but nothing she said made sense.

"No, I don't think I'll be able to *kill* you. You're an Arcane Sage! A *Sage*! I'm just a Sword Master." The woman sighed sadly. "You must be twenty levels higher than I am, at *least*."

Keith resisted the urge to say "I don't understand" again. Maybe it was the [Mana Burn] addling his mind, but he couldn't think of any words for this ridiculous creature.

The silence stretched on until she said, "So, um, should we fight in here? Or outside? I don't want to damage your property. That would be rude."

CHAPTER 3

Bridge Trolls Are a Delight

Henrietta

This wasn't going very well.

Sure, I'd somehow walked past all the automata patrolling the border, the highway, the village, and even the castle without them attacking me. I was thankful; I didn't want to fight them. I didn't want to fight anyone!

Especially when I could be touring the Dark Enchanted Forest and appreciating the sights instead. Seriously, this place was great! On the first day, I'd seen trees walking around, unicorn hordes blessing a lake, a dragon napping on a picnic blanket the size of an inn beside said lake, and dire wolves.

I had decided to set up camp close to the dragon, and while the dire wolves had woken me up in the middle of the night, they had steered clear of the fire-breathing lizard beside me.

It seemed human flesh wasn't worth waking up a dragon.

Then, in the morning, I'd met my first troll. Bridge trolls were a delight, and Gerda's riddles were hilarious.

What room had no windows or doors?

A *mushroom*! Brilliant!

The two of us had ended up having breakfast together, and Gerda had even let me use her kitchen. I might have been in there for a few hours longer than I should've been . . . but I loved baking, and the bimbleberry scones had come out particularly nice.

At least the lizardkin agreed.

When they'd seen me walk into the castle without activating any of the defenses, the two lizardkin guards had kicked up a small fuss. They didn't want to hurt an innocent traveler—it was bad for trade. I wasn't the only human in the dark woods, but I was probably the only one dressed in formal Drendil attire.

And our kingdoms weren't exactly on friendly terms, since my father kept sending over assassins . . .

I'd let them know that I had been sent here to fight King Keith, but it turned out their general wasn't available, and the guards needed further instruction.

So now, I was cooling my heels in the guard barracks. While I waited, I checked my character sheet to make sure I was ready to go.

Name:	Henrietta Doryn of Drendil		
Occupation:	Warrior Crown Princess		
Level:	67		
Experience Points:	15893/16750		
Hit Points:	1809/1809		
Mana Points:	1139/1139		
Bonded Item:	Jacqueline Tiamat la Fleur		
Class:	Sword Master		
Titles:			
[Human], [Noble], [Princess], [Crown Princess], [Warrior], [Aura Knight], [Sword Master]			
Attributes:			
Strength:	67	Intelligence:	17
Dexterity:	21	Perception:	19
Constitution:	27 (+2 Artifact: Ring)	Charisma:	29 (+4 Legendary Artifact: Earring)
Skills:			
Social:	6	Etiquette:	5
Leadership:	5	Bureaucracy:	7
+Swordsmanship: Parry:	1	Sword Aura:	7

Mastery:	2		
Perks:			
Sense Ally, Sense Lies, Calming Voice, Sense Motive, True Taste, Sense Ability, Inspire, Multitask, Quick Read, Resist Poison, Quick Step, Quick Draw, Force Thrust, Bludgeoning Cut, Harvest Kill, Sword Sense, Killing Intent, Aura Blade, Death Parry.			

I also peeked at my logs to see if my [Resist Poison] was responding to the tea they'd served me.

[You have activated the Perk: **Quick Step**.]
[**Quick Step** cooldown 00:00:12]

No poison, just a cooldown from my run here. I was ready as I'd ever be . . .

It had taken two hours, the *entire* lunch break, to find someone in charge. I'd felt terrible for wasting everyone's time, so I'd offered to share my baking, my basket full with enough scones to go around.

We chatted while we ate, and everyone was *really* nice.

"This is excellent, Princesss." Sithli, a lizardman with red-tinted scales and a long black ponytail, happily munched away at his bimbleberry scone. "I'd like a recipe for my kin in Kith Bog. My wife is with child, and often requestsss sconesss."

"Unfortunately, I've been sent to fight King Keith and probably won't make it back alive, but if I *do* survive, I'd love to visit your home!" I said, pleased that my baking was going over so well. "I'm not usually allowed in the kitchen at home, so I've never written down any of my recipes. I couldn't have Mother find them, or I'd get punished for baking in my spare time."

"That is unacceptable! Your mother punishesss you for baking in your ssspare time?" Chikli spoke over a mouthful of his own bimbleberry scone. He was larger than Sithli, with darker green scales and a short gray mohawk. His accent was less pronounced. "That is very disrespectful. It is your free time; you should be able to do with it what you will."

"That's right," Sithli put in. "You shouldn't follow ordersss from sssomeone who doesn't respect you and your time."

"But they are my parents," I tried to explain. "I'm supposed to listen to my parents. I know in some of the other kingdoms, children come of age at sixteen, but in Drendil, it's nineteen. They're still my legal guardians!"

"That is barbaric," Sithli said. "You mean to say that sssomeone can drink, join the army, or apprentice at a job, but they ssstill need a guardian?"

I nodded. "Anything that needs a signature: marriage, education, and career are all still controlled by my parents until my birthday this year."

"And they say we are cruel for abandoning our young at twelve." Chikli clicked his tongue. "Better to learn how to be responsible for yourself than to never make any important choicesss until you are old."

I didn't think either of these models were particularly great, but I also wasn't a lizardkin.

I was sad when news came that I could go in and challenge the Dark Overlord, but I had to do this. My whole life had been spent training to be a warrior for my king's use . . . even if my king was also my dad who wanted me dead.

Oh well, better to die a hero and all that. Finally be of use.

I bet my death would be reason enough for a war, and my father *loved* war.

Still, I hadn't been expecting a partially undressed Dark Lord squinting up at me over a cup of tea instead of over my dead body.

Seriously, why was everyone in this kingdom so nice?

I Would Be Disappointed
If I Had to Kill You

Keith

[You have 01:02:46 until Death by **Mana Burn**.]

"So let me get this straight. You were forced to train as a hero, even though you hate fighting. You leveled all the way up to Sword Master because your parents wanted a warrior heir, and I'm supposed to conveniently dispose of you to hopefully start a war?" Keith paraphrased.

He stared at the mysterious creature sitting across from him at the tea table, taking a sip of his hot cup of nettle tea, full of honey and cream, to calm his nerves. And then he noticed that Princess Henrietta Doryn of Drendil, warrior crown princess and the only child of the king and queen of his enemy kingdom . . . was staring longingly at the honey and cream. She held her own plain tea but made no move to take any.

He sighed and deftly switched cups with her plain brew. A *most* mysterious creature, indeed.

"Take mine, so you know it's not poisoned," he fibbed when she looked up at him in surprise.

She gave him a cute, dimpled smile and drank the tea so happily that Keith almost smiled himself. He liked his tea like he liked his cake, and she apparently shared his taste. He took her abandoned cup and deftly added cream and honey to his newly purloined porcelain.

The princess wiped some tea from the corner of her mouth. "Honestly, I'm not sure how this happened. One minute, I was disappointing my parents, and now, I'm here disappointing you—"

"I'm not *disappointed*. I just wasn't expecting company. Though I *would* be disappointed if I had to kill you." Keith paused. "It would leave an awful mess, and my necromancer is still on holiday in North Sumbria."

"Oh, yes, that would be an inconvenience, then. Should I come back later?" she replied brightly.

"No need. I'm actually very interested in learning how you managed to bypass my automata and guards. Would you consider staying so I can research how this happened?" Keith tapped his cup with one long finger. "You're the first assassin to get this far, you know. That's something to be proud of!"

Keith didn't know how to handle an emotionally fragile princess who smelled like cookies and expected him to end her . . . but even he could recognize that she needed a bit of praise for a job well done. She *deserved* it, too.

"You really think so?" She beamed at him with the biggest, brightest eyes he'd ever seen. "I could stay and help out until your necromancer returns? Though, is it alright if I wander about the kingdom sometimes? I'd love to have tea with Gerda, and Guardsman Sithli wanted me to share my scone recipe with his wife back in Kith Bog Village."

"As long as you don't cause a ruckus or hurt my minions, I don't think that will be a problem. One moment." Keith pulled out a generic contract for a laboratory subject from one of his workroom's filing cabinets. He had a lot of contracts squirrelled away from when he was younger and experimenting on people. He'd dabbled in magical prosthetics and enhancement enchantments before settling on full automata.

Keith scribbled down an extra clause at the end of the contract:

The undersigned will do all in their power not to cause a ruckus or kill the citizens of Nilheim.

There was probably a more legal way of putting it, but Keith didn't have enough energy to care; his [Mana Burn] was still ticking down. "Here. Sign this, and you can do whatever you want until I finish my tests."

"Thank you, Your Viciousness!" The princess glanced over the contract, noted the added line, and signed.

"Don't thank me just yet." Keith flinched as her enthusiasm caused a particular stab in his migraine.

[Mana Burn] killed people. It's why it was so hard to become a high class magic user. If the damage taken didn't outright kill the caster, then they were stuck having to sleep it off immediately—or risk having their mana continue to burn away until they ran out and died—assuming the caster had enough willpower to stay awake through the headache and exhaustion. Keith had a great deal of willpower. He knew this because he had suffered from [Mana Burn] a great many times, hence why he'd set up so many defenses around his workshop. Not that his minions knew that; they were simply told to steer clear and were paid to keep things safe and clean and running. As much as he *could* pop a ludicrously expensive potion and attempt to fight Hen—the princess, he might actually die if they fought right now. Not that he was going to tell her that.

"I'll set you up with a room, and we'll run the experiments tomorrow morning," he finished.

"What about now? I have nothing else to do if I'm not trying to kill you anymore."

"No!" He coughed. "I have to finish my current golem and clear the workroom."

That was technically true, just not what he was going to be doing immediately following this conversation.

[You have 00:53:28 until Death by **Mana Burn**.]

"Alright," she agreed.

"Good." Keith ordered one of his automata to ring in the guards' room, and they waited a bit before Chikli came running. The guard seemed anxious until he spotted Henrietta drinking tea with Keith.

"My liege."

"Show my new test subject—I mean, *guest* to the Nightshade Rooms. She has free reign of the kingdom except for my inner sanctum. Also, she has a sweet tooth, so plan accordingly."

The castle kitchens were barely satisfying his desire for desserts, so a royal princess probably wouldn't be satisfied either. Then again, he didn't know what she had been allowed to eat during her hero training.

That was everything settled.

"Good day, Princess." Keith nodded regally and swooshed dramatically out of the room . . .

. . . and straight into bed.

CHAPTER 5

Geran Grim's Ode to the Lace Kerchief

Henrietta

Chikli, the dark-green lizardman with the short gray mohawk, escorted me to my rooms on the second floor.

"Those rooms are out of bounds," he said, pointing across the inner veranda. "They are where His Viciousnesss residesss. Be warned, an alarm will sssound if you try to enter."

"I'm staying across from King Keith?!" I shot a look at the door to his room.

"Of course. These are the finest roomsss in the castle, Princesss," Chikli boasted. He opened the door to my rooms and ushered me inside.

I had not been expecting the beauty that I beheld once I walked into the Nightshade Rooms. The floors were covered in lush green-and-gray carpets embroidered in forests with a burbling stream stitched end to end. The bed lay in the middle of the room, headboard against the right wall. It was an elegant canopy-style bed with a silver inlaid leaf motif and green canvas pulled back by light silver tassels. A double bookcase took up the left wall, and a pair of vanities hugged the window to either side.

That's right, there were *two* vanities—one for jewelry, and one for hair and makeup. Jewelry hung on wire hooks on either side of the mirror, and trays of rings, brooches and jewels were delicately arrayed on the desktop.

Even *if* I knew how to wear makeup outside of "put this on lips," the cosmetics were old, crusty, and unusable. The place had recently been properly dusted, probably in the last month or so, and it wasn't too stuffy. Chikli scratched his cheek awkwardly. He assured me that a maid would be joining us shortly, and I could stay in one of the side rooms while they freshened things up.

"It's lovely, Chikli, really," I assured him. "But where am I supposed to hang up my sword and armor?"

"You can hook your sssword on the bed frame by your pillow, Princesss," Chikli replied.

I walked over and hung up my sword where he'd recommended. Just then, there was a knock, and we turned to see a young lizardkin maid in the doorway. She was tall, far taller than Chikli, with green-and-gold scales. Her eyes were also gold, and she carried herself with grace and poise.

"This is Lilith; she'll help you get sssettled in," Chikli explained. To the maid, he said, "The princesss wishesss to ssstore her armor. I'll leave you to it." Then he bowed and excused himself.

"We can put your combat attire in the wardrobe, Your Highnesss." Lilith curtsied primly, daintily holding the tip of her long tail as she did so. She spoke as her kind always did, with a love for the letter *S*. And I loved listening to it. "I'll go through everything as sssoon as possible and set aside thingsss that will fit you. Rinrin should be back next week to fix the master's buttonsss again. We can have her alter the dresses then."

"Dresses?" I asked in confusion.

"Through here, Your Highnesss." Lilith partially pulled out a copy of *Geran Grim's Ode to the Lace Kerchief* from the double bookshelf, and the whole shelf swung open into another room teeming with articles of clothing. "These are all well out of date, I'm afraid; no one has touched them since the Mistresss passed."

I stared at the collection before me: from pantsuits to ball gowns, hats to shoes, and fans to gem-studded purses. There were even sports clothes catered to fencing and hunting and riding, all in a variety of colors and fabrics.

Even while distracted by the finery, I remembered to stop and offer my condolences. "I'm sorry for your loss. Is King Keith really alright with giving me his late wife's room?"

Lilith coughed. "Beg your pardon, Princesss. These were Queen Vera's roomsss. *Mother* to our current Dark Lord and Master."

"Really? Is it alright for me to take Queen Vera's rooms? Won't I be intruding on a place filled with memories?"

I didn't know how long this room had been left unchanged, but King Keith looked similar now to when I'd first met him at my tenth birthday party. He had that "dark and haggard with a billowing cape" kinda feel. Ageless. I wouldn't assume to know his lineage, but there had definitely been a horn peeking through his dark hair. And some of the races lived hundreds of years.

"No, Princesss." Lilith shook her head. "Our Dark Lord hasn't any attachment to these roomsss. His mother died in childbirth twenty-four yearsss ago, and he grew up without ever knowing her."

The feeling of miscommunication clicked, and I realized with some shock that Keith Monfort, Arcane Sage, Shadow Magician, Evil Overlord, Dark

Overlord, His Royal Viciousness, and the ruler of the Dark Enchanted Forest of Nilheim . . . wasn't even a decade older than I was. "Then his father?"

"Unknown. Her Eminence Feliwyn, our Dark Lord's godmother, raised His Viciousnesss, then left when he came of age."

"Is that also when my father started sending assassins?"

"Yes, Princesss." Having finished taking off and storing my armor, we left the hidden wardrobe. Lilith closed it and showed me where my private washroom hid behind a catch door between the bed and the right-side vanity. It was sparkling clean, with a golden mermaid faucet and everything else made of marble. It was a marvel.

"Her Eminence is ssstill asleep at Lake Loria," Lilith added.

"I see." And I did see. There was only one "person" I'd found sleeping at the lake. Wow. "One last question, Lilith."

"Yes, Princesss?"

"Where is the kitchen?"

Let's Not Blow Up and Almost Kill Me This Time, Alright?

Keith

Keith awoke to the dawn song, a beautiful cacophony of phoenix melody and robin chirp. Usually, he would never be awake at this ungodly hour, but the sixteen hours of sleep—*two whole rest periods*—had left him full of mana and well rested in a way his nightly magic tinkering didn't often allow.

Keith stretched and sat up. He hadn't bothered changing last night, and he'd lost another button sleeping in his long work tunic. Rinrin would tsk, but honestly, there was nothing else to be done.

Until the arachne awoke from their diapause torpor in late spring, everyone had to make do with normal thread.

He activated his automata to let the castle staff on duty know that he was awake, and Tulith entered his rooms. She and Chikli had just gotten married, and Keith had to remember to post an ad for a new maid in the next year or so. He didn't want baby lizardkin running around his experiments and getting hurt.

"Have Panlith whip up breakfast while I take a bath," he instructed. "And find me something to wear that doesn't show grease stains." His creations always needed an unreasonable amount of grease to move.

"Your Viciousnesss." Tulith curtsied low. "If you wish, I have hot breakfast ready for you. Would you like cinnamon glaze pancakesss with honey cream while you sssoak in your bubble bath? It would sssave you time for tinkering."

Keith paused. "Since when does Panlith have my breakfast ready at dawn?"

"Oh no, my lord." Tulith curtsied again. "The princesss made the pancakesss. She's been in the kitchen on and off sssince yesterday, only ssstopping to rest for the wee hoursss."

"What?" His mind hadn't caught up with him yet. The princess. The daughter of his enemy who had come to kill him yesterday. That princess. In his kitchen.

"Yesss, Your Viciousnesss. She got up and made everyone pancakesss." The maid continued. "We've had them tested, and they are not poisoned."

Not that most poisons would do anything to him. Keith prided himself on his level nine [Survivor] skill.

It would almost be better if she *had* tried to poison him, since it might level up his skill to ten and grant him a new perk. Even if it *was* something lethal, his apothecary was full of the world's most dangerous poisons—and their antidotes.

Keith gave his approval, and Tulith returned with a stunning spread, including a side of hazelberry compote and two slices of salted sizzling pork cuts. Pork was usually separated into pies, steaks, or hock, but this was delicious.

Keith waved his hand and cast three spells in quick succession.

[You have attempted to use the Perk: **Cantrips (Cleanse)**. You have succeeded.]
[You have attempted to use the Perk: **Cantrips (Burning Hand)**. You have succeeded.]
[You have attempted to use the Perk: **Cantrips (Gust)**. You have succeeded.]

He purified and heated his bath, then poured in aloe and hard olive oil soap and used air magic to swirl it around to make bubbles. He added a drop of lavender oil and settled in for a long soak.

"Panlith got the recipe?" Keith handed off his clean plate, trying to figure out what to do with his new royal guest.

"Yesss, Master." Tulith smiled and offered, "Apparently, Her Highnesss only cares about baking and sssightseeing. As per your ordersss yesterday, we let her leave this morning. She sssaid she will visit Kith Bog and return at your usual afternoon work hour."

"I see." And he was starting to see more clearly by the hour. Oh well, he needed the morning to finish the automaton and clear space for his new research subject. "Just . . . don't let her into the inner sanctum until after lunch," he ordered. He didn't think he could survive [Mana Burn] twice in so many days. "And send someone to fetch her if she doesn't return by noon."

"As you command."

Keith finished his bath and made his way to his work room. He needed to finish the golem and clean off his enchanted worktable.

When one of the treants had fallen in a duel with Knolith, General of the East, the Treefolk tribe had kept the monster core and given the body to Keith as tribute. His enchanted table was made out of the treant's wood and a collection of the most magical ingredients he could find. It was of immense assistance in his Arcane Sage practice.

Though Keith thought that classifying a sentient race like the treants as a "monster" race just because they sometimes spawned in dungeons was very *rude*.

Still, he loved his desk.

Keith opened his character sheet and checked for any notifications before beginning [Construct Creation].

Name:	Keith Monfort of Nilheim		
Occupation:	Dark Magician King		
Level:	83		
Experience Points:	7140/20750		
Hit Points:	400/400		
Mana Points:	3570/3570		
Class:	Arcane Sage		
Titles:			
[Demi], [Royal Heir], [Dark Magician King], [Construct Wizard], [Golemancer], [Overlord], [Puppet Master], [Mechanical Enchanter], [Arcane Sage]			
Attributes:			
Strength:	16	Intelligence:	85
Dexterity:	42	Perception:	19
Constitution:	25 (+1 Artifact Bracelet)	Charisma:	19
Skills:			
Craft:	3	Bureaucracy:	5
Magic:	5	++Construct Creation: Large:	9
Command:	4	Survivor:	9
Mastery:	4	Enchantment:	2

Sage:	1		
Perks:			
Steady Hand, Quick Read, Multitask, Cantrips (Burning Hand, Gust, Dancing Lights, Cleanse, Mold Earth), Quick Chant, Shape Construct, Share Senses, Deconstruction, Fuse, Repair Construct, Modify Construct, Pure Concentration, List Automata, Construct Flight, Animate Object, Basic AI, Multitool, Identify, Mind Map, Remote Access, Ventriloquism, Resist Poison, Resist Mind Manipulation, Sense Motive, Sense Enemy, Advanced AI (Sentience), Reduce Mana Cost, Imbue, Quick Buff, Slow Burn.			

Everything looked good to go. He pulled out an inkwell of troll blood ink and a griffin feather quill to freshen up yesterday's enchantments, then got to work animating his newest golem.

He had even decided on a name.

"Hey there, Delilah, let's not blow up and almost kill me this time, alright?"

CHAPTER 7

This Is Madame Potts's Cast

Henrietta

After a lovely time familiarizing myself with the kitchen, I decided to go with Sithli to Kith Bog Village to meet his family.

I could have run the distance in half the time it took the wagon, but it was nice riding with Sithli. And no one bothered you if you were riding with the Dark Lord's army.

"Truly, Your Highnesss, we have a bimbleberry patch as long as one ssside of the castle wall! Early ssspring is the best time to go picking," Sithli assured me. "And my wife will be happy for the company; she misses Lilith and Tulith sssince they got work at the castle."

"Tulith is the maid who picked up King Keith's breakfast this morning, right? Did she say if he liked it?" Few back home in Drendil knew that their crown princess enjoyed baking. I had once mistakenly given my mother homemade biscuits when I was six, and she'd locked me up in the punishment room for a day. It was an empty stone room, with no windows or lights.

I became very, very familiar with that room. So familiar that after two years of screaming and ruining my nails trying to escape, I found a secret door leading into the servant's wing and out past the castle into town!

From there, I had been able to slip out and do whatever I liked doing! I'd also made my first friend, Bronwynn; she was an apprentice bard who knew everyone. She'd even set me up with baking lessons from Jeff, the husband of a famous baker. He helped his wife as an assistant, and I helped him when I wasn't off dungeon delving to level up my Warrior class.

And since I was punished at least once a week, I'd happily spent that time living my best life.

Now, I was living my best life baking for the evil hordes.

"He licked the plate clean, as I heard it." Sithli chuckled. "And he wasn't the only one. Please share your recipesss with my wife, Princesss, and I'll gladly swear to assist you in your hour of need."

"That's sweet, Sithli, but I'm sure I'll only be around for a short time. In the meantime, I'm happy to share any of my favorite foods with you and your family. If you hadn't let me in to see His Viciousness, I don't know *what* I would have done."

The thought of fighting the lizardkin left a sour taste in my mouth.

"It was our pleasure, Princesss," Sithli said. We turned a corner and suddenly found ourselves looking out over a beautiful wooden hut village built into and over the swampland. Wooden roads on stilts high above the soggy grass kept our wagon from getting bogged down in the . . . bog.

Sithli continued. "The gate golem didn't attack, and we figured that our most illustriousss and powerful Dark Lord would want to know right away if any foreign royalsss came to duel. It's all the rage in North Sumbria these days, you know! Our ordersss are to never enter the inner sssanctum, so as a royal, it seemed only right to let you deliver your challenge in person."

"Oh, um . . ." I realized how my declaration of, "I'm here to fight Lord Keith!" might have been taken the wrong way. I should have said something like, "I'm the hero, come to end the evil Dark Overlord cursing our lands!" or something like that.

Just another way I failed at being a proper hero.

Also, maybe I should've taken off the adorable hedgehog-print apron Gerda had given me and put down my basket of bimbleberry scones before making my challenge.

I'd taken them off before seeing King Keith, at least!

Anyway.

"Sithli, my love!" A very pregnant lizardkin who wobbled while she walked hurried over to meet us. She had beautiful golden slit eyes and darker magenta-and-green scales.

"Milith, how are you?" My lizardman friend jumped down and wrapped an arm around his wife to steady her. "I've brought someone to break bread with."

"I'm Henrietta," I said, unhitching the alligator-dog bog beast that was pulling our wagon. I led it into a muddy stable and settled it in. One of King Keith's automata looked at us from its half-sunken state near the town entrance, but it didn't otherwise react. I gave it a wide berth. "I promised Sithli some scone recipes in exchange for a tour of the village."

"A foodie?" Milith raised an eyebrow, smiling. "You'll want to try out Dithba's Laire. She is our kin's best."

With our things stowed, I happily followed after the pair while they explained why Dithba's twisted flake loaf was to die for. Namely, it was folded in garlic and cheese.

We reached the village square when the Village Crystal lit up.

Hello, this is Madame Potts.
This week's events are in! February edition.
There will be a special drop in the Depths of Despair Dungeon, on the third floor.
Crit rates in the Dungeon Valley Crest will have a +5% bonus if you are wearing red from now until the new moon.
Anyone interested in Grand Duchess Calisto's Spring Ball, you should have received your invites by now.
Marquess Dorset of the kingdom of Servalt *is* the slave trader you are looking for. Please catch him before he attacks the Filla Orphanage.
The king of Drendil has ordered the crown princess to go kill King Keith—or die trying! Luckily, mass murder has been avoided.
Peldeep's Lunar New Year will spark an interesting event this month: couples who confess in front of Julia's Grotto will have matching tattoos appear on their hands that can only be washed off with water steeped in Julia apple-tree blossoms.
This is Madame Potts, signing off.

Wow, Madame Potts's Cast had some really useful tips this time! It was odd that wearing red would give extra damage in Dungeon Valley Crest, but Madame Potts was almost never wrong. And even then, she only ever failed if someone worked hard to change her future predictions.

Five years ago, she had taken the continent by storm when all the Cast Crystals had lit up and Madame Potts's voice had emerged.

Hello? Can anyone hear this?
Sorry to hack into the Crystal Cast Network, but there's going to be a dungeon break in Frisia unless someone can find and clear it.
I would start the search on the southwest side of Mount Seagirt for the dungeon entrance.

The Mages Tower had been inundated with outrage that someone had *hacked*—which presumably meant illegally connected to—everyone's Cast Crystals . . . until an adventurer had followed the lead and found Dungeon

Malik on Mount Seagirt. The place had been teeming with ghouls and just mere days from a dungeon break.

It had been a near thing that could have wiped Frisia from the map.

Lizardkin from around Kith Bog had come out to listen to the crystal. They crowded around the village square talking about the predictions in various levels of curiosity and outrage.

Milith shook her head. "That King Simon never learnsss. Why doesss he throw away resourcesss attacking our lord like that? It's just foolishnesss, is what it isss."

"Masss murder?" Sithli stared at me in horror.

I blushed. "I mean . . . I was sent here to *kill* King Keith. I wasn't expecting everyone would just, you know, welcome me in and escort me to the inner sanctum!"

Sithli stared at me harder, reaching an arm around Milith.

"I'm not gonna suddenly mass murder everyone now!" I defended, a touch loudly. People turned to look at us, so I added, "Madame Potts said so herself! It's been *avoided*."

Milith, who caught on quickly, cut in. "So *you're* the crown princesss?"

She looked over my high-quality, warm and soft green lady's hunting tunic and lace-up floral print boots. All articles I'd found in the late queen's wardrobe.

"It's a long story," I said. Then I spotted a beautiful wooden sign hanging from a log shop with Dithba's Laire scrawled on it. I motioned toward our destination. "Wanna talk about it over garlic-and-cheese twists?"

CHAPTER 8

So Don't Be a Hero

Keith

"Is she back yet?" Keith pushed up his glasses and surveyed his clean work-room. They'd even managed to get the bloodstains out with some good, old-fashioned baking soda and vinegar. Sure, it had taken two treatments, but that was Tulith's job.

He'd finished Delilah, a defense-based golem with enhanced construction, and imbued it with [Sense Enemy]. It'd been immediately sent out to the western field. Then he'd just sat around refilling his mana pool while Tulith made his workspace presentable for experimenting on the princess.

Not that he was cleaning things for the princess, mind. Just that it would be easier to interrogate her while she wasn't sitting on a bloody, oily, arcane wooden bench.

That was the *only* reason.

"The princess was spotted entering the castle not too long ago." Tulith came back from disposing of the cleaning materials and brought with her a platter of snacks. She held it for the Dark Lord to nibble on as he contemplated dark things. "She was carrying two hampersss: one full of bimbleberriesss, and the other full of garlic."

"Garlic?" The Dark Lord scrunched his nose in distaste. "What dish requires berries and *garlic*?"

"I don't know, Master," Tulith said. "But you may ask her yourself; I can sssmell her approaching."

Henrietta peeked in through the open door before marching in with her head high and shoulders back, looking regal. Somewhere, she'd acquired new clothes, and the dark-green pants under the decorative, layered white-and-light-green hunting tunic suited her. The pant string on her waist bunched up, as the pants weren't exactly the right fit, but it worked well nonetheless. Her moment of poise was ruined when her stomach growled.

She blushed. "My apologies; [Quick Step] always leaves me hungry, and I didn't have time for lunch, excepting the bimbleberries."

"You can snack on this while I ask you some questions and run my first series of tests." Lord Keith motioned Tulith forward with her tray of cucumber sandwiches, candied fruit, sausages, and unigoat brie. Keith had already eaten the honey scones.

Henrietta looked beside herself with appreciation as she picked up a tiny sandwich.

Keith tried to ignore her adorable facial expressions and turned away to get his scanning tools. "First, we will determine how you got through my minions, then we will see your effect on my constructs. Take a seat on the worktable, please."

He'd been given a confusing report from the guards and read it twice before giving up and going back to tinkering. He could get information from the princess and then summon Chikli to his office that night if his tests were unsatisfactory.

He patted his work desk twice, and the princess jumped up to sit comfortably on its smooth, clean surface.

"Oh, um, I actually found out why I got past the lizardkin guards so easily," the princess tentatively offered. "At least, probably."

"You did?" Keith raised an eyebrow. He'd been reaching for a serrated knife set but changed his direction to a small carving knife hanging from an ornate display case. "Tell me more."

"It's all my fault." She slumped forward, looking miserable. "I am a terrible Hero of Justice."

"So don't be a hero."

"Pardon?"

Keith grabbed a quill and a tray of various ink bottles. He mixed a few together on a small seashell and put everything beside the carving blade. "If you want to be a hero, that's fine, but it's your parents forcing an identity on you without accepting your own preferences, am I right?"

"I mean, it's best for the kingdom if the heir is strong and manly . . ."

"Sounds sexist to me. Half of the Valarian continent is ruled by women. Even if you aren't counting Their Royal Highness Rowen of Peldeep, who switches between man, woman, or other at the drop of their fox tail." Keith shook his head and tsked. "So aside from your parents wanting a son and forcing you into some half-cocked princely mold, you've no other attachment to being a hero?"

" . . ."

"As I said," Keith continued when there was no ready response, "just don't be a hero."

Babble bubbled up and spilled out of her. "It's not that I don't like being a hero, and I *know* that a princess is just as good as a prince. I know women and men level up equally, so there isn't a difference between your Strength level sixty and my Strength level sixty—"

"*Sixty?*" Keith did a double take and looked the princess over slowly. She didn't seem to notice.

"—and I know girls can rule with an iron fist. Grand Duchess Calisto of North Sumbria is so tyrannical that her nobles don't get to keep *any* of their collected tax money. They have to put it into *infrastructure*. It gives my father a hernia just talking about it . . . but I don't like complicated magical memorization or killing people or backstabbing politics. I just want to go for long walks and meet interesting people and bake. Is that too much—" She cleared her throat. "Sorry, just give me a minute, and I'll pull myself together. What were we talking about again?"

"You." Keith took the empty tray of snacks from her and handed it off to Tulith, who disappeared out the door. "We were talking about you."

"Oh."

Keith waved a hand, and Henrietta lay down on the table. He dropped his brush in the ink and began drawing arcane symbols. The first spell was first level, requiring no concentration on his part.

"So tell me more."

CHAPTER 9

Who Could Turn Down a Free Back-Pain Relief Potion?

Henrietta

"You want me to talk about *me*? But I'm annoying—Wait, of course, you still need to know about the guards." I stared up at Keith from the table. It was probably foolish to let the Dark Overlord cast spells on me, but he could kill me any time he wanted, and there wasn't much point in fighting when I'd volunteered. I explained what I'd learned that morning. "When the castle's gate golem didn't attack me, everyone assumed I was just here to challenge you to a normal duel. They're all the rage in North Sumbria, or so I'm told."

"Really?" Keith looked taken aback, but he continued to carefully brush the spell around my shoulder.

"So said Sithli, and he knows a lot about it, since his brother Sethli moved there last summer." I resisted the urge to turn my head and watch him as Keith circled the worktable. It was a surprisingly nice worktable, and very comfortable to lie on. It was also the exact right size for me . . . Come to think of it, I was pretty sure this table had a house-sized golem on it when I was here yesterday. Best not to question a Dark Lord's table, though. "Did you know that Grand Duchess Calisto allows anyone with a certified trade registry to compete in a test to immigrate? Even apprentices!"

"I did not." Keith grimaced. "And I don't care to have my skilled workers poached like that. What could she have possibly offered them that was incentive enough?"

"Free health care." Just saying it left me in awe. My father would have had an aneurysm. "And a five-day work week."

"Pathetic," Keith scoffed, continuing to ink down the other side of my body. "*My* minions have a four-day work week. Everyone in the Dark Enchanted Forest knows that. *And* we have a necromancer who resurrects them or reanimates them in case of accidents. If it's reported fast enough, they can be revived with no side effects whatsoever."

"Still, who could turn down a free back-pain relief potion?" I said. Even growing up a royal, we didn't have very many pain relief potions—or maybe *I* just didn't have any. Mother was always saying things like, "Life isn't about having fun; it's about persevering through pain and suffering," or "If you thought having a broken arm was bad, you should try wearing heels instead of those ugly training boots."

Though now that I thought about it . . . a broken arm might actually be more painful? And Mother did have a personal royal apothecary that produced other potions at her leisure.

But I digressed.

Keith looked contemplative as he completed the ink trail down my side and around my feet. He looked away while he drew between my legs, up to my knees and back down again.

Leave it to an Arcane Sage to not even need to watch what they were doing while inking out a spell!

Keith finished connecting the circle of spell script with a flourish, then put aside his ink and brush. His eyes looked off in the distance, probably checking his character sheet or notification tab. A moment later, Tulith stepped into the doorway, waiting for direction.

"Send a group of raiders into North Sumbria and gather up any wayward minions who haven't already passed the duchy's citizenship exams," he ordered. "Also, Rufus should have just returned this morning. Find him and send him out to get me no less than three healers. I want it done by this time next week."

"Yesss, Your Viciousnesss." Tulith curtsied. "Right away, Your Viciousnesss."

"Well, that's settled." Keith smiled down at me. A very toothy smile. He had nice teeth.

I hesitated but asked, "You aren't going to drag back the ones who passed Grand Duchess Calisto's test? Why?"

If my father discovered that his taxable subjects had run off to another land, he would cry treason and haul them all back kicking and screaming. Then he would make a few into examples so it didn't happen again.

"Paperwork," Keith announced.

"What?"

"You heard me." The Dark Overlord shuddered. "My illustrious northern neighbor is a *sadist*, and her favorite thing to do is to send me large swathes of foreign rights and trade requisitions mixed with incredibly tempting intellectual tidbits. Do you think I could touch *anyone* who's completed the immigration registration into North Sumbria without having to go through a wagonload of bureaucracy for the trouble?"

"But you're the *Dark Overlord*!"

"I'm still king of Nilheim, ruler of the Dark Enchanted Forest. I can take time to master magic and create golems and foil assassinations because my carefully crafted system of oppression requires a *reasonable* amount of paperwork."

"I see." It made sense when he put it that way.

"Another reason for the four-day work week. Magic is my hobby, not my job." Keith waved at the ink surrounding me, and it began to glow. "Are you ready, Princess?"

I braced myself. "Ready as I'll ever be."

He smiled again. "Don't worry. This should only hurt a lot."

CHAPTER 10

This Was Going to Be a Lot of Work

Keith

Keith pulled out the teacup he'd given Henrietta just after her arrival the previous day. He held it up over the princess and used his free hand to continue manipulating mana into the spell script. Then he cast the spell by whispering a single word under his breath.

[You have attempted to use the Perk: **Quick Chant**.
You have succeeded.]
[You have attempted to use the Skill: **Magic**. You have succeeded.]
[You have attempted to use the Perk: **Sense Motive**.
You have succeeded.]

In order to test how Henrietta had been feeling during her arrival the previous day, Keith had inscribed an enchantment to connect her with something that she had interacted with. Namely, the teacup.

Keith used the [Imbue] perk to give each and every one of his creations [Identify], which revealed parts of the target's character sheet information, and [Sense Motive], which measured a person's killing intent.

They would scan the kingdom for trespassers and react appropriately. If an identified individual was not a citizen of the Dark Enchanted Forest of Nilheim, they were automatically scanned with [Sense Motive] and removed. Their motive, combined with how willingly they accepted removal, determined how dead they were when they arrived at the border crossing.

The advanced spell cast on Keith's defense golems reacted to any form of harmful intent toward his minions or his person, and to a lesser extent, his lands.

The thing about an enchanted forest, and a Dark Enchanted Forest at that, was that the land could take care of itself.

Keith expected only a little screaming as his spell activated, connecting the teacup and Henrietta. The mana would give her a shock equivalent to the strength of any killing intent.

He waited, but there was no screaming. There was also no zap.

"Princess . . ."

"Yes?"

"Did you *not* intend to break into my castle, fight my guards, and then kill me?" Keith walked around his magical worktable, looking for any sign of a response to his spell. It should have lit up the part of her body that she intended to attack with. For example, a politician would use her words or mouth, and a swordswoman would use her sword arm. There was nothing except the glow of his own enchantment on the table.

"Well." Henrietta shrugged awkwardly under his scrutiny but appeared otherwise unaffected. "I did intend to enter your castle, but I was hoping the guards wouldn't want to fight. They would get hurt! And I did intend to fight you to the death—my death. I mean, you're a *Sage*. The best I could do was maybe draw my blade before you roasted me." She then added as an aside, "I wear silk. I'm very flammable."

"I see." Keith had said that a lot these past couple days. "So your true intention wasn't to kill me or my minions, but to die a heroine's death?"

She had the grace to blush. "Maybe?"

"Well"—Keith contemplated his adorable enspelled princess—"that's unfortunate for you."

"Why?"

"Because now I have to run a few more tests." Keith broke the spell. "And when I'm done, you're getting locked up with Rufus in the dungeon."

"Didn't you just send Rufus out on a mission to find some healers?" Henri sat up and stretched, a single strand of her fluffy hair falling forward, begging to be tucked behind an ear.

Keith cursed and turned away to grab his spell-script materials.

"Then we'll finish my tests, and you can get locked up with Rufus when he gets back." He pulled down a few different bottles of ink and mixed them together. "In the meantime, you'll be my prisoner. Don't leave the castle grounds unless I say so."

"Alright!" the princess readily agreed, and Keith wanted to shake her for her lack of self-preservation . . . but it was better this way. He couldn't have her going off somewhere and trying to commit suicide for her parents' war. If she wanted to die for herself, that was one thing, but right now, he didn't think the princess knew herself well enough to make that decision. And his necromancer was *still* on holiday.

This was going to be a lot of work.

Keith finally understood why his automaton hadn't reacted and delt with Henrietta when she'd first arrived. And to a lesser extent, he understood why his minions had let her into the castle.

Chikli's report on how excited everyone was for their ruler to be met in honorable combat had been an about turn from the usual kill-it-with-fire attitude his minions *usually* had to assassins. It was still unbelievable that a hedgehog apron and a smiling princess had swayed his guards, but his tests on the golems had finally put all the pieces together.

His tight security procedures had been bypassed by carefree innocence, some freshly baked scones, and a series of polite misunderstandings.

And everyone in the castle had been over the moon that Keith had been challenged to a royal duel. Like it was a good thing! They had just been so proud that their king had been included.

In the end, he'd told them that any duel requests were to be submitted to his office, and the challenger shown to a guest room—even if they were visiting royalty.

Especially if they were visiting royalty.

This was the kind of foolishness that got put into storybooks, when the pure-hearted hero somehow managed to defeat the Dark Lord with the power of love or some other utter nonsense.

He was of a mind to act as a proper Dark Lord and do something befitting the title to show his minions that he required obedience. That when he told them to let no one into his inner sanctum, he meant *no one* . . . but that sounded like work, and he was off for the day.

When he finally finished testing the princess, he bid her goodbye, and then summoned Tulith again.

"Rufus has left already, hasn't he?" Keith took off his glasses and massaged his temple.

"Yesss, Your Viciousnesss."

"Sigh. And no word yet from Chloe?"

"I assume the necromancer will be gone for the rest of the month, Your Viciousnesss."

He actually sighed this time. "I'll need you to find a way to distract the princess until Rufus returns," Keith instructed.

"If I may, Dark Lord," Tulith replied. "I believe I have just the thing."

Keith nodded. "Alright, I'll leave it to you."

CHAPTER 11

His Viciousnesss Would Never Deny Someone Their Freedom of Speech

Henrietta

When King Keith told me I would be held prisoner for a week, I assumed he meant in the dungeon. I could handle being locked up in a dungeon much better than being locked up in a dark room, so I accepted my fate.

That was not the case however.

Instead, I continued my stay in the Nightshade Rooms, but with a full-time maid. Technically four maids, since everyone worked half days and only four days a week. I got along best with Lilith. She was brilliant at tying my apron in a way that made it not slip or come undone. The lizardkin woman was also a fair hand at sewing and had tailored some of Queen Vera's clothing to fit me.

Everything still looked two decades out of fashion, but at least I didn't need to wear the same traveler's kit I'd walked here in.

All in all, my time locked up in the castle had been very productive.

"Princesss! Your phyllo-pastry garlic-cheese pull-apart was deliciousss." Tulith entered the kitchen with a clean tray, again.

Ah, music to my ears; Keith liked my food! Having the most evil man on the continent, master of all lizardkin and trolls and the dark woods, eat my food every day and *like it* was such a novelty. One that I didn't think would grow old anytime soon.

"Thank you for letting me know, Tulith," I said. "And thank you for delivering my mail to my room."

"Think nothing of it, Princesss." The maid smiled a toothy grin. "It was fortuitousss that Madame Potts's Cast last week included your change of addresss, else you might have missed your invite to Grand Duchesss Calisto's ball!"

"I actually *did* miss my invite," I explained. I was gently sifting icing powder over cooled vanilla spice cookies, and paused shortly to get it all evenly distributed before continuing. "This was a copy. She included a letter asking after my new accommodations and whether I wanted to visit for tea."

"Please let me know when you're finished with your reply," Tulith said, "and I shall sssend it."

"If that's alright to write a reply?"

"Nothing to worry about, Princesss. His Viciousnesss would never deny someone their freedom of speech."

All that was left to do was place the cookies into little paper plates and carefully stack them in the cookie jar. She would serve them at afternoon tea beside jam tarts, cheesy scones, and cucumber sandwiches.

"Then I should send something out tomorrow. Do I have time to take a shower?" Baking with Panlith was fun, but recently he'd trusted me to work the ovens, and it got hot!

"Master is currently entrapping healersss into the Dark Lord's army," Tulith replied, "so he probably won't be free until closer to dinner. You have plenty of time to wash up."

I tensed. "Does that mean Rufus is back?"

I'd never met Rufus, but if he could kidnap three Healer-class mages in one week *and* bring them to the Dark Lord's castle, then he must be very powerful. What would happen when I got locked up with him? Torture? Training? Brainwashing? Or maybe he would try to get me to fight for King Keith's army.

Honestly, I wouldn't mind fighting for King Keith. I was supposed to be a warrior with a Warrior class . . . and it beat the slime out of fighting for my parents. I would feel bad for my battalion knights, though. Some of them had followed me into the dungeons during my training and fought by my side.

"Yes, Princesss." Tulith smiled. "General Rufus arrived thisss morning. He should ssstill be with our master."

"What's he like?" I probably should have cared enough to ask this before now, but I was busy and—honestly—putting it off. As soon as I'd found out that I got to keep my life and my rooms and my baking, nothing else had really mattered. It still didn't really matter.

"The general isss . . . How to explain?" Tulith tapped a long-nailed finger on her scaled chin. "He isss like a warm blanket and hot chocolate, but also like a ssslap to the face and a kick to your sssoul."

"He's the reason I'm still with my kin, and the reason Sithli's off the goatvine," Panlith cut in from plating lunch. He was a large tawny-brown lizardman who could pass for a dragonkin. His forearms were immense.

"True that, and we are all happier for it. Terrible habit, Milith was always complaining about the smell of smoke on his linens" Tulith agreed with the chef. She explained "Rufus and Chloe are the only onesss on call throughout the week.

They like taking off weeksss at a time, or even an entire month! I'd go batty with all that free time."

"Speak for yourself!" Panlith chuckled. "As the castle chef, I work more than everyone combined."

"You refuse to leave!" Tulith shot back. "The lot of you are nutty."

Panlith and I smiled at each other.

Honestly, it was already amazing to hear about a four-day work week . . . I couldn't imagine an entire month off. My own kingdom let people rest only on Wednesdays and holidays. Granted, we had a lot of holidays.

I took off my apron and hung it on the wall. "I guess this is goodbye, then." I felt very empty saying it, but that was that. "It was nice of you to share your kitchen, Panlith. You've got all the recipes I've used so far?"

The head chef squinted at me unhappily. "Why does it sound like you ain't coming back, Princesss?"

"King Keith has sentenced me to imprisonment with Rufus."

The lizardkin looked at each other knowingly. Finally, Tulith spoke. "If that's how it is, then there is no need to worry, Your Highnesss. Rufus only does one-hour sessions per person."

"Really?" That didn't sound so bad.

"Unless the sssituation is *very* dire," Panlith commented. "But it hasss to be an extreme case."

CHAPTER 12

Raise, Resurrect, or Revive

Keith

"She's been down there for two hours already, hasn't she?" Keith massaged his temple. It had taken most of the afternoon to organize immigration for his kingdom's four new healers—and to dispose of the fifth. He had six major bases throughout the forest, so all five would have been preferable, but Keith only needed three; they could split their craft between two locations each.

After he moved their families and all their worldly possessions here, of course.

The fifth healer had been appalled and told the others that they were sacrificing their families to the Dark Lord for gold in return. Their social security was bought on the lives of their loved ones.

But Keith didn't need their lives. Chloe might, though she preferred bodies already decomposed into bones over working with the recently deceased. At that point, it was a simple [Revive] and have a good day.

He still made her [Raise] his fallen minions after it was too late to properly [Revive] them. Sure, a zombie couldn't have children or grow old, but they could do pretty much everything else. At least they could after Chloe bound the wayward soul back to its body. Chloe had told him she thought it was a waste of mana, but to *not* do so would be a waste of *resources*.

Besides, if they died for him, then it was his responsibility to take care of their families and their last will and their replacement . . . and it was just a headache. Better to bring them back.

Raise. Resurrect. Revive, like he always said.

"Yesss, Master. I've just come from checking." Tulith curtsied. No one, including Tulith, was allowed in this area of the castle without a direct summon. But since he wasn't building attention-demanding constructs that required all his concentration to not *explode, and* he had a houseguest to keep track of, Tulith had been granted special permission to come here and report on Henrietta in the afternoon.

So far, his multitude of examinations on the princess had left a glaring but so far unsolvable problem for Keith. Henrietta, for all her assurance that she was *only* an eighteen-year-old Sword Master and *surely* no match for him . . . could punch him into oblivion if she had the mindset to do so.

And there was the problem.

She *didn't* have the mindset. So, while she was perfectly capable, she didn't think it was possible, and had thus walked right through his guards.

Usually, Keith didn't need to bother doing anything himself. His constructs protected his minions, and his minions relayed him news. He would get a report, and the body of any assassin sent into the Dark Enchanted Forest would simply be found lying at the crossroad into the kingdom of Drendil. Or whichever kingdom their character sheet said they were from.

There might be a few more killers disposed of and deposited in Drendil than originated from there, but if they had kingdom of origin, then Drendil could deal with them. He enjoyed reading their complaints more than he would admit.

This time, not so.

His highly trained, bloodthirsty crew of gore-crazy lizardkin guards had trusted the golems and let this assassin barge into his lands, into his castle, and even into his *inner sanctum.*

And there was no way he could devise a construct to [Sense Motive] a traumatized princess looking to get murdered.

Although maybe . . .

"Tulith, go tell Rufus it's time to wrap up for today." Keith rummaged through his shelves and found a mostly empty container of hens-teeth jelly. Next, he unearthed three sticks of cinnamon and a bottle of dragon's blood. "I know he's been working a lot, but tell him I have one last order of business to discuss before he's done for the day—Wait, actually, I'll be busy. I'll send him a note instead."

She waited while Keith scribbled out the plan for Rufus and his new [Construct Creation]. If it worked, Rufus would be getting more visitors.

Keith waved the paper so the ink could dry faster, and then handed it to the maid. "Give this to Rufus when you retrieve Princess Henrietta."

"Yesss, Master." Tulith went to do as instructed, leaving Keith alone with a new enchantment to figure out.

"Why does everything need to be learned by trial and error?" he groaned, not for the first time. "Why can't we just share our dark discoveries like reasonable people?"

He knew spells to inspire someone to take their own life. Spells for depression and anxiety and violence. His dark tomes were filled with blood magics and poison for the soul.

How hard could it be to craft a spell that would sense these things? He also needed to include an order that anyone caught in the new spell would be taken alive and thrown in the dungeon.

Rufus could sort them out.

With newfound vigor, Keith got to mixing ink and crafting mana circles until one came out with his desired effect.

He neglected to plan for the fact that this was not his usual afternoon, and he would have interruptions very soon.

CHAPTER 13

And How Did That Make You Feel, Princess?

Henrietta

"And how did that make you *feel*, Princess?"

"Terrible, Rufus. Simply terrible!" I took the kerchief Rufus offered me and blew my runny nose much too loudly for a royal. I didn't care.

I was reclining on a daybed in the dungeon across from a large beastman with golden hair, eyes, and aura. He was so big he almost didn't fit in his chair. He had dainty reading glasses on his wide, hairy nose, and took notes on a scroll in his lap. The scroll was secured to a thin slab of wood so he could work without a desk. The first hour had flown by so fast that I wouldn't have noticed except that Rufus' [Calming Effect] perk had expired. He was being awfully generous, letting me stay longer.

"I *know* I'm annoying, but why does Mother need to point it out in front of company?" Of course, Mother only did so in front of the queen's court ladies, those dames whom she trusted the most. She never would have done so publicly; that would have tarnished our family's honor.

It still hurt.

"Dismissing your opinion and criticizing your passion. Have you considered that you can be yourself now? You are outside the influence of your parents' house here." Rufus looked over the brim of his tiny reading glasses. He reminded her of Lord Tisbury, an uncle figure who worked for the Drendil Order of Phoenix Knights. They both exuded confidence. "Your parents did give you the tools to survive—lessons in social etiquette and sword skills. Perhaps keep what is important to you and leave the rest behind."

"I don't know if I *can*, Rufus." A week of baking and making friends had been magical . . . but I was supposed to further the agenda of the royal family. I had been born and raised to give my life for Drendil. "I have a mission, and I owe them so much."

"You *had* a mission," he emphasized. "Fight the Dark Lord. You came, you fought, you lost. Now, you have a new purpose: serving the victor to your duel. I'm told it's common in North Sumbria. Furthermore, no child *owes* their mother or father for being raised. That was their choice and their responsibility."

"I didn't actually fight Keith." I coughed and blushed. "I mean, I didn't fight *the Dark Lord.*"

"You didn't?" This was the first time his aura of confidence had faltered.

"We talked, and I got distracted, and before I knew it, I was here." I waved around me. "Maybe I *should* go fight him."

"Is that what you want or what's expected of you?" Rufus leaned back in his chair. "Is that what your parents want?"

I sighed. "I don't know anymore."

"Let's try an exercise," Rufus offered. "If you pretended to be honest with yourself, what would you tell me you wanted to do that you *don't* have to admit wanting?"

That convoluted question was easier than any of the previous. "I just want to make bimbleberry scones that turn out buttery and relax beside a dragon on Lake Loria. I want to help King Keith with his magic, and have tea with Gerda, and sleep in on Saturdays."

Rufus was writing again. He carefully blew on a small slip of paper. "Then I have your first prescription. Ah, there's Tulith now."

The maid walked down the stairwell and into the main dungeon hallway. Henrietta's cell was very close to the entrance, and the lizardkin was visible from between the bars.

"It's been two hoursss, Commander General," Tulith stated, opening the door to my cell. She held up a slip of paper. "And I've new orders from the king."

"Yes, yes, I've just finished. Here, read this."

Rufus handed Tulith his slip, and she passed over hers, then they both read their respective instructions quickly, nodding. When Tulith was done, she passed Rufus' writing to me. It was almost illegible, but years of reading court ledgers and scrawled bureaucratic missives had prepared me for this day:

> *No less than two hours of baking each workday.*
> *Required inner-kingdom travel on one rest day.*
> *Two full 8-hour rest periods on Saturday.*
> *By Order of Commander General Rufus Triever, King's Dogs of the Black Fortress, punishable by the First Order.*

Huh. It turned out, Rufus was actually the most powerful general in the Dark Lord's army. And he'd just bowed politely to me with a friendly, "Until next week, Princess," then left.

I looked at the slip in my hand, confused, then back up to the empty doorway.

"Wait, Rufus, wait!" But it was too late; I was alone with Tulith. The maid continued to hold the bars of the cell open and waited for me.

I wasn't ready. I needed a minute to blow my nose again, and I needed time to gather myself. "Can we swing by a wash station before I meet with the Dark Lord?"

"As you wish, Princesss." Tulith nodded, knowingly.

"Thank you."

I had a lot to think about before I met with Keith.

CHAPTER 14

Self-Destructive Suicidal Princess Come to Punch Him in the Face

Keith

Keith thought a spell to detect self-destructive suicidal princesses come to punch him in the face was too specific.

After a while, he did manage to configure a [Detect Suicidal Intention] spell. Now, all he needed to do was carefully trace it onto a new construct, and he wouldn't need to worry about this happening a second time.

He could leave it in the castle moat and move on.

If another Henrietta, not that there was anyone else quite like Henrietta, but if another person who didn't intend to fight but just die appeared, they would be captured and delivered to Rufus.

Along with anyone *else* thinking about ending it.

He used his once daily [Construct Creation: Medium] ability to reshape stone into the rough outline of an octopus and started sprawling ink designs over its back. To help capture intruders, he gave it the ability to scale walls and leap unnaturally far for its size. And a lot of arms—more than eight.

It looked like some tentacle monster from the Depths of Despair Dungeon off the eastern coast.

It was perfect.

He then reviewed his character sheet logs, and had to drag his attention away from calculating success rates. He hadn't really used his midsize construct skill much recently. Once he had hit level sixty, giant constructs had become available, and who would make horse-size creatures when you could make dragon-size golems that shook the earth when they walked?

No one, that's who.

Keith was preparing to activate the mana circuit when a knock sounded at the entry to his workshop, startling him.

Tulith escorted Henrietta in and curtsied before leaving. Keith really needed to set some kind of warning alert in case they interrupted him during another Great Work, or he might really get murdered by his wayward princess.

"Let's see it." Keith walked over to Henrietta and reached out a hand, waiting. She smelled like cinnamon, honey, and vanilla today. He resisted the urge to lean in closer.

"What?" She looked up at him with wide eyes.

"The prescription." Keith motioned with his hand again to give it over. Rufus always gave out post first-visit instructions.

"Ah, yes." Henrietta pulled a slip from her apron pocket.

Keith looked it over and sighed. "Well, that's easy. You can bake for half the week, go on an outing, then do a follow-up with Rufus and report back to me."

Thank goodness that was done. He could get back to work on expanding his Dark Army and have her delicious baking at the same time.

"Excuse me, King Keith?"

"Hm?"

"Why is this happening?"

"Why is what happening?"

"This!" Henrietta moved a hand between Keith and herself. "Why aren't we fighting?"

"I thought you didn't want to fight?" Keith asked.

"I don't! But it doesn't matter what I want." She drew herself up, standing taller and looking him in the eye. "Nobody cares what I want. I'm supposed to shut up and do what I'm told and not cause a fuss. *This*"—she waved between them again—"is causing a fuss. You don't need to do this. We can fight or duel or whatever, and then I'll be out of your hair."

"First off," Keith resisted a dramatic sigh. "*Of course* I don't need to do this. I'm the Dark Lord of Nilheim; I do whatever I want. And what I *want* is to eat bimbleberry scones—and to hire the excellent baker who makes those bimbleberry scones. I also want to avoid the war that follows your death. You think I have time to waste fighting your sorry excuse for a father? I am working on leveling up my ability to create automatons."

"No, but—"

He continued. "And my necromancer is *still* on holiday! She left three days before you arrived, and I don't expect her back for *at least* two weeks. No one is allowed to unalive themselves in the meantime, or it'll be a royal pain." Keith paused. "Sorry for cutting you off. You were saying?"

"I'm just . . ." Henri hesitated. "Can I really just bake and go around sightseeing?"

"What else would you be doing?" Keith raised an eyebrow. "And don't say fighting again. I really don't have the patience for practice battles, and I sent the healers out already. Besides, baking is an admirable job; much better than crown princess."

If she landed one hit on his glass-cannon min-maxed magician's body, there might not be enough left for Chloe to piece back together again. He should have kept a healer on hand at the castle. After this talk, he needed to craft a stronger amulet of [Repel Strike] or [Advanced Constitution]. They were a pain to create, since he didn't have any related ability, so maybe not . . . Maybe his godmother had left him something useful in her hoard before she'd flown off.

He'd been too careless. But then, a level sixty *anything* was nearly unheard of.

Henri pushed one lock of hair behind her ear. "I'd like to keep baking, even if I don't have any baking skills—"

"You don't have a skill?!" Keith interrupted her. Again. Her baking tasted divine and not from a simple amateur. He coughed and composed himself. "Pardon me. Continue."

"I have lots of *other* skills. I have [Bureaucracy] level six, [Leadership] level five." Henri began listing each of her noncombat perks on her fingers, "I also have [Sense Motive], [True Taste], [Sense Ability], [Inspire], [Multitask], and [Quick Read]. If not baking, is there something else I could help with? Do you have any monsters you need fought?"

She was honestly telling Keith, her kingdom's mortal enemy, all her skills and perks. Though one thing stood out above the rest.

Keith smiled down at the princess, and she blushed. "So what I'm hearing is that you want to bake for fun and get a job that utilizes your abilities?"

The princess nodded, and then for some reason, she wasn't looking him in the eye anymore but staring at his partially revealed left collarbone.

This was wonderful. If the king and queen of Drendil wanted to throw away their highly skilled and adorable princess, he'd happily accept her. As Godmother always said, "Only a fool would stop prey from walking into your mouth."

Keith might be a bit careless, but he was never a fool. "Then, Princess, I have just the job for you."

CHAPTER 15

You Do Know What Afternoon Tea Is?

Henrietta

That was how I found myself sitting with King Keith in an office, cross-referencing tax revenue forms from the previous year's accounting logs.

[**Quick Read** cooldown 00:16:35. Current Reading Speed: base
400 words per minute x Intelligence 17 = 6800 words per minute.]
[**Multitask** cooldown 00:09:50. 2/3 tasks utilized.]

The office was large, with two alcoves off to either side, like a *V* made up of three honeycombs. Keith's desk was in the central area, with two bookshelves and floor-to-ceiling windows that let in natural light. It was clear of clutter, with three neat stacks of paper on one side, and an ink station on the other. Every once in a while, one of his people would pop in and place more paper in one of the three stacks.

The alcove left of his desk was filled with records from the last ten years, divided into file shelves labeled Complete, Incomplete, and Missing Information. Each was internally sorted by region, time, and then by the office that had submitted them. It was a simple and straightforward system, and very like King Keith.

The right alcove had three smaller desks with no less than five assistants who came and went while handling any of the kingdom's affairs that didn't require the king's direct attention.

The three stacks of paper were in order of Requires Review, Requires Response, and Requires Immediate Action. I sat behind the desk, going through the Requires Review pile. Keith also sat behind the desk, going through the Immediate Action pile. We were practically sitting beside each other!

We were, in fact, sitting beside each other. And had been for two hours. I'd made it through almost all of my stack when a clock above the entry to the office let out a beautiful light strain of harp music.

The two lizardkin and one human stood up to leave. They passed a cat beast-kin and an imp walking through the entry. The two newcomers took over the empty chairs and got to work.

King Keith pushed back from his desk and stretched, then cracked his neck and stood up. When I didn't immediately follow suit, he looked at me question-ingly. "Well, come on."

"I just need to finish this. There are only a few more numbers to cross-reference."

"Hm." Keith gave me a look. He leaned over my shoulder to see the two points I hadn't completed, then pulled a red pin out of seemingly thin air and tacked it down where I was working. "Now you know where you were. Let's go."

Was it my imagination, or did King Keith just sniff? Was I annoying him because I couldn't complete the roster in time? I didn't even know there was a time limit!

"Alright." I jumped up quickly, and my chair missed King Keith's shin by a hair. He stared hard at the chair and then back up at me.

Keith had really nice eyes. He had really nice everything; long straight black hair that he sometimes fiddled with, and midnight-blue eyes that I could get lost in. Every time he ran a hand through his hair, my eyes were drawn to the small horn on the right side of his head. His nose was a bit awkward; it was a smidge small, and the ridge started just under his eyes. I liked it.

I coughed and backed away quickly. "Sorry. So, ah, what are we doing?"

"We are on afternoon tea."

"Tea?"

"Afternoon tea," he corrected, then he hesitated and asked, "You *do* know what afternoon tea is, don't you?"

"Of course I do. It's when the ladies of the court meet for socializing . . . over . . . tea?" The look on his face made me think I didn't know what afternoon tea was at all.

"Everyone in my castle," Keith stated, "works on a strict schedule, which includes a break every two hours. There are tea and snacks in the lounge, with time for a quick nap or a turn around the garden." He paused. "Though it's rec-ommended not to enter the garden if you don't have [Resist Poison]."

"Why?"

"Because the garden is filled with poisonous plants."

"No, why do we have to take a break every two hours? Doesn't that interrupt work? Why not work until the work is done?" I had never taken a snack break in Drendil. I did have a thirty-minute luncheon in my office or at the training grounds mess hall. And I did get to go to the queen's afternoon tea a few times. But that hardly counted as a break from work.

King Keith looked at me like I had two heads, but quickly composed himself. "Because I said so."

There wasn't much to argue with when the Dark Lord said so.

I followed Keith into the castle commons and spotted the other aides wandering into a side room. They stood around a table with sandwiches and a water jug filled with cranberries, sliced oranges and lemons and cucumber.

King Keith kept walking. I didn't know if I was supposed to join the others or follow him, but I didn't have to ask. As I slowed down, Keith faced me and said, "Your break time is yours. I like to walk in the garden." He pushed up his glasses. "Have you seen the garden yet?"

"I haven't." I didn't even know there was a garden before today.

"Would you—" He cleared his throat. "Would you like to see the garden now? I could point out anything that would kill you."

That sounded awfully romantic. Had the Dark Lord just asked me to go on a walkabout?

I hurried to say, "I'd love to!"

"Shall we, then?" Keith offered an arm, and I took it gently. I was holding the Dark Lord's arm! This day couldn't get any better.

Or so I thought.

CHAPTER 16

Who Swam in the Dark Lord's Moat?

Keith

Keith didn't know what had come over him. Perhaps it was the past week of delicious food, or the fact that Henrietta hadn't ever heard of a snack break. Or, perhaps, it was that he simply enjoyed her company.

Maybe it was the fact that she kept blushing every time Keith caught her staring at his chest where his collar had come open. He had never flirted with a man or woman before, but he liked to think that she was enjoying his company as much as his popped buttons.

It was hard to find love as a Dark and Evil Overlord. Sure, royals sent letters offering prospective husbands and wives, but those were just political marriages and not something he was interested in.

It wasn't healthy dating someone who had recently come into his employ, and partially forced at that. On the other hand, Henrietta was someone he considered an equal. She might be "highly flammable," but given the circumstances, either one of them could off the other pretty easily.

She was closer to him in level than most, and they shared similar skills, and she made him smile.

All of these things had come together in one reckless invitation to walk around the garden. And she'd said yes!

"The garden was actually cultivated by my godmother, Her Eminence Feliwyn," he explained as they stepped out into a veritable labyrinth of foliage. "She picked this courtyard, cracked the cobblestone floor, and filled it with dirt. Then she planted anything and everything that piqued her interest."

Henrietta nodded as he led her through a trellis of itching ivy. The leaves had hairs on the back that caused a violent rash wherever they touched. Keith explained the other plants as they went.

"And this area is for the crypt roses. They only bloom when you give them a dead body to feed on." The beautiful purple roses were a sight to behold. "It's lucky that we came today; Chloe buried some new bodies before she left, and they should bloom for another week or so before the flesh is fully dissolved. Easiest way to clean the bones, according to her."

"Chloe is your necromancer?" Henrietta stood transfixed, staring out at the stunning flowers.

Keith nodded. "She'll be back in two weeks. Her and Grand Duchess Calisto's daughter are close, and she's always gone for weeks whenever she travels north. Over here are the Venus water lilies; they eat anything that gets within reach."

Around the corner from the crypt roses, Feliwyn had dug out a pond and magicked a portal to the running water in the moat. The Venus water lilies kept popping up in the moat, and he was of a mind to let them. They reminded him of his napping godmother, and they rarely killed anyone.

Besides, who swam in the Dark Lord's moat? Ne'er-do-wells, that's who.

"What's this?" Henrietta asked excitedly as they turned the last corner and found the center of the garden. A hollow circle was shaped from a thick hedge, creating a private seating area where he'd had a long ornate bench permanently installed. There was a table with a single chair up in the middle of the hollow. A teapot covered in a green leaf cozy sat on the table beside one teacup and a three-tier tray of snacks.

Keith coughed and let go of Henrietta's arm. "Excuse me, Princess. Give me just a moment."

Keith opened up his character sheet and found the first spell he needed. Lifting one hand, he activated the perk.

[You have attempted to use the Perk: **Cantrips (Dancing Lights)**.
You have succeeded. You may create light x Intelligence 85. You
have chosen 6 lights.]

Floating lights appeared around the gloomy hollow. Then he scrolled through his skill list to find the other two.

[You have attempted to use the Skill: **Craft (Furniture)**. You have
succeeded. You may create basic furniture you have seen. Personal
aesthetics are determined based on your Dexterity 42 and Charisma 19]

Dirt and stone gathered from their surroundings to make a chair for him. It was pitch black and sleek looking. He made sure the seat was clean stone. Then he broke a branch from a nearby tree.

[You have attempted to use the Skill: **Craft (Small Item)**. You have succeeded. You may create a small item you have seen. Personal aesthetics are determined based on your Dexterity 42 and your Charisma 19]

The wood warped into a matching teacup with the one already on the table. He escorted Henrietta to the original chair and explained, "I don't normally have company. I'll make sure there are two place settings from now on."

"Thank you." Henrietta smiled up at him, and he mentally kicked himself to stop staring longer than was polite. Keith pushed her chair in for her and without thinking, reached out and pushed an errant lock of her hair behind her ear.

He stared at his hand, realizing what he'd just done. "I apologize for touching you without—"

"I don't mind," she interrupted. Henrietta was blushing again. She always blushed just lightly over the bridge of her nose and a little on each cheek. She had very light freckles—he assumed from her warrior training outdoors. Most princesses he'd met cultivated smooth, unblemished skin. Not that he cared, because her freckles only stood out when she blushed, and that was as adorable as she was.

"I see." And he did see. At least he hoped he saw. Still, consent was *important*, and it was inexcusable that he had acted without. He decided to ask for what he really wanted instead of accidentally slipping up again later.

"Princess," Keith hesitated only a second before asking, "may I call you Henrietta?"

CHAPTER 17

A Terrible Prophecy

Henrietta

Nobody called me Henrietta. I was still surprised my parents hadn't just named me Henri outright.

It all went back to before I was born. When the royal physician had announced that my mother was with child, my father's court astronomer had come forward with a terrible prophecy: that a magician would end the royal line of Drendil.

In fear and frustration, my father had gathered up any titled Magician in the kingdom and had them put to death. It'd happened so fast that there hadn't been any time for the Mages Tower to realize it was happening, and by the time anyone had, it'd been too late. That had proved to be my father's own undoing, as one of the condemned magician's managed to free himself at the last minute, casting a [Curse] upon my father with his dying breath.

The Cursed King Simon Doryn of Drendil would never sire another child in this life, and there was nothing he could do about it. After what had happened, there were no magicians left to undo the spell . . . and not one on the whole continent who was willing to try.

So when I was born, they immediately named me something that could be shortened to Henri.

Which was why I was momentarily at a loss and didn't reply to Keith's question right away. Did I want him to call me Henrietta? Who was Henrietta? The silence stretched on longer and longer, but he patiently waited beside my chair.

I decided, "I would like that very much."

If I was going to live in a new kingdom with a new life, I could have a new name, too. Or an old name, as the case may be. Either way, it was nice hearing Keith say it.

Keith nodded then took his seat with a flourish. "Then you may call me simply as Dark Magician Keith."

That was not what I was expecting him to say, so I did a double take. He looked away and covered his face, laughing. Was he making fun of me?!

"I'm sorry. I jest." He gathered himself and smiled at me. "Please, call me Keith."

"I don't know, *Dark Magician Keith*," I huffed. "That will depend."

"On?" Keith moved to pour each of us a cup of tea.

"I don't know, but when I do, I'll let you know." Honestly, I wasn't the best at playful banter. Even my etiquette teacher said I was too blunt for my own good.

Keith chuckled and passed me the cream and honey. He waited until I was done before preparing his own. "So, Henrietta, how was your morning with Rufus?"

Finally, an easy question! I was thankful for the change of topic. I preferred a slow approach to romance. If you counted calling each other by name *romance*. Anyway.

"Rufus is darling," I assured Keith. "And he's such a good listener!"

"He's thirty-two," Keith said firmly.

"What?" Another change in topic. I tried to keep up. "Really? He doesn't look like it with all the hair. I'm not the best judge with beastkin. I'm eighteen now, but my birthday is the day after St. Veralyn's Day."

Having my birthday so close to the famous holiday celebrating Dragon Veralyn the Green defeating the evil Sir George of Lindale meant that there wasn't much of a budget left over for anything except a small dinner with my parents and their friends each year. Sometimes, I would get in trouble and I could slip out, then Bronwynn the Bard would find me, and we would do something nice. I wondered if Gerda would like to have tea on my birthday?

I took a sip of my tea, a beautiful rosehip and Lady Green. Then I asked, "When is your birthday?"

"On the winter solstice." Keith was rubbing the bridge of his nose. Something he did when he was frustrated.

Of course the Dark Lord had been born on the longest night. It was only a pity I'd arrived here in February. I could have given him a present.

There was a moment's pause as we both drank tea and ate pastries. The bimbleberry cream tarts had come out delicious, if I said so myself. There was a little too much salt on the cucumber sandwiches, though.

Suddenly, the imp who had been working in Keith's office flew over a hedge and up to the entrance of our bramble hollow.

"Your Viciousness! You got a reply!" He stopped short when he saw me sitting across from Keith. "Ahhhhh. Beg pardon, Master, I'll just—"

"Stop hesitating, Gimtak, and give it here," Keith ordered. The imp dropped to the earth and scampered over. He handed over a scroll, bowing and scraping repeatedly. Keith waved a hand. "That'll be all. Back to work."

The imp flew away in a hurry.

I didn't want to pry, but Keith had been so adamant about taking a break during break time, yet he'd *still* accepted the letter. And in the middle of our teatime, too. That was technically very rude, but I didn't mind. I wasn't one for rigorous adherence to etiquette, and even now, my curiosity got the better of me.

"Who is it from?" I hadn't seen the seal before he broke it and had the scroll unfurled in front of him.

"Your parents."

"What?!"

The imp had said it was a *reply*, which meant this wasn't even the first letter!

Wait, of course the king of Nilheim exchanged correspondence with the king of Drendil. I didn't need to make everything about me all the time.

"It's from your parents," Keith repeated. He finished reading it over a second time and then tapped it, frowning up at me. "They want to know why you're not dead yet."

CHAPTER 18

Am I or Am I Not Your Prisoner?

Keith

What is the meaning of this, Monfort? That child's body should have come back in pieces, but I'm told Henri is still alive and well instead? You only have one job as ruler of the Dark Enchanted Forest, and you can't even get being an evil tyrant right. How hard is it to kill one measly Sword Master? Either combat our Hero of Justice or send them back.

Also, I don't understand that nonsense you wrote about scones. You are trying to mislead us, and I'll believe none of it. If Henri is rotting away in your dungeons, then kindly torture to your heart's content, but at least have the decency to end things quickly. If I don't hear good news by St. Veralyn's Day in one month's time, I'll be forced to take drastic measures.

Good day,

Simon Doryn, Sovereign King of Drendil

Keith hesitated only a second before handing the missive over to Henrietta. He never wanted to hear her get called Henri again. Reading what this flagitious imbecile had written made his blood run cold.

Maybe a new nickname would be better? Something unique, like Hattie or Ria would be a nice fit. Pending her approval, of course. And all in good time. Keith had only just been allowed to call Henrietta by her first name, so he would have to wait until they were closer before asking her about a nickname.

He would choose to forgo pet names altogether if it meant any hint of *Henri*.

Making a mental note to come back to this later, Keith watched her read the short letter.

She didn't seem upset by it. When she reached the end, Henrietta shrugged, handed it back, and asked, "That's Father, alright. So what are you going to do?"

Maybe Keith *would* go to war with Drendil. Conquer all their lands, step on their nobles, behead their royals, and burn their palace to the ground before salting the earth.

"I'm going to tell him the truth," Keith said aloud. "You're living in my castle, and only visit the dungeon a few hours a week . . . I *was* going to say that all future letters could be addressed to you personally, but would you rather I not?"

"That's very kind of you, but I'll write home." Henrietta shook her head, and Keith had a niggling of frustration that she still called that place home. He was being unreasonable, though; she'd only been here a week.

"As you wish." He refilled her teacup, and in a blatant effort to change the subject, he asked, "Now, where are you wanting to visit next? Kith Bog is nice, but there are these dolostone caves beside Thistlecrick that have a few thermal springs. The Naga clans live there, and their warriors would love the chance to battle a Sword Master."

"Really? I've heard about hot springs, but I've never been to one." Henrietta flexed her arm. "It'll be nice to work up a sweat on the practice field and then take a dip."

Keith coughed at the thought. He said, "Aside from Kith Bog and Thistlecrick, Gren's Keep is where most of the beastkin hail from, Plittsmouth is the underwater base below Lake Loria, and Frolin is the trading port to the northwest. We have an elven clan to the east, but it isn't anything different from walking around the rest of the dark wood."

Keith discussed the most scenic places to visit in the Dark Enchanted Forest until it was long past time to go back inside. He didn't worry about it, though; he had completed all his important tasks. And he could always just break his rules and work late tonight if it meant spending more time with the princess.

He was contemplating whether they should head back when Henrietta said, "Oh! I almost forgot."

"Yes?"

"I received mail today from Grand Duchess Calisto."

Keith raised an eyebrow. "I'm surprised she knew you were here."

"Didn't you hear Madame Potts's Casting from your Cast Crystal?" Henrietta asked.

"No." The only Cast Crystal setup was in the castle courtyard, where he would announce things to his minions . . . if he could ever find his godmother's Royal Crystal. "Though I am supposed to get updates when premonitions are related to Nilheim."

"She told everyone I was sent here to kill you." She blushed prettily. "Apparently, I was going to slaughter everyone in the castle."

"That's nice." Keith didn't let any emotion show on his face, remembering how close he had been to death's door when she'd interrupted him. He added "Having words with Tulith about what *related to Nilheim* meant" to his tasks. "No future plans to kill my minions or myself?" He said it with an air of jest, but they both knew Henrietta had been warring with herself up until now.

The princess took a deep breath and looked up at him. "No, I don't think so."

Keith nodded his approval.

"Anyways," Henrietta continued. "I've received my invite to Grand Duchess Calisto's Spring Ball."

"I have one as well," Keith said.

Henrietta looked at him expectantly. Was he supposed to ask her to the ball? That seemed a little fast, even if he was amicable to the idea. He didn't want to just assume—

"Can I go?"

"What?" Keith composed himself. That was right; how could he have been thinking she would want to be taken to the most exclusive ball in the known kingdoms by the *Dark Lord*. "Of course, why do you ask?"

She stared at him, hard. "Am I or am I *not* your prisoner? I'm confused."

Keith hesitated a second. "After everything that's happened, I was thinking along the lines of *royal guest* myself."

"A guest who's sent to the dungeons once a week?"

"You're in the capital of Nilheim, *everybody* gets sent to the dungeons *eventually*. Rufus is really good at his job, though, so it quickly moves to just a routine checkup."

"I see," Henrietta said. "So I *can* go to the ball?"

"If that is what you wish," Keith replied, then decided to throw caution to the wind and ask, "Would you like to go—to ride together?"

"I'd love to!" Henrietta exclaimed, and then coughed. "If it's not too much trouble?"

"No trouble at all." Keith decided this was a perfect spot to change the subject. He was getting good at changing subjects. "Then shall we finish our paperwork before dinner?"

"Oh, please!" Henrietta stood up and stretched. "I wouldn't feel right if I didn't finish at least those last two lines."

Keith offered his arm again, and the two walked back to the office.

That evening, a missive went out to all the castle staff. Gerda the Bridge Troll smiled when she received a personal letter from the king of the Dark Enchanted Forest, and a royal declaration was put up in Kith Bog and the other five cities under his domain.

Henceforth, Crown Princess Henrietta of Drendil shall be welcome as a guest in all the Dark Enchanted Forest of Nilheim. She shall be referred to as Princess, Your Highness, Sword Master, or simply Henrietta. Violation of this order will be met with punishment by the Second Order.

Signed and Sealed,

Keith Monfort, Dark Magician King of Nilheim

CHAPTER 19

Only an Idiot Would Declare War on the Dark Enchanted Forest

Henrietta

I immediately regretted not letting Keith mediate my correspondence. I also regretted writing home. One or all of my parents' letters might have ended up in my parlor fireplace over the next few days.

The Nightshade Rooms were just that, *rooms*. The suite had a parlor, a small library office, a walk-in wardrobe, marble bathroom, and an extra bedroom for a personal maid.

My days in Nilheim had passed by like a dream until this point. I would wake up and get ready, then enjoy baking in the morning, working with Keith in the afternoon, and sometimes having dinner with him in the evening. Then, I'd retire to my parlor and lounge on the very comfortable lounge.

Often, there would be lurid romance novels or sword-fighting manuals waiting for me, but ever since that fateful afternoon tea a few days ago, I also got *mail*.

The first was a short missive from Bronwynn asking if I was alright. I wrote her back to let her know about some of my escapades and that I wouldn't be returning to Drendil anytime soon—and that she was free to visit me whenever she liked. I'd even asked for permission from Keith to be sure and sent a border pass with the letter.

I'd also received a mysterious unlabeled package. Tulith had arranged for one of the golems to open it just in case it was a nasty surprise from my parents. Instead, it was a small handwritten book called *Out of This World Recipes*. As it promised, it was full of strange and delicious-sounding recipes I'd mostly never heard of.

I had immediately made the first recipe which included ingredients I knew were ready to go in the kitchen.

Boston Cream Donut

☐ 3 ½ cups all-purpose flour divided, plus additional as needed (438g)
☐ 2 ¼ teaspoons yeast (add 50g powder Goblin Lily to make it instant)
☐ ⅓ cup ground sugar (67g)
☐ 1 teaspoon salt
☐ ⅔ cup cow milk (157ml)
☐ 6 tablespoons melted butter (85g)
☐ 2 large eggs lightly beaten (room temperature preferred)
☐ ¾ teaspoon vanilla extract (substitute Bitter Star Fruit Juice)
☐ Vegetable oil for frying
☐ Boston Cream (pg. 86)
☐ Chocolate Sauce (substitute whipped Markle Berry spread)

In a large bowl (or the bowl of a stand mixer), combine 2 cups (250g)
of flour, yeast, sugar, and salt and stir to combine. Heat milk and com-
bine. Add butter, eggs, and fruit juice. Stir until dough clings.
Leave dough covered overnight or for one hour if instant.
Roll out dough, cut into circles, and fry in boiling oil one at a time.
Take Boston Cream (recipe pg 86) and use a piping bag to fill each
Donut.
Dip in Chocolate or coat in Markle Berry Spread.

Some of the foods listed in the book had been popping up in Drendil recently,
like *Ramen* and *French Toast*. They all began in North Sumbria, so it was believed
the Grand Duchess had a new chef.

I had no idea why someone would send *me* a recipe book, but I was too
excited to care! The day it arrived, I spent almost fifteen straight hours in the
kitchen, and it took a direct order from Panlith to get me to go to bed.

The book obviously wasn't a gift from my parents, but they did send me their
own letters.

The king and queen of Drendil were not happy. When I'd first arrived, I was
still torn between my duties to king and country and accepting my abysmal fate.
If I was honest with myself, some small desire to survive had made me jump at
Keith's original offer not to fight.

Now, I didn't want to go back to being Henri. Ever.

Keith and I had talked about it, and everyone had started calling me Henrietta, and it'd been nice figuring out who *Henrietta* was.

Which was why I'd decided to visit Gerda on my day off instead of exploring
some of the more exciting locales around the Dark Enchanted Forest.

"A kingdom without people,
A desert without sand,

An ocean without water,
What land is in your hand?"

"Oh, Gerda, that's a lovely riddle!" And it really was. I thought long and hard. "Is it . . . a map?"

"Your Highness is so good at riddles; I will have to try harder next time." The troll laughed and invited me into her home under the east bridge.

Bridge troll magic made for a lovely cottage in the space between the water and the stone arch. There was a cute door with a flower motif seemingly carved into the under arch, and when you reached up and held the doorknob, gravity turned you sideways so you could walk right inside. The first time had been terribly disorienting, but now it was just magical.

"I always look forward to your riddles, Gerda, but *please* call me Henrietta," I said, embarrassed. The pale-green woman laughed, and we both puttered around her kitchen, preparing for afternoon tea. I got out the cups and she boiled water. I plated the table while she brewed a berryleaf blend that smelled wonderful.

I had grown to love afternoon tea in the Dark Enchanted Forest.

"And I look forward to your baking." Gerda tucked a dark green braid behind her ear as she leaned closer and breathed deeply, appreciating the smell of ginger, cinnamon, and cloves wafting from the basket. "What did you bring?"

"Gingerbread cookies and cinnamon buns." I pulled the kitchen towel off my basket to reveal cookies shaped like trolls, knights, treants, and dragons. Separately wrapped in killer-bee wax paper were two sticky honey butter cinnamon buns coated in whipped sweet cheese. When I saw the recipe in *Out of This World*, I'd had to stop myself from outright begging on my knees for Panlith to order the ingredients. He'd been happy to procure what I'd asked for, no groveling required.

I'd needed citrons to add to the thick cheese topping, and flour milled from soft red wheat to make the dough chewy and light.

We sat down at Gerda's table and dug in happily.

"I don't know what else to say, Gerda," I said between licking my fingers drizzled in icing. "I'm just so happy here, but things aren't going so well."

Gerda frowned over her tea. "Is it the Dark Lord? I heard he had you locked up in the dungeon."

"No! I love spending time with Rufus in the dungeon," I replied. "It's the fact that St. Veralyn's Day is only a month away, and if I don't do anything by then, *my father will.*"

"I would pay money to get locked up in a dungeon with General Rufus Triever," Gerda sighed passionately. She shook herself and asked, "What will your father do?"

"Declare war?" I sighed, exhausted. "If I die, then it'll be a war out of revenge. If I live, he'll declare war because I'm supposedly being held hostage by the Dark Overlord."

"Wait, aren't you being held hostage by the Dark Overlord?" Gerda asked. "Last I heard, he didn't want to fight you until his necromancer returned and could clean up the mess, so you've become a magical test subject for his evil experiments while you wait for your death, all the while baking for his pleasure. That sounds pretty 'captive princess' to me, Princess."

She emphasized the last *Princess* while raising an eyebrow.

"It's not like that at all!" I slapped my palm to my face, instantly regretting doing so because then I had to stop and wash icing off my face. "I volunteered! Keith wanted to know how I got past his gate golem, and I couldn't go home without fighting him or dying. He was really nice and let me stay in the Nightshade Rooms when I wasn't in the dungeons. It's just—it's not as bad as it sounds, alright?!"

Gerda laughed so hard she hit the table, which creaked under the blow.

"It's not funny!" I protested.

"You're right," she agreed. "It's hilarious. But with all the mix up and kingdom gossip and war, there is one thing that's pretty clear."

"What?"

"Drendil isn't your home anymore, so it's time to let it go." Gerda shrugged. "When I came here, I left my family and my home behind, and I never looked back. My husband was a very mean troll, and not in a good way."

I settled in to listen.

"Sometimes, you spend your whole life trying to make your home a better place. You plant bioluminescent mushrooms to make it shine, you convince yourself your bruises are proud battle scars, and you take the job of protecting others from the ones you love," Gerda said sadly, her brown eyes distant. Her gaze grew firm when she turned suddenly to look at me. "But their choices are not your choices. And the only troll's—the only person's actions you need to take responsibility for are your own."

"There might still be a war," I spoke softly.

"Then there is war." Gerda nodded and finished off her last bite of cinnamon bun. She smiled a big toothy grin. "Though only an *idiot* would declare war on the Dark Enchanted Forest."

"Unluckily for us, I'm related to someone who resembles that remark." I nursed my now cold cup of tea. "Hey, Gerda?"

"Yes, Henrietta?"

"Thank you for sharing. And thanks for the support."

"Anytime." She nodded, her brown eyes twinkled when she continued. "Now pull out the gingerbread while I make us more tea."

CHAPTER 20

A Late-Night Potts's Cast

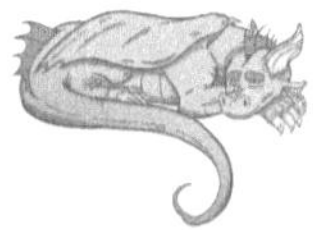

Keith

Keith was oiling tiny gears for his new planned construct when something very unexpected happened.

"Keith!" Henrietta burst into his workroom. "I've changed my mind!"

The princess wore a long green tunic with silver decorative embroidery at the open neckline, silver tights, and knee-high boots. She clutched a rolled and sealed scroll in one hand.

Keith carefully put down his gear and used a clean towel to wipe grease off his hands. When he thought about the princess in front of him, Keith changed tactics.

[You have attempted to use the Perk: **Cantrips (Cleanse)**. You have succeeded.]

He *really needed* to get himself an alarm to let him know when the princess and Tulith attempted to visit him in the afternoon. Or maybe he would install locks, then they could only interrupt him after he was ready?

"Good afternoon, Henrietta," Keith replied. "It's nice to see you too."

"Oh, stop." Henrietta was getting used to his teasing, but he liked that her ears still flushed a little red with embarrassment. "What I'm saying is that . . . I think I'm ready to cut off my parents. I don't want to get any more letters from them."

"I see." Keith stared at the scroll. And he did see. "And this is?"

"My last letter. I've told my parents that I'm giving up the throne and disowning them." Henriette offered it to him. "They can think of me as dead because I won't be returning to Drendil . . . So could you please mediate any more mail I receive?"

Keith took the letter and gave her a very big smile. "It would be my pleasure, Princess."

"Thank you." Henrietta stuffed a lock of her brown hair behind her ear. Tension left her shoulders, and she visibly relaxed.

"Just one thing, Hat—Henrietta," Keith slipped, almost using Hattie, one of the nicknames he'd been bandying about in his mind. He pushed forward when she just looked at him expectantly. "By mediate, do you mean that I'm allowed to read your mail?"

Keith felt that Hattie didn't fit right, anyway.

Henrietta nodded. "Everything I get from outside the Dark Enchanted Forest. I'm happy to read any mail so long as it's not from my parents. They might try to sneak in letters using intermediaries, so it would be best for you to check everything."

"Would you like me to reply to the letters, and did you want to know if there is correspondence for you?" Keith asked. "Or should I just dispose of it?"

"Reply however you want, and I don't care what happens to the mail. You can tell me if it's really important, like if they declare war or something," Henrietta explained. "But otherwise, I don't want to know."

"That reminds me." Keith sidled up beside her and offered his arm. "Have you considered becoming one of my minio—*subjects*? The benefits far outweigh the demerits."

"Really?" The soon-to-be-no-longer crown princess of Drendil took the Dark Lord's arm and walked with him out of the inner sanctum. "Tell me more."

"We have free revival, free health care, and a four-day work week," Keith offered. "And it comes with the Nightshade Rooms and an excellent office job." He waved her letter in his free hand. "You can file immigration forms while I arrange swift delivery of your letter."

"I'd like that." Henrietta sighed and looked up at him. "If only it were that simple."

They entered the main castle, and Keith paused to look at her. He asked her directly, "Why?"

"It's St. Veralyn's Day—"

"If you are worried about the war, Ria," Keith tried another one of the nicknames he'd been contemplating for days, and he thought it actually suited her very well. Since he had cut her off, he continued. "I apologize for interrupting, but if you're worrying about your father's threats, then don't. He has been threatening war since before you came here, and I have been planning for it since I took over the kingdom at sixteen. We are ready for an attack."

"No, no." Henrietta shook her head. "That's not what I was going to say."

They went through the common room, continuing toward his office.

"Then, again, I'm sorry I cut you off," Keith apologized. "Why can't you officially immigrate to Nilheim?"

Henrietta looked apologetically up at Keith. "Because I'm still eighteen until the day after St. Veralyn's Day. Registration for Drendil emigration starts at age nineteen or with confirmation from a guardian. I can't request a transfer of tax records until I come of age." A touch of hope filled her voice. "I could fill out the immigration forms today . . . but if I wait until then, I can submit them legally."

"So, what I'm hearing," Keith said, "is that it's not a *no*; it's a *not yet*."

"Yes."

If all they had to do was withstand a potential invasion and celebrate her birthday, he could wait.

He could also prepare.

Keith sent Henrietta out after she'd been helping in the office for a few hours, but then broke his own rule and stayed behind. He would need to finish as much paperwork as he could if he was going to create more golems for a war.

He was finishing up when Tulith appeared. She was on an evening shift, so this was the first he'd seen of her today.

"Master, there was a late-night Potts's Cast. I've done as you instructed and hired sssomeone to record them all for you."

Keith leaned back in his chair. He took off his glasses and rubbed his eyes. "What did it say?"

Tulith pulled out a small recording Cast Crystal he'd authorized for this purpose.

Hello, everyone, this is Madame Potts.
It's a little late, but I hope you'll excuse me.
The Peldeep adventuring guildmaster of Vitol stumbled upon
a new dungeon around Thia Falls and is trapped on the sixth
floor. He will die in nine days if rescue fails.
Thank you, this is Madame Potts signing out.

"Thank you, Tulith." Keith fiddled with the crystal in his hand. "Has anyone ever figured out who Madame Potts is?"

"No, but it's assumed she must be from North Sumbria," Tulith explained. "Sssince the Archwizard Jeffrey who created the Crystal-Cast Crystalsss lived there, it is thought that she found his Master Crystal and that is how she's making these announcementsss."

"Alright." Keith made a note to ask Grand Duchess Calisto when he went to this year's Spring Ball. He'd only gone once before, shortly after his coming of age, and he wasn't fond of the marriage-market aspect to the whole thing. Hopefully he could hide behind Henrietta's skirts this time. That was, if she chose to wear skirts. He should ask her what she was planning to wear so they didn't clash.

Keith knew he was going to be in his workroom late, so he dismissed Tulith early. She and Chikli were off the rest of the week, and there was no sense in keeping her late.

Then he got to work on an alligator-dog construct three times the normal size. Giant-sized creations were so much better.

CHAPTER 21

Sorry, Floofpoof Lv 6

Henrietta

After my letter arrived in Drendil, I was sure my parents had a lot to say and scream about. I feared my father would march the army into Nilheim as soon as he could muster the troops, but days went by with no word.

At least no word of an *army*. If my parents had replied to my letter, then I was blissfully ignorant, and Keith showed no sign that he'd received any correspondence.

Keith had been very busy after my father's threatening letter. He slept in and locked himself in his workroom most days. I was happy when we sat together in the office, but sad that we had dinner together less often.

Today was going to be completely different from my usual schedule. In fact, after I finished up in the kitchen, I was going to have my first Rufus-mandated excursion! As my first choice, I had decided to visit the village of Thistlecrick where the Naga clans lived.

But before that, I had some baking to do.

The naga were a monster race. Unlike beastkin, who always had animalistic properties like the lizardkin, or beastfolk, who could change from an animal at will like Rufus, the naga were a unique race unto themselves, like dragons or griffins. They were all born human above, snake below. As such, I'd been concerned about what kind of baking to bring, since regular snakes had strict dietary restrictions. They were also all carnivores. Not even *Out of This World* had a pure meat option.

That's when Rufus had come through for me! *The Carnivore Cookbook* he'd borrowed from one of his wolfkin clients contained a recipe for *fowl bread*.

Now, the question was: what was fowl bread, and why would someone call it something like *fowl bread*?

Well, in order to make the bread, I needed to find a number of ingredients that lived in the Dark Enchanted Forest, the first of which were forest fowl eggs. Panlith only had quail and duck eggs, so I'd started my day early and climbed about a hundred trees before I found sixteen forest fowl eggs. I didn't want to take more than one from each nest, but luckily, it was early spring, and there were a lot of nesting birds.

I'd also found, killed, and harvested the largest forest fowl I could find (Sorry, Floofpoof Lv 6), and then took it back to the castle kitchen.

I browned the meat, drained it, and pulverized it with my fists. Then I mixed in the four eggs, some baking powder and soda. I whipped it violently until it was a liquidy texture, and then baked it for forty minutes. Baked bread acquired.

The loaves smelled like a feast day. The terrible name didn't matter because it was one of the most delicious and fluffiest loaves of bread I had ever made. I made three more; one each for the three ruling families of Thistlecrick. Then I grabbed my sword from where it hung on my bedpost and tracked north from the castle. My blade was sheathed at my belt, and a basket full of unique baking was at my side.

While walking, I only had to use my [Killing Intent] perk eight times to convince predators not to attack me for the fowl bread.

I eventually found myself walking down a road with a lush canopy overhead. I turned a sharp bend in the road and came out of the dense forest path. Two great stone spikes as wide around as hippogriffs shot into the air and peaked together. Behind them stood a rocky cliff face covered in moss. The Dark Enchanted Forest had a few hills scattered around, but Thistlecrick was the largest, and the only one with known caves and hot springs.

Standing at attention at the base of each stone spike was a naga sentry.

They went on alert immediately when they saw me and crossed their spears to block entry into the village.

"Turn back lest you have business with the Naga clans," the one on the left spoke. She wore an impressive plate on her otherwise bare muscular chest, and a helm that blocked her face. "We don't want to have to kill you."

She sounded downright menacing.

"Greetings!" I didn't draw my sword but stopped and bowed dramatically—at least as much as I could while holding a large picnic basket. "I'm here to visit Thistlecrick. Have I reached the right place?"

"Yes," answered the naga on the right, who also wore plate on his otherwise bare muscular chest. His armor and helmet were a little rusty, and I was pretty sure there was a dent in his helm. "But we do not take kindly to strangers. Be gone!"

"I apologize. Let me introduce myself! I am Sword Master Princess Henrietta soon-to-be of the Dark Enchanted Forest, and I have come to greet the three ruling families of Thistlecrick with the permission of His Viciousness Keith Monfort of Nilheim."

Keith had told me that even if I gave up *the job* of crown princess, I should continue using *princess* while in his lands. He was very generous.

I lifted my picnic basket for the naga sentries and added, "I brought a gift."

The two shared a look, and after an imperceptible nod by the shinier sentry, her companion slithered away to presumably get someone in charge.

The remaining naga stood taller on her tail and looked me over. "If what you say is true, Princess, then we shall welcome you."

"Thank you!"

"But," she continued, "if you are a spy, no one will find your bones, for I shall use them as chew toys for my young."

"You have children? Congratulations! How old?" I was sadly an only child from a very small and cursed family. Still, I'd had a wonderful time with the children of my old adventuring party.

This perhaps wasn't the response the guard had been expecting because she paused for half a beat before saying, "Two and seven, Your Highness."

"Lovely. Maybe I'll get to meet them while I'm touring the village." We could hear the sound of the sentry returning down the path. "I've only met one naga while on delegation to the Peldeep Courts, so please excuse my ignorance of your culture. Do you have any recommendations for me while I'm here?"

The shiny naga tensed when I mentioned meeting her children, but she was a proper sentry and hid any show of emotion on what little of her face I could make out.

"Try not to die."

The less shiny sentry returned quickly with an entire platoon of heavily armored guards to welcome me.

CHAPTER 22

A Long-Standing War About His Buttons

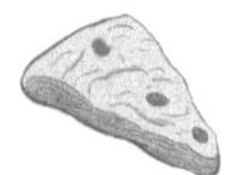

Keith

Keith slaved over another golem-style automaton, this one almost three stories tall and taking up the entirety of his inner sanctum workshop. He'd managed two alligator dogs before moving back to golems.

He ignored the sudden urge to move onto making small and easy constructs. That was just his rest-deprived brain being weak.

[Warning! You have the condition **Exhaustion**. You require base
1x3 mana for each working.]
[You have 01:15:38 until you Pass Out from **Exhaustion**.]

Keith was thankful once again for his huge mana pool, which let him work to his heart's content.

The room was large and circular, and usually had a variety of global time-pieces hanging from the ceiling to keep him on track of the sun, the planets, the moons, the day, the hours, the minutes, and the flow of mana in the Dark Enchanted Forest—but all of those had needed to be moved to fit his latest creation: Gerald.

Gerald was a part of Keith's newest line of automatons. Ones that fought.

His previous creations had all been designed to defend, but since Ria had almost blown up the golem he'd been working on that first day, he had designed more and more active models.

Take Gerald, for example; he had a level forty Strength. He could rip siege weapons in half with his bare hands. What Gerald lacked for in beauty or refinement, he made up for by being a giant thick-as-a-brick marshmallow man-golem thing.

Keith activated a spell to bar the inner sanctum. It was a new spell he'd created just in case any *unannounced* guests decided to drop in uninvited.

Henrietta was out sightseeing today, so it should be fine, but he wasn't going to take that chance.

Then he got to work animating Gerald.

[You have attempted to use the Skill: **++Construct Creation: Large**.
You have a 78% chance of success with a +10% modifier from
Skill: **Mastery 4**.]

The loading screen in his activity log took an hour before it finished. He couldn't wait until he was high-enough level that there were no more "chance of success" rates.

[You have succeeded. Please name your **Automaton**.]

"Gerald."

[**Automaton: Gerald** is now able to understand basic **Commands**.
Please give your first command.]

"Go to the clearing outside the West Gate and wait for my next [Command]."

[**Gerald** has received your **Command**.]

Keith kept a mental note of the number of characters in his [Commands] to ensure he stayed under the limit. A hundred and forty seemed like such an arbitrary limit, but such were the rules of magic.

After the workshop was cleaned up, and his various magical paraphernalia returned to its rightful place, Keith summoned Tulith. She had letters for him.

The first was from the royal capital of Drendil.

> *Henri,*
> *We have sent so many letters, and you haven't replied even once. The* impropriety *to not reply to your own mother! I have raised you since you were a child, fed you, and provided every opportunity, and you don't have the common decency to show proper respect.*
> *You are naive Henri, and you never make the right choices. No one is going to listen to someone who isn't able to complete basic tasks. Your father and I are incredibly disappointed in you. I feel like a failure as a mother. You*

haven't even managed to kill Monfort in a month under the same roof. You could at least escape and come home. Don't tell me that you can't break the bars with that disgusting sixty Strength of yours.

I shouldn't have to repeat myself. You are a smart child who listens to her parents. I expect to hear from you soon.

Queen Thalia

Keith felt immense satisfaction as he cast [Burning Hand], lighting the letter on fire.

The second missive was from Elder Clarissa from Thistlecrick:

Beg pardon, Your Viciousness,
Please let us know if we are to receive guests from the castle in the future.
Your faithful servant,
Elder Clarissa of Clan Lamia,
Thistlecrick

Ah, that was a mistake on Keith's part. He had honestly gotten so focused on creating an army to withstand King Simon's invasion that he had forgotten to inform his subjects that the princess would be visiting. She was a force to be reckoned with, and he shouldn't like to see anyone get hurt when Ria utterly destroyed those who refused her baking.

He really should find the Dark Enchanted Forest's Royal Crystal in his godmother's hoard . . . or he could just ask the maids to send notice ahead. They knew Ria's schedule better than he did.

He wished he could just send Tulith to sort Feliwyn's hoard, but who knew how many enchanted or cursed spatulas that dragon had? She also had a habit of not re-sheathing her knives and swords, just tossing them in the pile. It made searching her rooms a bit . . . dicey.

"Gimtak!" Keith leaned over his desk and called for the imp working in the aide alcove.

"Yes, Your Viciousness?" Gimtak jumped up and stuck a red pin into the page he was working on before flying over. "How can I serve you?"

"I need you to go find the maid Lilith and bring her here."

"Right away, Your Viciousness."

Gimtak was the best runner Keith had, mostly because he didn't bother with hallways and just flew in and out of windows. And he could search the entire castle in fifteen minutes with his [Scouting] perk.

Lilith came hurrying in. It used to be that she was never summoned to the Dark Lord's office, but it was becoming a frequent occurrence these days. She curtsied. "How can I ssserve you, Master?"

"How is Rinrin faring with the princess's wardrobe?" He pushed his glasses up. "And what is Ria wearing to Grand Duchess Calisto's Spring Ball?"

Lilith curtsied again and answered. "Rinrin has completed tailoring three day dresses, two adventuring outfitsss, a practice suit, riding clothesss, and one evening gown. The princesss has left it up to Rinrin to decide."

"Is Rinrin in now?"

"Yesss, Your Viciousnesss."

"Bring her to me," he ordered. "Please. You are otherwise dismissed."

Sometime later, Rinrin shuffled into his office.

"This Rinrin is here, Master." The ratkin was old, and her *th*'s were especially pronounced because of her broken front tooth. "How may I serve you, Dark Lord?"

Keith asked, "What is Princess Henrietta wearing to the Spring Ball?"

"Me thinks she will wear whatever she wants." Rinrin chuckled. "But this lowly one is making something special. Heheh, something special indeed."

"Why am I suddenly worried?"

"Have trust in Rinrin," the old woman said. "Now, does the Dark Lord want to match with the young princess?"

Keith flinched. She *was* young, and that's why despite their tentative flirtations, he wanted to wait as long as possible. Technically, after her birthday next month, they would only be six years apart, and worse marriages had been formed for king and country in the past.

Not that he wanted a worse marriage. Or any marriage . . . Not that she'd say yes.

Why was he even about thinking this?

Keith coughed. "Yes. No sense riding the same carriage if we clash."

"Just leave it to Rinrin." The ratkin nodded. "Clothes for the ball. Clothes for the ball . . . And His Viciousness? Will my Dark Lord treat his buttons nicely? You will be nicer to your buttons, yes-yes?"

"Of course I will," Keith lied. "Now, go back. I have work to do."

He wasn't just sending her away to get out of a long-standing war about his buttons. Keith did, in fact, have work to do.

CHAPTER 23

Silk Was My Guilty Pleasure

Henrietta

Practically the first thing I did in Thistlecrick was stab the Lamia chief's son in the throat.

He was wearing a gorget, so I wouldn't have crushed his windpipe even if my perfect execution of a sword thrust had failed . . . probably.

Honestly, Marik was a good Warrior. His spearmanship was excellent, and he didn't have to worry about poor foot work because, well . . .

Ahem, anyway, he deserved it.

After the naga delegation had been brought out by the guard, I'd introduced myself again and offered up my basket.

That was when one naga from Clan Lamia had immediately shoved to the front of the procession and accosted me.

Marik was a buff fighter covered in head protection, muscles, and nothing else. His scaled snake lower body had lifted him up to loom over me in a rather amusing attempt at intimidation.

He'd been so passionate with his, "They say you're a Sword Master, so prove it!" that I'd been startled, and a single loaf of bread had fallen out of my basket. Only my high reflexes had saved it from certain dusty doom. However, it *had* gotten an indent in the crust where I'd grabbed it, and I was embarrassed that one of the three ruling families would have less-than-perfect bread.

So now we were having a friendly spar, and I *definitely* wasn't taking it out on him.

"I concede," Marik said from where he lay curled on the floor. Or that's what I imagine he tried to say while choking violently from the force of my [Force Thrust]. He may have been suffering from a few cracked ribs, too, but he was a fighter—he'd be *fiiine*.

"I apologize for my son." Elder Clarissa of Clan Lamia thumped a fist to her heart as a sign of respect. "And thank the princess for taking the time to show him some pointers." The older woman had the same dark features of her boy, but her eyes shone with golden slits where Marik's were a deep brown. Two naga soldiers from Clan Lamia helped him up and took him away.

I knew who they were because each of the clans had different heraldry. Clan Lamia was an eye inside an oval egg, Clan Melusine had a twin-tail serpent like an upside-down heart, and Clan Kidna was a serpent head and fang with a single drop of venom.

I shrugged. "Anytime. King Keith let me know that you love to battle. I just wasn't expecting to be *asked* so soon."

"It won't happen again." The other clan leaders looked at Clarissa, who kept a calm face under the scrutiny.

"Thank you again for the gift, Princess," Elder Vance Kidna offered, presumably to move things along. "May we escort you? My daughter Mera would be honored to show you the hot springs."

Elder Draken Melusine cut in, waving a hand at a young naga teen wearing a beautiful silk vest trimmed with embroidered snakes. "And our Planta would be honored to show you around the town."

"That sounds lovely," I said, smiling at Planta. Quite a few of the naga were wearing silk, actually. Thistlecrick was right beside the arachnid dwellings, and most people didn't realize that spiderkin silk passed through here first. I knew; silk was my guilty pleasure. "Is it alright if I visit the town, then swing by the practice ring? I would love to work up a sweat before visiting the hot springs."

The Elders agreed, Clarissa looking relieved, and I set off with Planta. The young woman was very *fiery* in a way I'd never experienced before. "Princess, this haut pink is a wonder on you, and the cut accentuates your hips. You simply *must* buy it." Planta slithered around me, trying fabric and dresses up against me. We were at a small boutique in a sprawling merchant quarter carved into a cliffside. "I've heard that Grand Duchess Calisto ordered her niece a tea gown in this exact color. And Their Royal Highness of Peldeep imported a wagon load of this exact fabric from my clan for their newly renovated Rose Parlor. Can you imagine what it must look like?"

I really couldn't. It was a very . . . exciting shade of pink. Not that I had time to respond.

"Oh my, I just *have* to show you the accessories designed for this green day gown. They make you look like a woodland nymph! My cousin Sheila handcrafted the gold. It's real dwarven mined, too. We raided an illegal gnome transport vessel from the kingdom of Baldorin trying to cut through the Dark Enchanted Forest last fall, and now we have more gold than we can deal with even after the king's tax."

I will just say that the hour and a half I spent with Planta was more informative, more exhausting, and just *more* than any other social experience in my life. I came out of it with a surprising two *full* trunks of new dresses, stunning embossed leather greaves, a parasol, four pairs of shoes—alright, the black leather boots with silver vine threading made my heart happy—and a small chest of matching jewelry.

My wallet was a bit lighter, but honestly, I had been an active adventurer conquering dungeons for the past ten years, and I had the money to spend. My enchanted Valaria-issued Sales and Accounts card from the continental treasury of the Valaria Moniers Guild let me know that I could spend some more time with Planta and not worry too much.

While checking my purchases, I noticed something on my account that I had not accounted to find.

[February 5-15, Pre-Authorized Deposit of 20 Gold from the
Kingdom of Nilheim.]
[February 15-30, Pre-Authorized Deposit of 30 Gold from the
Kingdom of Nilheim.]

Keith was paying me? A wage? And how had he gotten an authorized signature? It must have been the laboratory aid contract! He'd been paying me for the test subject work, and at *two gold a day*.

Huh. So much for my [Bureaucracy] skill. It was embarrassing to realize I had overlooked it until now. I'd just assumed that my work over the last month had been without pay.

Sithli and Chikli were right: I needed to respect myself better.

"I'll have your clothes sent on to the castle, Princess." Planta smiled and tossed her long purple hair over her shoulder with flair, looking every bit the confident woman I'd come to admire. "But this is a special gift from *me*."

Planta opened one of the boxes and brought out a tight-fitting cotton swimsuit with a slight ruffle at the hip and matching white slippers. The second was a long purple silk bathrobe to wear over it all.

"Oh my goodness, Planta! You didn't?!" I reached out and caressed the silk robe.

Usually, silk was a terrible choice to wear while you were damp. The fabric was clingy and didn't absorb a lot of water. It quickly got wet, cold, and generally unpleasant. But this wasn't regular silk; this was high-grade arachnid silk from last season's weave. It was strong, waterproof, and easily regulated body heat. "It's beautiful . . . Thank you."

I suddenly wanted to cry. No one had ever given me such a wonderful, thoughtful, perfect gift before. I was moved.

"No, thank *you*," Planta said, blushing slightly. "For not killing Marik after he was so rude this morning. He's not usually that bad, but he does take being the strongest very personally . . ."

I see. I reached up slightly and lightly patted the girl on the shoulder. "No worries. I have no intention of killing anyone."

Planta put her hand on mine and smiled. "Then why don't I drop you off at the martial plateau? Don't worry about this." She waved at the trunks. "We'll handle everything."

"I'm ready!"

CHAPTER 24

Who Told the Future Like This?!

Keith

"I don't have *time* for this, Rufus." Keith pushed up his glasses and tried to wave away his demon general and closest friend. "Ria is going to be back tomorrow!"

"You *ordered* your own sessions," Rufus said, not budging from his relaxed stance in front of Keith's desk. "With a special enchanted scroll signed in blood. You aren't allowed to skip them unless I say so."

"But I'm *fine*," Keith insisted. "The paperwork is more important right now."

"Are you fine?" Rufus leaned over Keith's desk and stared him in the eye. "Or do you need relationship advice because *you've never experienced a relationship before?* And don't try to convince me you aren't interested in the princess. You gave her the *QUEEN'S ROOMS.*"

"She's a visiting *royal princess!* They were the only fancy rooms we had," Keith protested. It was the truth.

"And now that she lives here?"

Keith said nothing. He couldn't say that he liked the idea of her being there. Or that he didn't want to disturb her and make her move out. He also didn't want to say that the head maid had reported to him how much Ria loved her rooms or how happy he was that she was happy.

Also, it was nice that Ria wasn't stuck wearing adventuring travel wear all day. Though it would be nice to buy her something new . . .

Keith came back to the conversation and argued, "Still, I don't need relation-ship ad—"

"You wouldn't cast a spell without research," Rufus cut him off. "Or file these reports without understanding the math—and don't say you could do it. We both know Chloe is the only child genius. You would make a *mess* of Nilheim's reports without those algebra lessons."

Feliwyn's strict teaching hadn't just been relegated to Keith. She had kidnapped many lost souls while she was in charge of the castle and taught them reading and writing and arithmetic. It had irritated her that there were beings in the kingdom who couldn't read and appreciate her popular line of published romance novels.

"But—"

"No buts. I'll start the session here in front of your aides, or we can move somewhere more private," Rufus said. "You have so much to learn; the five love languages, the motivation wheel, interpersonal communication basics, and we can't forget conflict resolution."

Keith looked down at his mostly cleared desk and back up at the passionate beastman, then he sighed dramatically. "Fine! But you only get *one* hour."

"As you wish, my king." Rufus smiled. The two men repaired to a private room . . . and they were most certainly in there for longer than one hour.

Keith sat at a late dinner mulling over the difference between physical gifts and the gift-of-self as a display of affection when the shy lizardkin maid Winrith shuffled into the room.

Winrith was the nervous sort and shook violently in his presence. Keith always tried to speak gently to the woman, but usually, simple and direct worked best.

"Yes?"

"Y-Your V-Viciousnesss." She curtsied awkwardly and almost dropped something. She fumbled a bit then held out a sheet of paper. "F-For you."

Keith moved slowly to take it. "Very good, thank you, Winrith. You may go." She left and Keith read over the latest from the castle's Cast Crystal.

Hello, this is Madame Potts.
This week's events are in!
The griffins in Baldor's Peak have had three eggs stolen by
poachers and will start attacking the nearby dwarven outposts
by week's end. Find and return the eggs before the spring
equinox or else.
Thank you to the Servalt authorities for dealing with every-
thing in a timely manner. I really appreciate you.
Orion's Camp in the Grey Oak Hills has been overrun by Ban-
dit Bill and Jane. Be careful, Jane is an expert at long-ranged
weapons, and her husband is a proficient area-of-effect spell
caster. Rogue and Stealth types recommended.
The arachne will be awakening right before the Spring Ball.
While new silks won't be ready anytime soon, Their Royal
Highness Rowen of Peldeep has just received 36 bolts of pink

**arachne silk. This caster has it on the in that they've
earmarked a few rolls of silk as a prize for the Peldeep
St. Veralyn's Craft Fair.**

**Former Princess Henrietta of Drendil, Duke Wyldon of Ser-
valt, Master Thomas Martin of Servalt, Knight Commander
Bastian of Peldeep, and Countess Julia von Slyke of North
Sumbria are all making their first appearances in society at
this year's Spring Ball. Let's hope no one is foolish enough to
try poisoning someone this year . . . but please prepare your
antidotes all the same.**

**This seer wants to let King Simon know that *that* isn't a good
idea. But also, it might be Fate, and you will most certainly get
what you deserve.**

Hmm, I am messing up this telling . . . Oh well.

**Moving along, anyone visiting Hemlock Hill can touch the
Elder Hemlock Tree and gain a temporary +4 to any stat. This
is stackable with other buffs. The effect lasts longer based on
the Elder Hemlock Tree's favorability toward you.**

**Anyone looking for cornflower dew, there is a higher drop rate
in Dungeon Valley Crest this week.**

This is Madame Potts, signing off.

Keith didn't usually care about Madame Potts's Cast, even when it was about him. Everyone already knew how powerful he was, and his decrees were posted publicly. If he did do something noteworthy—like ordering Chloe to turn water into blood at a birthday party—then he usually had a good reason and didn't care if everyone talked about it.

He already knew King Simon's movements, and nothing Madame Potts said was likely to alter his plans.

But he *did* care that Henrietta's name was in the weekly events. What was going to happen this year that people needed to start carrying around *antidotes*? Who told the future like this? There should be *details*!

He was pretty certain any erstwhile poisoner wasn't going to be "Let's fight outside because it's rude to destroy people's property" Henrietta. Which meant that Keith was going to need to pack ready-made antidotes and send out spies to learn about the others mentioned alongside Ria.

Keith finished up his dinner of haggis with mashed potatoes and gravy. It was a new dish that was very popular among the beastfolk. After sending his regards to Panlith, he decided to swing by his personal apothecary.

He would, of course, pack his *own* poisons. You never knew when someone needed laxative in their tea.

CHAPTER 25

Which One of Us Would You Like to Fight First, Princess?

Henrietta

The fighting arena was carved into a plateau higher up on the mountain. A system of caves had been cut into the rock that included a resting area, some changing rooms, and a bathroom which I made use of. When I finished, I checked my gear for safety and then strode out onto the plateau.

There were men and women from all three Naga clans present. Some were fighting among themselves, and others holding practice bouts between families. Everyone came to a stop when they saw me.

"Um, hello," I said, giving a small wave. They all continued to stare at me in silence, so I scratched my head. "I was wondering if anyone wanted to spar?"

Suddenly, I was overwhelmed by very tall, very enthusiastic naga all looming over me. They argued among themselves until a member from each clan was chosen.

"I am Terra, from Lamia," Terra said. She tapped her fist to her heart in salute.

"I am Collin, from Kidna," Collin said. He tapped his fist to his heart in salute.

"And I am Shade, from Melusine," Shade said. She too tapped her fist to her heart.

"Excellent! I am Henrietta," I returned the greeting then waved toward a practice ring. "Shall we?"

The three shared a look before Terra asked, "Which one of us would you like to fight first, Princess?"

What a silly question, but I kept a straight face.

"I'll fight all of you, of course." I unsheathed my blade and checked my character sheet. My [Sword Aura] skill could last two hours before I needed a cooldown. "If I fight teams of three or four at a time, then I should get through everyone before dinner."

I closed my logs and looked up at my opponents. They wore a mix of awe, insult, and stoicism. Terra was the calm one, and immediately entered the ring. She unraveled her long snake body, freeing up her tail and looking ready to whip me. The others followed shortly.

"After what you did to my brother, I hope the three of us can give you a good warm-up," Terra said.

I cracked my neck and got into a casual fighting stance. "On the count of three?"

I won.

The girl, Shade, from Melusine had been the most challenging. She had a shadow-walker ability that let her teleport through shadows and into my blind spots. Terra fought similarly to Marik, with brute strength and heavy spearmanship. My [Quick Step] perk let me prevent getting blunt force trauma to the face from the butt of a spear, and my [Sword Sense] helped me [Parry] stealth cuts to the gut from Shade. Collin actually held off for most of the fight, and I didn't realize until later than I cared to admit that he was a sort of buff ranger type.

He could have enhanced his own weapon and attacked, but instead, he was defending from a distance and providing buffs to Terra and Shade. When I *did* realize what was happening, I jumped over the two in the vanguard and landed on Collin with a clean boot dagger.

I loved hidden daggers. No one expected a Heroine of Justice to fight dirty, so they focused mainly on the sword. Also, throwing knives at lesser targets while challenging a dungeon boss made it easier to clear floors faster.

Knives were wonderful.

I tapped Collin's nose, flat side down, and said, "You're out." Then returned to fighting the ladies.

Without their enhanced attributes, Terra and Shade were quick work. Honestly, with at least thirty levels between us, *everyone* was quick work. Still, I tried to give every warrior on the plateau a good fifteen-minute bout.

"Phew," I said after fighting the last challenger. "I actually worked up a sweat!"

My stamina was pretty big, and it refilled very quickly, but working against teams of enemies made for good exercise. Eventually, my [Sword Aura] had run out, but by that point I had been fighting the lowest-level newbie fighters, and I didn't need anything special to defeat them.

"Thank you again, Henrietta." Terra came forward and offered me a waterskin. I'd beaten a few heads together before everyone started calling me by my name. I liked being a princess . . . but I'd grown very fond of my real name. People might as well *use* it.

"My pleasure, Terra." I hesitated only a second before I asked, "How is your brother?"

"Embarrassed." The naga woman smiled. "But he'll feel better after he finds out about what happened here."

We both looked over the exhausted, bruised, and defeated group of naga—all of which were incredibly excited and already practicing ways to improve their fighting based on my recommendations.

"That's good." I nodded. "Tell him he shouldn't interrupt people like that. I almost dropped my gift!"

"Speaking of," Collin cut in. He and Shade joined them. No one had outright said it, but I assumed they were all pretty high up in their clan's hierarchy. "What *was* that? It was delicious!"

"I didn't get to try any," Shade sighed, "but I've heard from Janet, Planta's sister, that it was the most delicious bread they'd ever eaten."

I smiled. "That's good to hear. I got the recipe from a beastfolk friend, and I'd be happy to share it. I wasn't sure if you had any dietary restrictions . . ."

"Dairy," Collin answered. "We can eat most everything else. But something about cow milk just destroys us."

"Hm." I asked the first thing that came to mind, "Does having [Resist Poison] help?"

"No." He shook his head. "Though having a monstrously high Constitution does."

"Interesting."

"Well, Princess." Terra slithered around to Shade and put a hand on the naga's shoulder. "It's time that we return to our families for dinner. Collin will bring you to the hot spring house where his sister Mera is waiting to show you around."

"Shall we?" Collin bent down awkwardly to offer me an arm. I took it.

"That sounds lovely, Collin!"

Once I arrived at the stunning, carved wooden villa overlooking the springs, I was given my luxurious soft cotton bathroom suit and arachnid silk gown to lounge in while I ate chicken sausage, garlic stuffed olives, warm rye, unigoat cheese drizzled with honey, and a bowl of salted cashews.

I enjoyed the light charcuterie. They'd been all the rage last year, though no one had been able to figure out what *charcuterie* actually meant.

Then I was escorted to the hot springs.

Mera was in full professional tour mode, and after an hour at the pools and another hour getting a massage and mud wrap, we finally relaxed on an outdoor veranda to eat dinner.

The Kidna clan had set out an elaborate spread of roast lamb, truffle mushrooms in garlic hazelnut oil, and steamed vegetables in oyster sauce. Drinks included a glass of filtered mountain spring water and a smooth white wine labeled Beautiful Stars from one of Peldeep's famous vineyards called the Glass Apple.

"You know, Mera," I broached, "you don't have to play the host. I'm here to relax and just chat." Spending the day with Planta had *really* shown me how much time I'd spent with fake smiles and aristocratic etiquette. "Is there anything that you want to talk about?"

Mera warred with herself, and after a moment's hesitation, her demeanor dropped from rigid politeness to slightly conspiratorial. "There is one thing . . . Is it true that you came to challenge King Keith to a duel, and when you won, you asked to be the future queen of the Dark Enchanted Forest?"

I didn't spit take wine across the table because I had only just lifted the glass to my lips and hadn't actually taken a sip with which to spit.

"What?!"

CHAPTER 26

Interested

Keith

When Henrietta came back the next morning, she did not visit Keith.

In actual fact, he wouldn't have seen her normally because it was technically her day off . . . but even so, she had been joining him for lunch on her days off recently.

When he hadn't seen hide nor hair of her by late afternoon, he awkwardly inquired from Winrith.

Now, Keith was standing outside the Nightshade Rooms and trying to get up the nerve to knock.

After what was definitely *not* thirty minutes, he gave up. He could just talk to her tomorrow. He was turning to leave when Ria opened the door and poked her head out. "Hello, Keith . . ."

"Ah, hello, Henrietta."

Keith realized he hadn't bothered to hide his presence in front of a level sixty Sword Master. Her perception alone would have picked up someone standing outside her door this entire time.

"Do you want to come in?"

"Well, yes." He hesitated. "Would you like to talk here or go for a walk?"

Ria stepped back and motioned to come in. He noticed her ears were a little red, but otherwise, she seemed calm.

Keith had never been in his mother's rooms. He'd never met Queen Vera, and Feliwyn was his mother in everything but blood and title.

Ria led him to the parlor, and he made note of the interesting title of the book sitting on the table. He waved at it. "*Out of This World?*"

The princess smiled at the book. "It has every new recipe that's become popular in the last three years, and some that I've never heard of! The éclairs I made for tea last time were from this book."

The two sat down across from each other. "Was it from Feliwyn's book hoard?" Keith asked.

Honestly, that dragon loved the weirdest things. She kept three separate treasure piles: precious shiny things, from pebbles to gold; enchanted or otherwise useful tools, like swords and spatulas; and a book room full of romance novels and recipes. Oh, and a castle full of unique personalities.

"No. Actually, I got it in the mail."

"You did? From whom?" He didn't remember screening a recipe book, so this must have been when she'd first arrived.

"I don't know." Henrietta shrugged. "I haven't been able to confirm, but . . . Well, it's silly."

"Go on?"

"I think it might be from Madame Potts."

Keith started. "Why do you think that?"

"Well, Brownie sent me a letter at the same time and made no mention of it." Henrietta shrugged. "It's silly, I know . . . but who else could have known that I liked to bake? The postage is international."

"I see." Keith wasn't usually interested in recipe books, but this was a perfect opening for what he was actually here to talk about. "Speaking of Madame Potts, did you hear her Casting while you were away yesterday?"

"Sadly no." Henrietta shook her head. "I was fighting the Naga Warriors when it happened."

"Did you know you were in it again?" Keith tried to keep his tone neutral while he handed over the report.

Ria took it and read it over while Keith tried not to stare at her. She was adorable as usual, with her poofy brown hair pulled back by some type of headband. No loose bangs today. She wore a silk green vest over a lace-embroidered tunic with half sleeves. Her pants were a matching green to the vest, and she had on light peach-colored slippers.

"Does this mean that someone is going to get poisoned at Grand Duchess Calisto's ball? Because that's what it sounds like." Ria passed back the note.

"That's how I read it, too. Would you consider bringing some antidotes with you when we attend?" Keith brought out a few of his higher-level antidotes. They shined a vibrant red, and they were so potent they actually glowed in the dark.

Ria looked at the potions. She looked around the room. Then she looked at Keith.

He didn't know why, but he had a feeling about what was coming. "Ria, I—"

"Dark Magician Keith."

Oh no, that wasn't good.

"Do you know what everyone is talking about in your kingdom?" She frowned at him, and his entire person began panicking.

"I can explain!"

"I think you should." Henrietta nodded sagely. "I was worried that you didn't know."

"What?" Keith honestly thought she was talking about what Rufus had mentioned earlier: the fact that he'd let her stay in the Nightshade Rooms. "What don't I know?"

"Everyone is talking about how I defeated you in our duel!"

"But we never fought."

"That's not the point!" Henrietta sighed. "At first, everyone thought you won because I went to the dungeon. But now, I'm still here, and . . ." Henrietta paused, her ears growing crimson, "they thought that I won and asked for the position of queen as a reward."

"I . . . I can see why they might think that." Keith pushed up his glasses. "It doesn't help that I've given you Mother's rooms."

"Why *did* you—"

"Because you are a royal princess, and these are the only rooms that were up to standard. I couldn't very well give you Feliwyn's rooms! They're probably cursed." Keith pushed up his glasses. "And then, when you stayed, I thought they just fit."

Neither knew what to say.

Finally, Keith took a deep breath. "Listen, Ria."

She waited.

"What if I told you . . . Wait, this isn't the place to do this. This isn't how I thought—" He fumbled his words then took a deep breath. He just needed to follow his heart and communicate, just like Rufus had said. "I want you to know that I'm . . . interested."

"Interested?"

"Yes." Keith waved awkwardly between the two of them. "In us. In you. Maybe with some time. Maybe it won't . . . I like you, and I like that you are using these rooms, and I like the idea of you being queen of the Dark Enchanted Forest one day, and I'm just *interested*."

With that, he stopped putting his metaphorical foot in his mouth and put his face in his hands, not looking at her reaction. Worried about what he might see.

"That's good." Ria coughed. "Because I'm also interested."

"Wait, really?" Keith stood up, full of warring emotions and hope. "Not just in walks around the garden, but maybe more?"

"I mean, I *like* walks around the garden," Ria said. "I'm just also interested in other things."

"Like what?"

CHAPTER 27

Did I Want to Hold Hands with a Ruffled Dark Magician King?

Henrietta

I had spent the rest of my time in Thistlecrick with the knowledge that *everyone* thought I was going to marry Keith.

Marik had only instigated his challenge because he was a personal student to Derilla Vane, the General of the North, and he'd wanted to prove the rumors one way or another.

I knew that I'd have to talk to Keith about it when I got back . . . but I didn't have the courage to bring it up. It was *embarrassing*!

And then, the man just had to stand outside my door for half an hour. Probably because I'd missed lunch and he was worried about me.

I never expected that I'd be awkwardly sitting here after a heartfelt confession being asked what *I* wanted, again. Nobody ever cared about what I wanted.

"Maybe . . ." I blushed. "We could hold hands?"

That sounded like a good next step.

"Do you want to hold hands now? While walking around the gardens?"

Did I want to hold hands with a ruffled Dark Magician King and go for a walk in his man-eating flower garden?

"Yes, but what're we going to do about the rumors that we're getting married?" I also stood up, walking around the small table to stand beside Keith. "Also, I need to change into real shoes."

Keith bit his lip. "I could order a stop to the rumors on pain of Rufus or put out a detailed event of what happened."

"Would that even help?" I chuckled. "I'm living in the queen's rooms, filing kingdom paperwork, having private dinners with the king, and that king has in fact expressed *interest* in me."

Keith walked me to the door, and I slipped on the boots I'd left haphazardly by the entry alcove the previous night.

"You're right." He pushed up his glasses. "It probably wouldn't."

I hesitantly took his offered hand, and we headed to the garden. His hand was warm and had rough calluses over his palm and fingers from years of building magical constructs. He also had a slightly chopped-off pinky.

I was glad to have this chance to visit the garden today; the last of the corpse roses were wilting, and I was sad to see them go.

"There's one more thing I'm worried about," I broached. "What will people say when my father goes through with his threats to invade the Dark Enchanted Forest? He's raising an army as we speak."

"Ah, you heard about that, did you?" Keith sighed. "I was trying to figure out a way to tell you."

"Panlith was reviewing army rations when I swung by after I got back." It had been pretty obvious once I'd spent five seconds glancing over his shoulder. Logistics were my specialty.

Keith shook his head. "As I said before, he's been talking about this for years; it's why I have spies in Drendil. They sent word yesterday that King Simon is preparing an army."

"What are we doing about it?"

Keith shrugged. "I'm making attack-based automatons and sending out missives to the generals of each region to forward soldiers to the southern border. We can't guarantee they'll take the Great Road . . . though only an *idiot* would march through the wilds of the Dark Enchanted Forest."

"So no guarantee at all."

Keith nodded. "But I'm going to assume he'll take the Great Road, so I'll send our forces there. We have a few elven scouts skilled enough to survive along the border; they'll let us know if your father changes his mind. One of the generals should be enough to handle whatever Drendil has to send us."

"Hmm, let me think." My training had covered the tactical assault of an enemy, so I knew the general battle strategies commonly preferred by Drendil's forces. Most of the military resources were given to the Drendil Navy, as the seas along the southern coast were full of monsters . . . any army raised for land battles would be small and full of adventuring parties and mercenaries instead of soldiers.

After some time walking around the garden in silence, I said, "Alright. Here's what we can expect to happen and how to plan accordingly:

"The Servalt Kingdom to the east recently had a rise in crime and struggles with illicit trade. While the royal family won't condone my father's war, there may be some sympathizers who could be convinced to join the battle. It is, however, very unlikely. Stationing a scout party with personal Cast Crystals from the treasury should give us advance warning if they try to flank us.

"While those griffins are attacking the dwarven kingdom of Baldorin, I know for a fact that there are a few shady merchants that could use the opportunity to slip contraband through the Dark Enchanted Forest while we're distracted.

"Peldeep is our most successful trading partner. The nation as a whole is also pretty ambivalent to foreign affairs. Their Royal Highness might be an opportunist, but I think it's safe to say there will be no action from the west. They might even aid us.

"As such, if we move most of the western army to the southern border, and half of the eastern army to the Great Road between here and Drendil, then we will have two waves of defense. And, if need be, we can send the eastern army back to cover Servalt on short notice."

Keith stared at me. I was impressed that he'd listened silently through my plans all the way until we arrived at our usual sitting spot. I realized, sadly, that I needed to release his hand to take my seat, and I unconsciously squeezed before letting go.

"That is very well thought-out," Keith finally spoke, and I pretended not to see him wipe his hand while I also rubbed my sweaty palms on my thigh. We could be awkward together, at least.

We settled in and I continued. "Thank you. I figured the Naga clans are close to the dwarven trade routes and could be on the lookout for any movement there."

". . ." Keith pushed up his glasses. "Derilla Vane, the Northern General, won't be awake by then, but a general is already overkill. Any of the naga sentinals should be more than enough."

"Why don't we split the naga forces and leave most of them between here and Frolin?" My new battle-happy friends would cry when they heard that, so I added, "I know that leaving one half between their crossroad on the western road and this castle means they're better positioned . . . but I think we should move the others in between Gerda's bridge and the second line. Having dissatisfied and hotheaded troops in reserve won't do anyone any good."

"That won't work because the lizardkin are in charge of battalion defense, and they've decided to build traps, barricades, and spike walls in that area," Keith explained. "But we can send the naga as guards to assist the lizardkin defense line, giving them some action but mitigating our losses."

I nodded; that made sense. Strategic geographic troop placement was only viable if you knew the full picture. Gods, I loved logistics almost as much as baking pie. But not as much as making scones for Keith.

"Are we evacuating Kith Bog?"

"No." Keith shook his head. "The village might not have an active general, but it is quite a ways east of the Great Road. While it's technically between here and Drendil, it has no strategic importance. It's worthless swampland to anyone but the lizardkin. It's also one of my cities that likes to move around the most. It might not even be in the area by St. Veralyn's Day."

"Am I missing anything else?"

"Yes." Keith smiled a very big, vicious smile. He stood up and bowed eloquently, offering me his hand again. "Let me show you why they call me the Evil Overlord."

CHAPTER 28

Harbingers of Death and Destruction

Keith

After he had woken up from [Mana Burn], Keith had summoned all his wandering constructs from around the Dark Enchanted Forest.

Being near death had reminded him that just because no one had ever broken into his home before didn't mean it was impossible.

So, he had decided to rethink where all of his toys—cough—harbingers of *death* and *destruction* should live.

The reason he let them loose throughout the dark wood instead of hoarding them at the castle had to do with a few key factors, the first being that they were just plain *useful*. They maintained roads, they protected his villages and his minions, and they were his eyes upon the entire kingdom.

The second was that they were a physical demonstration of his power and a reminder to some of his more excitable minions that *he* was the king, and he could crush them under his feet if they thought to challenge him. Many clans, kin, and folk of Nilheim were used to being ruled by the smartest or punchiest or bloodiest among them, so letting them see dragon-size golems walking past their families let them know they were safe *and* they were weak.

The third, and arguably the most important, was due to a class perk that he'd gotten when he hit Master at level sixty at eighteen: his creations could gain *sentience*. Oh, it wasn't the same as talking to a real person. It was more that the essence of that creature came into being with it. Like a cat is a cat is a cat. A cat construct no longer moved like an inanimate wooden toy—it moved like a *cat*. And sometimes, it pushed things off the table and onto the floor; he didn't make many cat constructs anymore.

Keith could still give the sentient golems [Commands] and order them about . . . but it no longer felt like he was a puppet master making finger puppets dance. Instead, he felt like a mind magician making people dance against their will.

It wasn't pleasant, and it wasn't fun.

So he set them loose to go have adventures of their own. They had a job to do, much like everyone else, and basic rules they had to follow, just like everybody else . . . and he could reach out and contact them whenever he needed them.

Like now.

"Behold!" he said dramatically, waving his hand for added effect. They were standing on the top of the parapet overlooking the clearing west of his castle.

Beside him, Henrietta breathed a soft, "Wow."

Keith was immensely proud of his work.

They both stared out over hundreds of constructs, from a troop of mice sitting still in ranks, to the towering behemoths of rock or stone or wood that silently dwarfed the trees.

"I've stationed a large construct golem at every village in the forest, along with a flying-type scout to relay messages for us," Keith explained. "I've summoned all others here."

Instead of focusing on the legion of impressive feats of magic in front of them, Ria asked Keith the one thing he didn't want to talk about. "Keith?"

"Yes, Ria?"

"Why do you need relay messengers when you're the king? Why don't you just use the Cast Crystal like every other ruler?"

He scratched his head. "You know my godmother is a dragon, right?"

"Yes."

"She added the crystal to her hoard." He sighed. "And now we can't find it."

"You lost your King's Crystal?!" Henrietta stared at him incredulously, then giggled. Then doubled over laughing.

She obviously wasn't disappointed in him, which made this much easier. Keith explained, "I didn't know until it was too late and she'd flown off."

"Why not just hire the Mages Tower to make you a new one?"

"I didn't need it." Keith shrugged and waved all around them. "I can directly relay messages throughout the entire Dark Enchanted Forest—even places without a crystal—using my minions or constructs. It's a waste of money when I can just ask Feliwyn when she wakes up."

"When *is* Her Eminence supposed to wake up?"

Keith shrugged again. "She just wanted a light ten- to twenty-year nap."

"That's not helpful," Henrietta retorted; she looked back over his constructs. "But these are. I don't think my father has enough higher-level personnel in his army to get past the constructs, let alone the Dark Army. Even with mercenary adventuring parties added on. No wonder you haven't been worried."

"My hobby also happens to align with a healthy desire not to die," Keith joked. "Convenient when I'm so often sent assassins. Most of the smaller constructs were complete before I came into the throne."

Ria whistled. "Impressive."

"My plan was to mix them between the troops. Have the larger golems distract any powerful foes while buffed by Rufus's enhancements, then send in the midsize creations to take down basic ground soldiers. Most of the smaller constructs need my concentration to utilize, so I'll scatter them along the border where my elven scouts can't reach."

"Can I make another suggestion?" Ria grinned at the mice, bringing her fingers together in a look that would be *much* more menacing if she weren't such a cinnamon bun.

He would have to use that motion himself in the future. "Of course."

"How much do you know about battlefield logistics?"

CHAPTER 29

How Do You Audit Someone for Fun?

Henrietta

I reviewed the list of mice constructs Keith had given me. They were the smallest creatures in his army, and I had such wonderful plans for them. There were also a few moles that I'd decided to include in the mission.

After a quick explanation, Keith had readily agreed to send them where I wanted. Now, they all lay in wait beside the three small clearings between Drendil and the castle. One group was very close to the border, and the others were this side of Gerda's bridge.

With the help of one of Keith's raven constructs, I'd sent a letter off to my troll friend. It let her know where she could station and fight, or the best route for retreat. I didn't know her skills, and I didn't want to assume she was a fighter *just* because she was a troll.

"When do you think Father will attack?" I asked Keith. We had repaired to his office and were ignoring the work on his desk to review the battle plans.

"He did say he was going to wait until St. Veralyn's Day for word of your death," Keith reminded me, then he sighed. "But we shouldn't assume anything. He might strike early to catch us off guard."

"Or just because I stopped responding to his letters," I said before raising an eyebrow at the Dark Lord. "He is still sending letters?"

"Less than before." Keith shrugged. "I think he's finally accepted that you aren't replying, and now he's just addressing letters to you with an extra postscript for me." He flexed his fingers. "They are very therapeutic."

"How so?" I was curious how my parents' letters could inspire anything positive.

Keith chuckled. "I enjoy setting them on fire."

"Ah, I see." That did sound nice. "Now, as I was saying, we should make sure we have a grasp of the army's movement path."

Keith said, "If they follow the road, it will take them two days to march here. There isn't a village anywhere close by, so they'll be forced to sleep in the open."

We stood over a large map of the Dark Enchanted Forest. The forest sometimes moved around a bit, but everything attached to the roads stayed consistent, and the woods usually left monster lairs, lakes, and hills in the same area. Magical flower fields and ancient elm trees moved . . . but who knew if that was the forest or the flora itself.

"So one day to reach Gerda's bridge, and then another day to us?"

"Once they cross the bridge, they can march straight here or head east to Kith Bog. Though we might add half a day just to get over the troll bridge. It's designed for wagons crossing single file, which will slow them down a fair bit."

"What stops them from crossing the river directly?" I asked. I was going to do just that if Gerda turned me away.

"The water around a troll bridge is enchanted," Keith explained. "Anyone who crosses through it will end up back on the side they started."

"Really?"

"Yes, it's troll magic. The bridge troll—Gerda, was it? She'll presumably stay in her troll house while they pass. Even if Gerda *does* leave, the magic won't dissipate for at least a month. The bridge will simply continue to ask whichever riddle was used last to anyone crossing."

"So that puts a potential three days between when they enter the forest and when they reach us?" That would be plenty of time to strike.

"I think your plan is brilliant even without the added time from the bridge." Keith smiled at me, and I felt my face heat up at the straightforward praise.

"If it works"—I nodded—"we will have broken their spirits long before we get the chance to break their bones."

Keith and I rolled up the map and cleared the table, getting ready for his evening paperwork, which I'd offered to help with even though it was technically my day off.

I had figured out that while Keith *did* manage things well enough in his kingdom that he wasn't working *every day*, he still swung by the office just in case files with Immediate Action required his attention. Surprisingly, it wasn't as often as I'd imagined.

"In Nilheim, I only have a few cities under me, and each of those is ruled very differently based on the people who live there," the Dark Overlord explained to me. "Most of them are autonomous and simply report mandatory revenue and trade information, who was born and who died, who immigrated or emigrated, and any concerns. My spies are all golems whom I can see and hear through, and they don't require a transcript unless I'm using that knowledge to direct minions."

I eyed the three stacks of paper that had made it from the diligent group busy paper-shuffling in the corner. "What about the rest of it?"

"What do you mean?"

"Where does the rest of that paperwork go if you aren't going over it to make sure it's correct?"

Keith stared at me like he didn't understand, and I started babbling nervously, "I mean, how do you know if the documents are forwarded correctly and no one is breaking the law or committing fraud?"

"Simple." Keith smiled. "I don't, and I don't *need* to. My office assistants are from every corner of the Dark Enchanted Forest, and they are required to audit each other in a rotation. There was a magician named Ajax who retired two years ago who used to clone himself and audit everyone for *fun*."

"How do you audit someone for fun?" I couldn't fathom it.

"We have an enchanted abacus that calculates the input and output of anything it's set atop," he explained. "When it's your turn to audit, then you get to take a day off and wander through the previous two years' tomes checking that the budgets drafted for each month line up with the records. If you find anything amiss, you get a bonus, and if it's important, you get a paid two-weeks' vacation."

"And no one cheats?"

"Of course they cheat." Keith laughed. "It's politics. But I don't care as long as my constructs bring back news from across the kingdom that things are running smoothly. The generals run the kingdom, the clan leaders run the towns, and I just have to clean up problems by directly using my golems."

"And it works?"

"I wouldn't say it—"

"No one's going to welcome me back?" An adorable woman with long, curly sun-blonde hair and sparkling green eyes stood in the doorway to the office. "Or do I need to request a formal audience, *Your Royal Viciousness*."

CHAPTER 30

Leave My Captured Princess Alone, Chloe

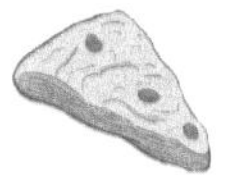

Keith

"Welcome back," Keith said, dryly. "Now get back to work."

Chloe Watercress and Rufus Triever had been Keith's best friends since he could understand what friendship meant.

While Rufus was the second son of the Gren's Keep clan leader and was all but *given* to Keith as a suitably aged playmate, Chloe was a literal stray brought home from one of Feliwyn's flits about the Dark Enchanted Forest.

A flight of fancy, as it were.

"Truly?" Chloe sauntered over and leaned against the desk. "You're going to war with Drendil after capturing their most-desirable-in-all-the-land to be your queen . . . and you can't even be bothered to introduce your most trusted advisor?"

Said princess coughed and reached for her waterskin. Keith smirked. "We both know Rufus is my most *trusted* advisor. *You* are just the most *powerful*."

"Damn straight I am," Chloe agreed. Then she winked at Ria. "Powerful, that is, not straight. Is Keith treating you all right, darling, or should I show you the dark delights a *real* black magician is capable of?"

"Oh my . . ." Ria had actually pulled out a traveling pack of nuts from her belt pouch and was happily snacking on them while looking back and forth between Chloe and Keith.

Keith rolled his eyes. "Leave my captured princess alone, Chloe; she's too busy to play with you."

"With what?" The woman tossed her golden hair over her shoulder and shifted her attention back to Keith.

"*Me.*"

Henrietta put up her hand to get their attention. "Hello, Chloe? The necromancer, I assume? Keith is correct, and we are . . . um, courting? Is that the right word?"

Keith nodded. "I think that works nicely."

"So I'm sorry that I can't return your interest," Henrietta finished. "But it's still nice to meet you."

Chloe stared at Henrietta very hard for a second, and then she burst into laughter. "It's nice to meet you too, Princess Henri."

"Henrietta, please," the princess requested.

"It's nice to meet you, Henrietta."

Keith felt the small worry he had secretly ignored up until this point fade away. It would have been a *disaster* if Chloe didn't like Henrietta . . . Though he was sure Ria would have won the woman over eventually by sheer volume of delicious snacks. But it was better to have everyone on the same page before the invasion.

Speaking of the invasion.

"Chloe"—Keith tapped his index finger on the table in front of him for attention—"just to bring you up to date, the invasion is set for two weeks from now. It'll take about three days to get from the forest entrance to our castle, and I've sent out instructions to the generals for troop placement and supplies."

He stood up and walked behind where Henrietta was seated, placing one hand on her shoulder. "The princess and I were just discussing Drendil war tactics, and I'm sure there is a lot to discuss. But first, how many undead soldiers do you have ready for battle?"

Chloe pushed off from the desk and reached up to scratch her neck sheepishly. "Actually? Almost none."

"What?" Keith wasn't even angry, just surprised.

"It's your stupid employment contract," Chloe huffed.

Henrietta cut in, "The one that says you'll [Raise], [Resurrect], or [Revive]?"

"That's exactly the one." Chloe nodded. "It also says that after death, we promise those we [Raise] job security and a standard of living for a natural life span—and then eternal rest. I just have some ghouls I've hired to do things.

"I *am* the most powerful person in the Dark Enchanted Forest next to our Arcane Sage golem-happy king here"—she pointed rudely at Keith—"but I've spent most of my resources over the last decade managing the population and resurrecting our minions. Which means . . ."

"Yes?" Keith asked.

"I have a binding magical influence over at least half your army through my [Life Boon] perk, and I could overthrow you easily if I had a mind," Chloe declared. "But I *don't* have a legion of mindless undead. Who *wants* a legion of undead, anyway? They smell funny."

"So what I'm hearing," Keith said, "is that you'll be useful on the front lines resurrecting people."

"Technically, I'd say the mouse trap is our first line of defense," Henrietta added helpfully. "So the second line would be a better fit, since that's where the mortal army begins."

"Quite right." Keith offered Henrietta a hand. "Now, should we head in to dinner?"

Henrietta accepted his escort, and Keith tucked her arm in his comfortably.

Chloe scoffed. "You're no fun. I'm not joking, you know; I could totally overthrow you! The ruler of the Dark Enchanted Forest is determined by strength, and that doesn't just mean level."

At this, Keith pushed up his glasses and looked Chloe over. Unlike Rufus, Keith actually needed glasses to see, and what he saw reassured him. He slowly smiled at his friend.

"Alright. If you *want* to be the king, then you'll be a great fit." Keith waved his free hand at his desk. "That means you'll be taking over the paperwork—something we both know won't faze you." Chloe had been the child prodigy of their group, and even impressed Her Eminence Feliwyn. "Of course, that also means no long vacations away from Nilheim, no month-long visits with friends, no more private budget. And you'll have to deal with the clan complaints, recruiting, and interkingdom *politics*—"

"Alright, alright, you've made your point." Chloe laughed it off as a joke, but she was actually flinching at his list by the time she cut him off. "Army babysitter it is."

"If it helps," Henrietta tried to console the beautiful woman, "you'll be leading your own group."

That made Chloe shake her head sadly. "None of my ghouls would—"

"Not undead. Sorry," Henrietta apologized for cutting her off. "You'll have four healers."

"Titled Healers? You don't mean Old Dame Juli—No, wait, *four?*" This got the necromancer's attention. "Since when did we have *any* healers in the Dark Lord's army?"

"Things change. You were gone for a month," Keith reminded her, walking Henrietta toward the office door. "We'll talk about this more tomorrow. Goodnight."

He heard Chloe grumble, "Don't you mean *you've* changed."

She wasn't wrong.

CHAPTER 31

To Confront or Not to Confront, That Was the Question

Henrietta

Two weeks was not a long time . . . but it felt like forever after I'd finished all the battle plans with Keith and had nothing else to do but sit around and *wait*.

Commander General Rufus and Necromancer Chloe had reviewed and given recommendations, but the preplanning was done, and now it was just checking in to see if people were getting into place and had the right supplies.

Everything was going well; at least it had been until I had a sudden surprise guest in the kitchen.

I was making *Out of This World* chai spice custard buns when a gentle knocking from the door caught my attention. Keith stood there. "Henrietta?"

I had my hair in a bun on top of my head and flour on my face, and I was wearing a very stained hedgehog-print apron.

The butter buns were hot out of the oven, and I was brewing chai on the stove. It was a lovely blend of spices and tea and cream that smelled amazing. I was supposed to whip eggs into the chai and then pour it into hollowed-out butter buns, and then bake them for ten minutes until it solidified into custard.

"Keith?" I quickly strained the chai so that it wouldn't over-steep and set it aside. Then I wiped my hands on a clean towel and joined him at the door. "What brings you to the kitchen?"

"Is now a bad time?" he asked hesitantly.

"No, no!" I assured him. "The buns need to cool down before I add the custard, so I'm not in a rush."

I was often tied to the oven until the baking and dishes were done, but today, I was trying a new *Out of This World* recipe, and I liked to give each recipe my full attention.

"Good, because there's a favor I'd like to ask," Keith broached. "Have you been to Amarinth Glade?"

"No, that's just east of Kith Bog, right?" I crinkled my nose in concentration, bringing up a mental map of the Dark Enchanted Forest. Not that it mattered when things were always moving.

"No, it's moved east of Thistlecrick at the moment," he said, reaching out one hand and grabbing mine. He slowly traced a finger on the palm of my hand as he explained, "I've just got word from my raven automatons that a suspicious group has set up camp in the glade. I've just finished relocating all of our troops and I don't want to send them immediately back east. Especially when they are at work building barricades. Knolith, the General of the East, is still in closed door training and I need someone strong enough to control the situation."

He cleared his throat. "You have [Quick Step], right? Would you consider popping over? I know it's not the usual sightseeing, but it's best if someone competent—"

"I'd be happy to help," I cut him off, squeezing his hand in assurance . . . and to stop him from distracting me with his fingers. "Thank you for trusting me."

He smiled at me and visibly relaxed. "I'm grateful that you're on our side, truly. It's like we suddenly have an extra General class—though I don't want to pressure you into fighting. You've had enough of that."

"Well, *I'm* grateful that you're not just locking me up in a castle like any *other* princess." My Aunt Beatrice was like that. Kept in the castle until she was married off and then kept in her husband's castle until his untimely demise, no matter how many times she demonstrated her political prowess. Cousin Francis took after his father and I'd never even met his wife.

I thrust out my jaw in determination. "I might not be the real cause for my father's war, but I'm still a part of it. I *want* to help."

Keith squeezed my hand back. "Then I'll let the closest scout group know you're on your way. You can travel with the raven, Hubert, and he'll be able to keep us connected on your trip."

"Alright," I agreed. Hubert was a lovely name for a bird. "I'll finish up these buns while Lilith readies my backpack. It shouldn't take longer than an hour. I'll meet you at the front gate?"

"I'll see you there."

Usually, when traveling long distances, the best option was a strong horse. But I was faster than your average horse, and mildly allergic to the beasts. It was nice that the Dark Army used alligator dogs to pull carts and get around, as it meant less horrid sneezing on my part.

I was a *lot* faster than an alligator dog.

The road from the Dark Lord's castle took me straight east, and by early evening, I was in the vicinity of Amarinth Glade. As this was the Dark Enchanted

Forest, there were no guarantees it would still be there; though Keith had assured me it wouldn't wander far. In fact, it turned out to be only a ten-minute walk from where the raven had last seen it.

A scout with the ability to fly was very handy.

The two of us crouched behind some bushes, listening in on a rowdy bunch sitting and drinking around a fire. There were about ten people, four horses, and two wagons. Shortly after we arrived, the pot of stew they had going on the fire was ready, and everyone gathered round for dinner.

"We're almost home, ladies and gents," a happy voice boasted. It belonged to a large woman in a blue vest sitting on a makeshift log. She was eating the first bowl of soup served. "Which means only one drink each, and then let's get an early bed."

There was a groan from the other campers, but no one argued.

"Hey, we'll all be living like kings when we meet Duke Lector in Servalt," the woman consoled them. "Easiest gold we've ever made."

"Speak fer yerself, boss!" a young man missing a great many teeth chimed in. He had a large scroll map out in front of him as he nursed a cup.

"Come off it, Warren. You can't expect places to stay still in the dark woods. You know that."

"And what about those damn *bluffs*," another grumbled. He was short and lithe and chewing on hay grass. "*You* didn't 'ave to climb tha side of a friggin' canyon drop to get the goods, now didja?"

"We all appreciate you getting the eggs, Darryl," the leader said. "And you didn't die, so it all turned out fine in the end."

I'd heard enough to piece together a picture from one of Madame Potts's Castings. Now, I just needed to think about how I should go about this.

To confront or not to confront, that was the question.

CHAPTER 32

Treasure Hunting

Keith

Keith focused on keeping Hubert seated on a branch beside Henrietta.

He had finished his office work, then spelled around in his workroom for a few hours until it was time to see Henrietta.

He moved the raven to hop onto her shoulder and gently ran its beak through her hair, reminding her that he was still there if she needed him.

The bird's eyes were enhanced with magic, and he could see the princess as clear as day even in the dark night of the forest. She was deep in thought but reached up to stroke his construct's feathers. Keith was pleased that he had used real feathers for the aesthetic.

Keith didn't care about the mercenaries or the eggs, though he supposed returning them would be a great political boon in his relations with the dwarven nation.

He just wanted Henrietta to be safe. Not that he should really be worried.

She came to a conclusion and sent him flying. She crouched low to the ground and burst into a light-footed silent sprint farther away from the group.

When she was alone at a distance that no one could overhear, Henrietta stopped and lifted one hand in front of her. Keith flew down, careful not to dig the talons into her flesh.

"Keith?"

"Yes, Ria?" The raven simply opened its maw, and Keith projected his voice using [Ventriloquism].

"These are your lands, so I was wondering if you have a preference?" she asked. "Kill? Capture?"

Keith projected, "I don't mind whichever."

Henrietta leaned forward, resting her head against the raven. "I don't like killing."

"Then don't," Keith replied. He'd asked her to go on this run because . . . Well, he had a list of reasons, starting with Rufus suggesting a distraction.

Though the moment she'd left, he'd regretted it and immediately wanted to call her back.

But Rufus was right, and he wasn't really worried about a small mercenary troop fighting against a Sword Master. Honestly, he wasn't even worried about her fighting in the *war*, just fighting against *her people* in the war.

Henrietta placed his raven gently back on her shoulder.

"Alright," she whispered, "Here we go."

Keith used the moment's pause to take flight. His reinforced automaton was perfectly capable of staying with his princess while she battled, but he wanted to enjoy her prowess from the air.

There was a burst of [Sword Aura] that emanated from Ria and wrapped delicately around the encampment, questing for sentries. In a blink, Ria kicked off in a [Quick Step], all but teleporting her to the three sentry mercenaries scouting the perimeter.

Each went down with expert strikes to the temple that brought her opponents to their knees. Or would have, if she hadn't scooped the now comatose men into her free hand.

By the time the dust settled from her perk, Ria was standing back at her starting point. She gently dropped her victims to the dirt and then focused her aura toward the camp.

Ria cracked her neck and reached for her sword, then hesitated. After a sigh, she just patted the hilt affectionately and then kicked off again.

She was beautiful. She was graceful. She was deadly.

Even if she didn't kill anyone.

Keith admired Ria as she let her [Sword Aura] wash over the mercenaries. She eliminated the entire camp one person at a time with a simple punch.

"Sorry."

"Let me just . . ."

"Pardon me."

The first few were taken unawares as she executed a perfect surprise round. The boss roared to her feet and barely popped out her therianthrope wolf ears before she fell flat on her face. Darryl and Warren weren't yet finished with their soup, and they splattered the broth everywhere as they were taken out.

"Phew." The princess patted her hands together and placed them on her hips in a power pose. "That was a good warm-up."

Henrietta surveyed the bodies that had fallen haphazardly about her with a self-satisfied grin. She took the time to properly remove the bubbling soup from the fire so it wouldn't burn. She sniffed at the soup, and whatever she smelled there, she disapproved of.

And then her whole face contorted.

"*Achooooo.*"

The sneeze echoed through the quiet night, and Ria cast an annoyed glare at the horses. One whinnied in upset at the loud sound.

"What now?" Keith alighted Hubert beside her.

She smiled again. "We go treasure hunting!"

The first wagon had room for passengers and a few packs and crates and a keg. Keith watched the princess easily pop the lid off each box, ferreting out their quarry with brute force alone. Luckily, they only had to search the first wagon because nestled in a crate of straw were three blue eggs, each the size of a teapot.

"Keith?"

"Yes, Ria?"

"Can you reinforce this box?" His princess carefully packed the eggs back into place and nestled them with more hay to keep them from jostling on the journey.

"Yes, but there are limits. I'm currently using up all of the spell slots for Hubert," he explained, "but I could switch out one. I'm using [Construct Flight], [Ventriloquism], [Share Senses], and [Remote Access]."

"I can carry you in the wagon."

"Then allow me."

Keith spent some of his leftover mana.

[You have attempted to use the Perk: **Quick Buff** on Wooden
Crate. You have succeeded.]
[Warning! Mana has dropped below 10%. Rest is recommended,
or you may suffer Nausea, Heartburn, Indigestion, Upset Stomach,
or Death.]

Keith ignored his lower-than-normal mana. He was a Sage, and ten percent of his mana pool was still three hundred and fifty mana . . . He just *maybe* should have rested after activating his new alligator-dog construct, Berry. And micromanaging half his automaton army with small, innocuous [Commands] hadn't helped.

Why was he constantly abusing his powers?

Henrietta closed up the straw crate. The princess had easily removed the nails sealing it, and now, she simply pressed her thumb on each nail to hammer it back shut.

Henrietta tucked the now buffed and padded box back in with the rest. Then she squealed with glee at something she found tucked behind the crate.

"Oh, perfect! I found rope!"

CHAPTER 33

Special Delivery for You

Henrietta

The rope was almost enough to carefully hog-tie every mercenary I'd felled. Except for the boss, who was knocked out mid-animorph and took up as much rope as three of her companions.

I gave up trying to make her fit within what little rope I had, and instead punched a hole through one of the larger crates. It was quick work to shove her through the opening and have Keith reshape and reinforce the wood. She could still use her legs, so I threw her in the wagon first and dumped the rest of the mercenaries on top of her. A few groaned but they were otherwise still below 10% health and unconscious.

It was harder to manage the horses. I just *couldn't* abandon them . . . as much as I so desperately wanted to. Keith had let me know that the scouts were half an hour behind me at my pace (or four hours at theirs), and there was no guarantee the horses would still be here if I didn't bring them.

Aaaaachooooo.

"Gods save me. Why am I doing this! ARGH."

Sniffle.

My plan was simple. Load up everything (including the people) into one wagon, then cover the eyes of the four horses, and guide them into the now empty armored wagon. The armored wagon was likely meant for the mercenaries to fall back to in case of a fight. Not that it had helped much against me.

This wasn't my first rodeo. I had a bit more experience pulling horse-laden wagons than most, I assumed, since I often transported the knights mounts back in Drendil.

"Keith," I sniffled and blew my nose into my kerchief. My eyes were water-ing something fierce, and I had to rub them a few times before I could focus on

Hubert. I'd need to deliver the eggs as soon as possible if I wanted to head off the griffin attacks, but it would be nice to check in at the castle on my way past. "Will you be available if I arrive around midnight?"

There was a long pause and no response. "Keith?"

". . . No." Keith's voice was strained. ". . . Sorry."

"Is everything alright?" My heart skipped as I waited longer and longer for his answer. What if an assassin had attacked while he was connected to Hubert? Or the invasion had started early? I could abandon the mercenaries, but even then, it would take a few hours—

". . . Just . . . need rest," he finally answered. "Disconnecting . . . Hubert."

Magic took a lot out of mages, even arch mages. I could only imagine how many spells Keith had going at any given moment, let alone on top of crafting new automatons for the army and joining me for part of my mission.

Hubert shook himself after his master left, going back to being a construct raven. He didn't seem fazed and shuffled softly on my shoulder as I walked to the front of the wagons. It might be a bit of a bumpy ride for the mercenaries, but the horses were more important.

I carefully stepped into the wagon harness, draping it over both shoulders and carefully tightening the straps. The rest dangled behind me. I wasn't a horse after all—no matter what Mother always said—but that was fine. I was just happy that I'd had Keith clean everything before I touched it. His [Cantrips] were so useful!

With two hitched wagons in tow, I ran back up the Great Road.

"Princesss!" Sithli came forward to meet me at the crossroads. I didn't have the best night vision, so I *may* have wrecked a bit of the road coming to a quick stop. The horses were *not* happy.

The lizardman guard was part of the team patrolling from the castle to the front line further south. He met me with ten other lizardkin guards; I only recognized Yulith, a short gray-green lizardkin with a Fu Manchu and a love for butternut rum balls, another castle favorite from *Out of This World.*

"Sithli!" I smiled at the lizardman. He stared a bit wide-eyed at the whole affair and scrambled to catch my reins as I tossed them at him. I needed the entire affair lifted slightly to better unveil myself of the straps.

"This is Lieutenant Franni," Sithli introduced the leader of the scouts, a tall lizardkin with purple-tipped scales and short red hair.

"Princess." The lizardkin bowed.

"Special delivery for you," I quipped, waving a hand at the two wagons. "I just need to grab the griffin eggs, and then I'll be on my way."

I unearthed the crate that held the eggs from the front of the horse wagon, hugging them to my stomach and said, "Sorry I can't stay and chat, but I need to head out if I'm going to have enough time to get everything done. Though . . . do you have any snacks?"

"Right here." Sithli handed over a muffin. I freed a hand to take it and unceremoniously shoved it in my face. The lizardman saluted. "Fair-weather travelsss, Princesss."

"Send my regards to your wife!" I finished the baked good, nodded at everyone, then kicked off again. My [Quick Step] was on cooldown, but I could go pretty fast with my stats alone.

I kept my eyes opened for a rest stop along the way and eventually found a small clearing off the side of the road. There was a fallen tree at the far end that would make for a nice windbreak and backrest. I settled in for the night.

The Spring Equinox was approaching, and the nights were above freezing, but still carried a refreshing cold. I kept the chill at bay with a sturdy woolen cloak. Hubert disappeared into the forest.

I checked on everything before I fell asleep.

The three eggs were gray with beautiful blue swirls, and I gently ran my hands over each. My [Mastery] and Perception nineteen were enough to find the heartbeat in each. I worried they would get cold overnight, so I sat cross-legged and tucked the eggs under my shirt. I let my body heat warm them as I wrapped my cloak around my legs and hugged them gently.

It wasn't comfortable, and I didn't mind. I nodded off under the moon and the starlit sky.

Something brushed my ear, and I came awake. Keith was nuzzling my neck. "Keith?"

Pardon me, I meant Keith's *automaton* was nuzzling my neck. Hubert didn't reply, simply hopping off my shoulder so I could stretch. Clearly, Keith hadn't possessed the automaton again yet, and I blushed at my misunderstanding. And at the absolutely lurid thoughts that followed it. What would it be like to have the *real* Keith nuzzling my neck? I put the eggs gently back into the crate and grabbed my pack. I slaked my thirst with a swig of my waterskin, ate from a small pouch of dried strawberries, bananas, and roasted nuts, then got ready to head out. The eggs were secure, so I lifted the crate gently and hugged it to my chest.

Hubert flew overhead.

The forest was lush with early spring, and flowers bloomed all along the Great Road that stretched east to west through the Dark Enchanted Forest. I had passed the exit to Keith's castle an hour back down the road, and I would need to travel almost all the way east to reach the dwarven stronghold's turn off.

I could run the entire distance from Baldor's Peak and back again with plenty of time before the griffin attack. And the war wasn't for two weeks, so I thought it fine to slow down and enjoy some sight-seeing as I went.

I walked leisurely down the road for half an hour before Hubert flew down and alighted on my shoulder. "Good morning," he greeted in Keith's dark and comforting voice.

"Good morning, Your Viciousness."

"Ha," Keith said. "How was your sleep?"

I shrugged, careful of the bird and the eggs. "Alright. I'm thinking I'll be out here for a few nights while I return these."

The raven eyed the crate. "I'll send word that you're on your way to the dwarven delegation."

"Thank you."

We walked in companionable silence for a while. I had the feeling that Keith came and went a few times, but I couldn't be sure, so I just waited for him to initiate conversation again.

"Henrietta?"

"Yes, Keith?"

"Chancellor Grimly will meet you at the dwarven outpost at our border in . . ." Keith hesitated. "Two days?"

"Sounds fine."

"Well." Keith coughed. "Have fun."

"See you when I get back."

The raven nodded with human flair, and then Keith was gone. Hubert took off from my shoulder perch and flew down the road.

He was right; I would have fun.

CHAPTER 34

How to Care for Carnivorous Weeds

Keith

Keith broke contact with Henrietta and glowered at the curly-haired blonde woman staring starry-eyed at him from across the table.

"I still can't believe it." Chloe laughed. "*You!*"

"Shove it, Chloe," Keith ordered, looking down at his desk and the work piling up. It was perfectly manageable, just larger with the war preparations.

He wasn't usually in the office this early; his day started with a leisurely bubble bath, delicious food, a fun jaunt in his workshop to get the creative juices flowing, then lunch, paperwork, an enjoyable walk through the garden, more paperwork, and dinner. He ended the day with a nice cup of tea and a good book. Not one of his godmother's draconic romances, but something educational, like *50 Ways to Disintegrate a Body so It Can't Be Reanimated* or *How to Care for Carnivorous Weeds,* and more recently, *Nine Habits for Having a Good Marriage.* Rufus was adamant that the Habit books were excellent resources, and Keith was actually enjoying some of the more calculated recommendations.

Things like *holding hands once a day builds intimacy.* He *liked* holding hands. With Henrietta, that was. Not his persistent and annoying necromancer who wouldn't leave him alone.

"The Dark Lord of Nilheim," Chloe teased. "In love!"

"Did I give you this much trouble when you started dating Grand Duchess Calisto's heir?" Keith finished processing a request for intercity business licensing from one of his kingdom's largest merchant guilds after the arachne, the Pixie Prim. The lesser fae roaming his lands loved to cultivate beautiful gardens in roving flower fields across the forest, and they were happy to designate a portion for potion materials and rare ingredients.

Again, why did common vernacular refer to the average fae as *lesser*? He could never understand. He supposed there were fewer greater fae ruling the cosmos from their courts. Perhaps it was also his penchant for confusing the definition of lesser and fewer. Chloe was still chuckling.

"I know you have work to do," Keith said dryly. "Maybe you should go do it?"

"If you mean meeting those healers, then it's done." Chloe sighed. "They are all excellent, but none are powerful enough to resurrect anyone . . . yet."

"It's your job to fix that."

"I know, I know," Chloe said. " That's why I've sent them through one of the dungeons."

Keith glanced at the smaller kingdom map he'd had commissioned, sitting above one alcove. "Hm . . ." he hummed, contemplative.

"What?" Chloe followed his gaze. "Is there a specific dungeon Your Viciousness would have me dump them in?"

"Henrietta spent a lot of time dungeon delving," Keith mused. "I wonder if she'd like to see ours?"

Chloe said in mock shock, "You're hopeless. Besides, didn't you say she doesn't like fighting?"

"She doesn't like *killing people*," Keith corrected.

"Are you saying monsters aren't people?" Chloe teased. "How unlike you."

"That's not what I meant, and you know it. It's entirely different. I have it on good authority that Ria had a wonderful time fighting the Naga Warriors." Keith sighed and finished processing a request for land-resource negotiation renewal between the unicorn hordes and the merfolk. The forest had moved their area north of their usual watering hole from the Kemp River, and they would need to cooperate with the merfolk to use Lake Loria a little longer than planned. "I just think dungeon delving would be a nice distraction . . . I could use a distraction myself. Maybe I'll go too."

"Only you would think of dungeon delving as a great place for a *date*." Chloe tossed her hair over her shoulder and checked her perfectly manicured rose-pink nails. It matched the white dress with embroidered roses along the hem that came down to her calves. "Is that what you're doing now? Distracting her?"

"Yes." Keith made no move to deny it. He ran a hand through his hair, careful of his horn. "It's still weeks until the battle, and she was getting restless. Rufus recommended giving her something to do . . . so easy level ten bandits it was."

"I thought you said she doesn't like killing people?" Chloe countered. "Your mission seems in poor taste."

"She didn't kill them. She captured them and hauled them back to the army. Now she's delivering their cargo to the dwarves," Keith countered back. "She gets to sightsee *and* feel useful on an important diplomatic mission."

Chloe stared at Keith until he became self-conscious and stopped reading documents to actually look at her. "What?"

"It's just the way you said that." Chloe frowned. "I can't tell if it was *meant* to sound that insulting."

"Insulting?"

"The way you said 'she gets to feel useful' like that." Chloe shook her head. "I think you're making a big mistake if you think a Heroine of Justice who has dedicated her entire life to a cause just needs you to give her tasks to 'feel useful.' She's a grown woman."

"That's not—She's not—" Keith started, then he took a breath. "She's not like *you*, Chloe. Ria still has a 'need to be helpful, or she thinks people won't love her' trauma that she's working through. You know that's dumb. I know that's dumb. But if that's what she needs, then I'll follow Rufus's recommendations. Even if I need to make some myself."

"I still think you're making a big mistake." Chloe shrugged. "But you're the boss, and she's your wife."

"Wife?!" Keith choked. "We aren't even engaged yet!"

Chloe rolled her eyes. "*Yet*. You're so far gone, it's only a matter of time."

"I think it's time *you* actually got back to work." Keith waved a dismissive hand at his friend. "And let me do the same."

"Fine. But Rufus isn't the only person qualified to give you advice," Chloe warned, huffing and turning to walk out of the office. Over her shoulder, she said, "And maybe you should listen to your friend who's already in a happy relationship instead of the forever-alone therianthrope?"

"Goodbye, Chloe."

CHAPTER 35

The Pounce Protectorate

Henrietta

I walked steadily until just about noon before I came across anyone else on the road, and then a trickle turned into a flood of travelers heading down the Great Road.

So far, I'd seen a family of field mice wearing tiny straw hats riding a small wagon pulled by a lizard, a lone wolfman who looked at me with suspicion, a caravan train of three carriages carrying ten lizardkin and cages filled with livestock, and an elf walking and reading a book at the same time.

We had a few half elves in Drendil. Sumbria was ruled by elves, but I'd never visited their courts. My parents enjoyed attending their royal gala every year while I challenged the Dungeon Valley Crest. I'd met a few elves on delegation to Peldeep, but they were all stoic political figureheads. This was the first elf around my age I had come across.

She wore long pants with a half skirt cut like a leaf over her right leg, and a leather protective chest plate over a loose shirt. Her brown hair was in an elaborate set of braids, and she had darker green skin than the half elves I'd met before. A delicate circlet perched on her brow.

I veered to the opposite side of the road so I wouldn't startle her, but I needn't have bothered; she kept her head in her book the entire time. She appeared shortsighted and had it up to her nose so she could read the words.

Did elves not have glasses?

Hubert was just a normal construct most of the time, flitting about overhead, and only rejoined me when Keith used him as an intermediary.

It was mid-afternoon, and I was halfway between the castle and the dwarves when I met with trouble.

"Here, you!" A beastkin in a helmet and leather gambeson marched over to me from a group of combatants I assumed were headed to the battlefield.

"Yes?" I tensed. I'd only seen a handful of humans since entering the forest, and I was surprised people didn't call *spy* anytime they saw me.

The beastkin—I couldn't tell what kind, since his ears and tail were hidden by armor—loomed over me. "Are you Princess Henrietta of Drendil?"

I wasn't expecting *that*. I repeated, more tentatively, "Yes?"

He turned to his compatriots and hollered, "IT'S HER!"

Suddenly, I was surrounded by enthusiastic beastkin.

"Did you really defeat the Dark Lord in single combat?"

"What level Strength do you have?"

"When's the wedding?"

"Have you fought Rufus yet?"

When they first approached, I had immediately taken a guard position so I could escape before the eggs became compromised . . . but it was quickly apparent the group were more interested in gossip than fighting.

A midsize beastkin who came up to my shoulders did a cartwheel over the group and landed with a flourish in front of me.

His voice carried over. "Alright, you lot, back it up."

There was a bit of grumbling, but everyone complied. The man was a calico catkin with three tufts pointing off each ear. He wore a casual white shirt under an embossed silk and leather vest, and his dark-brown pants tucked neatly into knee-high boots. Two knives and a short rapier hung off his belt. He wore a very fashionable hat; it even had a small collection of feathers. He purred his *R*s subtly.

The catkin bowed eloquently, taking off his hat as he did so. "Princess Henrietta, it is an honorrr to meet you." He gave the motley crew behind him a hard stare until most of them realized he expected them to bow as well. Then he smiled back at me. "What brings Yourrr Highness this way?"

"Greetings and well met." I lifted the crate holding the eggs. "I'm delivering these on diplomatic business for Ke—His Royal Viciousness."

He bowed again. "Where are my manners! I am Alistair, and this is my adventuring party, the Pounce Protectorate."

"Adventuring?"

"Why, yes!" Alistair exclaimed. "There are three dungeons in the Dark Enchanted Forest, and so we have a very active adventuring guild."

"THREE?" How had I never heard of this? How had this never come up? "Where are they?"

"The Hollow Gorge and Deep Shoals Dungeons are in Gren's Keep terrritory; Green Oak is beside the elven capital," Alistair kindly explained. "We don't offer access to adventurers from other kingdoms because they are only accessed through our home cities . . . and *you* know how people get with the Dark Enchanted Forest. I shouldn't say that's always the case, though; Grand Duchess Calisto sometimes sends us a batch of herrr adventurers to help train them up."

"Excuse me, Miss—Ah, Your Highness," the first beastkin who'd approached me earlier spoke up. "Is it true what the rumors say?"

Alistair tutted at the man. "You shouldn't believe in rrrumors, Cory."

I cleared my throat. "Well, I challenged King Keith . . ." All eyes looked at me expectantly. ". . . Just not to a duel," I admitted. "I was *technically* sent to kill him."

"Rrreally?" Alistair cocked an eyebrow. "And did you?"

"Kill him? Of course not! *He's the Dark Lord.*"

The Pounce Protectorate nodded knowingly. Alistair cocked his head. "So did he kill you?"

"No," I replied. "His necromancer was still on holiday."

More nods of understanding. Alistair gave me an appraising look and concluded, "Alright. Thank you, Princess. Shall we see you at the upcoming battle?"

"Of course." The fact that he hadn't pressed for more information made me relax my shoulders. "Does that mean I'm almost at the turnoff for Gren's Keep?"

I peeked down the road, but only saw more woodland and overhanging tree branches.

"Sorry, Princess, but our city is closerrr to the western borderrr." Alistair frowned, considering. "If you walk there at yourrr current pace, it'll take you almost two full days just to rrreach the connection at the Great Road, and then it's another half day's walk."

"I see." Perhaps it was worth running to the dwarves just so I would have the time for a visit to the beastmen capital. "Thank you, Alistair. I think I'll stop by on my way back. There should be enough time to spend a day or two in Gren's Keep before the war."

"If you hurry." Alistair nodded. "While visiting Gren's Keep, be sure to swing by the Damp Gizzard. Despite the name, it's a local favorite. We are heading there ourselves."

"I'll keep that in mind."

"One last thing." Alistair leaned in and asked, "How good are you at rrriddles?"

"Fair."

The catkin smiled and tipped his hat. "Then you should be alright. Farewell, Princess. It was lovely to make yourrr acquaintance."

The rest of the Pounce Protectorate seemed disappointed that our conversation had ended without more juicy gossip about Keith or myself, or Keith and myself . . . but I ignored their puppy-dog eyes and continued on my way with a polite goodbye.

With newfound purpose, I clutched the crate more securely and kicked off, activating [Quick Step].

CHAPTER 36

You're the Dark Overlord!

Keith

Keith stared hard at his plate of bimbleberry scones. Very hard.

Was it the nut megera? No, maybe the cinnamon? Perhaps there wasn't enough sugar? Or too much floof powder?

Whatever it was, Panlith's scones just didn't *taste* right.

"If you sigh one more time," Chloe stated firmly, "I will take it away and eat your bimbleberry scone *myself*."

"You know it's more than the scone, Chloe," Rufus put in while Keith glared at the necromancer. They'd joined him out of the blue for his afternoon tea in the garden; they'd even brought their own chairs.

"Alright, you two." Keith pushed his scone aside and opted to drink his luke-warm elderberry and nettle tea with honey instead. "Why are you interrupting my break? Because if you are just here to tease me, I'm sure I can find something exciting for you to do."

Rufus cradled his own delicate teacup and started, "The most important thing—"

"We thought you might be lonely," Chloe cut off the beastkin, flipping her long golden locks of curls over her shoulder. She did that a lot, and Keith always wondered how it never managed to hit anyone. "What with the princess away."

Rufus sighed. "Chloe, that's not why we are here at all. Ignore her, Your Viciousness."

"I usually do." Keith rolled his eyes and nodded at Rufus. "Go on."

"It's two weeks until the invasion." Rufus frowned. "I've seen your orders, but they aren't the way you usually handle these affairs. Why aren't you just creating a wall of impenetrable defense at the Drendil border and wiping out the enemy before they cross into our territory? Not to mention a *three-line defense* between the border and the castle? Any one of the three of *us* could destroy the Drendil army with our eyes closed, without risking our people. Without a hero on their side of the board, Drendil is almost laughably weak!"

"Your princess could defeat them," Chloe put in. "It would be delightfully ironic."

Rufus took another sip of his tea and continued. "There is no reason for this war to begin with. You could just marry the princess tomorrow and be done with it."

"That is assuming she would have me," Keith said dryly. He knew all of this, but still intended to go forward with the current lineup.

"Please." Chloe laughed. "You two are so into each other, a bridge troll could use you as the answer to 'Who's the most pining couple in the land'?"

"I do resemble that remark." Keith nodded. "But I don't *want* to crush and kill the entire Drendil army . . . Though I am of a mind to throw the royal family off a cliff."

"Explain," Chloe demanded, not caring that she was being rude to her king. Keith didn't particularly care, either; he liked being alive more than he liked being pandered to. His generals knew their lord valued competence and straightforwardness above all else.

"*If* I destroy the Drendil army with my almighty power *before* they even step foot into the Dark Forest, I will no longer be acting in self-defense, and that would cause controversy among the Continental Council."

"So?" Chloe picked at her nail, uninterested.

"One of whom is Grand Duchess Calisto. The grand duchess who is hosting the Spring Ball. A ball that would be Ria's debut to society. A ball which she is *immensely* looking forward to—as am I. Since I will be going with Ria," Keith pointed out. "I've already ordered our outfits."

Chloe waved her hand dismissively. "Mother-in-law would never deny your entry just because you killed a few thousand people. You're *the Dark Lord*."

"Since when did you start calling her *mother-in-law*?" Rufus turned on Chloe. "You and Julia aren't even engaged yet!"

"Duchess Calisto has let me know that I must call her that or she'll be incredibly disappointed in me," Chloe said, looking very pleased with herself. "It's now a race to see who proposes first! It's almost a guarantee I'll be wedded and bedded by this time next year." She raised an eyebrow at Keith. "So if you want to go first, you'd better be quick about it."

"I'll keep that in mind." Keith was happy for Chloe, and he pushed down the sudden feeling of nausea that churned his stomach. He tried to keep his tone casual. "Will you be moving to North Sumbria, then?"

"Julia isn't thinking of inheriting the duchy, so we'll probably live here most of the year," Chloe said.

"We're getting distracted," Rufus spoke up, leading the conversation back on track. "Explain to me in a way that makes *strategic* sense, why we aren't just destroying the Drendil army?"

"Because," Keith replied slowly, "Henrietta has worked with the Drendil army for her entire life—just as you have trained with ours. What do you want to bet that she's friends with half the armed battalion sent our way?"

"And?" Chloe argued. "We're just going to kill them a little. Death happens, and then you get over it."

"Not everyone has a level fifty-seven necromancer in their army, Chloe," Keith pointed out. "Unless you are volunteering to resurrect everyone on *both* sides?"

"So how do you intend to win the war without killing all of Ria's friends?" Chloe demanded.

"Ria came up with the idea, actually. I just needed to reset the automatons to capture and separate the army into segments, dragging the victims through the dark wood and depositing them at random along the border. That will demoralize the army and should force them to retreat."

"If the plan involves your automata, why are the lizardkin and naga battalion stationed on *this* side of Gerda's bridge?" Rufus inquired, pointing at the map. "And why the line of beastkin set up at the crossroad to the castle?"

Keith smiled, recalling how passionate Ria had been telling him the plan. "Honestly? Theft."

CHAPTER 37

I'll Never Turn Down a Bit of Gossip

Henrietta

I came upon the bridge a few hours later and stopped to refill my enchanted waterskin—dysentery was no joke.

If you've crossed one bridge in the Dark Enchanted Forest, you've crossed them all. I discovered this when a familiar figure hopped onto the path in front of me and drew herself up.

> I face the shadows,
> The light as well,
> Control all water,
> Without a spell.
> Who am I?

"Gerda?!" I squealed with delight.

My favorite bridge troll winked at me. She was wearing a loose white tunic with a floral print vest on top and a pair of loose tan pants tucked into calf-high brown leather button-up boots. "I'll not count that as your answer to my riddle. Who am I?"

I scrambled to remember the riddle that had flown past me. After a moment I hesitated and asked, "The moon?"

Gerda chuckled and stepped aside, waving a hand to show I'd guessed successfully. The troll quipped, "I gave you an easy one because I'm a kind and patient troll. Don't let me catch you off your game a second time!"

"Oh, you did it on purpose?" I countered, not really angry. "What would you have done if I got the answer *wrong*?"

"I believed in you," Gerda said, ignoring my question. "Now, did you want to head on or stop in for a bit of tea and gossip?"

"I'll never turn down a bit of gossip."

Gerda grabbed the ledge of the sideless bridge and swung herself over. I climbed carefully down the bank and found a familiar door under the bridge. A bit of troll magic later, and I was carefully placing the crate of eggs safely beside my boots inside her enchanted spacial cottage.

"So, are you in control of just these two bridges, or are there more?" I asked, taking a seat at her kitchen table.

Gerda placed a cup of dandelion tea in front of me, and I added a spoonful of honey. She set out a bowl of fresh huckleberries for a snack.

"There are more." Gerda smiled, looking very pleased with herself. "At least four, though I won't tell you where. It's more entertaining that way."

"What about the other bridge trolls? Don't they get upset that you're hogging all the bridges?"

Gerda chortled. "Princess, I'm the *only* bridge troll."

"In the whole Dark Enchanted Forest?"

"In the whole Dark Enchanted Forest," she said. "Most of the trolls live in the mountains or work in the army. We don't have a city, just our own caves scattered about. The last bridge troll was an ancient old coot named Larry. He's retired now, and I happily took over."

Gerda sipped her own tea. An interesting thing to watch, as the woman had stunning lower canines that peeked just over her upper lip.

We shared a companionable silence for a minute, drinking tea and eating berries. Then I asked, "So . . . gossip?"

"You'll never guess who is on their way to the castle right now!" Gerda said.

"Who?"

"Countess Julia von Slyke of North Sumbria!"

I tilted my head. "Grand Duchess Calisto's daughter?"

"Yes!" Gerda looked at me like she was sharing an inside joke that I didn't understand.

"But why?"

The troll eyed me and popped a berry in her mouth. "Someone at the castle has a long-distance relationship with the countess . . . and I have it on *the best authority* that Julia has come here to get the jump on her lover—and propose!"

"It's not Keith, is it?" I panicked, wondering who else I knew eligible enough to woo Grand Duchess Calisto's daughter.

"What, of course not!" Gerda shook her head, sending her many dark-green braids toppling over her shoulder. "It's Chloe! After Julia heard about the war, she threw on her armor and mounted her fastest horse, setting off for Nilheim as quick as she could. You might still make it back in time to see her arrival if you hurry. She only just passed the border today."

The thought of running all the way back to meet Chloe's girlfriend was tempting, but . . . "I really want to visit Gren's Keep," I said.

"If you are going to Gren's Keep then you have to visit the Damp Gizzard. Olen's rumblepot stew is heavenly . . . though I don't recommend their tea. 'Stout or get out,' as the old man likes to say." Gerda chuckled, a deep growling rumble.

I sipped my tea and listened while Gerda told me more about Gren's Keep and its unique shops. Out of all of them, I was most interested in Verily's Vases, Logan's Noodle House, the Damp Gizzard and Thulebert Thorn. The last was a special surprise I didn't expect to find in the Dark Enchanted Forest.

"Thulebert Thorn moved here from Peldeep about three years ago," Gerda explained. "He wanted to be closer to the dwarven outpost without having to actually *live* at the outpost."

"What's wrong with Frolin?" This was as good a time as any to ask for information on my destination.

Gerda thought for a second, tapping a finger on her chin, then explained, "The dwarves are very happy to meet with outsiders in Frolin, but they aren't *quite* so happy when people monopolize the space for other things."

"So they want travelers to buy their wares, not set up shop and become competition?" I reasoned.

"Exactly." Gerda nodded. "The place is very big, but there's no suburbia. You have a shop, and you sleep up top."

"Good to note. Do you know Chancellor Grimly?" My hope was to arrive, drop off the eggs with the chancellor, and then make it to Gren's Keep for dinner. I could do it if I left here in the next half hour and pushed my mana to the limit with repeated [Quick Step]. "The ol' dodger will be at Grim's Golden Greaves," Gerda said. "If he's at the shop."

"If he's not at the shop, who else is in charge?"

The bridge troll shrugged. "No one's 'in charge.' They're dwarves."

I'd met with the dwarven trade delegation in Drendil many times, but I'd never visited the dwarven nation before. It wasn't that they didn't accept outsiders per se, just that my parents were racist against most of the rest of the continent, and since Drendil was cut off from the continent by the Dark Enchanted Forest, we did almost all international travel by boat. Sumbria, Servalt, and North Sumbria stretched up the eastern coast, with Peldeep to the west. There was a trade delegation from the dwarven kingdom that passed through Nilheim to Drendil on occasion, but there wasn't much travel the other way. As such, I said, "I don't understand."

"The dwarves," she explained, "have a king, but the king isn't a hereditary title; it's a job to complete the ancestral ceremonial rites. It is often passed down in one family, but when the king of the dwarves dies, the title is given to the next dwarf who is most qualified. The actual kingdom is run by a council of elders."

"I see."

Gerda leaned forward, offering me the last of the huckleberries in the bottom of the bowl, and I shook my head. She ate them and then took the plate to her kitchen sink to wash and set out to dry before coming back to join me at the table. She continued, "Frolin is actually run by a merchant council. They take turns each session being first speaker, but that just means the rotation of who gets to talk in which order changes. They are all on equal footing."

"That sounds like a nightmare for getting things done . . ." I didn't like a lot of my parents' choices, but I also had seen the amount of time it took a committee to come to any conclusion.

"It is," Gerda agreed. " But I'm sure you'll have no problem finding Chancellor Grimly."

CHAPTER 38

A Good Plan Made in Jest Is Still a Good Plan

Keith

Keith rubbed the bridge of his nose, exasperated.

"But we're ready to fight!" Lieutenant Patina insisted. She was head border guard of Plittsmouth in Lake Loria. "We can attack from the shores and drag—"

"No," Keith cut her off. "No. I don't want to clean up drowned bodies; they're a disgusting mess."

"We could eat them." Patina smiled a shark-toothed smile. Her selkie blood let her walk on land, but her sharp grin and her smooth brown skin as soft as seal hide gave away her ancestry. "Once the bones are picked clean, I'll even deliver them to Necromancer Chloe—"

"I said no."

Telling his army the plan was very different from *telling* his army the plan. Obedience was expected, but some were more persistent than others for an audience. And it was very hard to send away this particular individual.

"You don't think I'm strong enough to fight on the front lines, do you?" Patina accused. "Come on, cousin, don't punish my people just because I'm leading them."

"I'm not saying you *can't fight*," Keith explained slowly, "I'm saying you can't drag the entire Drendil army to a watery death."

"But *whyyyyy?*"

Keith sighed. "Because I don't want to overthrow Drendil. That would be a nightmare . . . unless you want to take over their kingdom and reform the government from the ground up?" The look of abject horror on Patina's face told him how she felt about that. "Which is why the answer is no."

If he said it once, he said it a hundred times. That line worked *wonderfully* on his minions. He'd need to remember it the next time some fool asked him to consider world domination.

"Then what did you want us to do?" Patina asked. "Sing them to sleep?"

"No, of course not—Wait, actually yes!" Keith stood up from behind his desk and walked toward his cousin. She was actually another godchild of Her Eminence Feliwyn, but they had been raised as cousins, and they would forever *be* cousins, even if no blood was shared between them. "You're brilliant, Patina."

"You know I was joking, right?" She gave Keith a long-suffering look while he patted her on the shoulder.

"A good plan made in jest is still a good plan," Keith replied. "That would save me so much time and effort! I can't wait to tell Ria when she gets back."

"While we're on the subject, who *is* this Henrietta What's-Her-Name?" Patina squinted up at Keith, who was caught gazing wistfully out a window. "And *what* has she *done* to you?"

"You'll understand when you're older," Keith teased, redirecting his stare at his cousin. "Suffice it to say, she is strong, competent, and she is *staying*."

He hoped . . . That he was still self-doubting meant he needed another session with Rufus.

Patina scoffed. "You're barely a month older than me."

"Yes." Keith smiled. "And that means I'll forever be older and wiser than you."

"You still haven't answered my questions," Patina pointed out.

"You noticed that, did you?" Keith looked up at the clock above his office door. Right on time, harp music sounded throughout the office. "Too bad, but would you look at that? It's my break."

"I know where you have afternoon tea." Patina stalked after him as he exited his office and walked down the stone corridor. "You can't get rid of me that easily!"

"Are you sure about that?"

"Patina!" Suddenly, a lyrical voice called out from the break room where a beautiful blonde woman was happily snacking away on tarts. "You're here!"

A violent shiver raced through Patina's whole body at the sound. She had just enough time for one scathing look at her king before Chloe shot out of the break room and tackled her. Patina caught the necromancer with ease but had to politely bend down so Chloe could better wrap her arms around the selkie's bicep in a hug.

Chloe glomped onto Patina and spoke a mile a minute. "I'm so happy you're here! You can't believe how bored I've been since I returned! Let's go get manicures—I know your nails *need* the love. You're so beautiful, darling! You should take better care of yourself!"

Patina gave Chloe a strained smile. "Please Chloe, not now. I'm trying to have words with my cousin . . ."

"None of that," Chloe said sternly. "It's break time, and you need one! *Look at your hair!* We simply *have* to go see Winrith for a spa day."

"But—"

"Don't worry." Chloe dragged the muscular guard off down the hallway. "I'll tell you *all about* the princess. I know all the gossip. You're going to love this."

Patina actually relaxed at that last bit. "You promise?"

"*Every last sordid detail,*" Chloe assured her, ensuring Keith could hear every sibilant syllable.

"Then I'd be happy to get my nails done with you, Necromancer Chloe."

Keith was suddenly wary as Patina shot him a vicious smile over her shoulder. He might come to regret siccing Chloe on his enthusiastic cousin.

Hubert was a good raven. And Keith enjoyed connecting to him for a literal bird's-eye view of the forest. He'd [Commanded] the raven to keep an eye on Henrietta and guide her should she need it.

The Dark Enchanted Forest liked to play tricks on people sometimes, but he wasn't too concerned because Henrietta was . . . Well, she was Henrietta.

She could take care of herself.

What Keith was not expecting to find when he connected with Hubert during his afternoon lunch break was the absence of his wayward princess. Hubert was sitting in a tree overlooking the western bridge, with no Henrietta in sight. He sent the raven flying for a better view of the road.

Keith was just about to panic when a magical enchantment activated under the bridge, and he watched Henrietta climb up from below. The magic was very delicate and intricately put together by someone of incredible craftsmanship. It was only perceptible to Keith because he was an Arcane Sage. This must be the natural [Troll Magic] skill he'd read about.

Henrietta was smiling happily and still carrying her crate full of eggs.

"I'll see you when I get back!" she called down below the bridge.

"Have fun in Gren's Keep and tell Olen I said hello," a voice replied. "And be ready! I'll have a harder riddle for you when you come back this way."

Keith sent Hubert swooping down to alight on Henrietta's shoulders. The princess smiled at him. "Keith?"

"Hello, Ria."

"How are things back at the castle?" She carefully freed a hand, careful not to jostle the crate in her arms, and ran her fingers through his raven's feathers.

"Things are going as usual." Keith sighed, trying not to be distracted by the feeling of her touch. "Though I had some unexpected company."

Henrietta looked shocked. "Julia arrived already? Is she riding an enchanted horse?"

"No? Wait." Keith felt a headache coming on that for once had nothing to do with [Mana Burn]. "You don't mean *Countess* Julia of North Sumbria? She's coming *here? Now?*"

Henrietta nodded, "I heard it from Gerda. Julia's on her way to see Chloe."

"Oh no." Keith realized Hubert was rubbing his raven temple with a wing, mirroring Keith's own habit. He let the raven resettle itself. "And Chloe has no idea."

"We think Julia's here to propose," Henrietta exclaimed brightly. "Isn't that marvelous?!"

"Of course she is." Keith sighed. Again. "And that battle maniac chose *now* to do it for multiple reasons . . ."

"Is this going to upset our plans?" Henrietta asked.

"You have no idea." Keith shook himself and continued, "But there's no rush to come back. You're stopping by Gren's Keep after you deposit the eggs?"

"If I have time." Henrietta hesitated. "You're *sure* I have time?"

"Absolutely. Don't worry about a thing!" Keith used Hubert to nuzzle Henrietta affectionately. "Take as much time as you need."

"I'll still be back before St. Veralyn's Day," the princess assured him.

"As long as you're back the day *after* St. Veralyn's Day, that's all that matters." She nodded. "For the war."

"For something much more important than a war." Keith poked her cheek with a wing. "It's your birthday, remember?"

CHAPTER 39

I'M HERE ON A QUEST

Henrietta

Gerda was lovely, but duty called!

I said goodbye after I finished my tea and headed up the road a ways to the turnoff.

According to the bridge troll, the exits to Gren's Keep and Frolin were just a stone's throw apart on either side of the road. Right for the dwarves and left for the beastfolk. The forest had moved a bit recently, but it *should* remain as it was for a few days.

We hoped.

The western wood thinned out as I got nearer Peldeep. The usual lush green-wood gave way to young evergreens and the occasional berry bush. Off in the distance, to the north, I could make out the Baldorin Mountains. The stark peaks that jutted to the sky were reminiscent of a ridgeback ice dragon I'd met when I was fourteen. I'd been leveling up in the Depths of Despair Dungeon, and I'd taken the opportunity to slip away while my escort knight Sir Havork was resting. We'd just cleared level six of ten, and I had my guard down. It wasn't often that I had the time to play by myself.

Then I'd fallen through a trapdoor.

It had taken an hour of fighting through unknown snowy territory to find my adventuring party and escort knight, all the while certain it was the end for me. Luckily, my kit was warm, and my training had paid off! I could handle most of the mobs with pure swordsmanship, and any trying foe with a [Force Thrust] or [Bludgeoning Cut] . . . until I'd come upon the dragon.

She had been beautiful and majestic and sentient as all of her kind, but over-come with dungeon madness, as all monsters who spawned inside a dungeon were. I didn't defeat her easily. I'd barely survived with a missing leg and all of my emergency potions gone. The only reason I was alive was because I'd gotten her at a disadvantage. I'd led her through a series of tight-fitting rock edifices and brought our battle below a deep cornice of ice and snow. The low curved peak had prevented her from flying out of my reach, and she had been too enraged to let me go.

What was *really* awesome for me was that the ridgeback had scales that bristled out like a cat's. That meant her scales were sharp and deadly, but less fortified than other members of dragonkind. In exchange for her claws ripping off half of my leg, I'd grabbed onto her belly scales and pulled one loose. My blade had sunk deep inside the exposed flesh, and the rest was history.

The worst part was the scolding I'd received.

Alright, and the leg wound—but I got better!

Hubert joined me from the air and signaled that he could see the exit just ahead. I didn't know why it bothered me, but the road to Gren's Keep and the road to Frolin were across from each other—an actual *stone* apart. They *almost* lined up . . . but for a hand length on either side. The dark forest was truly a *dark* place.

The almost-but-not-quite-a-crossroad made me antsy, so I didn't dillydally.

The path turned craggy, and it eventually met up with the river that ran downstream to Gerda's bridge. The Frolin outpost came into view, and I paused to look on in appreciation.

Before me was a giant door intricately carved with runes and set into the mountainside, with shops bordering it in a perfect symmetrical half-moon. The buildings were of varying sizes; from three-story stone shops to short and wooden tavernesque cabins.

It was midafternoon, the sun was hot, and foot traffic had moved inside. After confirming the eggs were still in one piece, I sauntered into town with the crate in my arms and a raven on my shoulder.

"HALT!" a voice boomed from the rocks beside me. Suddenly, a dwarf rose up and towered overhead. He looked like your typical dwarf: stocky, short limbs on a large, burly frame, but he was more than twice my size.

Having only dealt with political dwarven ambassadors in a tea parlor, I'd heard of but never witnessed the famous dwarven skill [Control: Size].

"Greetings!" I swept into a polite bow, careful of my cargo. "I am Princess—"

"WHO GOES THERE?"

"I am—"

"AND WHAT IS YOUR BUSINESS IN FROLIN?"

The dwarf probably couldn't hear me from up there. I waited until he'd finished and then repeated myself, louder.

"GREETINGS. I AM HERE TO SEE CHANCELLOR GRIMLY."

I took a breath to yell some more, and the dwarven outpost guard used that time to ask, "WHAT BUSINESS HAVE YOU WITH THE DWARVEN

COUNCIL, HM?" He leaned down and eyed me with a frown. "YOU SURE YOU AREN'T HERE TO SHOP?"

"No—I mean, NO, I'M PRINCESS HENRIETTA, HERE ON A QUEST FOR KING KEITH—"

"Well, why didn't you say so?" The dwarf popped out of giant mode and stood before me on the path. "We were right worried you wouldn't make it in time!"

"Oh, how are things with the griffins?"

"Not good, actually." The guard shook his head sadly. "We had to rebuild two shops just last night! It would have been much worse without Madame Potts's Cast, I tell you what!"

"Sorry I'm late, then. May I know your name?"

"You can call me Nolin." The guard tugged on his long ruddy beard, twiddling the end. "I'm with Hermin's Gold Emporium." He pointed to the second shop on the left of the giant stone door. "We've just got in a collection of rare rose-gold quartz. I'll put in a good word for you, and maybe you can get a discount. You'll visit us, yes?"

I had every intention of window-shopping for a bit before heading out again. I knew I wasn't in a rush, but I *felt* in a rush . . . Still. Rose gold sounded pretty. And strangely enough, even Hubert was positively vibrating with excitement. "Alright."

"Excellent!"

"Nolin!" An aged dwarf ran out of one of the wooden buildings to the right of the stone door. "Is that her?"

Nolin nodded. "Aye, Grimly."

"Thank the bedrock, we're saved!"

At the same time, an ear-piercing screech resounded over the outpost.

CHAPTER 40

My Necromancer Can't Resurrect Ashes

Keith

"Do we tell her?" Keith tilted his glass of elderberry cider at Rufus. The two were sharing a drink after dinner and had gone up to a secure place to have a very serious discussion. Keith had warded their conversation against spying. Twice.

Rufus shuddered in the way only a beastman could. "I'm not going to. Are you?"

"If we *don't* tell her, then she will be furious . . ." Keith replied.

"And if we *do* tell her, she'll try and decorate the entire castle in flowers. She'll stop all work on kingdom business to send runners out to the fae glades for ever-blooming daffodils, and she'll start pestering you to make automata welcome-singing doves."

"I remember."

"She might even succeed at finally painting the entire castle blue, since you're so distracted with your *own* partner."

"Good point."

The two men stared out over the black stone crenellations of the parapet. Chloe was in the garden below, laughing with Patina about something. And by something, they were laughing about Keith and Ria and the absurdity of it all. The *Drendil* princess with *their* king. Patina was of a mind that Henrietta was just waiting to stab Keith in bed . . . but Keith had to purposefully stop thinking about *that*.

He threw back his cider to slake his sudden thirst

"So we just wait for the storm to arrive?"

"I guess so." Rufus downed his own drink. For an entirely different reason.

* * *

The Dark Enchanted Forest had been Keith's home since he was born, and as the ruler of the Dark Enchanted Forest, he had many tasks.

None of which seemed all that important right now.

"Your Viciousnesss, Kith Bog peat and fishing reportsss for the first quarter have arrived," Chikli tried to get his attention, but Keith simply waved at him to put them with the Review Documents pile.

"Your Viciousnesss, I've prepared your glazed citron tartsss with a side of vanilla pudding." Panlith almost begged Keith to eat something. He was eating just fine . . . it was just a shame that he had eaten the last chai custard bun, and he wasn't in the mood for food.

He should have savored them over the few days Henrietta would be away.

"This Rinrin asks Master . . . why? Why do you do this? The poor buttons . . ."

Keith was wondering if he even *wanted* to be here when Julia arrived. The whole affair was becoming a bother. And more so than usual. Even his automaton tinkering didn't bring him much joy.

"I'm going back." A beautiful siren with long curled hair and delicately shaped purple fingernails stood at attention in front of his desk. "And I'll expect a *proper* military order to arrive by week's end. There isn't much time left to prepare."

"Goodbye, Patina."

"And you should seriously consider the fact that you are marrying someone you don't even know that well! And I haven't met her yet."

"If I marry her, you can meet her at the wedding," Keith countered. "Or maybe she'll be by during the war. Who knows."

"Really?" Patina resisted the urge to pout, and Keith commended her self-control. She really was growing up. "I think something's wrong with you, Cousin. You aren't usually this . . . distracted?"

"I'm fine," he countered.

"Sure you are," Patina replied sarcastically. "Or maybe you've been cursed."

"I'm just busy with being king," Keith said. She was right, though . . . maybe he wasn't just pining pathetically for Henrietta to come back. Maybe this wasn't the honeymoon phase that Rufus had warned him about. Maybe he *was* cursed.

He could always check with his spells . . . Asking Chloe would be faster, but the necromancer would laugh herself silly if he broached the topic now.

"In all seriousness," he changed the subject, "you probably will see Henrietta during the battle. Also, could you figure out a way to prevent anything from disturbing Feliwyn?"

As much as he teased, Patina was a strong and capable military leader. Her skills were invaluable—and putting the army to sleep really was a stroke of genius.

"I'll *try*."

They both shared a look. Feliwyn *hated* being woken up from her nap. It would be a disaster if they disturbed her. Maybe Keith would write to the

Drendil army letting them know what any loud combat or errant missiles around his godmother would end with.

He pulled out a quill and jotted down a quick letter he'd been putting off since Gimtak delivered his mail that morning.

> *Dear Knight Commander Havork,*
>
> *As per our last missive, I am not available to forward any messages to Princess Henrietta from the Drendil Court. However, I can assure you that she is well. Perhaps you should ask yourself who is really a danger to her safety? I had thought you would already know the answer.*
>
> *Should Simon decide to continue his plans, I'm sure you will see her again soon. In that line of thought, please consider a cease-fire due south of Lake Loria . . . Her Eminence Feliwyn is still resting beside the waters, and I would hate for anything to wake her.*
>
> *My necromancer can't [Resurrect] ashes.*
>
> *Signed,*
>
> *Keith Monfort of Nilheim, King of the Dark Enchanted Forest*

Keith summoned Gimtak to handle delivering the letter, then leaned back in his chair.

Honestly, it might not be that bad if Drendil *did* wake up his godmother. She was an absolute grouch when she was awoken, yes, but that wouldn't be directed at *him*. And, once she had finished raining down terror and fire and destruction . . . she would be in *excellent* form to meet Henrietta.

Speaking of Henrietta, he should take a break soon to see how everything was faring with the dwarves.

CHAPTER 41

One Dwarfess Held a Whip

Henrietta

A veritable symphony of screeching griffins descended upon us.

Nolin immediately activated his [Control: Size] skill and charged into battle. The aged dwarf, Chancellor Grimly, I presumed, had run over and was gripping his hair on both sides of his head as he wailed, "Not again!"

My first instinct was to draw my sword, but that would require dropping the *very important* crate of eggs. Instead, I stood there awkwardly debating what to do as seven winged monsters attacked the now very upset outpost of some twenty dwarves.

For their part, the dwarven guards were impressive. They brought out forged-steel netting and all manner of excellently crafted weapons to stave off the monsters.

The griffins turned over roof shingles and carts, dodging the occasional thrown axe or spiked boot as they did so.

An expert-level crafted spear that glowed with a +1 Strength modifier went flying past my face. That was when I decided it was time to act.

I leaned over to get in Chancellor Grimly's face and told him, "Hold the eggs!" shoving the crate into his arms.

He took the crate with both hands and looked ready to faint.

"Excuse me." To help, I reached out and grabbed an armored dwarfess running past. She looked like some manner of authority figure and had been yelling, "Vanguard to me!" when I did so.

The look of pure insult at being dangled from my hand turned into menace as she activated [Control: Size]. I dropped her as the dwarfess promptly dwarfed me. "You *DARE—*"

"GRIFFIN EGGS!" I pointed at the crate, then back at her. "Keep them safe, please!"

Her expression dawned with realization, and she ran over to help.

I was already gone.

[You have attempted to use the Perk: **Quick Step**. You have succeeded.]

Three griffins were in combat with eight dwarven tankers who had weapons drawn and varying levels of [Shield] deployed. I jumped high and landed on a raised spear, a shocked dwarf holding it as I stood on the tip and stopped there.

"Hello," I said as I drew my sword and let my [Sword Aura] cover the two sides.

[You have activated the Skill: **Sword Aura**.]

[**Sword Aura** field is currently Strength 67 + Perception 19 = 86 ft diameter. You are able to lock on to targets equal to your Strength within the **Sword Aura** field to evaluate their threat level. Information available to you is based on the level difference between you and your target. You may use Sword Perks on any locked-on target. Targets with Perception equal to or greater than yours or targets you choose will feel your **Sword Aura**.]

[You have chosen: **All Targets**.]

I ignored the usual skill pop-up and focused on my targets.

There weren't any especially dangerous numbers among those in combat. The dwarfess I had sent to guard the eggs was one of the most powerful at level thirty-one. Nolin was just behind at level twenty-eight.

And all of the rest were under level twenty-five and every one of them below thirty Strength.

The three griffins attacking the line of tankers focused on me. One swooped in and tried to rake me over the shoulder with its claws, but I simply reached out with my free hand and grabbed its taloned foot.

"Sorry about this!" I told it as I jumped to the ground, bringing the griffin with me and bashing it into the rocky earth as I did so. I tried to control my Strength so the monster was left with enough hit points to survive, and I was pleased to see it was mostly unbroken.

I dropped the talon and launched toward the next griffin.

A collection of cheers rang out from the dwarven fighters.

While I was busy subduing the second with a choke hold, a dwarf with golden armor ran forward to finish off the griffin I'd left on the ground. As the griffin was a member of the Nilheim populace and the dwarf was not, I acted accordingly.

[You have attempted to use the Perk: **Force Thrust.** You have
succeeded.]

I thrust my pommel in his direction. My [Sword Aura] carried the force of
the blow across the distance until it met golden armor and broke one of the ribs
underneath it. The dwarf was sent flying into the line of tankers behind him.

The dwarves stopped cheering.

I finished choking the second griffin into submission and tossed him on top
of the first that I'd just saved. The third griffin had climbed higher into the sky
to try and avoid me.

The few dwarven tankers who hadn't fallen helped their comrades to their
feet and all turned their weapons my way.

"No killing!" I chastised the dwarven tankers.

"Says who?" one yelled back.

"Princess Henrietta, that's who," I said, then turned my attention behind
them. The vanguard had circled to the shops and were fending off two griffins
trying to wreak havoc. Nolin was busy fist fighting another griffin, and the last
griffin was awkwardly flying between fights trying to join in. It was younger than
the others and had no sense for battle yet. My [Sword Aura] told me it was still
only level eighteen, compared to its feathered friends who all had levels close to
mid-twenty.

I flicked my sword at it from across the town.

[You have attempted to use the Perk: **Bludgeoning Cut.** You have
succeeded.]

The young griffin was within my [Sword Aura], making it an easy target. A
number of its primary flying wing feathers were severed, sending it pinwheeling
through the air. It was thrown off so much so that it landed somewhere among
the mountain rocks out of sight.

The third griffin was flapping desperately toward its newly fallen kin, searching the area outside of the dwarven outpost, so I left it and turned to the vanguard.

They were trying to mitigate shop damage.

"As one!" an older dwarf with red locks and a bushy moustache called. The
group tossed a metal net at a griffin as it swooped down to try and destroy
an overturned cart. The net found its target, and the monster was successfully
detained. As one, the vanguard jumped onto it with sword and spear and axe and
mace and dagger. One dwarfess held a whip and gave out a particularly fierce
battle cry as she cracked it down toward the captured griffin.

"I'll just stop you there," I said, stepping in between the griffin and whip.
I pulled it from her hands and tossed it casually aside. Then I turned to the

monster and reached for the net. With a flick of my wrist, I lifted the metal and flipped it back where it came from, trapping the dwarves underneath.

They would be perfectly capable of escaping, but it gave pause to the combat. With the vanguard, the tankers, and most of the griffins now complaining and eyeing me warily, I finally had the chance I was looking for.

"EVERYONE STOP! I HAVE THE GRIFFIN EGGS!"

CHAPTER 42

Obnoxious Micromanagement Was a Skill

Keith

The first thing Keith saw when he [Shared Senses] with Hubert was a strong, beautiful, confident woman utterly dominating.

Dwarves were knocked off their feet. One griffin was sent tumbling into the craggy rock. A heavy metal net that took four dwarves to throw was casually tossed back over the group.

It was a sight.

The eggs were safely held by Chancellor Grimly. They were guarded by an angry-looking Corporal Nova, who seemed ready to murder somebody. She was *not* happy when his princess tossed a dwarf into the shield wall.

Keith sent Hubert flying. When Ria loudly proclaimed that she had the griffins' eggs, there was a sudden stillness that fell over the chaos. Keith chose that moment to alight onto her shoulder.

"Keith?"

"I'm here."

"Perfect timing," she said, then sent out another burst of [Sword Aura] to hopefully get everyone's attention. "I AM PRINCESS HENRIETTA, COME TO RETURN THE STOLEN GRIFFIN EGGS."

The dwarven vanguard crawled out from under their net while the tankers lined up neatly in front of them, still with shields deployed.

The griffins who could landed opposite the dwarves. A few clawed the earth restlessly, while others still had hackles raised and were eyeing the ensemble like they would pounce at any second. One had gone to assist the griffin who'd hit the earth. It could barely stand, but once it made it to its feet, it hobbled over to join its companions. The two that had disappeared into the jagged rocks had still not returned, but Ria didn't seem to mind.

She stood in between the two groups.

"Bring the eggs!"

Corporal Nova walked forward, Chancellor Grimly right behind her. The dwarfess had taken the crate, and she pulled the top open, revealing three eggs nestled inside to everyone there.

A mixture of relief and joy screeched from the griffins, and the dwarves hesitantly lowered their shields, though they had not deactivated anything yet.

"We found the eggs and have journeyed to return them. The dwarves did not steal them," Ria proclaimed. Keith didn't interrupt. Even if he was the Dark Lord, giving people the chance to do things without obnoxious micromanagement was a skill he had learned at his godmother's flank.

Feliwyn gave direction, and if someone tried and failed, she would support them until they were confident enough to do it right every time. Or she would eat them. But that was a rare occurrence; minions usually did as she asked.

The dwarves waited until the griffins settled themselves. A female griffin with a sunset-red lioness head, golden haunches, and a catlike sandy tail walked forward. She was the one who had half collapsed a roof and knocked over a cart.

With a sniff, she slowly inspected the eggs. A delicate wing tip reached out and slowly brushed one egg. Visible joy overcame the griffin mother, and it reared back, letting loose an ear-piercing eagle screech. Its companions all took to the sky—even the injured one—as the griffin nodded regally at the princess. Then it gripped the crate in its talons and launched into the air.

Keith nudged Hubert to nuzzle Ria as a sign of support and approval. He loved watching her work. Also, he *might* have spent extra mana so he could smell in [Shared Senses].

Ria whispered to him, "That's one thing done. Now I can go to Gren's—"

"Princess." Corporal Nova cut in front of them and stood, angry, at attention. "Why did you injure my men in the fight? Thomson has three broken ribs, and Dame Helga almost lost her eye when the netting hit her!"

"Excuse me . . ." Ria put away her sword, and Keith used the opportunity to tell her the dwarfess's name. "Corporal Nova, are you not merchants and ambassadors stationed in the Dark Enchanted Forest?"

"Yes. Which is why—"

"And do you regularly seek to kill citizens of Nilheim?" Ria cut her off this time.

"They're *monsters*," Corporal Nova retorted. "Monsters who attacked *first*."

Keith sighed. This was a long-suffering argument.

"Then is that how you do business with other kingdoms in Valaria? Taking the law into your own hand?" Ria stuck both hands on her waist and stared down at the offended corporal. "Is killing each other going to stop a griffin from attacking, or will it just bring back more griffins that wish for vengeance?"

"They started it!"

"Well, I'm finishing it. Please take these three advanced healing potions to use among the injured. No one need suffer long—"

A bloodcurdling screech resounded over the crowd as the young griffin who had fallen earlier shot out from between some mountain rocks. The griffin who had left to search for it was nowhere to be seen.

Keith hopped off Ria's shoulder and on to Corporal Nova's forearm.

Just before the griffin finished his downward assault on the group, Ria grabbed onto it. She swung her body neatly around to sit near the wingspan at the young griffin's neck. She subdued it with her second choke hold for the day.

"She's impressive, isn't she?" Keith asked the dwarfess awkwardly holding Hubert the raven.

"*Agh!* Wait. King Keith?" Surprise turned into shock which turned into tentative placating. "I mean, she's very strong."

"She handles my subjects very well," Keith sighed happily.

In front of them, Ria was petting an exhausted and cowed griffin youth trying to catch its breath. Ria was saying encouraging words to the creature and letting it know the eggs had been returned.

"Then I'll get Chancellor Grimly to report the situation," Nova finally sighed, the anger subsiding as a look of displeasure played across her face. "Now it's time for the hard part . . ."

Keith tilted Hubert's head.

The dwarfess swept her gaze around the outpost. "Cleaning up the mess."

CHAPTER 43

The Unigoat Fell Apart in My Mouth

Henrietta

The battle had been fun, but now it was done, and something very important had to happen.

Food. I was *starving*.

This was the norm when I did intense dungeon delves as well. I came off cooldown from my [Quick Step] and [Swordsmanship] needing a full waterskin and a loaf of bread. My rations were pretty scarce at this point, and what with everyone running around trying to get the outpost back in order, I was left in a bit of a sorry state.

Which was why I may have come back to Keith pleased but a touch hangry.

"I've straightened out the young griffin, and he'll head out when he gets his wind back," I told Keith and the dwarfess holding Hubert. "He intends to find his brother—that's the griffin who followed after him into the mountains—and report back to the flock. Or pride?"

"You speak griffin?" The dwarfess looked surprised. She sounded surprised, too.

"No, but I have a very high [Social] skill, which includes interpersonal communications. It promotes the capacity for empathy and understanding between two individuals," I explained. The [Social] skill had been the skill that I was born with.

Individuals usually received their first skill at level one. The only thing on their character sheet to base that skill off of at that point was their species, name, and any titles they might be born with. Dwarves were unique in that their famous [Control: Size] skill started out pretty useless as just [Control] until level ten. Instead of receiving their second skill at level, their [Control] skill raised to [Control: Size] without having to spend years leveling up the skill. They resumed gaining a new skill every ten levels just like everyone else after that.

"Princess." The dwarfess had crossed her arms and was looking rather irked. "I thank you for your help with settling the feud between us and the griffins. However, I really must—"

"Sorry to cut you off," I cut her off. "But do you have a shop in the outpost that sells food?"

"Excuse me?"

"Ria," Keith reminded helpfully, "her name is Corporal Nova, and she would be *happy* to take this conversation to Polman's Tavern. Wouldn't you, Corporal Nova?"

The dwarfess gnashed her teeth. I had rarely seen someone who wore their expressions so openly. I couldn't understand why she was so angry.

Alright, picking her up probably hadn't been the best first impression.

"I'm sorry we got off on the wrong foot. But could we *please* go get something to eat?" My stomach rumbled, proving my distress. "It's usually fine, but I've been pushing myself to the max to get here, and I'm honestly starving. I had berries for lunch."

"I have to get back to things here," Keith told me. "Are you staying in Frolin overnight or heading out to Gren's Keep?"

"Is there an inn? I like the idea of a real bed tonight . . ."

"There are a few rooms at the tavern. Usually for those too far gone to walk out at closing time," Corporal Nova said.

"Perfect." It was better than sleeping with sticks and rocks poking you.

"I'll check in tomorrow," Keith bid farewell, and Hubert took off to the skies.

Corporal Nova led me around the group righting the overturned carriage. Nolin was doing most of the heavy lifting, as he was still in his giant form. We exchanged nods as I passed. I was happy I hadn't needed to crush him into submission during the fight, as his battle strategy had involved defending with his fists and not felling foes.

Polman's had gotten off lightly with just a crooked sign where an errant boot had flung out of line and hit it. The building had two entries; half the entire tavern entry wall opened on sturdy hinges, and a smaller-than-I-sized pair of swinging doors in the middle of the bigger door. I opened the bigger door instead of opting to duck.

Inside, the room was a mix of the two sizes. Two giant chairs at a giant table in the first row, dwarf-sized everything else behind. The table was as tall as King Keith, and we walked under it to find a place to sit.

"Now, Princess." The corporal seemed much more at ease once she was comfortable and holding a drink. Hers was a stout, and I had a refreshing lemon radler. "As ambassador to the Dark Enchanted Forest and council member of this outpost entry into the dwarven lands, it is with every diplomatic delicacy that I wish to issue a formal complaint."

"I'm listening," I said. I was listening, but my focus might have been on the bowl of mountain unigoat stew being plated behind her at the bar.

"The Frolin designation is considered under the Baldorin Council. As such, any harm inflicted on our citizens is in violation of our treatise with Nilheim. The penalties of which—"

"I'm going to stop you right there, Corporal Nova," I told the military dwarfess. "I am not a citizen of Nilheim."

"But King Keith—"

"Was simply making sure that everything was delivered properly," I rudely interrupted her again, conscious of the stew now being carried our way. "I'm also sure that provision for the 'execution without trial' of any Nilheim citizen in Frolin would breach the same treaty?"

"But they are *monsters*." The dwarfess shook her head. "They aren't *people*."

"You know my father feels much the same way about dwarves," I said offhandedly. That definitely did *not* win me any diplomacy points. Trade was open between Baldorin and Drendil, but that didn't stop prejudice. "And *he* is wrong, too."

Finally, the stew had arrived. I reverently picked up my spoon and dipped it into the bowl. The unigoat, parsnips, potatoes, and thick broth smelled divine.

"I can't believe you just said that to me." Corporal Nova slammed her fist on the table, rattling my bowl and knocking over her own tankard.

I braced the stew with my free hand and sent her a look that probably mirrored my [Killing Intent] perk. "Watch it!"

At the same time, one of the dwarves waiting tables yelled, "Mind the beer, Nova!"

The dwarfess took a deep breath and resettled herself. I finally took my first bite of the stew, and all else faded away. The broth was thick and rich. The herbs earthy. The unigoat fell apart in my mouth. The vegetables were soft but still held substance. It probably had too much salt, but after my travels, it was exactly what I needed.

I appreciated the taste so much that a delicate sound of pleasure escaped me. Corporal Nova looked on in disgust but ordered her own bowl.

"You know, it's hard to be irate with someone who likes my husband's cooking that much," she told me.

"Is Polman your husband?" I asked around a mouthful.

"No, that was his grandpappy," she replied. "Marvin runs it now, but he kept the name."

"Listen," The stew did wonders for my mood and as I regained myself I tried to employ the etiquette skills my mother had beaten into me. "Corporal Nova, I apologize for any injury my part in returning the eggs has caused to the dwarven outpost. I would like you to know that I acted in good faith and would like to keep good faith with the dwarves going forward."

Corporal Nova eyed me for a long second and then sighed again. "Alright Princess. I'll accept your apology on behalf of Frolin, but I don't appreciate how cavalier you are with us and I expect you to show respect and dignity to my countrymen in future."

"That I *can* promise." I emptied the bowl and waved the server for a second serving.

I spent the rest of dinner chatting with the prickly corporal and meeting Marvin and some of the other crew. At one point, Chancellor Grimly came in to greet me and let us know most of the damage had been repaired and everyone could go on with their lives.

Which meant I could go shopping around the outpost before bed!

I just needed to follow my very important must-follow rule: don't buy more sharp, shiny, pointy things. I could do this.

CHAPTER 44

His Never-Ending List of Kingly Duties

Keith

The morning sunrise was a terrible thing that Keith never had to experience because he'd purposefully chosen rooms facing the western sky.

That morning, however, he wasn't snug under a plush comforter enjoying a peaceful sleep. No. Instead, he was glaring against the light in Henrietta's room.

In front of him knelt a trussed up and slightly battered spy whom his lizard-kin maids had found hiding in Ria's closet.

He couldn't be certain if the woman was an assassin or simply there to gather information. Either way, this was the closest any such outsider had come to the castle since . . . Well, since Henrietta herself.

"Why is this happening?!" He pinched the bridge of his nose, slightly lifting up his glasses to do so. "And why at this *ungodsly* hour of the morning?"

"Perhapsss it's because we sssent out all of the automaton guardsss?" Lilith suggested. She gripped the rope of the tied-up individual in one hand and held a knife to their throat in the other. The spy glared up at the Dark Lord, but her mouth was gagged. "She must have ssslipped through our defensesss."

"I kept some behind!" Keith argued.

He'd learned his lesson, and a midsize snake golem now lived in the rafters of his workroom. And there were still the gate-golems for anyone foolish enough to walk in through the front draw-bridge. "Still, again? I thought I covered every base with the princess's extra tests!"

"Shall we move this one to your inner sssanctum, my liege?" Lilith asked.

"Yes, yes." Keith waved a hand flippantly. "I'll be by after breakfast. You may throw her in the pit."

"Right away, Your Viciousnesss."

It'd been so long since he'd used the pit under his workroom, he didn't know how clean it was, and he didn't really care.

He considered the merits of going back to sleep.

"Your Viciousnesss?" Chikli poked his head into entry to the Nightshade Rooms. "Were you going to make time to interrogate the egg-napping mercenar-iesss today? Or should I leave them with Rufusss for one more sssession?"

Keith let out an exasperated sigh and stalked toward his never-ending list of kingly duties.

"I won't say. Ya can't make me! *Ya can't make me.*"

"I would never *force* you, Warren." Rufus's calm voice came from inside a cell when Keith arrived at the dungeons shortly after breakfast. "If you don't want to talk about how hard it is being the navigator, we can change the subject, but the subject does seem to eat at you."

The beastman reassured the panicked youth sitting across from him in the locked cell. Warren was missing a great many teeth, and his words slurred with spittle.

"It's just not right. They wanted me to navigate *the Dark Enchanted Forest.* And the boss kept yelling at me whenever we had to backtrack," Warren grumbled. He took a swig of water and then asked, "How do you *live* here, General Rufus?"

Rufus smiled. "I can only say that you get used to it."

"Well, I don't wanna get used to it! I wanna go home," Warren said. "How is taking *eggs* breaking the law? Nobody complained when I harvested floofpoof eggs!"

Rufus began listing off the laws that he had, indeed, broken, "Article Twenty-Three of the Classification of Nilheim Districts, Section Two of Citizen and Denizen:

> *Monster races which maintain communicable soul sapience are to be treated as native citizens of Nilheim.*

"And further, Article Seventy-Eight of the Classification of Collection, Section Six of Harvest and Hunting:

> *Hunting denizens or citizens of Nilheim by foreigners shall be punishable by the Secord Order.*

"Which is why you have been deposited here for questioning."

"But eggs can't communicate. So's they ain't a citizen or a denizen or which-ever," Warren argued. "They's just *eggs.*"

"And you are just a mercenary. With no one to hear you scream," Keith commented offhandedly from where he stood, leaning against the cell and smiling viciously. To Rufus, he said, "Why not quote childhood labor law? Section Two:

The action of using for profit any offspring, living or dead, not yet of age, shall be deemed illegal unless approved by a merchant guild application."

"I was going for the long-winded, roundabout approach where you convince someone to change their mind through their own dealings." Rufus sighed. "But yes, Section Two does apply."

"Does that mean I ain't going home?" Warren shriveled up under the look Keith sent him.

The Dark Lord smiled a very toothy grin. "Depends on who hired you, now, doesn't it."

"It were merchants!" Warren offered. "Servalt merchants. But merchants."

"Excellent. I've been looking for an excuse to deal with the corruption from Servalt bleeding into my realm." Keith speared his general with a gaze of iron. "When the war is done, Servalt is next. And you'll be in charge of cleaning it up, Rufus."

The therianthrope kept his professional demeanor in front of the prisoner but gently sighed. "Of course, my liege. Right away, my liege."

Keith left the dungeon, satisfied that things were going to be solved without much need for interference.

CHAPTER 45

You Aren't Napping on My Bridge, Are You?

Henrietta

I admit it.

I bought *so many* shiny, pokie things. In my defense, the dwarves made *very nice* shiny, pokie things.

After dinner, I went on a romp about the outpost, and I came back with three new throwing daggers, a silver boot needle, a hair tie with dangling lock picks, a mithril-plated fan with a belt hook, and a small polish kit for my Hero sword.

Craigy Hammerbottom, who had sold me the polish kit, had even offered to throw in the first polish for free! He might have drooled a bit as I handed over Jacqueline Tiamat la Fleur. She was a very beautiful [Hero Sword] that I'd pulled out of a stone dragon mural in the Depths of Despair Dungeon. Her hilt was made of fine twists of orichalcum, and her blade was mithril. The grip was made out of sea drake hide, with a sea drake scale curved pommel.

Jacqueline wasn't a very big talker for a magic sword. She spent most of her time sleeping, but when she was awake, she could be quite a handful. [Water] was her primary element, but on a critical success, she gave out [Void] damage.

She was my key to defeating the Dark Lord.

Keith's mother had been a nephilim; half demon general and half seraph paladin. If he took after her in any capacity than he was unlikely to possess [Void] damage resistance.

I had learned a lot about him during our afternoon tea breaks, including a bit of his history. While nobody knew who Keith's father was, he'd been born with only partial demon and human traits. One horn, strong magic, but no wings. He was a demi, someone who maintained both sides of their heritage. This was a rarity, as the System usually only kept one of the parents' titles to pass on. If you had a catkin mom and an elf dad, then you were born a catkin *or* an elf.

Keith's mother being a nephilim was also a rarity.

Speaking of Keith, I searched the outpost for my erstwhile raven companion but didn't see Hubert anywhere. If I was going to have time to stop at Gerda's place for breakfast, I would need to leave soon. I wanted to give her the present I'd bought her last night.

"Corporal Nova," I said.

"Yes, Princess?" she grumbled. She had gotten up to escort me out of town. I got the feeling her husband was a morning person, while Corporal Nova was not.

"Thank you for showing me around. I have to leave now. Could you let Keith's raven know I've left for Gerda's bridge?"

"I thought you were going to Gren's Keep?" the dwarfess all but accused. I had a feeling she didn't like me, but I enjoyed her company, so I wouldn't hold it against her.

"I am," I told her.

When I didn't say more, she sighed and replied, "Whatever. Have a safe trip."

I waved goodbye and took one last look for Hubert before starting down the trail.

I cost you nothing, and only you know the cost.
I am worth more than gold or silver, but hold no value after I'm lost.
I can be traded, and I can be difficult made,
By king or peasant, I can be easily gave,
And while I cannot hurt your flesh or bone,
When broken I destroy your heart, your name and home.

I actually sat down on the bridge for some thirty minutes to think of this one; Gerda hadn't pulled any punches for her riddle this time. "Argh." I flopped onto my back and looked up at the sky while my friend stood patiently by. Honestly, I was lucky that I had found the bridge exactly where I'd left it last night and didn't need to go searching, so a little extra time solving the riddle wasn't too much of a hassle. I thought aloud. "It's not . . . maybe friendship? Reputation? Hmm."

Eventually, Gerda got tired of waiting and leaned over to stare at my face. I opened one eye to see her fawn-brown eyes staring back. She had a few white freckles on her nose that made me think of deer. If deer were pale-green.

"You aren't napping on my bridge, are you?" Gerda teased.

"No!" I countered. "But I think I'm ready. Based on the *broken* bit, I'm going to guess . . . a promise?"

"Well done, Princess." Gerda reached out a hand to help me up. She patted me on the shoulder. "If I'm going to have to wait so long every time, maybe I'll just stick to the beginner-level riddles?"

"Don't you dare!" I shot back. The two of us climbed under the bridge and into her kitchen. "I love your riddles!"

"But will you love it if I can't let you cross the bridge?" Gerda set the table with some of her own freshly baked gingerbread cookies and a snack tray of nuts and fruit. "You'd have to defeat me to get past, and I'm warning you that troll magic is no joke."

"What's a little combat between friends?" I said, happily munching away on nuts.

"As long as you are alright with having to trek a mile off the path to cross the river, it should be fine . . ." Gerda pulled out a beautiful oak box with little jars of assorted dried tea leaves. "Now, which tea would you like?"

"Ohh! This is new!" I admired the tea and the cute labels scrawled with each flavor. "I'll have some rasp-elder berry, please."

"Thank you, I took a walk to Glendale in North Sumbria to buy some supplies after we spoke yesterday." Gerda chuckled. "I don't think I mentioned this part, but Countess Julia couldn't figure out my riddle. She also couldn't defeat me . . . so to save time, she offered me money and a favor to jump off the bridge myself. I, *of course,* would never stand in the way of true love."

"Does someone just need to get you off the bridge to 'defeat' you?"

"For the lower level riddles, yes." Gerda smiled a very big and self-satisfying smile. "I've never been defeated."

"I thought you just said—"

"Jumping off myself doesn't count," Gerda countered. "Ah, the tea should be steeped. Let me grab us some teacups."

"I also have a present for you!" I used the opportunity to pull out a small cloth I had rolled up and stuffed in my belt pouch. "I saw these in Frolin and thought of you."

I handed over the cloth. She put it on the table and unrolled it to reveal four crystal tea set spoons carved with mushrooms on the handle tip.

"I thought of you and the first riddle you gave me," I said, slightly nervous that she wouldn't like them. Gerda usually used little wooden soup spoons for mixing honey and cream into the tea, so I hoped she liked these.

"They are beautiful, Ria!" The troll reached out and delicately picked one up to inspect it. "Thank you."

"*Thank you,*" I replied. "For being the first friend I made in the Dark Enchanted Forest."

I pretended not to see the troll rub one eye. She gathered up the spoons to go rinse them in her kitchen sink so we could use them right away.

All in all, today was looking to be a great day.

CHAPTER 46

Why Is Everybody So Enamored with the Princess's Socks?

Keith

Keith was having a very bad morning.

A very bad morning indeed.

Again.

It had started at an hour too unbearable to even consider calling it morning.

They'd found another spy. This one was a half-elf guard repositioned from the Servalt border closer to the castle.

He'd *also* been found in Ria's closet.

"Why is everyone so enamored with the princess's socks?" Keith demanded to know. He didn't expect an answer.

"Maybe they want to leave a poison needle in one?" Chloe offered.

"Or perhaps they think she's stolen a kingdom treasure and hid it in her unmentionables?" Rufus added.

The necromancer and commander general had joined him for breakfast. Keith could never be sure if Chloe would come down for breakfast at the same time he was there. He didn't know Chloe's sleeping schedule, and neither did she; it was a free-flowing nebulous thing that switched between worshipful "beauty sleep" and staying up all night sewing minions back together after a wagon accident.

Chloe had to have all the pieces attached properly for most of her spells. It also made everything cost less mana. Resurrecting someone with just a finger *was* possible, but dangerous. First the body needed to be magically healed piece by piece starting at the finger, and *if* it was reformed in time, then the necromancer would have to invoke higher level spells than she could safely cast. She told everyone that she couldn't do it, and that they'd better do their due diligence and bring her the *correct* pieces to put back together.

Nobody wanted to end up with two left hands or Uncle Jimothy's bunion toes.

His commander general more often than not had eaten and gone about his day long before Keith came downstairs. Rufus was the early-to-bed-early-to-rise, five-small-meals-and-exercise kind of man. No wonder he was still single.

"I wasn't being serious," Keith groaned. He took a sip of his tea and let the hot honey and smooth, creamy liquid warm him from the inside out. Lady green tea was a key ingredient in the Awakening potion, and he savored its natural effect. "Though I wouldn't put it past Drendil to attempt a poison sock needle."

"Did you learn anything from the first spy?" Chloe asked around a mouthful of cheesy flake pastry.

"I learned that her favorite snack is dehydrated apples, she works for Ven Larsen as a tailor, and that her mother's name is Lola Higgins." Keith sighed. "She isn't under any enchantments, so I'm no use. Rufus will have to take a go at her spy perks. I'm pretty sure she has [Liars Palace]."

"I love a good challenge." Rufus grinned and carefully cut a piece from his avocado toast. "It's rare that we get a spy who's mastered the talent to create a fake identity so well they can take on the fake personality as truth."

"Give her to me, and I'll sort it out." Chloe said. "I could get an answer—"

"That's against the Valarian Council," Keith put in. At the same time, an angry Rufus warned, "No mind control!"

"If you own their soul,"—Chloe waved him off—"they tell you freely."

"Enough, Chloe." Rufus stood up quickly and slammed a fist down on the table. The room went quiet at his outburst, but Keith wasn't surprised. Everyone knew how Rufus felt about freedom and *ethics*. He was Nilheim's standing representative at the Valarian Council. Whereas Chloe just treated almost everybody as if they were just a body. It sort of felt like she forgot people were real people sometimes.

Chloe had the grace to blush. "Alright, alright, sorry. I was just joking."

"It was in poor taste." Rufus settled back down in his seat. After a moment, he said, "I'm sorry I lost my temper."

Keith watched his two closest friends. They fought a lot, but they also fought side by side when it mattered. He wouldn't be surprised if Rufus was asked to be her best man.

Speaking of, if he finished up early today, maybe he could take his own vacation before a certain Paladin arrived . . .

Keith had worked himself stupid in the vain hope that he might—just might—have a chance to slip away for a few days.

He liked to think that if Drendil had King Simon running everything all year, then Keith could probably leave for a few days, and the Dark Enchanted Forest wouldn't burn down.

That was, if he stopped having spies and family drop in . . .

Julia was set to arrive any minute; who could really tell how long it would take. She could have a magical horse or stamina potions or any manner of magical aids.

"Your Viciousnesss." Lilith had come to deliver an afternoon snack and found him staring at the wall. "Is sssomething bothering you?"

"I'm not cursed," Keith let her know. Not that she had asked, but he'd tested. And he wasn't under the influence of a spell either.

Lilith set down the tray and curtsied. "So nothing is bothering you?"

"Actually," Keith stood up, leaving the office and his snack behind. "I'll be in my inner sanctum. I should be busy for an hour."

He hadn't visited Ria yet, and it was midmorning. Time flew when you had spies and paperwork and anxiety. And a whole bleeding kingdom to run; thank the gods for competent minions.

Not that he was getting anxious about things. Keith had prepared for war with Drendil for about a decade . . . a war he'd originally intended to stop at the border, but who was counting?

Henrietta was counting. On him. To make her a part of the team.

Keith ignored his chaotic inner thoughts and connected with Hubert. The raven had stolen something shiny and was creating a nest in a nook among the rafters of one shop. The automaton had let its nature distract it, but all of his higher sentient creatures did so. He couldn't blame the raven for behaving like a raven.

He *could* and *did* panic when Henrietta was nowhere to be seen. He had Hubert fly around the town, high overhead. There was no trace of her, so without waiting around, Keith sent Hubert up the trail.

. . . Missing the fact that a dwarfess who'd just sat down to lunch and a beer at Polman's Tavern might've had a message for him if he'd bothered to say anything to anyone before he flew off.

As it was, Keith didn't check in. He simply flew off toward the Great Road, proceeding directly to Gren's Keep, pushing to catch up with his missing princess.

CHAPTER 47

The Flat of the Blade Across My Throat

Henrietta

After a lovely cup of rasp-elder berry tea, I said farewell to my bridge troll friend and set out west for the Gren's Keep turn off.

I wasn't in a rush, as there were still a few days before I was needed back at the castle . . . and even then, I wasn't really needed. I ignored that train of thought and sauntered up the road at a casual pace.

I tried not to look at the crossroad that wasn't a perfect crossroad because it was still off by one stone on either side of the path. That was a foolish thing to do, because I may have tripped, and barely had time to catch myself.

My Dexterity was high enough that my flailing save looked more like an elegant sway, but it was still awkward to just flail about while walking.

I glared down at the path; I was very sure that rock hadn't been there a moment ago . . .

If the path found my glare insulting or amusing, I couldn't tell. In either case, it chose not to speak to me.

A voice coughed in front of me. "Excuse me, miss."

Or maybe it did? I looked up and found five armored elves riding unicorns in front of me. My cheeks went red, and I moved to one side of the road.

The elf at the front of the group nodded. He was very proper and had a look about him that said anything and everything disappointed. He was riding the unicorn bareback, and gently patted the creature as he asked me, "Have you seen a young girl on the Great Road?"

I assumed he meant an elf girl, and I had seen one earlier. "I saw a girl reading a book back toward the king's castle. She had brown hair and was wearing a circlet—"

"Thank the gods." The prim elf visibly relaxed, and his companions did the same. He turned to the rider just behind him on the left and said, "She'll probably beat us back to the Hollow. What say you, Hazel?"

"Let's make haste," Hazel replied. Then she said to the unicorn she was riding, "Brightstar, I'm sorry you had to take us all this way."

Her unicorn tossed its head, and Hazel smiled. "You're right. Thank you."

I could have activated my [Social] skill, but I didn't want to intrude. The group seemed very worried for the missing girl. I hesitated to call her *young* myself, as she looked about my age. Still, it wasn't nice to presume.

They rode off up the path, and I continued on my way to Gren's Keep. I was a little worried that I hadn't mentioned that I'd seen her *yesterday*, but hopefully, that wouldn't make too much of a difference.

It made a difference.

I ran into the elf girl with brown hair and a circlet on her head not an hour later. She was reading a new book. It was purple, and this time, I was close enough to make out the title: *Gradient Flora of Green Oak* by Olen.

If I remembered correctly, Green Oak was the dungeon outside the elven city in Nilheim.

"Greetings!" I hailed the elf maiden as she approached, her nose deep in the book.

She didn't look up.

"Excuse me!" I tried again, but to no avail. Finally, as she was about to pass me, I reached out a hand to gently tap her on the shoulder.

I was suddenly on my back on the road staring up at the sky. I'd managed to get a finger onto the flat of the blade before it landed threateningly against my throat, but otherwise, I'd been completely taken by her surprise attack.

The elf looked as surprised as I felt. She was straddling me with the open book in one hand and her dagger in the other.

"Oh my gods!" The elf turned beet red as she jumped off me and flicked her book closed. She hopped twice on one foot as she stuck her knife back into a boot sheath and continued. "I'm so sorry! I didn't mean to throw you, Princess. Please forgive me!"

"That's fine." I laughed it off and stood back up myself, dusting off my clothes.

This was just another reminder that my perks and skills meant nothing if they weren't activated. I checked to make sure nothing had fallen out of my pockets before turning back to the elf.

She looked like she was about to cry, and I quickly waved away her fears. "It's alright! I'm fine! It's my fault for not blocking. And for trying to touch you. But I did call out twice."

The elf looked even more mortified and hid her face behind her book. Her ears peaked out on either side, a darker green from blushing. "I'm *so* sorry."

"I'm actually impressed. That was a wonderful throw!" I told her. I wasn't lying; it was a very good throw. I didn't usually get thrown, so I was doubly impressed. Abilities only took you so far, and she who reacted faster lived. It was my fault for not expecting danger at all times; my tutors would have been mortified.

I was tempted to use [Sword Aura] to try and get a sense of her level, but that would have been rude if she was strong enough to notice the skill.

"Really?" She looked at me over her book, hopeful.

"Really, really," I assured. "So, um, should we introduce ourselves?"

It wasn't the most graceful way of asking for someone's name, but I wasn't very graceful today. And I was tired of calling her "elf girl" in my head.

She took a deep breath and bowed so low her hair flopped forward and her circlet shifted slightly off-center. "I'm Lady Amaryllis Elm of Green Oak Hollow, but please call me Amy, Princess."

I hadn't misheard that first time. She *did* know who I was.

"It's nice to meet you, Lady Amy."

"*Eeeek!*" Amy made a squealing noise before collecting herself. "I'm sorry, Princess. I'm just such a huge fan."

"What?" I could only imagine what news had made it to the secluded elven home in the Dark Enchanted Forest. Maybe I didn't want to know; all this gossip about me was getting bad for my heart.

"Of your work!" Lady Amy's eyes lit up. "You defeated the Depths of Despair Dungeon when you were fourteen. And you soloed Dungeon Valley Crest by the time you were sixteen! Sixteen! It took me a decade of training to solo Green Oak Dungeon, and it's a lower-level dungeon! I just can't believe it's really you! Can I ask you some questions? Do you have time? I can walk with you back to Gren's Keep if that's where you're going? I won't be a bother, I promise. Did you know that when you defeated the phoenix of level fourteen in Dungeon Valley Crest, my father won the auction on some of its feathers? We also collected a blue scale from the ice dragon you killed. It's the dagger . . . in my boot."

Amy trailed off again after that long-winded ramble.

I could see why an adult elf would consider her still a young girl. And why he probably considered me a young girl, too. With that in mind . . .

"Alright," I said. "But first, you should know that there's a group of elves looking for you. They're riding unicorns down the path in that direction." I pointed.

Lady Amy visibly panicked. She gripped her book to her chest and whispered, "Oh no!"

CHAPTER 48

Paint the Castle Pink

Keith

It was a beautiful morning to fly over his kingdom, and Keith enjoyed the view. It helped that he'd had tea before this flight with Hubert, or he wouldn't have been in such a good mood.

Being at nearly a hundred percent mana for the first time in a long while might have also helped.

This also gave him an excellent opportunity to see how the roads were faring in the west, with most of the soldiers moving around in preparation for battle. There was significantly more mundane foot traffic than he would have assumed with a war on the horizon, but Gren's Keep was far from the Drendil border and full of beast people who could take care of themselves.

He did note seeing Sir Vainbark and Lady Hazelglade of the elven Hollow in passing. They were riding unicorns of all things, and Lady Hazelglade was actually riding the young heir to Goldenhoof's herd. It still made Keith uncomfortable that he couldn't remember the colt's name, so he made a mental note to check his physical notes later.

He couldn't wait to get the report of what they were doing on his desk . . . though he could guess it had something to do with Duke Briarthorn's daughter. She was notorious for going missing during her lessons.

Keith didn't panic when he arrived in Gren's Keep and still hadn't seen Henrietta. They had probably just missed each other somewhere on the road.

Keith wondered, was it just him, or did he spend a lot of time not panicking about Henrietta?

He settled Hubert in an elm close to the town's entrance and disconnected. Just in time for the chaos that awaited him back at his inner sanctum.

* * *

There were twelve days left until St. Veralyn's Day, and Keith was wondering if he should scrap the plan and just go destroy Drendil now.

No one would even know. Alright, everyone would know. And everyone would also tell him "I told you so." Which he couldn't be sure was worse than his necromancer having a nervous breakdown in the castle lobby.

"What do you *mean* Julia is on her way? Rufus!" The petite blonde paced back and forth, roiling black tendrils lashing out subconsciously as she waved her arms about with delicate, dramatic flair. "*How could you not tell me?*"

The commander general looked pained. "Her rooms are already made up. Please, Chloe, this isn't the first time Julia has visited—"

"Nothing is ready! I'M NOT READY! Dear gods, what am I going to *wear!*"

Keith was halfway down the stairs when she noticed him. He flinched.

"And you!"

"Listen, Chloe," he started. "We were wondering how to tell you—"

"With your *words*," the necromancer said. "Like an *adult.*"

"Chloe, I've something important to tell you." Keith joined them on the main floor.

She looked leery. "What?"

"Julia is on her way here to see you," he told her. "I'm sorry I didn't tell you sooner. We thought you might try and paint the castle again."

Chloe deflated a bit, grumbling, "You owe me one."

"I do." Keith nodded.

"I don't," Rufus teased. "I was just doing as I was told."

Keith pushed up his glasses to rub the bridge of his nose. Chloe glared at the beastman.

Suddenly, there was a ruckus outside the main castle entrance, and they all turned toward the castle's double doors. They burst open violently, one heavy wooden door hanging slightly off its hinges.

"Chloe!" A woman taller than a bridge troll but shorter than a giant dwarfess ran up to the necromancer and swept her into a twirling embrace. "My love!"

"Julia?!" Chloe couldn't help but laugh. "Hey, watch the armor."

Keith and Rufus looked away politely as the two reunited. Rufus leaned in close to Keith and said, "You know, she *could* use that favor to paint the castle pink."

"She wouldn't."

"But she *could.*"

"If she *did*," Keith surmised, "then maybe Drendil wouldn't recognize us and just march right on past."

"Ha! As if anyone from Drendil would make it this far." Rufus chuckled.

"What about the two sock thieves we found loitering at dawn in Henrietta's wardrobe?"

Rufus scoffed. "They don't count. They aren't a part of the army."

"How are things coming along with them?" Keith peeked; Chloe and Julia were still passionately saying hello. Julia was the only woman that Keith had met that could be more . . . just *more*, than Chloe. At the same time, the countess really grounded his necromancer—when Chloe wasn't having an existential crisis that Julia might visit, that is.

"I've mostly broken the first." Rufus shrugged. "She was instructed to kill Henrietta and/or retrieve all of her Drendil possessions."

"And they assumed everything would be in her sock drawer?" Keith asked incredulously. "Or that she was hiding in her closet?"

Rufus shrugged. "Maybe that's where she kept things at home. I haven't gotten that far yet. Honestly, I don't think I'll properly break them before the war. Not if we want useable intelligence. And I'm not willing to do that."

"I see." And he did see; torture gave poor results. Rufus's techniques could give actionable information, but took much longer.

"Your Viciousness! General Rufus! Greetings and good fortune." Julia hailed us. The two were *finally* finished. As was expected, the countess immediately got to work. "Where do you want me in the war efforts?"

He respected that in a person.

"First, I'll have Chloe show you to your room," I told her. "She only *just* found out you were coming, so there might be a bit of . . . remodeling left to do. To suit your tastes."

The second they were finished, Keith was sure that Chloe would tear Julia's room apart and put it back together again. At least now she would only do it once, and not every day leading up to her visit.

Julia blushed slightly at that. The dark skin of her ears turning a ruddy pink.

"I'm sorry I didn't properly call ahead," she apologized.

"You could have at least told me," Chloe pouted prettily. She was still holding Julia's hand.

"For the second," Keith continued, "I'll have you defending Chloe. I don't want you involved in the greater war effort; that could be politically costly for your mother."

"I don't need—" Chloe began hotly.

Keith cut off his necromancer, "Since she'll be *busy* running around resurrecting people."

Julia smiled and squeezed Chloe's hand. "No arguing, love."

"Since that's done." Keith pushed his glasses up and surveyed the three individuals in front of him. "I have an announcement to make."

Rufus, Chloe, and Julia all looked at him expectantly. Keith smiled.

"I'm taking the weekend off."

CHAPTER 49

Keith's Godmother Was Trying to Kill Him?

Henrietta

Lady Amy peeked behind me and frowned. "Are they coming this way?"

I waved back the way I'd come. "No, they rode toward the castle."

"Great! Then I'll definitely be available to walk you to—Wait, did you say *rode*? Brightstar, that traitor!" The elf tossed a few sun-streaked brown braids that had fallen forward over her shoulder and let out a huff.

Starting at her widow's peak, two braids swept out and hugged her heart-shaped face with wisps of straight loose hair. The braids looped behind her head and tied into a high-top ponytail that fell in partial braids to her waist. A few flowers and vines had been woven into the strands in places, and the whole arrangement made her look like a proper elven princess.

If you ignored the breastplate, that was. I assumed a real elven princess would be in full armor riding a unicorn into battle, not running around the Dark Enchanted Forest in half armor with her nose stuck in a book.

"The search party seemed very concerned. Are you sure—"

She interrupted vehemently. "I'm absolutely sure. They're not worried about me. They're just upset that I'm not sitting around looking pretty like I'm supposed to."

"I see." That sounded familiar. We started walking at a reasonable pace, though it looked like instead of arriving at noon, we'd reach our destination closer to sunset. "Then sure, join me on my quest."

Lady Amy looked at me with bright eyes. "What is your quest?"

"I'm debating," I told her honestly, "between ramen from Logan's Noodle House or rumblepot stew from the Damp Gizzard."

"Oh." Disappointment flitted across her face. Then she perked up. "If we eat at Olen's, then he gives a discount for a room."

"Then let's aim for the Damp Gizzard. I like sleeping on a real bed."

The trip was longer than it needed to be, but Lady Amy was anything but boring.

"And then His Viciousness walked out of the Green Oak covered so heavily in Venus violents pollen that his skin was dyed purple for a week!" she finished a daring tale of the first time Her Eminence Feliwyn had sent King Keith to test himself against the dungeon in the Hollow.

"Really?" I couldn't imagine how cute a ten-year-old Keith running around casting [Quick Chant] spells must have been. For the better part of the afternoon, Lady Amy had regaled me with stories about the dungeons around the Dark Enchanted Forest. And, even better, stories about King Keith.

"Really! Father was hosting Her Eminence with an elaborate feast when he burst in." Amy giggled. "He was still Royal Heir at the time, and Rufus could beat him with one hand tied behind his back."

"So are you friends with Chloe and Rufus and Keith?" I tried to piece things together.

"Me?! Oh no! Oh no, no, no, no, no," Lady Amy protested vehemently. "My . . . um, duties kept me from doing more than simply greeting the prince with all the other children. Her Eminence chose Rufus as our king's closest confidant, and it's a good thing she did."

"Why?" The forest around us had become overgrown with brambles and bushes and holly so thick that it was getting hard to see anything but a wall of green.

"Everyone knows how solitary and introverted our king is," Lady Amy explained. "Necromancer Chloe challenged him intellectually, but General Rufus trained with him and handled most of the assassins."

"I thought the assassins didn't start until Keith stepped up as king at sixteen?" I asked.

"Where did you hear—Ah, wait." The elf chuckled. "Yes, Drendil started sending assassins around that time. But no, I meant the other assassins."

"What other assassins?"

Lady Amy listed them off on her fingers. "Royalists during the Sumbrian revolution, the Servalt first prime minister's private army, Her Eminence Feliwyn's shadow corp—"

"Wait?!" I interrupted. "Sorry, did you say Keith's godmother was trying to kill him?"

"I don't think she was trying to perma-death him. She was just sending shadow assassins after him."

"Not to kill him?" I asked, again.

"More like training?" Lady Amy shrugged. "It's the usual upbringing for prospective rulers of the Dark Enchanted Forest. You can't be weak if you want Lithnilheim to acknowledge you."

"Who is Lithnilheim?" I could understand the training. It was actually a wonder my parents hadn't thought of it.

"The forest." Lady Amy nodded respectfully to the general area around us. "It's the elven name for the Dark Enchanted Forest, and where Nilheim comes from. The elves were here first, serving the Hollow, long before the towns or the castle.

"They learned that Doreen the Devourer, Demon of Gluttony, had been mortally wounded and hid in the forest to spend the last of her days. After a few raiding parties tried and failed to drive off her and her minions, a sort of truce was formed because she only had some fifty years to live before her wounds would overcome her.

"But then she had children—a lot of children—and more groups settled here. There have been a mix of kings and queens of all races going back hundreds of years, but every once in a while, the bloodline breeds true and a powerful demon resurfaces. King Keith is only a demi and could have easily been overthrown as a child if Her Eminence hadn't stepped in. But it was a bloodless rise to power, since she did."

"Unless you count the assassins," I said.

"Yes." She chuckled. "But who counts assassins?"

CHAPTER 50

Keith Is Going on a Date

Keith

Keith gently pushed the knife point away from his throat. "I *told* you; I'm not cursed. I already checked!"

"Exactly what someone who is cursed *would* say," Julia tsked. "[Identify] him, Chloe."

Chloe already had her hands up casting the spell. Behind them, Rufus was doubled over trying to hold in laughter. After this, Keith was going to find the most boring problem under the dark moon and send Rufus to go fix it.

"Don't fight it," Chloe ordered her king. "Or we'll have to resort to drastic measures."

"Yes, yes, just get on with it already."

Chloe cast [Identify] and then [Dispel] and then [Soul Link] and Keith let her. In the back of his mind, he was actually relieved to have secondary confirmation that he wasn't under some kind of spell.

He passed all the tests, but Julia still looked unconvinced. "Maybe we should also test for poison?"

"Julia, he's not cursed." Rufus finally stepped forward. "Keith is going on *a date*." Awareness dawned. "With whom?"

"Princess Henrietta of Drendil," Keith cut in. "And if I'm going, it's *now*. So would you please sheath your blade?"

Julia took the point off his neck. "Well then, congratulations. Henrietta is a good sort."

"Thank you." Keith nodded and shook out his cloak. "Now, if you'll excuse me, I'll be back in a few days. Send any important updates to Gren's Keep."

"Wait!" That's when Chloe started yelling. "You *can't* leave now!"

"Watch me."

* * *

Keith left a hot mess of confusion and anarchy behind. Among his generals, at least.

His workspace was clean, organized, and primed for his absence.

In a way, Keith wished that he had stepped out that morning instead of wasting time flying Hubert all over the forest. He could have found Ria faster if he'd left—and he wouldn't have needed to argue with Chloe about leaving.

Did she care that he was abandoning his work, the castle, or the war preparations? No. She was livid that Keith wouldn't play host to Julia.

Honestly, that was just another reason for him to run away . . . or vacation, as he'd informed the group.

Chloe had gone so far as to fake faint into her lover's arms at the unfairness of it all, but she would get over it.

So Keith shook out his old dungeon delving kit and grabbed his satchel, went up to the lookout platform, and headed out for Gren's Keep.

For his tenth birthday, Feliwyn had gifted Keith a collection of monster parts. From it, he had created his favorite magical prosthetic construct. He had dabbled in replacing limbs at that point, but for this he'd crafted himself a set of wings.

They were black wyvern membrane tissue bound to mechanically enchanted treant bones, for added flexibility and mana circulation. The wooden bones were also easier to carve spell script and enhancements into for a ten-year-old.

Keith unfolded the set and slotted them into holes precut into his adventuring tunic. [Flight] was a higher-level spell, and it cost a lot of mana to maintain. Activating the wings, however, meant he could fly around and not risk plummeting to a painful collision with the earth if Henrietta distracted him.

Planning ahead was always important when dungeon delving.

It took a bit of trial and error to get a feel for his temporary extra limbs, but less than half an hour later, he was flying west.

Keith arrived at Gren's Keep before dinner.

It was next to impossible to go unnoticed in the Dark Enchanted Forest when you were the king of the Dark Enchanted Forest, so he didn't bother trying to be stealthy.

He landed outside the town. Folding his wings down, he clipped the tips to his belt so that they wouldn't sway around awkwardly while deactivated, and then he simply walked in through the front gates. He told himself it would make it easier for Ria to find him if everyone and their human knew he'd arrived. Secretly, he enjoyed the chaos it caused.

Unfortunately, the General of the West found him first.

"Yourrr Viciousness!"

A tigerkin in full beast form went from casually napping on a building roof nearby to bounding over fully transformed and landing on one knee in front of him, his voice rolling the *R* as many of the feline beast folk did.

"General." Keith nodded imperiously, but he wasn't looking at Quinton. He was sweeping the crowd for any sign of Henrietta.

Quinton rose to his full height in beastman form, a little taller than Keith, and awkwardly scratched his head. "We weren't expecting you?"

"I'm taking a vacation."

Quinton's mouth dropped open; he didn't appear to believe what he was hearing. "A *vacation*?"

"Yes." Keith nodded.

"You?"

"Yes."

"Here?"

"Yes?"

"But . . . why?" the general asked. "We don't have any golems needing rrre-pairs, and there aren't any new monsterrr types spawning in the dungeon. If you needed ingredients for yourrr automata, you could just say so."

Keith couldn't see or smell his princess anywhere, so he made the next most obvious choice. "Quinton?"

"Yes, Yourrr Viciousness?"

"Take me to the Damp Gizzard." Keith knew that the first thing Henrietta would do would be to find food after her [Quick Step] cooldown. So if she wasn't here yet, he should wait in the most obvious place.

"Yes, um, of course." Suddenly, Quinton looked like he'd been caught between a rock and a hard place. "Right now?"

Keith only saw his general sweat like this for one reason and one reason alone. He ordered, "Tell me."

"It's no problem. Just . . . I need to tell the wife first, you know? I'm supposed to be watching the kits after I get off guard duty . . ." Quinton looked off toward his house and then back at Keith. "Of course, Yourrr Viciousness comes first! I'll have someone send word to Lina."

"How old are Bastian and Bastet now?" Keith remembered the twins from the last time he'd visited. Lina had shoved a fluffy Bastian at him so she could tend to Bastet clawing the couch legs. The young tigerfolk had spent the better part of thirty minutes telling Keith all about the animals he'd seen and tried to hunt that day.

"Six, but Calypso is two and quite the handful now." Quinton chucked. "But she's cute and can get away with murderrr."

"How many murders?" Keith joked. The two started walking to Olen's, and the crowds dispersed politely to let them through. "Is she hunting already?"

"Ha! She's taken afterrr her old man and caught her first rrrabbit this week!" Quinton smiled with pride.

The general signaled someone to take over for him on guard duty, and a veteran named Puma stepped forward. Keith approved. As the saying went, *No one checks for assassins quite like Puma Checks.* She was renowned across the entire forest for her stealth, her deadliness, and her high Perception.

It became a saying due to her so aptly appropriate last name.

He was just about to have a word with her about keeping an eye out for his wayward princess when he heard a familiar voice call out behind him. "Keith?"

He turned around and saw Ria running up to him with a big, surprised smile on her face.

Puma, in natural guard form, attempted to stop Ria from approaching the king without proper protocol or invite . . . It didn't go well for the beastwoman.

Ria had chosen Perception as her dump stat . . . and Puma's entire arsenal was fueled by high-level stealth skills. Ria didn't realize the guard was on her until Puma had a dagger drawn on the princess's neck.

Within half a second of the knife landing, just before it touched her flesh, Ria reacted with a startled flinch, grabbing Puma's wrist and using her momentum to throw the guard over her shoulder.

Which would have been fine, if Ria's Strength stat wasn't sixty-seven . . .

They all watched in impressed horror as Puma flew far, far away into the forest. Just before she dropped out of a sight, the guard's armor caught the sunlight and gave off a beautiful sparkle.

"That was *amazing!*" the young elf girl who was standing right behind Henrietta spoke first. She turned to General Quinton and exclaimed, "Did you just see that? She just threw Mistress Puma! *The* Mistress Puma . . . Should someone go check that she's alive?"

Wait, was that Duke Briarthorn's daughter?

Keith looked at the busy town, the general, and Lady Amaryllis. All of whom were interested in tagging along for his reunion with Ria.

He suddenly had a wonderful idea.

All This Just to Go Get Someone Who's Been Yeeted into the Woods?!

Henrietta

I looked down at my hands in shock, then up at Keith.

He took one and held it firmly. Like he was expecting I'd run off. He tried to make me feel better by saying, "It was a natural response to being startled, Ria. It will be alright."

It didn't work. And I was suddenly tempted to run off and find Puma and bring her back myself. "But—"

"He's right, Princess Henrietta!" Amy nodded. "Puma is almost level forty and second to none but General Quinton here."

Amy pointed at the tiger beastman standing close by. He had a pained expression on his face as he shaded his eyes with one hand and gazed off into the distance after Puma.

What Amy had said sunk in, and the general turned to me. "You are Princess Henrietta?"

"Yes, ah, sorry." I gently waved with my free hand. "Nice to meet you, General Quinton . . . Sorry about the mess."

I'd said sorry twice and felt twice the fool.

General Quinton just ran his hands through his white hair, a soft contrast to his dark-gray complexion in human form. "It's alright, Yourrr Highness. Puma will land on her feet. She could probably make it back here by tomorrow, but I should go check on her." He turned to a few beastkin who had gathered by the gate. "Who wants overtime?"

"Actually." Keith squeezed my hand. "Why don't we go and grab Puma for you?"

I felt immense relief wash over me and gave him a thankful look. If I mistakenly inconvenienced someone with my abilities, I wanted to make sure they were safe. "Really? It's not too much trouble?"

"Of course not." He smiled back.

Lady Amy nearly jumped out of her boots with excitement and proclaimed, "An adventure! My body is ready!"

There was an awkward silence as I realized that Lady Amy, *who didn't have [Quick Step]*, wanted to join the search party.

"I don't think—"

"You aren't coming—"

Keith and I both replied at the same time. He nodded at me to go first.

"Listen, Amy, our plan is to race to Puma and come back as fast as possible. It won't work unless everyone can travel at the same speed . . . and I don't think you can keep up." I tried to say it as gently as I could.

"There's no need to worry about that." Amy smiled. "One of my [Ranger] perks is [Tree Walker]. I'm not the fastest on the roads, but I could get to Mistress Puma and back far quicker than any of you, since she fell in the forest."

Keith suddenly smiled a very big, very toothy grin. "You could?"

"Of course!" Lady Amy said proudly. "I even have tracking skills! It'll be a breeze."

"That's excellent!" Keith said. "Then we can trust you to find her and bring her back tonight."

"What?" Lady Amy's face fell into shocked horror.

"General Quinton has a previous task, so it was looking like Henrietta and I were going to have to miss dinner to go and find the guardswoman. But with you offering to go, and with the assurance of your skill and history, I am offering you this quest."

If Amy could track and find and bring back Puma for us, that would mean I could go to dinner with Keith knowing the search party was in good hands.

My desire to have dinner with a handsome, winged Dark Lord in leather *might* have been at war with my natural inclination to do what I thought was right. This kept happening, and I didn't know if I was just weak to Keith or learning to take my own desires seriously for once . . .

It wasn't *just* the prospective dinner date; I decided that if she was more skilled for the job, then it would be a relief to have someone who knew what they were doing out looking.

Lady Amy's eyes unfocused in a telltale sign that she was busy reading a System Prompt. Keith must have used his Dark Magician King title ability to give her an official quest.

"All this just to go get someone who's been yeeted into the woods?!" Amy looked between me and the air where the prompt would have popped up. "Five hundred experience points and a random artifact?"

Keith pulled off a black bracelet with golden thread entwined throughout. "Not just any random artifact. This has a +1 to Constitution on it."

I was extremely jealous. My father never offered me experience points or official quests when he gave me tasks . . . and watching Keith offer a beautiful elf girl jewelry wasn't making it easier.

I stomped down on the negative emotions, convincing myself that it was fine.

Everything was fine.

"Done!" The elf accepted. She did a little stretch and turned to walk back through the gate. Amy glanced over her shoulder and told us, "I'll be back before you can say, 'Adventurer, I'm on My Way.'"

The song immediately popped into my mind, and I groaned. That earworm would be stuck in my head all day.

No matter where you're trapped,
I'll find you.
I'll battle levels higher,
For you.
I'm just a humble bard, they say.
But, Adventurer, I'm on my way!

Bronwynn the Bard, my best friend back home, also known as Brownie, had released an entire new evening's worth of songs for her performance at Peldeep's Lunar New Year show. It must have been a huge success if people were already starting to sing the lyrics here.

I, of course, had gotten to listen to all of the songs before anyone else.

We waved Lady Amy off. General Quinton arranged the guards, and Keith tucked my hand into his arm.

"Ready for the best stew in the entire Dark Enchanted Forest?" he asked.

"Lead the way."

Keith took a second to wish the General of the West a good evening with his children, and then he led me up the road to the Damp Gizzard.

I wasn't expecting things to get steamy. I also wasn't expecting the glitter.

And I certainly wasn't expecting the musical number.

CHAPTER 52

A Real Princess

Keith

Keith led Ria through the main street of Gren's Keep and pointed out the shops that might interest her.

Keep was a bit of a misnomer, as it was the remnants of an old fortress once owned by Grendelyn the Grey. He'd been a crotchety old sorcerer who'd collected interesting people. The people, including an unorthodox amount of beastfolk, had not been impressed.

They'd burned it down and cleared it out and built a quaint country town on the spot of the ruins. It had been the first metropolis of beastfolk on the continent, and over the generations, more people had moved there. Apparently, they kept the name because the old sorcerer had always despised being called Gren.

And then the Pixie Prim had moved in.

The entire city now overflowed with flowers and vines and beautiful gardens thanks to the influence of the Prim. Even the Damp Gizzard had morning glory dangling off its low-hanging eaves.

Keith gently guided Ria off to the side of the entrance as he pushed open the front door to Olen's place. A mug missed his head by a full hand's length and crashed into the street.

There was a brawl going on inside that came to a comical stop when Keith walked in. A partially transformed bearman in the process of wrestling an angry drunk ratkin to the ground looked up at them. "Yer Viciousness, I didna see you there!"

"Don't stop for me, Olen. I'll grab us a seat." Keith brought Ria over to a table against the wall close to the bar.

"Oh, is Olen from the north country?" Ria asked upon hearing his dialect. It resembled the folk north of the Baldorin mountain ridge. "And did that otterfolk just smash Olen over the head with a chair? What if he breaks the chair?"

"He has to pay for it or repair it," Keith replied. He contemplated pouring them a cup of water while they waited, but Olen had already tossed the drunk ratkin out the conveniently still open door and picked up the otterfolk to do the same. They would have their drinks shortly. "And I think he inherited the Gizzard from his uncle. He moved here about a decade ago to take over. If I'm remembering his paperwork correctly, he's from the bearfolk village, Orsons Pass."

Olen Orrin clapped his hands together twice and wiped them on his apron. He gave the room an intense once over to make sure no one else was getting uppity. Either Keith's presence had settled things down, or no one else was in the mood.

"Sorry about that, my liege." Olen picked up the not-broken chair and pulled out a notepad that looked tiny in his giant bear paws. "What can I get you for dinner?"

"Let's start with drinks. Ria?" Keith tried to get his princess's attention.

Ria was staring, captivated by the bearman's clothes. "What? Oh. Did you know I have the same apron?"

Olen gave a self-satisfied grin. "Did you win it off Gerda in a tablero game?"

"No!" Ria laughed, and Keith settled back, enjoying her enjoyment. "She gave it to me after we baked bimbleberry scones together. What's tablero?"

"It's—"

"Master Olen." A squirrel hopped up onto the ledge of the serving hatch window leading into the kitchen. "Orders up!"

It hopped back down at the same time two bluebirds flew out of the window with napkins, alighting on a table and cleaning it. They chirped, and Olen told them, "Lyle's mug flew into the street."

More chirping.

"No, I'm busy. With the *king*."

Chirp.

"Well, he's mine, so I'll do the thing and then be right back."

The two birds twittered, one grabbing both cleaning rags and the other flying off in search of the missing mug.

Keith cut in before Olen taught Ria the rules of tablero . . . a game for which he was sure she'd drink everyone under the table. Another night. "They have some lovely berry teas and a sparkling mint liliput. What do you think, Princess?"

She rolled her eyes at the title and said, "I'll take the sparkling. And your famous stew!"

"Make that two, Olen."

"Right away!" The bear beastman nodded. "We'll chat later."

Olen ambled over and slapped their order down on the ledge before grabbing several plates and bringing them out.

Someone started singing in the kitchen, and the light aria filled the tavern.

Ria leaned in close. "I thought that beastfolk couldn't get smaller than a cat?"

"They can't," Keith replied. "Those aren't beastfolk."

A purple lizard no bigger than Keith's hand slithered onto the window ledge, its scales shimmering despite the fading light from outside. It carried a tiny oak wand with an amethyst at the tip. With a swish, it cast a long spell, and suddenly, all of the Damp Gizzard's lamps blazed with light.

"Wait!" Ria grabbed a hold of Keith's tunic and exclaimed. He resisted the urge to cover his face with one hand from how adorable that was. "Is that Lavender the Lizard Wizard?"

"Yes."

"The one and only!" Lavender bowed from her perch. She turned and slithered back into the kitchen.

"That means . . ."

Olen went through the kitchen door, revealing a sheer menagerie of woodland creatures inside.

"It means," Keith finished, "that Olen married Princess Penelope of Peldeep. And now his entire restaurant is run by her animal friends."

"He married a *real* princess?"

"I'm having *dinner* with a *real* princess," Keith reminded her. He chuckled as Henrietta almost fell out of her seat trying to get a better look. Luckily, she was still holding his sleeve.

"You know what I meant," she countered. "Someone who can sing like a nightingale, make friends with beasts of all kinds, and overcome her traumatic past by besting evil to find her happily ever after."

Keith just stared at her.

"I can't sing to save my life," she protested, her cheeks blushing pink.

"I also wouldn't call my minions *beasts*. That's a bit rude, even if the shoe fits." Keith ran a finger and thumb along his chin. "Especially for Chloe."

"Isn't she human?" Ria questioned.

"Yes." Keith nodded. He stood by what he'd said.

The song in the kitchen came to a full crescendo, and the doors burst open to reveal a beautiful black-haired princess dressed in a blue day dress complete with short poofy sleeves, and a pristine white half apron around her waist.

Olen came up to stand beside his wife, holding the bowls while she held the drinks. Purple sparkles danced across the cups as the last remnants of Lavender's [Bubble Blitz] spell finished.

Princess Penelope curtsied low. "My king, my queen, allow me to present your dinner!"

Keith quite liked the sound of *my queen*. Ria choked on air beside him.

CHAPTER 53

A King-Size Bed

Henrietta

Yes, Keith and I were courting. And besides the fact that he was very pretty, he was also very good company.

We were of similar stations, so my parents couldn't complain—excepting the whole mortal enemies, assassins, and kingdom war part. I didn't have any fiancé waiting for me back home, although my mother had brought up a number of court lords and ladies as marriage partners over the years, mostly as a threat to get me ready for the next dungeon delve.

"If you can't level up faster, the least you could do is marry someone *actually* competent. How about Lady Luise? She'll make a fine jewel for the kingdom when you're king," she'd say.

"Lady Luise beat her maid to death last week with a candelabra. I don't know if she'd make a good queen?"

"Tut-tut, she'll need that determination to rule beside someone as weak as *you*, dear. Now, go level up properly—if you can't grow a backbone, you can at least get strong enough to be impressive to hide your disgusting naivete."

It wasn't much of a threat; I'd always assumed my marriage would be a political marriage—with no offspring because of the curse. Any partner would just be for show, and with my parent's tastes I knew I wouldn't enjoy the match.

While I was very seriously considering Keith's . . . *interest*, and I was getting used to the idea that people were encouraging our relationship, that wasn't the same as outright being called queen of the Dark Enchanted Forest by a beautiful princess.

Penelope's long black hair was tied in a ponytail that braided down to her knees. Her eyes were slim and delicate like her fox heritage, though she didn't show a hint of any tails.

"Thank you, Penelope," Keith told the woman. "The *princess* and I will let you know if there is anything else."

"We are at your service!" If I didn't know any better, I'd say Penelope smirked at Keith before grabbing Olen's arm and dragging him back to the kitchen. "I hope you like your drinks with extra glimmer?"

"It's wonderful, thank you." I praised.

Lavender was back at the bar, enchanting drinks. *The* Lavender. The last time I'd heard of the Lizard Wizard, she was in a party of adventurers in the Depths of Despair Dungeon. Not many talking animals went from helping deserving lost heroes to becoming legends in their own right. If I recalled correctly, Lavender had started by giving directions to a seventh son.

I pulled my eyes away to focus on Keith. He was watching me with that *look* he sometimes got. The one that said he was very happy and content. He'd finally relaxed a bit with food in front of us.

"Thank you." I braced myself to sample the stew.

"For what?" Keith tilted his head. He lifted a spoonful of broth and blew on it gently.

"For letting her know I wasn't the queen yet in a way that didn't cause a spectacle." I eyed my own bowl.

Keith shrugged.

This was my second tavern stew in as many days, and I had to immediately apologize to Marvin because there was a reason *this* stew was talked about across the entire Dark Enchanted Forest. It was golden, creamy, and slightly sweet. I tasted hints of curry mixed with cardamom, and the spices heated my tongue without being uncomfortable. The potatoes were soft deliciousness infused with the flavors of mushrooms and carrots and onions. The beef melted in my mouth.

The broth was unique and flavorful in a way that I'd never tasted before. I moaned with pleasure. Keith twitched.

"This is amazing." I finally had enough cognitive function to speak. "Do you think Panlith would forgive me if I hired a singing princess and beastman to cook at the palace once a week?"

"Panlith hasn't taken a day off since he took over that kitchen five years ago," Keith told me. "His house collapsed during a heavy rainstorm, trapping him and his family under the bog. His wife and children could be [Resurrected], but his body was washed downstream and took too long to find. After Chloe [Raised] him, he showed up and hasn't left the kitchen since. I think he would fight tooth and nail to keep it that way."

"Wait, wait, wait." I coughed on a sip of the bubbling spritzer. "Panlith is *a zombie*?"

"No." Keith enjoyed another bite of stew. "He's a ghoul lord. He's obviously retained his intelligence."

"Huh." I'd had no idea. Though I'd wondered why he was always in the kitchen even when everyone else took days off. "Are there any other undead that I know?"

"Gimtak is also a ghoul lord." Keith listed on a finger, "Phillip the Skeleton Porter, Brian the Vampire Accountant, and Milith the Wight."

"Do they all not follow the four-day work week?" I'd seen Gimtak delivering Keith's mail every day. Though I only knew of Philip and Brian in passing. Milith was rarely in the kitchen, and only to grab something and run away.

"Just Gimtak and Panlith. That imp actually spends most of his time relaxing in the library or snacking in the break room. He's so fast and his [Teleportation] so high that he only needs a few minutes to deliver the royal mail each day. He has an army of winged delivery workers who do the rest of the kingdom work, and his son handles everything else. Gimtak is practically retired . . . Honestly, he might *be* retired and just doing it every day out of boredom. I'm surprised he hasn't asked for eternal rest yet."

My mind tried to wrap around all of the undead happily working about my new home. It was one thing to know Chloe was a powerful necromancer and another to know I was surrounded by creatures of evil. "Wow. I never would've guessed."

They were all so *nice*. My father would've had the army hunt down any *hint* of an undead in Drendil. He was particular about "keeping the kingdom *clean*," as he put it.

I was growing more and more sure of my decision to embrace evil every day.

Penelope returned with a beautiful glass jar piled high with ice cream, markle berries, whipping cream, and two connected-via-the-stem cherries on top. A shimmering glow of blue mist danced around the dish, compliments of Lavender's magic.

"On the house, dear royal guests," Penelope declared. Then she handed us two tiny dessert spoons. "Is there anything else you need addressed?"

As she asked, two bluebirds flew about her in graceful swoops and picked up our light wooden bowls. A chipmunk sat on her shoulder watching the dining hall, presumably to whisper in her ear should anyone be in need of service.

Keith looked at me, but I was happy and didn't need anything else. I eyed the ice cream and blushed a bit when I realized we were going to share it. Keith turned back to our hostess and said, "Yes, Princess Penelope, we would like to stay the night. Two rooms, please."

"Please, my king, I am your loyal subject and have been since I married Olen, last I checked . . . Penelope or Mrs. Orrin will do." Penelope's voice suddenly took on a very concerned pitch, though her face retained a smile as she told us. "And *oh dear*, but while you were enjoying our stew, a few guests arrived whom have taken our second to last room. We only have one left upstairs—but it does have a king-sized bed and a chair."

CHAPTER 54

Phrasing, Penelope, Phrasing!

Keith

It was Keith's turn to almost spit take, though he maintained his composure in the face of the two princesses with a barely concealed eyebrow twitch.

The years of training under his godmother Feliwyn had come in really handy of late.

Penelope was just as much a tease as her parent, Their Royal Highness Rowen, and Keith needed to be sure she didn't realize how much her words had affected him.

Like the adorable Ria was affecting him right now. She happily placed one of the two cherries into her mouth and popped the stem off with her teeth. Then she let out a happy sigh that made him painfully aware of just how hard it was to look away. He had to drag his gaze back to their hostess.

"That is unfortunate," he told Penelope. "Perhaps we could book the room for Lady Amaryllis and find accommodations elsewhere."

Penelope shook her head sadly. "It is a *shame*, but the armies marching around have sent more merchants to our town. Everyone is steering clear of Drendil's border, and the whole of Gren's Keep has no—"

"Sorry, my liege." Olen ambled up behind his wife just in time to cut her off. "We'll make room for you and Princess Henrietta upstairs. The Bobbin Brothers were going to have a room each, but I'll let them know there's been a change of plans."

"I appreciate that," Keith said, at the same time Henrietta asked. "Are you sure?"

He was taken aback by the implications of her question and stared at her, then remembered to close his open mouth.

She blushed. "I mean, I've slept in a chair before; it's not too much of a hardship . . ." Ria shrugged it off with much more rationale than Keith could muster before continuing. "And besides, we'll be sleep—*camping* together in the dungeon tomorrow, won't we?"

"Unlikely. We could easily complete the Hollow Gorge in a single day. It might be a close call in the Deep Shoals Dungeon," Keith explained. "But we can still try—they've set up portals on each floor so that anyone can hop out when they're ready. We use the dungeons for revenue, and it's safer for the porters that way."

Keith took a second to pop his own cherry. He savored the taste.

"But then we'd have to start from the first floor again the next day . . ." Henrietta watched Keith eat very intently, and he wondered if he should've let her have both cherries.

"That is true." Keith nodded.

"So are you two sleeping together, or do you need separate rooms?" Olen scratched his head and then squeaked in a very high-pitched voice when Penelope elbowed him in the ribs.

"Separate, please," Keith insisted. There was no way he could sleep if Ria was there. She might watch him sleep . . . He might watch her sleep. This trail of thought needed to stop.

"Alright, Your Viciousness," Olen replied, rubbing his side as his wife face-palmed. "I'll let the brothers know. Give me a bit of time to clean up your rooms; you can head up in an hour. I'll leave the keys with Lavender."

"Thank you, Olen," Henrietta said before Keith could. "And thank you, Penelope, for this *delicious* dinner. I'm seriously impressed! Everyone across the Dark Enchanted Forest was raving about you, and I can see why."

"And you are a very kind guest," Penelope smiled with pride. "You come back anytime, Princess."

Henrietta leaned forward and peeked over at the bar. "Can I ask, how did you get Lavender the Lizard Wizard to work at your restaurant?! She's amazing!"

Penelope chuckled and tossed her long black braid over her shoulder. "I dueled her in a wizard fight at the Peldeep Festival of Lights. She was so determined to learn my illusion spells, so she set out to find me again, and, well . . ."

"I found her first." Olen wrapped an arm around Penelope. "And I carried her off to the Dark Enchanted Forest to be my wife."

"More like I rode you like a horse," Penelope replied dryly. "He was in his bear form, of course."

"Phrasing, Penelope! Phrasing!" an elderly otterfolk lady at the table beside us called out. "Also, I'd like dessert, please."

"I'll be right there." Penelope gave Keith and Henrietta a small curtsy and patted her husband affectionately on the arm. He released her to go back to work.

"Enjoy the rest of your dessert," Olen told them. "I'll go up and get your rooms ready."

When they were by themselves again, Ria asked Keith, "So which dungeon should we hit up first?"

"The Hollow Gorge is closer. Its entry is in the pass that leads down toward the Deep Shoals," Keith explained. He knew that Henrietta had completed the Depths of Despair Dungeon off the eastern coast, but he wanted to be sure, so he asked, "Can you swim?"

"Of course!" Ria said between a mouthful of whipping cream. She licked a spot of cream off the curve of her lip. "I spent many years—"

"I'm back!" Lady Amaryllis burst into the tavern with Guardswoman Puma right behind her.

Keith sighed. All he'd wanted was a peaceful dinner with the princess he was courting.

Ria stood up to greet them. "Thank goodness . . ." She paused and looked at Keith. "Or is it 'thank evilness' in the Dark Enchanted Forest?"

Keith shrugged. "I've never heard either saying."

Henrietta continued, "Anyway, I'm thankful everything worked out. I'm so sorry, Mistress Puma. I completely reacted on instinct. Do you forgive me?"

"See!" Lady Amaryllis cut in, sounding smug. "I told you she wouldn't hold it against you."

Henrietta argued, "Amy, she hasn't even—" at the same time Mistress Puma said, "Lady Amy, now is *not*—"

The two women stopped and stared, realizing their confusion. They decided to ignore the elf girl entirely.

"Princess." Mistress Puma bowed. "I'm sorry for not recognizing you upon your arrival."

"And I'm sorry for throwing you into the woods," Ria replied.

"Think nothing of it." Mistress Puma smiled. "If you'll excuse me, I must resume my shift for the evening."

"Of course! Don't let us keep you!"

Mistress Puma left, but Keith noted with disappointment and a hint of annoyance that Lady Amaryllis was pulling up a chair to join them.

"So what's the plan?" the intruder asked.

Ria waved for a server to come take their new guest's order. She told Lady Amaryllis, "I have a room upstairs tonight. Want to share?"

Keith was suddenly disappointed in, annoyed at, and very envious of Lady Amaryllis. He regretted giving up the shared bedroom idea and decided that he would need to get rid of this young elf travel companion *as soon as possible.*

As soon as they went upstairs, he connected with a golem and left a message in Green Oak, the elven city. They could come collect their errant saintess sooner so *he* could have a romantic date with Henrietta.

Not that it mattered, because Fate had other plans.

CHAPTER 55

A Walking Glow-in-the-Dark Mage

Henrietta

The morning was bright and beautiful and green. Actually, the arm and leg thrown over me were green.

Lady Amy had tossed and turned all night. At some point, she'd kicked off her blanket and was sprawled out in her breast band and bunched-up leaf skirt, hair in a braided state of disarray.

I left her lightly snoring in our bed and slipped on my clothes before popping out to the bathroom.

Between staying up late chatting with the elf, being woken up multiple times from her tossing and turning, and my excitement of going dungeon delving today with Keith, I *might* not have slept very well.

I wandered downstairs in search of strong tea.

To my surprise, Keith sat at a table nursing his own cup of tea and reading. He looked as tired as I felt, but he also had an air of frustration about him.

"What's wrong?" I asked, slipping into a chair at his table.

Keith put down the report. "Gimtak dropped off two reports. Ria, do you have a habit of hiding things in your sock drawer?"

"I do . . . but how do you know that?" Keith was here, not rifling through my drawers, so there must have been a story behind his question.

"We've found some spies in your closet back home." He waved a hand over the papers. "I got a report letting me know another was found today. They also managed to kill one of our own before they were captured."

My heart dropped out of my chest. The thought of one of my new friends not being there when I got back hit me hard. My voice wavered a bit as I asked, "Who?"

Keith double-checked the report. "Chikli. He got stabbed a few times."

"Oh no!" I couldn't believe it. Chikli was one of the first people I'd met at the castle. "How is Tulith?"

"She's fine, why?" Keith cocked his head to the side, giving me a confused look.

"Aren't they married?"

"Yes?" He was still confused.

We stared at each other in some obvious form of miscommunication long enough for me to just break down and ask, "Wouldn't she be upset if her husband is dead?"

Keith realized and laughed. "He's not *dead*. He just died. Chloe probably sorted it out after they found his body. Considering it was day of? He's probably been [Resurrected] or [Revived], depending on how much mana Chloe had left after showering Julia with affection. Worst case I left a few revival potions."

"I can't believe I forgot you do that for staff. My father never found the expense worth it." I dropped my face into my hands. "I need tea."

Keith waved over a girl in an apron who was waiting tables. Olen and Penelope were nowhere to be seen yet. I ordered a sweet tea and raspberry muffin.

"So?" Keith prompted after I'd been poured a giant mug of black tea and sugar and honey with some specialty in-house hazelnut syrup. Lavender wasn't there to magic up fun drinks, but I would accept any hot, sweet, morning wake up in a cup.

"Not that I should be telling you, and I'll have to find a new spot now . . . but whenever I take off my grandfather's heirloom jewelry, I always stuff them in my socks. This grants a +2 modifier to Constitution." I held up my pinkie to show Keith a small black ring. Then I lifted my poofy shoulder-length hair and revealed one earring with a mithril chain linked with emeralds draped over the ear. "And this grants a +4 modifier to Charisma."

"A plus four?" Keith leaned across the table to look closer at my ear. "Who made it?"

I could understand his interest; anything over a plus three was *legendary*. Literally. It had the [Legendary] tag. "My great-great-grandfather dabbled in jewelcraft."

Keith raised an eyebrow. "More than dabbled, I'd say."

"I probably wasn't supposed to take it, but I needed everything in my arsenal to take you on." I sipped my tea with a contented sigh. "Too bad I didn't take the whole royal set."

"Then I'm assuming the spies your father sent are after your earring." Keith finished his own tea and watched me patiently finish the rest of mine. "We'll plan for that when we get home."

"What was the other report?" I asked. He'd said there were two.

He pushed up his glasses and tapped the second page on the table. "There was another Madame Potts's Cast while we were traveling yesterday."

"Really?"

He pushed over the piece of paper.

Hello, this is Madame Potts.
This week's events are in!
One month until Grand Duchess Calisto's Spring Ball! Debutantes from around the continent are gearing up to make the trip. By air, by land, and sea . . . those sailing off the western coast should consider *not* going by sea, as there's a 50% increase of tentacle encounters in the area from now until May 1st.
Servalt authorities found a group of catkin children in Westhills, and three Peldeep human youth in Colwood. This madame thinks it would be wise to look at repeat known offenders.
The war between Nilheim and Drendil is coming up, and commerce is booming! If you're in Gren's Keep or Kith Bog, you can expect a 10% discount on most trade goods until the Great Road clears and normal traffic resumes.
The Emerald Caves Dungeon of Baldorin is about to experience a Monster Surge. Gem-cutter ants and razor-teeth worms averaging level four are spawning at an increased rate.
The village of Bryn in Peldeep will be celebrating their 75 Year Celebration next week. Everyone visiting the celebration will be granted +1 Favorability with Peldeep.
Pirate Abra and her band of Misfit Undead were seen off the Sunshine Coast of Sumbria. Batten down the hatches and send out the navy because Abra is known to attack coastal villages. For someone who lives in the water, she has a strange love for setting everything on fire. Recommended: outfits that are flame resistant.
If everyone thought the Goose Incident of last fall was bad, then I have troubling news for you: A golden goose was spotted flying over Sumbria yesterday. The bird's whereabouts are currently unknown, but this madame is certain it won't stay hidden for long.
This is Madame Potts, signing off.

I handed the paper back to Keith. "It's going to be a busy month for everyone."

"So it would seem." He folded the reports and tucked them into a vest pocket. "For now, would you like to go explore a dungeon with me?"

I stood up, ready. "I thought you'd never ask."

There were four different types of dungeons in Valaria.

First, there were tower dungeons, great buildings that stretched to the sky, and each floor brought you closer to the top. Tower dungeons could go up into the sky, like Green Oak, or down into the earth, like the Depths of Despair. These were the most common and stable.

Second, there were labyrinth dungeons, elaborate mazes that expanded outward. These were important to defeat quickly, as they continued expanding until the dungeon was completed.

Third, there were monster dungeons. They served as home to a growing race of monsters who would pour out as a stampede when the dungeon could no longer contain them. They were the most dangerous for obvious reason.

And lastly, there were portal dungeons, seemingly small dungeons from the outside, but inside housing whole, unique ecosystems on every floor, and the only way to get to the next level was through a dungeon portal. They were accessed through a portal platform or gate.

Keith had let me know that Deep Shoals was an underwater labyrinth dungeon that stretched under the lake just south of Gren's Keep. He'd assured me that pockets of aerated land popped up all over the maze.

The thought of being trapped in a tight space underwater while man-eating fish tried to eat me gave me a cold sweat. It did *not* sound very fun—even if I did have a walking glow-in-the-dark mage and unlimited air.

As such, and after very little debate, Keith and I headed west to the Hollow Gorge.

I couldn't wait to check it out, especially after I learned that the Hollow Gorge was a portal dungeon. A *portal dungeon.* They were very rare, and an adventurer's dream because of the ecological diversity and the variety of monsters. It made for a great challenge.

This was going to be so much fun!

CHAPTER 56

You Stab Things, I Light Things on Fire

Keith

Ria and Keith had decided that it might be faster for her to run and Keith to fly. While it would have been nice to take a walk through the Dark Enchanted Forest together, Keith was hoping they'd be long gone before Lady Amy woke up.

In her excitement, Henrietta *probably* hadn't forgotten that she'd left the elf sleeping in upstairs. And since she *probably* hadn't forgotten, he *probably* didn't need to remind her.

Honestly, his desire for some quality time with the princess might have turned him into the scheming Dark Lord his godmother envisioned. He pushed the feeling of existential moral dread aside and activated his wings.

The construct wings were not as fast as a high-level [Flight] spell, but they saved him hundreds of mana and allowed him the freedom to let his mind wander. He didn't need another spell exploding when he tried to cast it because he was too distracted by the princess . . . [Mana Burn] was *not* a joke.

It would've ruined their date.

He watched Henrietta from the sky. She ran so fast that dust flew off behind her. Creatures from all over the forest somehow felt her approach and cleared the path long before she got there. Everyone excepting a few adventurers, whom she simply ran past on her way.

Keith kept up with her and dove down to arrive just as she did.

"So this is the Hollow Gorge!" Henrietta stood with her hands on her hips. She surveyed the bustling market set up outside a giant platform with three crossed ornate trellises. While they watched, an adventuring party walked up the short stairwell to the platform, and a shimmering blue light engulfed them and portaled them away.

"I suddenly have a strong *need* to defeat this dungeon," she said seriously. "I've never fought a portal dungeon. This is going to be *awesome*."

"Would you like to solo the dungeon? Or should we do it together?" Keith asked.

"Good question." Ria smiled up at him and tentatively reached out to take his hand. "Want to do it together?"

"As you wish."

They started walking toward the registration booth when Henrietta tugged on his hand.

"Let's check out the dungeon quests!" She pointed excitedly to a large notice-board tacked all over with posters requesting monster materials, harvest ingredients, and an assortment of dungeon loot.

Keith didn't know why she bothered; they weren't in need of money or dungeon items themselves. Well, technically, that wasn't true. Looking at the board revealed a number of his own personal requests. His powdered gem-cutter ant carapace was running low, and he needed a few phoenix feather ink brushes.

"Is there something you need from the dungeon?" Keith asked as Henrietta read the board.

She shrugged. "I was thinking it might be fun to collect some of these ourselves."

Keith hesitated. "Wouldn't a porter slow us down? I have a dimensional storage ring, but it's full of mana and health potions and snacks for the trip. I still need an Escape Scroll and a Revive potion."

"I have a Revive potion," Henrietta said. "And I don't think we'll need the Escape Scroll, do we?"

"Not technically; there are Escape portals on each floor, and one if you defeat the boss."

"That's fine, then." She smiled up at him. "My [Harvest Kill] perk comes with its own storage. Anything I help defeat can be stored."

"That is an incredible perk." Keith raised an eyebrow. He turned back to the board to give it a once over.

In the usual way of things, some quests were only allowed to adventurers, and not just any dungeon delver. A professional adventurer specialized in challenging dungeons to hunt and harvest materials, while a dungeon delver was any one time visitor.

Keith didn't worry about being denied any quest on the board; he was the Dark Lord after all. And sorting out the loot afterwards also wouldn't be too much hassle.

After exiting the dungeon, the quest materials could be sold directly to those who'd made the request or dropped off at the local guild attached to the quest board. The guild would act as the middleman and charge ten percent, but it was better than hunting down all of the buyers individually.

Ria was in high spirits and dragged Keith through the stalls to buy extra snacks for the trip. He recalled her appetite after a fight and purchased a few candied hazelnut rolls himself.

Then they were finally ready to head over to sign in at the register and get their badges.

Keith filled out the paperwork and slipped the guild attendant a gold coin with an extra order. Then they walked over to the platform.

Henrietta asked, "So, did you bring any golems with you? Aside from your epic wings?"

Keith grinned. "No, I'm going full Dark Magician today. I brushed up on my spells just for this."

What was the point of having a giant draconian library with piles of spell books if you didn't sneak around memorizing them throughout your childhood? Keith hadn't wasted the opportunity and studied hundreds of the things.

His [Quick Read] perk and Intelligence eigthy-five weren't to be laughed at, and he had taken an hour to refresh his memory on the spell words and casting requirements.

The average wizard had access to the kingdom's regular library and was free to study as they would . . . but your average wizard was level fifteen. Even famous adventurers known throughout the continent, like Lavender the Lizard Wizard, were only in their level thirties.

Keith checked his character sheet. His experience points gained from hunting and harvesting had slowed down in recent years, as he'd focused on golemancy and tinkering and running the entire Dark Enchanted Forest.

As you do.

"I can cast whatever you like, but I'm atrocious at healing. Though I can use the perk [Quick Buff] to enhance or buff your items durability by +1? Or better yet . . ." Keith lifted the hand he was holding and thumbed the heirloom ring on Ria's finger.

Unlike his [Cantrip] perk, which only had five spell slots for an instant cast, the regular spells he knew were not limited to anything except his own capacity for learning. Each had complex formulae that were essential in shaping his mana into the spell diagram, and then a long verbal component he could thankfully skip with his [Quick Chant] perk.

"[Wearer's Luck]."

[You have attempted to use the Skill: **Magic (Wearer's Luck)**. You have succeeded. 50% debuff applied to all Rogue-class Abilities attempted on this item.]

He watched his mana deplete and spent a bit more to make the basic buff last for twenty-four hours.

Henrietta looked her ring over, pleased. "Can you do my earring as well?"

"My pleasure." Keith reached out and delicately ran a finger along Ria's ear as he cast the [Wearer's Luck] spell a second time. "Should I enchant your sword as well?"

Before he could touch it, Ria jumped a bit and waved a hand over her sword protectively. "Oh no, Jacqueline doesn't like to be disturbed like that."

Keith didn't take it personally. Enchanted swords almost always came with personality. More so than his golems, even. "That's fine. So you stab things, I light things on fire, and between the two of us, we'll have a great time?"

"That sounds lovely, Keith!" Ria squared her shoulders trying to look professional, but she had a bounce in her step as they hopped onto the platform.

Ria looked out over the market while Keith distractedly checked his own equipment. As lines of blue light wove around them, he heard Ria mumble under her breath, "Oh shoot. She saw us!"

CHAPTER 57

Not Very Heroine of Justice

Henrietta

The idea of a date with Keith, walking hand in hand through a dungeon while a trail of monsters stretched behind us and the glow of [+1] experience points illuminated us in the darkness . . . *might* have been a deciding factor in my choice to abandon Lady Amy this morning.

"Abandon" was a *strong* word. I'd only agreed to go with her to the Damp Gizzard, and I'd done just that. We'd talked and had a lovely sleep—or at least she had—and I'd been happy to let her sleep in while I popped out to conquer a dungeon or two.

Alright, I was making excuses; it wasn't kind to run off before she woke up. I'd let a moment of selfishness overcome me, which was *not* very Heroine of Justice of me. Granted, I was only human. Maybe living with the Dark Horde was making me a little bit evil?

Something told me she would be there, waiting for us, when we finished the dungeon, and I would need to apologize. I was very good at apologizing; I'd had a lot of practice.

I would enjoy a lovely delve with Keith, and then regroup with my new . . . friend? We'd only known each other for a single day, but that seemed to fit. Were friendships always formed so quickly? Most of the people I'd met in the Dark Enchanted Forest had become my friends over the few weeks I'd been here . . . when back in Drendil, I just had Brownie and a few knights under my command that I could joke with.

Come to think of it, perhaps it was sharing a room. Back in Drendil, some of my knights had slept together every time we'd stopped at an inn on route to our quest. They'd told me they were friends with benefits. I always shared a room with the Knight Commander Havork, who slept on the floor or, if there was one, a chair.

So I guessed Lady Amy was my friend with benefits.

In the meantime, I waved an apology to the elf as Keith and I portaled to the first floor.

A field of golden flowers bowing to the wind under a blue sky dotted all over with racing clouds greeted us. My hair picked up in the wind and blew into my face.

I was going to let go of Keith's hand and try to fix my hair, but he squeezed it and said, "[By the Grey-Scale Wing, Tame the Elements]."

Magic settled over me, and my hair and clothes stopped whipping about. Keith, with his long black hair in a ponytail, stood pristine beside me. He smiled and waved with his free hand. "Shall we?"

I think I already loved dungeon delving with my Dark Magician King.

The second we stepped off the platform, I contemplated activating [Sword Aura] so I could see where all the monsters were, but finally decided against it. That would have been overkill on the first floor of a midlevel-strength dungeon. The best we'd find here was a level five, and that would be the boss monster for the floor.

"This floor is covered in goblin lilies, so watch where you step," Keith let me know as we walked through the ankle-high grass. He blushed a bit and continued, "Ah, my apologies. You're a veteran, so I won't talk your ear off with every little dungeon detail."

"Just because I'm a veteran doesn't mean I know everything," I teased him. "Are the local goblin lilies poisonous?"

"Yes, but they aren't lethal. The thorns have a paralytic effect to slow down their prey long enough to eat them alive. They take root in the grass." Keith pointed off to our left. "There's a lake off in that direction where most of the larger monsters mill about. And over there"—he pointed to our right—"is a floofpoof nest."

"Hmm." I looked around but couldn't see anything but grass. "Where is the boss?"

"With the floofpoof nest," Keith said. "Are you close to leveling? Should we clear out every floor or race to the stronger levels?"

I checked my character sheet.

Name:	Henrietta Doryn of Drendil
Occupation:	Experimental Subject Minion
Level:	67
Experience Points:	15994/16750
Hit Points:	1809/1809

Mana Points:	1139/1139		
Bonded Item:	Jacqueline Tiamat la Fleur		
Class:	Sword Master		
Temporary Status:	[Tame the Elements]		
Titles:			
[Human], [Noble], [Prince], [Crown Prince], [Warrior], [Aura Knight], [Sword Master]			
Attributes:			
Strength:	67	Intelligence:	17
Dexterity:	21	Perception:	19
Constitution:	27 (+2)	Charisma:	29 (+4)
Skills:			
Social:	6	Etiquette:	5
Leadership:	5	Bureaucracy:	7
+Swordsmanship: Parry:	1	Sword Aura:	7
Mastery:	2		
Perks:			
Sense Ally, Sense Lies, Calming Voice, Sense Motive, True Taste, Sense Ability, Inspire, Multitask, Quick Read, Resist Poison, Quick Step, Quick Draw, Force Thrust, Bludgeoning Cut, Harvest Kill, Sword Sense, Killing Intent, Aura Blade, Death Parry.			

"Keith?" I frowned, noticing something.

He saw my face, and whatever he saw made him anxiously ask, "Yes?"

"What does 'Experimental Subject Minion' mean?" The new occupation confused me. Had he started the paperwork to transfer my citizenship without my approval? That wasn't very nice.

Maybe people would say I shouldn't expect the Dark Lord to be nice. I'd say they were wrong.

"Oh! That." Keith pushed up his glasses then scratched behind his slightly pointy ear. "You signed the Experimental Subject contract a while back, and I finally finished registering it yesterday. It allowed me to immediately start paying you through your moniers guild registry the day you signed it, but it just sat in the inner sanctum until yesterday when I was cleaning things up in preparation for this trip. Now that it's official, the contract also allows me to dismember you and put you back together properly, to provide you with restorative care such as [Revive], [Resurrect], or [Raise], to credit your contribution to any published work, and to contact your next of kin as a retainer."

"Wow, maybe I should have read that contract more closely." I looked over my character sheet for anything else, but it all looked fine.

"We can write up a new contract? As the castle's baker or secretary. Or we could draw up a . . . Well, maybe that's too soon," Keith trailed off. His cheeks turned very red, and he coughed to clear his throat.

"Yes?" I couldn't imagine what had made him so uncomfortable.

"Nothing. So? Experience points? I'm not even halfway there."

I hadn't been tracking the experience points from defeating the mercenaries, griffins, or dwarves. "It looks like I'm 756 EXP from leveling."

"Let's party up to clear the dungeon," Keith recommended. "I don't know if it'll be enough after we share the experience points, but it'll get you close."

I glanced behind me to the platform and sighed. Our date wasn't going to last as long as I'd hoped.

"You don't have to worry," Keith told me. "We have the dungeon to ourselves, give or take one or two adventuring parties who arrived before us."

"Really?!" I skipped ahead and turned to face him. With a flourish, I pulled out my sword and gave it the habitual practice swing.

Keith pushed up his glasses with his free hand and then held it aloft. He chanted, "[Fireball]."

The light flickered in the wind that blew across the field of golden flowers.

"Wait!" I cried. "I have the best idea! You're an Arcane Sage . . . could we just burn down the whole level?"

"As you wish."

CHAPTER 58

There Was Something Inherently Delightful About Lighting Everything on Fire

Keith

There was something inherently delightful about lighting everything on fire.

Henrietta was spellbound to the flames, making impressed noises every so often as it all burned.

Also, anything caught in the fire was consumed as experience points.

[You have defeated a **Goblin Lily (Level 2)**. +1 EXP]
[You have defeated a **Floofpoof (Level 1)**. +1 EXP]

"[Fireball]."

[You have attempted to use the Spell: **Fireball (Level 1)**. You have succeeded. Damage 5 x Skill: **Magic (Level 5)**.]
[You have dealt 25 damage to **Floofpoof (Level 1)**. +1 EXP]

He had to say the spell aloud each time, as he'd never bothered to pick up [Silent Chant], only [Quick Chant]. He'd chosen it because chanting all of "Oh spirit of the eternal flame, hear my plea and grant me [Fireball]" every time he wanted something roasted was a bother. He still needed to bring up the diagram for the mana movement in his mind's eye, but that wasn't a problem for him.

Now, he wondered if he *should* have chosen [Silent Chant]. It would have been more impressive to just raise his hand and rain fire down upon the earth without having to say [Fireball] every other second . . .

Maybe he would pick it up the next time he leveled up his [Magic] skill and qualified for a new perk.

A level one [Fireball] cost him barely any concentration and only ten mana. He didn't even bother using his perk [Reduce Mana Cost]. Keith had three thousand mana points to spare, even *after* carrying Henrietta one-handed and operating his wings to keep them in the air.

The only real contest to his concentration was the princess crushed against him, with her arms around his neck. She smelled like freshly baked cookies. He was beginning to feel hungry, and he wasn't sure it was just for sweets.

It was enough of a distraction that he didn't even bother trying the [Multicast] perk.

They flew together over the red-and-gold fields as he lit everything aflame.

They'd formed a party, and the EXP share was fifty percent, so Henrietta received half of every kill. Experience rounded up, which promoted teamwork, especially in the lower levels where each experience point was especially valuable. It was too bad that the division maxed out at four party members.

If they took their time and stayed a few days, it would've been fun to walk around each level picking off all the beasts. Unfortunately, Henrietta *really* wanted a chance to eat at Logan's Noodle House. Keith didn't mind where they ate; he just wanted to spend alone time with Ria.

Still, they would breeze through the lower levels and take their time with the bigger prey further on . . . and Keith didn't know if he was as ready as the princess to sleep together in the dungeon.

"I've never flown before," Henrietta spoke into Keith's ear, and his current [Fireball] fizzled out, burning his pinkie and hitting him with backlash damage. Not enough for [Mana Burn] or anything serious, just enough to sting. [Mana Burn] required a critical failure of a spell strong enough to rip open the mana channel, not something a failed [Fireball] could do to an Arcane Sage.

He ignored the burn and replied calmly, "How do you like it?"

"I love it!" She leaned into his chest and sighed. "I love wide, open spaces. You can't get much more open than the sky."

Keith waited until she was settled before activating another [Fireball].

[You have defeated a **Floofpoof (Level 5)**. +3 EXP]
[**Dungeon Boss** defeated.]
[**Level 2 Portal** activated.]

Keith closed his notifications and tossed the last [Fireball] casually into the blaze below. The monsters on the first level only had about five to ten hit points, so it was a bit overkill. The heat and the smoke were only manageable because of the strong wind that fanned the flames. For comfort, Keith thought through some of his harder memorized spells.

"[Elemental Barrier]."

With that, the smoke started to wrap around them as if they were protected by a giant bubble.

They didn't wait for the blaze to die down, simply descending to the glowing platform that would take them to the next level.

"I'm happy no one else is challenging the dungeon today," Henrietta told Keith. "How long until the floor resets?"

"Two hours and everything will start putting itself back together," Keith replied. "The dungeons around the Dark Enchanted Forest are all midsize. Green Oak is weaker, and monsters respawn every four hours or so. The Deep Shoals Dungeon restarts every five hours."

"That's a lot of time to collect monster materials." Henrietta nodded. She would have plenty of opportunity to loot in the coming levels.

They touched down on the glowing pad, ready to take on level two.

Keith enjoyed the sheer joy that lit up his princess's face when she saw the white sand beach stretched out before them.

A tropical sun beat down and made the waves dance with reflected light on the sea.

"I'll be right back." Henrietta tore off her adventuring boots and dipped her tiny, adorable toes in the sand.

Then she ran down the beach, enjoying the hot day. There was a moment when a giant crab popped out of the sand ready to attack her, but she punched it in the face and blasted it into pieces.

[Your party member: **Henrietta Doryn of Drendil** has defeated a
Giant Crab. +2 EXP.]

"Come on, Keith!" The princess rolled up her sleeves and started pulling out the giant crab's legs with her bare hands. "We can have crab for lunch!"

Lunch wasn't for an hour yet, but he wouldn't pass up on Henrietta's cooking.

"The beaches should have a few more giant crabs"—Keith waved around them—"if you want to clear the area before going inland."

She nodded, harvesting the last crab leg into her storage. "Perfect. We can eat some of these and sell the rest to the merchants outside."

They finished up and headed down the beach, Henrietta dealing with anything that came their way in a quick, clean, professional manner. Keith had a moment where he remembered the first time they'd met.

He was insanely grateful she hadn't punched *him* into lunch meat.

They were halfway around the beach when there was a scream that echoed out from the tropical forest. "Help! Please! Somebody?! Anybody!"

Henrietta took Keith's hand and dragged him toward the voices. "Let's go check it out!"

Keith mentally sighed. His alone time had ended so soon.

CHAPTER 59

Some Sort of Impressive Kingliness Skill

Henrietta

I was used to saving people. In fact, it was kind of my job. I grabbed Keith's hand and activated [Sword Aura] to make sure it wasn't an ambush.

The number of times I'd been ambushed with a plea for help was seven.

It wasn't that the ambushes had stopped at seven. It's just that at some point, I was a high-enough level that my skills prevented me from getting jumped.

The point was moot because there was no ambush. Instead, there were three dead adventurers and a healer crying in a tree as a giant crab tried to eat him.

The healer let out a high-pitched scream and threw a fruit at the crab.

The crab happily caught and ate the fruit, and another, and another. It was about to eat the healer when I picked up a rock and used a bit of strength. The rock smashed through the giant crab's skull, and the monster crashed to the ground.

[You have defeated a **Giant Crab**. +3 EXP]

"Oh, thank the gods. I'm saved!" The healer, a tanned young man who looked and sounded like he came from Peldeep, slowly climbed back down the tree. He tried to fix his robes, and then he got a good look at Keith behind me. In an instant, the man was ramrod straight. "Your Viciousness!"

"You should probably worry more about your party members, Healer Bowen," Keith pointed out.

"Ah, well. About that." Bowen pulled out two yellow glowing potions. "I only have t-two Revive potions . . ."

We all looked down at the three dead adventurers.

Keith raised one eyebrow. "You can't use [Revive] yet? What about [Resurrect]?"

"N-neither." Healer Bowen turned an uncomfortable shade of pale and splotchy. "I'm s-still level seventeen."

"Hasn't it been a month?" Keith asked. "And you've only levelled up twice?"

"Yes, Your Viciousness." Bowen uncorked one potion and went to the biggest of his party members, a brown-haired beastman with a wolf's tail and ears. "I'm just not a very g-good adventurer."

I asked, "Are you the only one with potions? What about your party members?"

"No, miss." Bowen finished pouring the bottle into the big man's mouth. "They told me it's my job to supply the potions and the buffs, then I'm to get to safety."

"Argh!" The beastman coughed and rolled over to his hands and knees and sprang into action. He was actually impressive for someone who'd just been dead. "Bowen, where's the crab?"

"It's alright, Striker." Bowen patted his arm and shoved a thumb at us. "The king took care of it."

"Technically," Keith pointed out, "Princess Henrietta killed the giant crab."

They both bowed to me respectfully and I shoo'd them. "None of that, now. Go finish helping your party members."

Bowen dragged Striker over to their fallen comrades: an incredibly short human—shorter than a dwarf, even, but her status definitely said full human—and beside her what looked like a cat girl rogue. I was interested enough to listen in on their whispering even while they deliberately spoke under their breath.

"Should we wake up Sara or Priscilla?" Bowen waved at the two women.

"Sara," Striker said, pointing at the human. "If we revive Priscilla and carry Sara, we'll never hear the end of it."

"Good point. I'll find her arm."

Bowen used the potion on the short human, and after a few seconds, the woman shook herself awake. She slapped her face with her newly attached arm and groaned, "What happened?"

"Giant crab," Striker told her, offering her a hand up. "The one we defeated wasn't alone."

Sara sighed. "Give me a second."

The woman sat up and looked around. Her eyes went wide when she saw us.

"Don't mind us," Keith told her. "Henrietta decided to save you."

I rolled my eyes a bit at that. "And Keith wanted to stay around to see if you all got healed."

He smiled at me. "That's right. And now they're all revived, and we can go."

"What about Priscilla?" I asked. The cat girl was safe with her adventuring party, if still very dead.

"They can bring her to the market outside and get a potion there." Keith shrugged. "And then report back to me later tonight on why they aren't leveling my healer properly."

The three flinched at that, but Bowen argued, "That's n-not true, Your Viciousness!"

"Oh?" Keith raised an eyebrow. I felt pressure burst out of him, hitting the man with some sort of impressive kingliness skill.

"Y-Yes!" Bowen stepped in front of the party and stuttered harder than before. "It's m-m-my fault! I d-d-don't *want* to fight. I'm a *healer*."

"And?" Keith asked.

"So he stays out of danger and heals us properly after every fight," Sara cut in. She walked up and put a hand on Bowen's arm. "We can't increase his share of the experience any more without him doing some of the killing. But we'll train him up eventually, even if it takes longer than the rest."

Keith nodded. "Good."

The Dark Lord turned away from the group and lifted up my hand, gently swirling a finger on my palm. "If that's decided, should we get back to our date?"

I didn't swoon. I thanked my Constitution twenty-seven. "Alright. But this time, I get to clear the floor, alright?" I turned to the shocked faces of the adventuring party. "Can you teleport out? Or do you need to go back through the first floor . . . which might still be on fire."

"Oh no, Your Highness," Sara told me. "We know where the exit teleporter is on this floor."

"Thank you. This is my first time in a portal dungeon," I explained. I hesitated but thought I might as well ask what was on my mind. "Excuse me, but are you under a curse?"

The party tensed up, but Sara just smiled a crooked smile. "Because I'm short?"

"Yes." No sense beating around the bush.

"I'm not cursed. I'm not half dwarf, and I'm not under any spell," Sara declared vehemently. "I was simply born this way."

"Oh." I didn't know what else to say. I'd had my fair share of curses, so I thought I'd ask. "Well, that's that then. Sorry if it was a sensitive subject."

"That's alright." Sara smiled. "You can imagine it comes up a lot.

I squeezed Keith's hand. "Well, it was nice to meet you all. Stay safe carrying your friend to . . . um, safety."

"We will. Now, get to lifting, boys! Priscilla ain't gonna carry herself out!"

I watched the group get themselves up and gone, and I waved goodbye as they disappeared into the trees.

When we were alone, I turned to Keith and asked, "If we cook up this giant crab for lunch, that'll give them enough time to get out of the dungeon, right? Then we can see how fast I can clear the floor. You cleared the first level in what, thirty minutes?"

"Twenty-eight." Keith raised his free hand, and it lit on fire. "Should we boil the crab in one of the island's small lakes, or cook it from the inside out?"

I licked my lips. "Boiled? I have garlic butter for our bread, too. We can make a dip."

"I like the way you think."

CHAPTER 60

Crushing His Skull Between Her Thighs

Keith

After a nice lunch, Henrietta got to clearing the dungeon.

Keith enjoyed watching. It was no joke that she was the Heroine of Justice, and he was reminded again how fortunate they were to have come this far without her crushing his skull between her thighs.

They were very nice thighs, but that was beside the point. Also, he needed to stop using the word *nice* for everything when it came to his princess. His godmother had taught him etiquette—dragons required a great deal of etiquette, or they might eat you.

Luckily, Feliwyn was a patient sort, and she rarely ate people.

Henrietta activated [Quick Step]. She didn't bother using any of her other skills or perks, relying purely on her abilities to cut down every living thing on the second floor of the dungeon.

Keith still thought that having a dungeon named Hollow Gorge and an elven city named the Hollow, and having them both be on opposite sides of the kingdom—most days—was an irksome choice. However, that decision had taken place centuries ago, and perhaps the confusion had been the intent.

He still didn't like it.

While they lived at the castle, Keith was still under the belief that he and Henrietta—despite her thigh-crushing Strength sixty-seven versus his Intelligence eighty-five used for spell casting—were a pretty equal match, even without his golems to protect his body. After watching her capabilities, he was beginning to doubt.

She took on most of the floors by herself and cleared them in record timing. The unique ecosystems made for a nice . . . a *fun* variety of challenges. But with Henrietta almost sixty levels higher than the monsters, there wasn't much challenge on a fighting level.

The third floor was a midnight pine forest, and they shared a walk under the stars while dire wolves howled at the full moon. Henrietta told Keith about her times in the Depths of Despair Dungeon, and when he started to discuss the upper levels of the Hollow Gorge, she listened. He noticed she was a bit quiet afterwards, but he didn't think anything of it.

He thought she was just strategizing or enjoying the beautiful scenery.

The next floor was arid and a cut mix of rocky desert with some scattered trees. It not very comfortable—dust got into everything if it wasn't magicked properly. Henrietta had a great time hunting spiked armordillos and punching holes in their shells while dodging their pointy tails.

That was not the normal way adventurers defeated the nigh-impenetrable scale hide of an armordillo . . . but most adventurers who challenged this floor were level ten to twenty.

After hitting level ten, each of one's attributes were level ten (or thereabouts). Then every level up only granted two attribute points. A normal adventurer at level fifteen might have:

Attributes (10):			
Strength:	14	**Intelligence:**	12
Dexterity:	11	**Perception:**	11
Constitution:	11	**Charisma:**	11

And anyone who chose to min-max at level fifteen, putting all their points into Strength or Charisma or Dexterity to cater to their class . . . were very easy to kill. If Keith judged correctly, with Henrietta's Strength sixty-seven, her other attributes should be around twenty to thirty.

Nothing down here stood a chance. Dungeon monsters were all creatures born of the dungeon core's magic and suffered from dungeon madness. As such, they were mindless killing machines who wouldn't be able to strategize a victory. Strength and skill were what determined the winners.

After the desert, they portaled to a steep cliffside, and Keith took over flying them around. Level five unigoats and griffins covered the mountain, and Henrietta's [Sword Aura], coupled with her [Force Thrust] perk, could one-shot the murderous goats off the mountain side. It became a game, between her strikes and his [Mana Arrow] spell, to see who could hit the most monsters.

They stopped at level six to have dinner. The old growth forest was filled with bloodthirsty treants and their smaller plant nettlekin cousins, who attacked them without mercy.

The leaves of the nettlekin made for a delicious pesto sauce. Henrietta cut the bark flesh off the treants and roasted unigoat meat on the heated boards. Keith was in charge of the fire, while Henrietta managed the knife work. She used twined herbs to brush the nettlekin pesto over a roasted leg.

"You were saying there are ten levels to the Hollow Gorge, right?" she asked.

Keith had magicked them up some chairs and a table and a teapot and two earthen cups. He let the fire go to burn naturally and turned his attention to his lavish dinner. "There are eleven. I think the last two might actually give you a challenge."

"Really?" Henrietta happily enjoyed her food and continued between mouthfuls, "Do you think we'll be done by tonight?"

They had about four hours left before they needed to think about leaving. If they could manage the rest of the floors in the same amount of time as the earlier floors, then they would be back in time for the last call for supper at Logan's Noodle House.

They had spent too much time enjoying themselves in each level and had only made it halfway.

"I think that you could solo it, but it might cost us time," Keith said. "Shall we continue after this, and I'll help if we run out of time?"

"Alright."

"How close are you to leveling up?" he asked. Keith felt a little bad that him being there took away half her experience points, but he wouldn't have given this up for anything.

"Close, actually!" Henrietta's eyes glazed over a bit as she looked at her character sheet. "I need just over a hundred."

"Perfect. There are fewer monsters in the floors ahead, but they will be six to ten experience points apiece, and even halved that should push you over." Keith drank his tea, not bothering to look at his own character sheet. He needed at least ten thousand points before he would level up. "Have you gathered everything you want? How is your dimensional storage?"

Henrietta was in charge of any and all harvesting because she had the [Harvest Kill] perk. It was fast. It was efficient. It meant they weren't bogged down by storage. The only downside with the perk was that it only harvested items from something Henrietta had personally killed. Which meant Keith was still in charge of magically crafting tables and chairs and cups and teapots every time they stopped.

He could have stored those things in his smaller dimensional ring, but honestly, it kept him from just sitting around and staring at Henrietta while she did her own things.

It worked out very well.

So they continued through an elemental water serpent and man-eating trout lake on level seven, and a nest of phoenix and rock lava golems on the side of an active volcano on level eight . . .

Keith was under the impression that they would continue through the entire dungeon this way.

He was also under the misguided impression that they would be evenly matched in combat if Henrietta's might was put up against just his magic . . .

When they hit level nine, Keith discovered just how wrong his assumptions were.

CHAPTER 61

No One to Hear You Scream

Henrietta

The second we passed into level nine, I felt the slow creep of dread climb up my back.

I looked down a dimly lit cave path and played off the shiver as a reaction to the coldness from the cloying damp. The path was wide enough that Keith and I could still hold hands while we walked, but I admitted that I grabbed his arm a little harder than I meant to. I'd been preparing since he mentioned the underground level earlier in the day, and everything should be fine.

I was totally fine.

"Ria?" His breath tickled my ear as he leaned in closer. "Is there something the matter?"

Usually . . . Usually, only Sir Havork traveled with me on these kinds of levels. He knew that I had a—a *thing* about small spaces.

I *could* handle them. Dungeons with open spaces, bright rooms without windows, and dwarven tunnels lit with bioluminescent moss and mushrooms and glow stones didn't bother me very much. Even Rufus's office was comfortable over cloying.

It was just the dimly lit dungeon floors with very breakable lanterns and trap doors that dropped you into blackout rooms that had no way out and *no one to hear your scream*—

Time to take a deep breath. *Usually* wasn't *now*, and Keith was waiting for a reply.

"It's . . ." I could tell he was concerned, his eyes patient and kind. "I don't really like these kinds of levels."

"Why?"

No anger. No pity. Just a pure and honest question.

"I'm not a fan of the dark," I explained. "Or tight spaces."

"Alright." He nodded and lifted his free hand. He didn't say any spell, and suddenly the entire tunnel was filled with dancing lights. They were the same ones he used to light up the area we liked to sit in to have tea in the gardens back home.

"Thank you." It wasn't perfect, but the light and Keith's presence beside me made a big difference. I let go of Keith long enough to unsheathe Jacqueline, then reached out and gripped his hand again.

It was a lifeline.

I took a practice swing to see how far my reach was, but it was too tight to do most of my normal moves. I'd be limited to lunges and thrusts with no cuts.

"[Mana Shield]," Keith cast on himself. He asked, "Are you ready?"

I shook my head. "One second."

[You have activated the Skill: **Sword Aura**.]

I chose [All Targets] and immediately noticed the two creatures clinging to the top of the cavern ceiling just down the tunnel. I would activate my other abilities closer to the combat.

"Pyre bats to the right," I told Keith. "Do we have some way to breathe if one of them ignites while I'm fighting them?"

"You can leave that to me," Keith assured me. "Or do you want to leave the whole floor to me?"

I shook my head. "No, it gets easier every time I face it myself. I'm better now. You should have seen me the first year they threw me into . . . Well, I'm better now. I can do it, and it's better if I keep challenging myself."

"You said 'better' three times," Keith pointed out, squeezing my hand. "But I'll respect your decision. Just let me know if it becomes too much."

"Alright," I lied. "Let's go."

The pyre bats were each level nine, and they were grooming each other upside down while clinging to the ceiling of a small alcove. They were half as tall as Keith and known to attack with sound- and fire-based attacks. I focused on them using my skill and ignored everything else.

If they got upset, they tended to light themselves on fire, so while the pyre bats themselves weren't a problem, the [Vacuum] area of effect—caused by fire in an enclosed space—could trap me, with no air, on the ground as the cold stones dug into my broken fingernails and no one came—

"Ria?"

I'd stopped and stood there with my eyes closed, shaking. But it was fine, this was normal! It just took me a bit to gather myself. I gave Keith my best smile. "I'm just thinking about how to defeat the bats without igniting them. The second we turn this corner, they'll see the [Dancing Lights] reflecting down the path. I'll have to activate [Quick Step] now, and then I'll only have a few seconds to jump them."

"Can I just kill the dumb things?" Keith almost growled in his grumble. "I have so many dragon spells memorized that any one of the air-based cutting attacks could do it. Or I could magic the alcove to collapse on—"

"No!" I yelled. Then I realized what I'd done as my [Sword Aura] turned each pyre bat red in my senses. They knew we were here. I continued, quieter, "No, it's fine. They're coming now. How—How about you take the one on the left, and I'll stab the one on the right? One hit each?"

Keith sighed but agreed. "As you wish."

The pyre bats had let go of their perch and were flapping down the path. They flew in a jagged angle up and down, the one on the left slightly ahead of its partner.

It let out a screech just as we turned the corner, and I realized that I hadn't actually activated [Quick Step] yet.

[You have taken 21 Sound-based Damage. HP 1788/1809]

The attack bounced off of Keith's [Mana Shield]. He looked at me and frowned. With a wave of his hand, he cast the spell, "[Air Cutter Blades]."

Before I had time to chastise myself and activate [Quick Step], the air gathered into ten blades and cut *both* pyre bats into ribbons.

[You have defeated a **Pyre Bat**. +4 EXP]
[You have defeated a **Pyre Bat**. +3 EXP]

"Hey!" I turned on Keith. "My bat!"

"You took damage," he countered. "You weren't ready."

"So! I could take a hundred of those hits and be fine." I crossed my arms.

Keith pushed up his glasses, "Could you? At Strength sixty and presumably thirty-something Constitution, you have eighteen hundred hit points. By my calculation, a hundred hits from a pyre bat should be almost exactly enough to kill you."

"You know what I meant!"

Keith looked at me. I was stubborn and continued to hold my own. *He* was overreacting.

Finally, he sighed. "I'm sorry. I didn't mean to steal your kill."

"Apology accepted." I nodded. "Let's go. I'm sensing some mole dogs further on. I can handle all three of them. *Alone.*"

He reached out a hand, and I hesitated only a second before I took it.

We walked along, and I pushed down the impending dread that stayed with me as we walked farther into the caves.

CHAPTER 62

Let Me Out

Keith

Keith knew Henrietta was *not fine*.

Despite her monstrous Constitution and overly powerful Strength, she was unconsciously shivering and sweating at the same time. When they'd first arrived, her hands had gripped his sleeve so hard she'd warped the fabric.

He was lucky she hadn't outright broken his arm.

Still, no matter what he tried, she insisted that she was fine. And then she just stood there and took an attack, completely distracted.

He was reassured when they fought . . . when *she* fought the mole dogs. The thigh-high monsters with wicked spikes on their arms liked to dig under unsuspecting adventurers, but Henrietta managed to defeat them all in an instant and with her usual flair. However, Henrietta didn't harvest the bodies. She left them behind to rush back to the bright lights floating around Keith. She smiled again, but it was like she was proving to herself she could do it despite her obvious internal struggle.

"How about we take a break and drink some water," Keith suggested, rubbing her palm as he usually did. He liked to distract her, but this time, he did so because it seemed like it helped her focus on him. They'd walked far enough down the cave tunnels to turn a few corners but *not* reach a new batch of monsters.

Henrietta shook her head and let go of him. "We can't stop, we're almost to the next group."

Keith felt the absence of more than just her hand. They were losing their sense of teamwork as she sunk deeper into her own anxieties. "What's the next group?"

"I'm sure there'll be another soon," she assured him. She let go of his hand and walked ahead, but still within the range of the lights. Her fingers were gripped into fists so hard that they were turning white.

But he didn't know how to help her other than speeding through the dungeon as she wished. He cursed the fact that he couldn't teleport out of dungeons on his own. He should have brought an Escape Scroll, but there wasn't a herd of monsters in the dungeon he couldn't solo, let alone with Henrietta. The two of them could face it all in their sleep, so he hadn't brought one.

Just then, the stone where Henrietta stepped gave way, and the entire tunnel floor collapsed underneath them.

Keith cast, "[Feathered Fall]."

The spell hit all members in his party, slowing both of their descent into the pit trap. There were a few jagged rocks below that would have done a number on either had they landed wrong.

"Ria?" They both touched down at the same time, but Keith ran over to the young heroine as she collapsed into a sitting position, hugging her sword. A part of her shirt was cut by the blade, and a line of blood ran down from her collarbone. "Ria, I'm here; it's alright . . ."

"Let me out." Her voice broke, and something inside Keith broke with it, shattering his heart like jagged glass. "It's too dark."

The same [Dancing Lights] were still following them and illuminating the pit, but Keith didn't think Henrietta was talking about their surroundings.

"Listen, Ria," Keith tried to speak calmly. "I'm going to—"

She started crying, and Keith paused as her enchanted sword started glowing white . . . but not with holy energy. A flash of light filled the area, and Keith let out a surprised grunt as he blinked spots out of his eyes.

When he could see clearly again, Henrietta stood in the pit, sword in hand. *"Let me out."*

She swung her sword, and a sword slash of [Void Damage] hit the pit wall at an angle, wiping it and a portion of the ceiling higher up out of existence. She swung twice more haphazardly and opened huge rents in the terrain.

Keith resisted the urge to run. Demi and dragon spells were made out of mana and pure System energy. The energy of the universe. [Void Damage] was the antithesis of his entire magical stats makeup.

But Henrietta was still crying, the silent tears trailing down her cheeks as her eyes turned swollen and puffy. Her sword was humming as she tried to walk up the slope her cut had made in the wall. So Keith did the dumbest thing he'd ever done.

He activated his automata wings. Flying came naturally after hours of playing [Fireball] toss that morning.

He flew up behind Henrietta and tried to approach her slowly and with a running dialogue so as not to startle her.

"Ria, Ria, I just need you to close your eyes. Just close your eyes, and I'm going to fly us out of here. I'm going to pick you up now, alright?" He reached out and placed a hand as gently as he could on her shoulder.

She didn't react as he'd hoped, jumping and swinging her sword precariously in his direction. The Void energy cut through his [Mana Shield]. He didn't know any chaos magic or holy magic, so he was next to powerless as her sword sliced by his bicep. He thanked the gods it had only grazed him.

[You have been **Critically Hit**. You take 150 Void-based Damage.
HP 250/400]

Keith leaned in and whispered into her ear, his hair falling forward and tickling her cheek. "Princess, wake up. I'm here to let you out."

"Keith?" Something he'd said caused her to pause long enough for him to scoop her into his arms. One of which burned with pain from his wound. He ignored it.

"I've got you," he whispered, making a decision. The automata wings weren't going to be enough; whatever this was, he needed to get her out of here as fast as possible. "By the Great Wyrm Who Breathes Air into the Sky, [Flight]," Keith spoke the high-tier spell aloud. His perk [Quick Chant] did not apply to the most powerful spells he knew. After he lifted off, he sunk fifty percent of his remaining mana into the [Flight] spell, propelling them up and through the tunnel at breakneck speeds.

He didn't know where the exit teleporter was on this level, and the tunnel system made it harder for him to just sense magic in the area. He would have to search the whole level or defeat the boss . . . It might be faster to fight the boss.

Keith could defeat the boss himself. And as long as Henrietta remained in her current state, he was sure he could get them out in record timing.

Anything that got between Henrietta and the portal out of here was going to have to die a very quick and final death.

He summoned [Air Blades] in advance. They trailed after him with the [Dancing Lights].

With an urgency he hadn't felt since his youth, Keith raced for the exit teleporter.

CHAPTER 63

Stabbed by Your Date

Henrietta

The ground went out below me, and the entire world went dark.

I was suddenly in *that room* again. The one I'd spent six hours locked up in every time I was caught behaving poorly or questioning my parents. They knew what was best for me, and if I couldn't accept that, then I needed some *alone time* to think about it.

While the punishment room had been an unpleasant experience, it'd eventually become the gateway to my newfound freedom. I'd spent enough time there that I'd come to know every pebble and every divot . . . which meant one day, after years of scrabbling around in the dark, I'd found the escape tunnel. After that, I would sit against the cold stone wall, watching the door slowly close, then close my eyes and count to one hundred.

Just in case they came back and opened the door.

They never did.

Then I'd reach out and press a pebble-size stone on the floor, and the wall behind me would open up into a low passage. On my hands and knees, I'd crawl in the pitch-black hidden passage until I reached the end. I repeated a mantra in my head the entire time, over and over and over, reminding me to keep my eyes closed. To just keep crawling. To push up and open the wooden board that led into an abandoned storage shed.

After that, it was simply dressing up like a maid and pretending like I belonged. My perfectly respectable brown hair and brown eyes blended in well, and the freedom to explore the world outside of lessons or a dungeon was worth the . . . discomfort.

Now, all I could feel was the sense of pressure in my chest. My hands shook violently as I reached for Jacqueline . . . and my panic woke her up. *Close your eyes, dearest,* a motherly voice settled on my consciousness, blocking everything else out. *Just swing my blade and kill them all. Cut down everything until the sun is on your face. I am here with—*

"Ria?" A voice whispered in my ears, startling me. At the same time, something gently touched my cheek. It smelled like lavender oil and cotton and *Keith.* Arms wrapped around me and carried me close. I didn't let go of Jacqueline, who made a few protests about not being satisfied without tasting more blood. But she only grumbled and then went back to sleep.

I didn't know how long I remained like that. It was more than a hundred seconds. The notification tab let me know that I had important things to check . . . but I couldn't do anything but hold on and hope.

Eventually, Keith stopped flying and touched down. The world changed, and a cool breeze touched my cheeks. Sunshine pressed against my eyelids, letting me know that we'd made it out of the cave.

I wasn't immediately alright, but I was coming out of myself. I could feel the tears running down my cheeks. My eyes *hurt,* and my nose was stuffed. I tried to rub my face and realized that I was still holding Jacqueline.

Keith was talking to someone quietly, and then we were alone again. He sat down in a chair with me in his lap, something that made my cheeks burn to think about.

"Ria, we're here. You can open your eyes."

I looked up into a very scary face. Keith looked ready to kill someone. I leaned Jacqueline against the table and reached up to rub the crease between his eyebrows. It was better when he smiled at me.

"I'm sorry," I said simply. There wasn't much else I *could* say. My weakness had ruined a perfectly lovely date.

Keith grabbed my hand and sighed. "No, *I'm sorry.* I didn't bring an Escape Scroll, and it took me a while to beat the floor."

"With no help from me," I grumbled, fascinated with the way he was playing with my palm. He always did that, and it was always distracting.

We sat there awkwardly. He'd found us a tent with a carpet, two chairs, and a low table. It must have been a resting area in the market outside the dungeon.

We hadn't gotten to finish the delve because of me.

I resisted the urge to apologize again. The arms holding me weren't as strong as a knight's, but they were comfortable. I needed to get up and take my own seat soon . . . or even now. I thought about it, but I wasn't *ready.* In a moment of selfishness, I sniffled and pressed my face back against Keith's collarbone.

Keith sucked in a breath. "I'm going to need to move you."

I pushed away from him. It wasn't what I wanted to hear, but I was a burden, and of course I'd already overstepped. I stomped down on my growing need for someone to comfort me. As I was convincing myself to get up, Keith reached between us and unclipped his wing automaton straps. He had to shimmy a bit to get the contraption off each shoulder.

He sighed in relief as the wings fell onto the carpet behind his chair. He stretched his shoulders as best he could and then cracked his neck.

His arms wrapped back around me, and I sniffed again. It came out louder than I'd intended. He leaned close, touching our foreheads together.

"Henrietta, you are in so much trouble," he said, matter-of-factly.

"I'm sorry." My heart raced. I knew it; he was going to tell me I was a disappointment, that I'm not strong enough to—

"And," he continued, "I'm throwing you in our dungeon when we get home. You need more sessions with Rufus."

I put up both hands then and pushed him away. "You're not—Your shoulder! What happened?!"

Even through my barely recovered vision, I could see the stark red blood that matted his sleeve. A blade had cut through his clothing. I leaned closer and felt a wave of relief; there was only a nick in the flesh of his bicep.

"Someone," Keith whispered into my ear, dragging back my attention, "deals [Void Damage]. My greatest weakness."

I blushed. My father's spies had guessed that information, which was why my father had sent me into the dungeon to find Jacqueline. It was something I'd planned to mention to Keith someday. *Today*, actually. When we'd reached the top floor of the dungeon, and I could let loose.

It probably wasn't the best way to find out . . . being stabbed by your date.

"One more thing," Keith said, looking strangely intense. I braced myself. "Did you level up?"

CHAPTER 64

The Bloodthirsty Urge to Go Burn Down Drendil's Castle

Keith

[Error! High Tier Spell: **Dark Flare** has failed. You take base mana cost x3 modifier damage to Health.]
[Warning! You have **Mana Burn.** You will continue to burn mana until you Rest. Mana burned at 1/3 base rate due to Arcane Sage Perk: **Slow Burn.**]
[You have 01:18:42 until Death by **Mana Burn.**]

The dungeon boss on level nine had spawned mini bosses. While Keith was distracted blowing them up, the boss had managed to slide a tentacle of darkness around his leg—which he couldn't see very well, since he was holding a princess in a princess hold in his arms.

This was the first time he'd tried to fight while protecting someone, and it was very distracting.

The tentacle broke Keith's high-level "By Draconic Flame that Bursts Forth, [Dark Flare]" cast, and he felt the spell rebound.

Every time. He'd had more spells fail since Henrietta had shown up at his castle than he'd had in the last *decade.*

It was the work of willpower to clean up the boss through the [Mana Burn] pain, down a health potion, and teleport out of there.

By the time they were back in the market outside the dungeon, Keith was fighting a pounding headache and the still-burning sensation where [Void Damage] had sliced his arm.

After he sat down with Ria, Keith shuffled a bit and popped a green high-grade mana potion. He sighed as he recovered a hundred mana, giving him extra time before he passed out. He could force himself to stay awake until he died from the mana bleed, or he could let sleep take him and start recovering . . . Unfortunately he'd be out for a good sixteen hours and he didn't want that.

Better to push it to the last minute and use mana potions to get back to Gren's Keep. Safer too, when assassins were still running around the forest.

He was seriously resisting the bloodthirsty urge to go burn down Drendil's castle. He didn't know what exactly had caused Henrietta's crippling phobia, but her begging him to, "Let me out," implied this wasn't simply an I-got-trapped-in-a-dungeon-pit-for-too-long fear and more of a someone-locked-me-up-and-wouldn't-let-me-out type of response.

He could hazard a guess as to who could lock a princess up in a dark room until she broke.

As much as he wanted to go off and destroy everything . . . Keith still had Henrietta to see too and a bed with his name on it. For now.

His shoulder's still hurt from where the wings had dragged behind him. He'd dropped a good amount of mana in order to sustain his [Flight] spell at its highest speed, and his construct wings suffered from getting whipped behind him. The floor boss had even torn one of the wings trying to pull him from the sky, not realizing it was actually a spell keeping them aloft.

He'd made the wings when he was *ten*. They were useful and looked impressive, but they were not durable or a replacement for the actual high-class magical spell.

After portaling out, he'd ordered a private tent for them and set about taking care of Henrietta.

Which led to their current conversation. He meant what he'd said. As soon as they were home, he was going to drop her off straight into their dungeon for another Rufus session.

Before she could get upset over attacking and injuring him, Keith changed distraction tactics.

"Did you level up?"

Henrietta opened her mouth to say something but then closed it again. "I think so. Let me check."

Notification tabs were usually annoying when there were important matters to deal with. Case in point, his own incessant [Mana Burn] reminders. He held her a little tighter as she got a faraway look, reading the updates.

"I'm level sixty-eight!" she let Keith know. "One second."

It took longer than a second to go through everything she needed to finish leveling up. Her character sheet must have been as long and obnoxious as his, what with her being over level sixty.

As a person grew, at each new level they gained one attribute point in Strength, Dexterity, Constitution, Intelligence, Perception and Charisma—until the end of childhood. That was age ten for most races. After that, the system granted two attribute points per level up to put where anyone willed.

Keith resisted the urge to tense as he asked, "Are you keeping with your current trend of having the same level and Strength?"

The idea of her crushing diamond into powder came to mind. It was glorious to imagine.

"Actually . . . I think I'll put it into Dexterity and Perception. I'm tired of traps," she admitted.

"Would you like me to find a professional Rogue to teach you some tricks?" He didn't have any on staff since the Goose Incident. But there were a few famous adventurers in Gren's Keep who could be convinced.

"Good plan," she said, still reviewing her character sheet. "I get to choose a new perk, so I'm just reading the list now."

Keith sat back, much more comfortable now that he wasn't juggling Ria up front and wings in the back. He wondered if he should make her a pair? A flying, sword-wielding Henrietta ready to cut her foe in half from across the battlefield would be a sight to see.

That was another thing. Keith stared down at Jacqueline, the magical [Void Damage] sword, perfect for completely and utterly destroying him.

He suddenly recalled the exact words in Madame Potts's prophecy. *Mass murder* indeed.

All of the spells he'd learned that were mid or high level were from his godmother's hoard. They were all of them dragon spells, and they were all of them *useless* against Jacqueline's crit damage.

If she attacked him . . . could he win?

His golems might be able to hold up long enough for him to escape. He could also use his wits to defeat Henrietta by trapping her or taking her sword. There were hundreds of golems that he could summon to fight the Heroine of Justice if he were prepared to do so.

[You have 00:48:42 until Death by **Mana Burn**.]

Keith pinched his nose. He needed twenty potions to last until they arrived back at the Damp Gizzard, and he needed them *now*. In less than an hour, he was going to pass out on the floor or just stay awake until he died.

His necromancer wasn't on holiday anymore, but she was clear across the kingdom and wrapped around Julia's dark sword-calloused finger. He would have to hope Henrietta would use her Revival potion on him . . . and that thought was almost as embarrassing as admitting he was dying now. She already had enough worries.

And he didn't want to admit his weakness.

The most obvious choice was still to make it back to Gren's Keep intact and then get some rest. So while Henrietta was choosing her perks, Keith used his skill [Share Senses] with Hubert.

The crow had followed them to the Damp Gizzard before wandering off to do *crow* things. Now he was riding along, he sent the crow to pick up some health and mana potions. Merchants were willing to give things to the construct after Keith projected his voice, and soon, Hubert was carrying a sack filled with life-saving jars to their tent.

Keith left Hubert with instructions on where to go. He should arrive before Keith outright fell over.

He would get Henrietta settled, empty the potions from his storage space and from Hubert, and then they could be on their way.

At least, that was the plan.

CHAPTER 65

Arrest This Human!

Henrietta

If Keith hadn't lost interest because I'd snapped at him or because I'd shown weakness and let my fear get the better of me, or because I'd cut him . . . then I thought it might be nice to use my points to reflect my new life.

Honestly, the chair cuddles gave me hope.

It would be nice to have perks that were useful while living in the Dark Enchanted Forest. Dexterity and Perception were vital for paperwork and helped significantly with my baking. And if I was going to continue living in the castle, I should also prepare for the job I was aiming for.

[You have leveled up the Skill: **Leadership** to Level 6.]
[**Leadership** affects Perception 20 x Charisma 29 targets who are under your command = 580 targets. Those under the influence of **Leadership** will hear what you say, understand your instructions better, and act upon them naturally. Targets with **Leadership** or Perception equal to or greater than yours, or targets you choose, will know they are under the effect of the Skill: **Leadership**.]

Please choose from the following Perks:
Natural Poise: You look like the person in charge. +1 Charisma when active. This effect targets individuals equal to your new Charisma x **Leadership** = 180. This lasts for a number of minutes equal to your Charisma.
Management: You effortlessly direct others and aid them in completing a task with ease and efficiency. Grant +1 to a chosen

Attribute for those following your direction. This lasts for a number of minutes equal to your Charisma.

Battle Call: You lead your troops with vigor. All members of your army can hear your words, no matter where they are on the battlefield. +1 Charisma when active. This effect lasts for a number of seconds equal to your Charisma.

Still no culinary perks. The System had offered me [True Taste] when I'd leveled up [Etiquette], but that had been the only time it'd recognized my passion for baking over my titled jobs.

It seemed that spending a few afternoons in the kitchen was nothing to days and weeks leading knights in drills and conquering dungeons.

I looked at the offered perks and read them through a few times before settling on the one that I thought would help me best moving forward.

[You have chosen the Perk: **Management**.]

My new character sheet read:

Name:	Henrietta Doryn of Drendil
Occupation:	Experimental Subject Minion
Level:	68
Experience Points:	29/17000
Hit Points:	1809/1809
Mana Points:	1139/1139
Bonded Item:	Jacqueline Tiamat la Fleur
Class:	Sword Master
Temporary Status:	[Tame the Elements]
Titles:	
[Human], [Noble], [Prince], [Crown Prince], [Warrior], [Aura Knight], [Sword Master]	

Attributes:			
Strength:	67	Intelligence:	17
Dexterity:	22	Perception:	20
Constitution:	27 (+2)	Charisma:	29 (+4)
Skills:			
Social:	6	Etiquette:	5
Leadership:	6	Bureaucracy:	7
+Swordsmanship: Parry:	1	Sword Aura:	7
Mastery:	2		
Perks:			
Sense Ally, Sense Lies, Calming Voice, Sense Motive, True Taste, Sense Ability, Inspire, Multitask, Management, Quick Read, Resist Poison, Quick Step, Quick Draw, Force Thrust, Bludgeoning Cut, Harvest Kill, Sword Sense, Killing Intent, Aura Blade, Death Parry.			

[Mastery] had been an incredible boon, converting my mana pool to Intelligence x Strength instead of the usual Intelligence x Dexterity. Blunt force mana was more my style than attempting to delicately manipulate matter.

All in all, my character sheet reflected me quite well. And maybe when my [Etiquette] skill hit level six, I'd get the chance to pick up more culinary perks.

I could only hope.

"THERE YOU—Oh my gods."

I closed my notifications tab and looked up to see a head poking into the tent. Lady Amy had waited the entire day for us to come out, and now she was blushing and covering her face. It was almost evening, by the looks of the sunset reds against the tent.

Keith was currently holding me on his lap, absently fiddling with my fingers.

"I thought I said we weren't to be disturbed?" Keith grumbled under his breath behind me. I made to jump off his lap, and there was a slight resistance from him, but only slight. Standing let me know that I'd mostly recovered from my weakness and could pretend normalcy again.

I ignored my burning ears at getting caught cuddling the king of the Dark Enchanted Forest in a tent.

"Lady Amy! I'm so sorry we went ahead before you arose." Placations came naturally. "Keith—the Dark Lord and I had planned a private trip and didn't want to wake you."

Just because I'd recovered a bit from my . . . *moment of weakness* didn't mean I was suddenly better. It wasn't something I could just *get over* and be one hundred percent moments later. But, even if I wasn't focusing well and still felt out of sorts, it didn't mean I couldn't stand up and deliver.

I considered activating one of my [Etiquette] perks like [Calming Voice] to help ease the situation, but thought better of it. She was a duke's daughter and potentially had a higher level [Etiquette] than I. As I knew from my own experiences, attributes didn't define a person. I myself had Intelligence seventeen, an incredibly high level for anyone not learning [Magic] . . . but my patience for memorizing was nonexistent.

What I was trying to say was that Lady Amy could shove her foot in her mouth and come off as an excited puppy, but I had no doubt she would turn around and put on a mask and act properly if required of her. There was no telling how high her skills actually were—and she'd already admitted to soloing a dungeon.

Lady Amy looked hurt by my apology; like she was trying not to pout but failing. She glanced between Keith, her king, and I, her hero, and her shoulders slumped.

"I'm sorry for interrupting." She politely curtsied from the open doorway flap of the tent. "Perhaps I could accompany you in a dungeon delve tomorrow?"

I heard the hidden words of immeasurable disappointment at being left behind that remained unspoken in her address—or maybe that was me feeling a *little* bit guilty about choosing a date with Keith over my new friend. Still, we hadn't made any plans.

And as of now, my dungeon escapades were probably best left behind us. "I'm sorry—"

"THERE SHE IS!" a new voice called out, and Lady Amy visibly panicked. She jumped nearly a foot in the air, turning around ready to make a break for it. It was too late, however, as the entrance was surrounded by people, their shadows falling against the canopy.

"Saintess Amaryllis, I'm so happy we found you."

Keith mumbled, "About time . . ." and I turned to him in shock. He grinned, showing all his teeth. "What? I just *casually* let her father know that we'd met while traveling. Who could have known she was on the run?"

"You did *not*! When?"

"After you went to bed," Keith replied innocently. "I was sending out routine paperwork, of course."

"Duke Briarthorn is eagerly awaiting your return." The elven paladin whom I'd met on the road the day before stepped into view. "If you'll just come with us, my lady—You!"

He saw me standing in the tent slightly behind Amaryllis and frowned, righteous fury in his tone. "I did not think that you had deliberately misled us, but now I see you were aiding the saintess. By your pathetic appearance, are you one of those foolish Drendil soldiers? You might try to influence our saintess with your corrupt ways, but we will not have it!"

"Wait, no—" Lady Amy tried to explain, but the older elf cut her off.

"Guards, arrest this human!"

CHAPTER 66

Death by Mana Burn

Keith

[You have 00:17:33 until Death by **Mana Burn**.]

The effects of [Mana Burn] were hitting him harder now. His hands had a light tremor, his head hurt, and exhaustion was eating away at his senses. As it got closer to zero, he'd be fighting harder to stay conscious.

In a way, Keith had brought this upon himself. Sir Vainbark was a stern force to be reckoned with; he would pursue a matter to the ends of the earth if tasked to do so. The elf was standing just out of site behind a tent flap, but his anger was apparent.

"We shall see what nefarious ploy Drendil has when Lady Hazelglade gets through with you," the elvish paladin told Henrietta.

Amaryllis was doing her best to dissuade him, but her "You're making a mistake!" went completely ignored.

Of course, Keith would not allow Sir Vainbark to mess with his princess.

Ahem, *the* princess.

Keith stood, towering behind Henrietta, and placed one shaking hand on her shoulder protectively. "Tell me, why are you arresting Princess Henrietta Doryn of Drendil?"

Everyone stopped. As expected, none of the older elves bothered to bow. They nodded politely while the young ranger in the back only bowed halfway before getting elbowed by his neighbor. The elves were the original inhabitants of the forest, and while they called him king, they did so only as a formality.

Sir Vainbark looked between Henrietta and Keith. He raised an eyebrow and demanded, "If this is the Henrietta you announced to the Dark Enchanted

Forest last month, then I have to question your love life. This woman led us astray in our quest to locate Lady Amaryllis and return her to the safety of the Hollow Sanctuary."

"Actually"—Henrietta put up her hand and waved for everyone's attention— "I told you nothing but the truth. I *did* see Amy walking toward the castle. I just forgot to mention it was the day before."

"A likely story," the paladin scoffed.

"It's true. Also, I did run into her shortly after our meeting, and I chose not to do anything about it," Henrietta finished. "Because Lady Amy is an adult under Nilheim law, and free to act accordingly."

"She is Duke Briarthorn's daughter, and the saintess. She will never be free to do as she pleases. Her responsibilities are her life," Sir Vainbark countered.

"Is this true?" Henrietta looked up at Keith.

The matter was of political delicacy due to the peace treaty between the elves and Nilheim. It granted the Hollow a respectful autonomy of the elvish culture—including their saintess. Still, he wasn't in the best mood, and that reflected in his answer.

"It is true that a person is free from their parents' guardianship after they come of age, and Lady Amaryllis is certainly older than sixteen," he began, "but the saintess is a title and a job. As such, it has restrictions much like we face as king and princess."

Lady Amy deflated, though Henrietta simply waited for him to continue. She knew him so well already.

"Of course, it is not my business how she spends her *free time*," Keith said. He was happy that he had one hand braced on Henrietta now because a wave of nausea hit him, and he resisted the urge to just fall over. "I do wonder what parts of her job are so arduous that I learn of her escape every month or so?"

Sir Vainbark grew red, an amazing sight as the flush ran to the tips of his green ears. "It is her duty to meditate in the Sanctuary. No harm comes to her or any of our people."

Everyone looked at Lady Amy. She mumbled, "I would call isolation a form of torture. If boredom doesn't count."

"You are surrounded by attendants!" Sir Vainbark barked.

Keith knew the solitary life of those in power but had expected that she should have been given playmates much the same way he had. This was the first time he'd heard otherwise and felt a touch of sympathy for the young elf. He resisted the urge to grip the bridge of his nose; his temple pounded.

"Still," Keith declared, "as a working citizen in the kingdom of Nilheim, you are entitled to three days off each week. I'll assume that the Hollow elves did not forget the employment legislation they accepted and agreed to in our updated treaty five years ago."

"What?!" Lady Amy practically screamed but barely contained herself to a reasonable volume. "No one told me that!"

Sir Vainbark jerked back as if physically stricken. "That is . . . Wait. That shouldn't apply . . ."

Keith frowned at the paladin. "It applies to *everyone*. Including myself."

He wasn't going to mention that he ignored the rule some of, if not most of the time. He should've considered making it hour based and broken the four days up over the entire week to keep abreast of kingdom matters. His perks made managing day-to-day tasks the work of a few hours. When they weren't about to go to war, that was.

He was getting distracted.

Sir Vainbark was considering his words as Keith continued, "I've only known Lady Amy to be traveling for these three days. As such, there is plenty of time for her to return back to work for tomorrow. I see no reason for you or your men to abduct a member of the elven court against her will and in my presence, no less."

"But we were tasked with bringing her home!" Sir Vainbark argued. "It's not abduction—"

Lady Amy cut in, "It is! I'm an adult even by elven standards now that I'm twenty-five."

She looked at Keith and Ria, her eyes red with the beginning of tears. "If what King Keith says is true, then I'll gladly return to the Hollow in time for my prayers." She whipped around to glare at the paladin. "But you'll have to wait until I'm ready to leave to escort me."

It was with effort that Keith didn't let out a sigh of frustration. This all but guaranteed Lady Amy would want to spend time with Henrietta before the elf left that night to return to the Hollow.

Granted, it would be nice if Henrietta had more friends in the Dark Enchanted Forest. As much as he would like to spend all their free time together, he knew the importance of having companions to rely on. It would also make Nilheim feel more like a home, so she would be less likely to leave him—it.

Keith got another notification alert as a wave of exhaustion hit him.

[You have 00:03:23 until Death by **Mana Burn**.]

"If that is all, everyone get out," Keith snapped, beginning to rush. "Henrietta, can you escort Lady Amy back to Gren's Keep? I'll catch up with you at Logan's Noodle House."

Disappointment flashed on Henrietta's face and hurt his heart, but he was a minute from passing out. He managed a smile that was probably more like a grimace.

"You can't—" Sir Vainbark argued when a hand reached out and patted him on the arm. Lady Hazelglade stepped into sight "Come on, Vain, let's escort our lady to dinner with her new friend. We'll have much to talk about with the duke when we get back. Your Viciousness." She nodded at Keith in a polite greeting.

He nodded back. "Lady Hazelglade."

"Alright," Sir Vainbark finally accepted, following everyone out into the market.

Henrietta looked back at Keith. "It'll be slower to walk back with Lady Amy."

"They have unicorn mounts," he replied, reaching out and holding her hand up to kiss the palm. "Perhaps you can get the story of how that's possible. Goldenhoof's herd is notoriously proud."

She chuckled. "I'll ask."

"I just have a few things to wrap up here; I'll catch up eventually," Keith assured her. He let her go, and she ran out to catch up with the others.

[You have 00:00:22 until Death by **Mana Burn**. You may expend
Hit Points to stay awake.]

Keith collapsed, catching himself on the chair. He reached into his storage and popped a mid-grade mana potion, barely drinking it in time.

[You have 00:03:10 until Death by **Mana Burn**.]

He sighed and lifted the bottom of the tent flap, letting a large construct raven hop inside pulling a bag of potion bottles behind.

"Perfect timing, Hubert. Let's see if we can't postpone this bothersome unconsciousness until this evening."

CHAPTER 67

King's Hold

Henrietta

I sensed Hubert joining Keith in the tent but didn't think much of it.

Lady Amy was beside herself, babbling about how much this changed everything, and how she'd like to come visit the castle on her days off if I was free for lunch. I didn't mind; she made for excitable company, and I was happy to have more friends. Maybe I could visit the Hollow, and she could show me around.

In the back of my mind, I felt a touch of irritation from Jacqueline. I slapped my forehead, realizing I'd left my blade behind. "I'll be right back!"

I lifted the tent flap, peeking my head inside. "Sorry, I forgot—*Keith?!*"

The Dark Lord was half collapsed on the floor with his body draped over the seat of a chair, Hubert clinging to the back. Potions spilled out on his lap, and he clutched an open mana potion in his hand.

Keith was startled by my appearance and actually looked . . . guilty?

"Ria, I can explain." He sounded guilty too. He didn't continue but threw back the potion as fast as he could. His hands were literally shaking, and when he was finished, he tried to put the bottle down but dropped it at the last second.

He glowed as the potion took effect and a bit of color returned to his pale face. For the first time since I woke up, I took the time to really *look* at him, and I kicked myself for assuming an all-powerful Arcane Sage would never overdo things.

"Here, let me help." This wasn't my first time seeing a mage who had reached their limits. Instead of rushing, I carefully stepped forward and knelt down beside him. I picked up the used bottle, recapped it, and put it aside properly. I grabbed another one, opened it and brought it to his lips. "How much mana do you have left?"

He stared at me with a mix of emotions. Embarrassment and frustration and exhaustion were the easiest to identify. Slowly, he opened his mouth and let me pour the contents inside.

Another glow, but no response to my question. He was already looking much better, but his hands were still shaking. I prepared each bottle thereafter and handed them over one at a time so he could drink them himself.

I debated feeding him the rest myself but thought better of it; he still hadn't answered my question.

He went through *ten* high-rank mana potions and a couple mid rank he pulled from his dimensional storage. Even after downing all of them, Keith still looked the worse for wear. He rubbed the bridge of his nose, and a small frown creased his brow.

Mana headaches were bad, but this—

"You have [Mana Burn], don't you?" I asked, no longer waiting for him to explain. A hint of anger made its way into my voice.

He flinched at that, but then looked down. "Yes."

"How much mana do you have right now?"

"Around nine hundred . . ."

"And how long until you run out?" I demanded. He hesitated. "Keith, how long do you have until you need to rest. "

He mumbled, "Two hours . . ."

"Don't you burn mana every three seconds?" The [Bleed] effect was similar and I had been stabbed enough to know. I tried to do the math but I hated math. I still thought that two hours was an overly generous estimate. I'd guess it was closer to one hour at most.

"Eight seconds, technically."

"Really?" I gathered the empty bottles and shoveled them all into the bag. I also took the time to grab Jacqueline and put her back in her sheath where she belonged.

He explained, "My perk from Arcane Sage is [Slow Burn], and it's made it feasible to survive longer before I pass out."

"How many times have you had [Mana Burn] that you actually got it as a perk choice?"

Keith hesitated. I got the feeling he was counting, but he wasn't forthcoming with any numbers.

I didn't know what made me more upset: that he put himself in danger that often, or that he remained silent when I asked him hard questions.

I ground out, "But *why wait?* You could have popped the mana potions while I was here?"

"I was distracted getting here, then we had company . . ." Keith groaned, trying to get up but stumbling a bit. I caught him with my shoulder under his arm and helped him to his feet, hugging him around the waist for extra support. He admitted, "And I didn't want to worry you."

As a bit of payback for worrying me, and because it looked like he could barely stand as it was, I made up my mind on my next course of action.

"That's it," I said, sweeping his legs out from under him and dropping him into a princess—I mean, a *king's hold*. "I'm taking you back to the Damp Gizzard and straight into bed. Your bed, I mean; I'm putting you in your bed. To sleep." I would have blushed if I wasn't so upset.

Keith made an undignified noise and flailed his arms, then groaned as a new wave of headache must have hit him from the sudden movement. I ignored his, "Wait! RIA! You can't—" and carried him toward the tent flap.

"You shush," I told the Dark Lord—quietly, because I knew how much headaches were affected by loud noises. Over my shoulder, I said, "Hubert, take care of the bag of bottles," then I stepped out of the tent and into the glare of sunset as the last bit of light started to fade behind the mountain range to the west.

Outside, the elves were preparing to leave. Lady Amy was in the process of arguing with a unicorn; something about betrayal and learning how to read runic script . . . but it wasn't important to me right now.

Everyone stopped what they were doing when they noticed us.

"Something came up," I said. Keith had the strength to nod politely at the group, as if he weren't held in my arms with his legs dangling. I addressed Lady Amy specifically. "I'll see you back in Gren's Keep!"

With that, I activated [Quick Step] and took off.

The sooner I could get Keith into bed, the better.

Into *HIS* bed! To sleep!

Actually Communicate

Keith

Keith had *not* been expecting to fall into Henrietta's arms and get carried to bed . . . but apparently, that was what happened.

The weight of his headache mixed with his exhaustion had caused him to nod off even before they arrived back at Gren's Keep.

He probably should have protested; he didn't, though. Henrietta had let him carry her around, so it only seemed fair.

It took him two full rest cycles before he woke up in the afternoon of the next day. A part of him regretted losing so much time, but he wouldn't have done anything differently.

Alright, maybe he would have drunk the potions sooner. Still, it wasn't his first near death from [Mana Burn], and it wouldn't be his last. With Chloe around, it didn't seem like too much trouble, aside from the headache.

He flinched when he remembered the anger in Ria's voice last night. He'd have to apologize.

The door to his room opened at the same time he tried to sit up.

Henrietta stood there, holding two cups of tea.

"Good morning . . . afternoon," Keith corrected himself. He awkwardly stuffed a stray lock of long black hair behind his ear. He realized that a portion of his hair had tangled around his horn, and he started to pull it all straight.

"How did you sleep?" Henrietta came forward and put the tea on the bedside table.

"Like the not-dead," Keith joked. He could tell it fell flat. He didn't know if that was cultural or if she was still angry at him. He would bet the latter. "Listen, Ria, I want to apologize for upsetting you yesterday."

"Just for upsetting me?" Ria sat down in the chair across from Keith and looked him square in the eyes. Her voice was calm and collected like a scholar, belaying any hurt or sarcasm. "What about how you didn't tell me you had [Mana Burn] and almost died, alone in a tent, mere inches away from me?" Here she let a small amount of frustration show. "I know how hard it is to show weakness, but I hope you know I'm not going to just stab you when you're down?"

"Actually, I do know that," he whispered softly. "Thank you."

Keith finished detangling the last of his hair and flipped it back over his shoulder. He threw the covers off and swung his legs over the side so he could sit facing her. One of the relationship counseling books Rufus had forced on him—and that he'd read six times—was very clear about this sort of situation.

"Let's talk about what happened and make a plan going forward," he told her, hoping communication was, indeed, the best course of action. "It's just that when you had an anxiety attack in the dungeon, I panicked. I moved to get us out of there faster than I've ever cleared a floor before, and I overdid it. I admit it. And afterward, I didn't want you to worry. I thought you were already kicking yourself to apologize for something you didn't need to apologize for."

Keith paused. He might have rambled on longer than necessary, but better to actually communicate now than risk misunderstandings later. He did add, "I thought that I could just refill some mana and go to the Noodle House, and it wouldn't be a big deal."

Henrietta took a deep breath. "Why does everyone in this kingdom think that dying isn't such a big deal?"

Keith lifted a finger to point out the obvious, but Henrietta pushed on. "There was no Chloe to [Resurrect] you if you died in that tent. What if something happened with one of my father's assassins? What if you didn't drink the potions in time? Were you just going to leave it to Fate?"

"Fate is one of my patron goddesses . . . but no," Keith admitted. "Honestly, in a worst-case scenario, I had trusted *you* might give me your Revive Potion. My minions are loyal, but the strongest reigns and all that . . ."

Henrietta crossed her arms. "Of *course* I would have. If I wasn't half way back to Gren's Keep with Lady Amy by then."

Keith pushed on. "And in the same vein, I wish that *you'd* told *me* before going into the dungeon that there might be difficulties if we encountered tight, dark spaces . . . but I understand why you didn't."

"So I didn't tell you I was . . . *weak* to dark spaces, and you didn't tell me you had [Mana Burn], so it's fair?" Henrietta picked up her cup of tea and blew on it.

"No." Keith shook his head. "All is fair between us because comparing like that won't help anyone."

"I was worried . . ." Henrietta sighed. "This is the first time we've inconvenienced each other. Thank you for not leaving when I was being less than fair."

"Inconvenience might not be the word I would use . . . but I think we both felt that way." Keith picked up his own tea. It was already prepared perfectly, and he smiled a bit as he took a sip. "So should we get to the planning part next?"

Henrietta smiled to herself, tapping her mug with one finger. The motion drew his eye, and he suddenly felt the urge to hold her hands. Something he'd been struggling with a lot lately.

"I let you know if something is bothering me before I go catatonic and stab you?" Henrietta teased. "And you let me know if you're on the verge of dying from overdoing things?"

Keith chuckled. "Do you think we'll actually be able to follow through with that?"

"We can *try*," Henrietta replied. "And if we fail, then we talk about it? That is . . . if you really *are* alright with my . . . struggles? You're *sure*?"

"Everyone is afraid of something," Keith said. He himself had been struggling with his own fears ever since Henrietta had showed up at his castle smelling like freshly baked scones and suddenly becoming a part of his everyday life. He would talk to her about that too. Soon. Probably.

When he figured things out and had answers.

Henrietta relaxed a bit. "And I'm still interested. In us . . . But I think there is one more thing you'll have to do as punishment."

"What is that?" Keith raised an eyebrow.

Henrietta smiled. "I'm not the *only* one who's going to get thrown in the dungeon when we get home."

CHAPTER 69

Perrrfect Timing

Henrietta

The noodle broth was a blend of warmth and spice, rich undertones of hearty vegetables simmered in herbs and topped with sliced roasted boar, sprouts, mushrooms, and a boiled floofpoof egg. I couldn't resist making an appreciative sound as I sipped a spoonful of the broth.

Keith choked on his tea, but he did that sometimes. On the topic of tea, this blend was light and seeped in jasmine. I'd never had green niku bark tea before today, but I was determined to find the supplier and stock up before we left.

There had been an awkward moment after our discussion in Keith's room, but then I'd decided it was time to eat.

I'd waited long enough!

Logan's Noodle House was near the Damp Gizzard and full of happy beastfolk enjoying giant wide-brimmed bowls designed for eating ramen.

I'd never eaten ramen, as it was a popular new dish that had only started popping up a few years ago. My father didn't like new things "destroying the time-honored traditional foods of Drendil," which were various forms of roasted and boiled meat and vegetables and tubers. He'd put up a ban on selling ramen, sushi, tacos, lasagna, kimchi, poutine, and any other strange dishes that made the rounds. Seriously, there was some wildly creative chef living in North Sumbria who was changing food culture for the better. Ramen was *delicious*.

Keith and I enjoyed our meal while the room filled with locals and a few adventuring parties, two of which I recognized!

"Priscilla, how many times do I have to tell you that crabs hunt in pairs?" Sara said to the catkin beside her. "You almost got us killed. *Again.*"

"You know this wouldn't be such a problem if we stuck to the first floorrr?" Priscilla smiled a feral grin. "I like hunting floofpoofs."

"Sorry," Healer Bowen mumbled, rubbing the back of his neck.

"You have nothing to apologize for," Sara told him matter-of-fact, reassuring him with a kind smile. "It's our job to level you up. It's just faster on the second floor."

"But don't cha think it would be easier to clear the whole first floor for EXP instead of rushing to the second floor?" The barbarian-type fighter was the last to take a seat, having grabbed everyone's menus. I may have forgotten his name already.

"No." Sara shook her head, then noticed us and paused. As with many of the folk in Gren's Keep, as soon as they saw Keith, they got a *look* and then nodded or bowed or curtsied in his direction before going back to doing whatever it was they were doing. It was better than the expected groveling back in Drendil, and I appreciated the fact that it was a show of respect from a distance—never interrupting or drawing attention to itself.

In this case, Sara bobbed her head before going back to defending her choice to tackle the second floor for higher EXP. I knew how hard it was to clear dungeons from my childhood and thought both ways had their merit . . . the second floor just cost more in Resurrect potions.

Keith leaned over and whispered into my ear, "Are you wanting to go say hello?"

I got the impression he was being polite and didn't actually want to. As much as I enjoyed listening in on other people's conversations, it was our last day together before we headed back home.

"No." I placed a hand on his arm. "I'm happy just sitting here with you—"

At this point, the doors swung open, and the second group of adventurers I knew walked into the eatery.

"Logan, a rrround of bowls for my companions here, as we've just come back from patrolling!" A calico catkin led the large group of beastfolk inside. He placed one boot on a chair dramatically, keeping an eye on everyone as his group took over most of the establishment. I would recognize that hat anywhere.

"It's Alistair McKraken and the Pounce Protectorate!" I heard Priscilla sigh dramatically into a swoon. "He's so dreamy."

I had to admit, the feathers in his hat were *very* fashionable. I smiled up at Keith and finished, "Though if it's this busy, we might want to go for a walk?"

"Princess!" One of the protectorate, a lion beastwoman with golden hair and golden eyes whom I didn't know the name of, noticed us and bowed awkwardly from her seat. "Yourrr Viciousness!"

The entire group paused and turned to look our way. A sudden deafening silence replaced the chair shuffling, rough housing, and banter.

Alistair put his foot down and swept into an elegant bow, taking off his hat with extra flourish. "Please, forgive this crowd of rrruffians, Yourrr Viciousness!

And Prrrincess, I'm so glad to see you could stop here on your travels. How is the soup?"

"Delicious, thank you, Alistair." I nodded back. "We were just finishing and heading out for a walk."

"Perrrfect timing." He flashed us a stunning smile. "The Pixie Prim are doing their rrrounds in about . . . fifteen minutes? You won't want to miss it."

I looked up at Keith, who pushed up his glasses scholarly. "Do you want me to explain what that means, or would you like it to be a surprise?"

There was no need to consider; I loved surprises. We bid farewell to everyone at Logan's Noodle House and took to the streets.

Gren's Keep really was a beautiful cottage village, with cobblestone streets, herb gardens, and all over painted with delicate murals of shapes, flowers, or animals. It was midspring and everywhere was full of blossoming trees.

As we walked, I could hear cheering nearby. Keith pulled me into a small community garden filled with lavender and milkweed and bees. We stood alone in the shade of a cherry tree; new buds covered the canopy like snowdrops. All up the street, beastfolk threw open windows and stuck out their heads while children paused from their play to watch expectantly. I followed everyone's gaze and saw a swarm of colorful pixies letting off golden pixie dust as they swept through the streets.

Flowers turned their faces upward, blooming brighter. Trellises lifted delicate vines out, and leaves unfurled as if drinking in sunshine. Trees swayed, and the carrottops in the garden next to me shook gently.

The pixie dust was sparkling glitter that fell over the city, and more magical still was the fact that it disappeared after it touched down, leaving no mess.

Keith asked, "So, is this a nice surprise?"

"It's perfect." Something came over me, and I leaned my head against his arm and sighed. "It's beautiful."

Keith replied, speaking softly, "Yes. Yes, it is."

There was a gentle breeze. I glanced up, and Keith was staring at me. His blue eyes were searching mine as he whispered, "Can I kiss you?"

I didn't answer. Instead, I reached up and wrapped my arms around his neck. He leaned down to assist me, and I pressed my lips to his. We were awkward at first, and his stubble scratched my cheek, but I didn't care. He tasted like warm honey and tea.

We stayed in the garden long after the Pixie Prim had flown on and everyone had gone back about their day. Eventually, he broke away and pressed his forehead to mine.

"Ria, let's go home."

CHAPTER 70

What If She Betrays You?

Keith

When Henrietta and Keith returned home, there was a new energy to their courtship and a comfort in their conversation that hadn't been there before.

He could still taste her on his lips, and feel where she had tugged a little too passionately on his hair. If he had the option, he would be sitting with her in the garden right now, instead of locked up in the dungeon talking to a smug fluffy beastman.

"Can we get on with this?" Keith perched awkwardly on the daybed, not utilizing its comforting recline because . . . well, because he didn't want to. "I still have work to do."

Of course the first thing Henrietta had done when they returned was tell Rufus that she and Keith needed a session. As far as punishments went for nearly getting unalived by his own careless attitude, it was a bit much.

He didn't think it was *that* bad.

"After hearing from Henrietta this morning"—Rufus tapped his notepad with a claw—"I have to say I'm impressed."

That managed to pique his interest and he glanced at the notepad. Keith had not been privy to her session and could only guess what she had told his general. "Why?"

"Henrietta snapped at you, lied to you, almost killed you . . . and yet you're concerned for her?" Rufus flipped through his notes.

"Yes?" Since the beastman neglected to mention the kiss, Keith would assume that Henrietta had not disclosed that part of their trip. He was momentarily distracted by the thought of her soft brown eyes and—"And you still want to pursue her?"

"People get upset when they're afraid, Rufus," Keith countered, dragging his mind back to the present. "According to Green, there is a difference between lashing out in fear and lashing out in anger."

"And yet they still result in the same outcome." Rufus dipped his quill into fresh ink and jotted down something, smiling to himself. He continued, "I have to say I wasn't expecting you to read *every* book by Mola Green, but I shouldn't have been surprised. They are overdue, by the way. Scholar Violet told me you've taken out all the relationship counselling books in the library; how did you find Green's book on the childhood origin of self theory?"

"We aren't talking about *me*. We are talking about why I'm not upset that Henrietta lied to me about being fine in the dungeon—which is where you are wrong, because I was upset. Very upset." Keith pushed up his glasses and crossed his arms. She'd had him so desperate to save her that he'd pushed himself to the limit and almost reaped the consequences. They weren't even engaged yet! He needed to slow things down. "Which is why we confronted each other about things and talked it out. Like reasonable adults."

"You certainly are reasonable, I suppose," Rufus teased. He hesitated a breath and then he took on a serious demeanor. "Also, I'm happy you're not dead. [Void Damage]? Really?"

"Really really." Keith sighed. His arm was barely healed after a high-grade potion last night.

"How will you counter it if she betrays you?"

Keith didn't respond, the thought of Henrietta turning on him was more unbearable than he wanted to admit.

Rufus noticed his difficulty and changed tactics. "Or if she goes catatonic again?"

"If she gets locked up in a dark space, I'm going to find the culprit and rip out their still beating heart—*after* getting her out." He frowned. "If she doesn't kill me in the process. Bringing us back to the point."

"That your princess could easily kill you during a lovers spat?"

Keith sighed. "I'll have to reach out to other enchanters, since there won't be anything useful in Feliwyn's hoard . . . maybe Violet can reach out to her uncle Lorthar in Hemlock Hill? I wouldn't be surprised if the Witch of Winter's End has a spell or two, and I know Slake Drakeford, adventurer extraordinaire has a bunch of weird spell books in his loot collection . . ."

"Don't tell me, tell Scholar Violet. Have her reach out to anyone and everyone if you have to - Just do *something*, or I'm going to continue nagging you until it's done." Rufus put his notepad aside, taking off his reading glasses and placing them on top. Stretching, he said, "Let's go get lunch."

Keith eyed the beastman warily. "But we just started, and we haven't talked about my issues yet."

"Keith, I've known you since you were *five*." Rufus chuckled. "I *know* what your issues are. *You* know what your issues are."

He waved at Keith, sitting there in a defensive position on the edge of the daybed. "Are you ready to talk about them today? How about you get over them right now and go beg your princess to marry you because you lo—"

"Don't say it," Keith interjected. "Not yet . . . I need more time."

"I think you're ready." Rufus chuckled. "But why waste my time when you refuse to accept it? You've already promised to work on things with her. You have a plan: take better care of yourself and stop running away from relationships."

"When have I ever run from a relationship?" Keith protested.

The reply dripped with sarcasm. "Ah, yes. You'd have to actually *allow* one for you to run away from it. My bad."

"I put up with *you*, don't I?" Keith griped.

"As you said; you are a *reasonable* adult." Rufus opened the door to his dungeon office and waved out the king of the Dark Enchanted Forest. "You know when you're doing things that are dangerous. You just don't care. Start caring. If you don't, you'll hurt the people who *do* care."

Keith left Rufus to his own devices after lunch, when his commander general proposed going for a refreshing swim in the moat.

Rufus liked to chase sticks and wrestle monsters as a nice afternoon exercise and was insane. Henrietta was taking some time to herself. Julia and Chloe were lost in each other's company, and he wasn't sure if they even knew he was back yet. So, the Dark Lord grabbed a few cream puffs and sought out a quiet space to think.

After everything that had happened yesterday, Keith couldn't get the image of Henrietta out of his head; from her smiling up at him in that garden to her behavior in the dungeon to just . . . Ria.

And when he thought of their difficulties in the dungeon, that actually made him like her *more*.

The fact that she knew his less-than-ideal traits and *still* wanted to continue the courtship was reassuring. Being the king of a magical realm meant he was under a lot of pressure. He'd had his fair share of marriage offers from many prospective partners around the continent. Few had piqued his interest. Their letters went from boring dowry lists to long pages full of dreams to conquer said continent. Was it too much to imagine that he wanted *more* than world domination? Keith was impressed that he could sustain a single country's mixed populace without civil war—and that by sheer will of paperwork and oppressive strength.

Not his actual Strength, of course; just his level was security enough.

Henrietta enjoyed his company, and her struggles were something he wanted to support her through. Everyone got angry. Everyone lashed out in their own way. Aside from [Void Damage] utterly murdering his ass in a moment of anger, he knew that they both liked to talk things out, so that shouldn't be a routine occurrence.

As for the other stuff . . . Well, he'd just have to let go and let Henrietta in. Maybe.

He finished his cream puff and headed for the library. He had some books to return.

CHAPTER 71

Far, Far Away

Henrietta

When I finished my morning session with Rufus, I felt raw and angry with an overwhelming sense of frustration. At my parents. At my life . . . At myself.

My usual disposition kept my spirits up; I could embrace a well-balanced life juggling parentally enforced naivete with the power to crush skulls in one hand and organize battle formations with the other . . . It was a wonder I'd been able to survive this long. Rufus had given me some book recommendations that might help with that, but most of them weren't in the library at present.

"I'm sure His Viciousness will be done with Ms. Green's *Findings on Childhood Trauma Theory* soon," the librarian, Scholar Violet, assured me. She was a dark-skinned human from North Sumbria who kept her frizzy black hair in a partial updo. I half expected the librarian to be wearing glasses, but instead she had a spyglass hooked to her belt and dangling from a chain.

"Thank you, Violet. I'll just take a look around, then." I nodded, leaving the scholar to her work.

I'd been to the library a handful of times since arriving, mostly when I needed to look up things that came up in the kingdom reports I wanted to research . . . Or checking out their culinary section. As much as I enjoyed the odd story, I preferred baking in my spare time and looking up fun new recipes!

The library was enclosed so as to prevent sunlight from wearing the spines of the books. Floor-to-ceiling bookshelves were set up like the spokes of a wheel, granting the librarian at the center a full view of the room. An aisle wound around the outside, and the outer walls were a collection of books and scrolls and tools for lend, as well as maps and all manner of knickknacks.

Small doors in the alcoves let out into pocket reading rooms overlooking the carnivorous flower garden, with very comfortable daybeds to relax on—the same as in Rufus's office.

The library was in the castle wing between the gardens and the village outside so that anyone could come and enjoy the knowledge it held. There were a few magical stone wyvern golems to deter theft, and their heads followed any who entered with a watchful eye.

I was standing there in front of the Monster-class Anatomy section, reading about the different types of toe bones that each species of dragon had, when a hand holding a book dropped in front of me.

"Violet said you were looking for this?"

Keith was right behind me. I took the book and turned to face him, smiling. He looked a little disheveled; his usual Dark Magician King robes were missing a top button, and the second one from the bottom was gone now, too . . . I pulled my eyes away from his bare chest and straight to his lips, which didn't help. "Thank you."

"It's an interesting read about how your childhood defines you." Keith raised an eyebrow. "I wonder how close we are? Both single children, raised to take over a kingdom someday. Though my mother is dead, and yours is better off—Um, far, far away."

I chuckled. "I am enjoying being far, far away from my parents, so I'll give you that."

"As it is," Keith continued, "we have a lot in common."

I found myself leaning into him and wondered if he was struggling with the same desires I was. I gripped the book tighter.

Keith leaned closer too. We were in plain sight of Violet, and I didn't even care. I just wanted him to kiss me. My cheeks grew hot, and the only thing stopping me from outright grabbing him were the books in my arms.

Before it went any further, however, Keith drew in a deep breath through his nose and rocked back. He asked, "Why don't you read the book and then we can talk about it over tea tomorrow?"

"Sure." A little disappointed but understanding that we were in public view and he was probably uncomfortable, I broached, "How was your time with Rufus?"

"It went well." For some reason, he looked . . . guilty? I eyed him harder, and the tips of his short pointed ears darkened. "We mostly talked about making a plan."

"A plan?"

"Yes." Keith coughed. "A plan."

I ducked around him. "Why don't I check these out"—I lifted up the books—"and you can tell me more about the *plan*?"

Keith followed. "I'd rather hear how your session went? Is there anything I can do to help? Are you . . . ready? For next week's battle? We have, what, six days until St. Veralyn's Day?"

"Hmm," I hummed. But I wouldn't press him on what he'd talked about with Rufus. Just as I didn't want to talk about how much I'd been overcome with emotions that morning, being told that my trauma was probably a tool to control me, and that it was a form of abuse that I should consider unjust instead of normal. Something inside me knew that if Rufus had said this when I'd first arrived here, I wouldn't have really listened.

Being surrounded by nice people . . . Actually, maybe I should change that thought to *being surrounded by normal people* had really opened my eyes to how toxic and corrupt it was back home.

As much as I'd fought to save people in my father's court from his injustices—like that maid I'd rescued the day I left—I had always been blind to the idea of *change*. That was just the way it was . . . and it had never crossed my mind that it could be any other way. My defiance was rebellion, not a desire for *normalcy*.

I stopped in the stacks halfway down the aisle to the checkout desk. "I'm ready for the battle. I'm ready to cut all ties with Drendil, and I'm ready . . ." I stared at Keith, hovering awkwardly close as he absently pushed his glasses back into place after the sudden stop. "I'm ready for more things. *Interesting* things."

Keith jerked and almost knocked off his glasses entirely. He nodded and gave me the most forced smile I'd ever seen. It was conflicted and frustrated and yearning all in one, and I wondered what had changed since yesterday. I was confident that our kiss in Gren's Keep had been magical, and that we were courting—unless this hesitation was being brought on by his meeting with Rufus?

I cursed at the beastman in my heart but smiled back at Keith. "Whenever we are both ready, of course."

"Of course . . ." He hesitated as if he meant to say more, but whatever griffin had caught his tongue made him close up again.

Since he had a tendency to remain silent with his thoughts when he wasn't ready to share them, I let him keep them. For now. I cradled both books in one arm and reached out to take his hand before continuing down the aisle. His palm was sweaty, and he hesitated a second before entangling our fingers together and squeezing my hand like he normally did.

He walked with me to check out the books, still silent.

When we left the library, he turned to me and said, "I forgot something. I have to go."

It was an excuse, I knew. I tried not to worry about him as he walked off at a determined pace.

CHAPTER 72

The Semi-Naked Beastman Lounging on a Daybed in the Dungeon

Keith

"Rufus!" Keith burst in on the semi-naked beastman lounging on a daybed in the dungeon.

Rufus was wearing a red silk robe and some comfy slippers while he drank wine and read one of Her Eminence Feliwyn's sordid romance novels. He looked at Keith over the rim of his tiny reading glasses. "Yes, Your Majesty?"

"Are you day drinking? Never mind, I don't care." There was a moment while Keith tried to find the words to say why he was there. Finally, he settled on, "You were right."

"I know that." Rufus closed his book and sat up. "But it's always nice to hear. What changed in the last hour that made you realize I'm right?"

Keith didn't *want* to say that he'd seen Henrietta in the library and had wanted to push her up against the shelves and kiss her silly. And what was worse . . . she'd looked like she expected him to do just that.

Everything was happening so fast. Too fast. He'd never expected a young, adorable warrior princess who smelled like freshly baked cookies to waltz into his life and then *like* him instead of *murder* him.

All the beautiful women sent his way until this point had secretly aimed a knife at his heart or poisoned his tea. She'd carried him to bed and nursed him back to health herself when he'd gotten injured.

Even though Henrietta Doryn of Drendil *was* like other girls in many ways, including the fact that she technically *had* been sent here to kill him . . . she'd become one of his closest—well, they were more than friends at this point.

Keith sighed.

She was funny and smart and highly skilled, and he had become addicted to her baking. It wasn't that he didn't remember what it was like before she came here two months ago—he didn't *want* to remember.

"I don't know what I'm doing," Keith confessed. "But I'm falling in love with the princess."

"I told you so. Now, tell me about it." The beastman put aside his reading and stood up, motioning Keith to take a seat on the daybed in his place. Rufus somehow managed to look professional as he took up his seat, cross-legged and still in a silk robe. "Are you alright if I use some basic perks to help?"

Keith agreed, and the two settled in for a second session that day. Keith felt the wave of [Calming Effect] wash over him. He didn't fight it, but then, he noticed another spell subtly influencing him. Keith raised an eyebrow at Rufus and accepted the second unknown spell. Honestly, he would trust Rufus with his life on top of his well-being. The man was Keith's most trusted advisor and best friend, even if the beastman *did* have terrible taste in literature.

Suddenly, words came easier, and his thoughts were unbared by anxiety and frustration.

"The princess smells delicious," he heard himself say. "She's so cute that sometimes I just want to ruffle her hair or kiss her. Now, it seems like that's all I want to do." His true feelings spilled out in a jumble and so did his fears. "I'm worried that I'll make a terrible mess and keep crossing the line without her permission."

Rufus raised an eyebrow at that. "You crossed a line?"

"I can't stop touching her." Keith dropped his head into his hands.

"Without permission?" Rufus's voice was harder than he'd ever heard it. But Keith kept going as if something was inspiring him to let it all out.

"I pushed her hair behind her ear," Keith confessed. "And sometimes, I grab her hand before I've asked. And it's becoming harder and harder to resist kissing her after she kissed me in Gren's Keep."

Rufus lifted a hand to cover his face. He looked like he was in pain for some reason. Keith had to wait for the beastman to compose himself.

"Go on."

"I am not ready." Keith lay back on the daybed and threw his hands in the air. "But I spend five minutes in her company, and that's all I can think of. I almost kissed her in the library. We aren't engaged yet, Rufus. This is serious!"

"And how did Henrietta react?"

"I . . ." Keith rubbed the bridge of his nose. "She . . . she told me she's interested in doing more."

"I see." Rufus nodded sagely and leaned forward. "So you've come here to rub it in your best friend's face that you are about to get married and live happily ever after?"

"What? No!" Keith sat up so fast he needed to readjust his glasses. Maybe he should get them refitted with how many times that was happening. "I came here because I needed advice on how to not mess this up!"

"Well, for starters, you could *not* run to me every time you want to kiss your girlfriend," Rufus advised. "If you don't want her to get any weird ideas, you could also just talk to her."

"I do talk to her!" Keith protested. "I told her I like her and I'm interested in a relationship, maybe, and that we could go slowly."

"How slowly?"

Keith looked away and stared hard at a potted plant in the corner of the dungeon cell. Seriously, why did Rufus like living down here so much? "Until we both know what we want?"

"And what do you want? What do you want *her* to want?" Rufus asked.

"To stay." Keith felt a small tightness in his chest and tried to ignore how much saying it cut.

He was the Dark Lord and he locked himself up in his tower and he ruled with an iron fist and he did not need anyone.

He had no family. As much as he knew his friends and subjects liked him, it wasn't the same. Even Her Eminence Feliwyn had always been destined to leave. She had been tasked with training him to become king, and then she was free to go wherever . . . and she did. She flew off the afternoon he turned sixteen and had been napping beside Lake Loria ever since.

"You *are* thinking of marrying her?" Rufus broached. "Or at least settling an engagement?"

"What? Now?" Keith's ears burned. "We've known each other less than two months!"

"So?" Rufus tilted his head. "Marriage is about family. In the beastfolk tribes, you can do whatever you want, whenever you want, with as many partners as you want. We don't discriminate. We just accept who we are, and we are honest about it with our partners. We marry when we find someone we want to marry, no sense beating around the bush."

"I know that already," Keith replied curtly. "So why aren't *you* married yet?"

Rufus looked a little contrite. "You try being the most powerful beastman in the Dark Enchanted Forest. I take one step into Gren's Keep, and I get swarmed with challengers."

"So what are you doing on those week-long getaways, hmm?" Keith pressed. "No romance?"

"Sadly, no." The commander general of the Dark Lord's army smiled broadly. "I took Chloe's advice and got a hobby that wasn't work related."

"What?" Keith realized how much he'd fallen into himself over the last decade that he hadn't bothered to keep up with Rufus outside of their once-a-month sessions or the odd dinner in the dining hall.

"Music," Rufus said the word almost reverently. "I've been traveling the continent listening to famous minstrels, concerts, and plays."

That wasn't what Keith was expecting. "You leave for a week so you can cross the continent just to hear someone sing?"

"Yep." Rufus chuckled. "Sure, I find company sometimes, but there is a lot to learn about being with my kind. I haven't found the right person yet."

Speaking of finding the right person . . . Keith felt guilty how he'd left Ria standing there in a hallway.

"Hey, Rufus?"

"Yes, boss?"

"Do you want to grab a drink at Scowls sometime?" Keith chose the castle tavern where the two used to run off to in their younger years.

"Your treat?"

"My treat."

Keith stood up to leave but paused at the cell door. "What was your new perk?"

"[Honest Heart]. It's not compulsory. It just makes it easier to find the words to express one's inner self. The revelation sent Keith deep into thought. Now, go ask your princess to marry you," Rufus ordered his king. "And talk to her about your feelings!"

"Actually, I don't think I will."

"What, why?!" Rufus was taken aback. "Didn't we just have a moment? We just had a moment! What happened?"

"I *am* going to talk to the princess. And I *am* going to ask her . . . to the Spring Ball." Keith grinned. "I'll propose there. She's her own person, and she might decide to go back to Drendil to clean up after the upcoming battle—or she might not. I don't want to tie her down and make that choice harder."

"You are an idiot," Rufus told him. "But at least you're a *reasonable* idiot. And that would be a perfect time to ask."

"*And*," Keith stressed, "it means we can announce it in front of the council."

"You're going to do it in front of everyone, including her parents?" Rufus let out a laugh. "Not the most romantic, but it will serve them right."

"Now, if you'll excuse me, I have to figure out how to talk to Henrietta without messing things up."

"I still think you should just marry her and be done with it," Rufus called after the Dark Lord, but Keith was already walking out of the dungeon.

CHAPTER 73

You Don't Look Like a Sadistic Freak Bent on Destroying Our Lands

Henrietta

[**Quick Read** cooldown 01:45:13. Current Reading Speed: base 400 words per minute x Intelligence 17 = 6800 words per minute.]

Shortly after Keith left, I went to his office . . . our office to finish up the pile for Requires Review. I was tempted to look through his Requires Response or Requires Immediate Action pile . . . but that would be a bit rude; I wasn't queen of the Dark Enchanted Forest.

Yet.

I told myself not to think of that. My king of the Dark Enchanted Forest seemed like he was having second thoughts, but maybe I just didn't know how this all worked. Maybe he had gotten upset at something else? Maybe he had indigestion? Or bad breath?

Or maybe the kiss had only been good for me?

Thirty minutes passed with me just awkwardly sitting there doing nothing, and then I pulled out and reread the battle plans over again. At some point, a shy lizardkin maid shuffled in.

Winrith was in a bit of a panic.

"Your Viciousnesss!" She stopped short when she saw that it wasn't Keith sitting behind his desk. I was expecting her to continue, but she simply froze. Now that I knew she was undead and I'd spent time with more lizardkin, I could see the subtle tells. Her eyes, when you could see them, glowed green and leaked wisps slightly at the edges. Her pupils were pits of the unnaturally vibrant green as well.

She was a *very* high-level undead.

"He's gone to check something, Winrith," I told her. When she remained in place another minute without saying anything, I offered, "I could take a message? I'm sure he'll be back—"

"Ria!" Keith walked in. I was glad; I thought Winrith was going to faint soon. "I need to talk to you!"

"Keith."

"Your Viciousnesss!"

"Winrith?"

The maid stammered, "I've b-been sssent to t-tell you. The guardsss have captured sssomeone from Drendil!"

"What?" Keith and I said at the exact same time.

"They h-have them in the g-guardhouse by the c-castle g-gate," Winrith managed. Honestly, this was the most I'd ever heard her speak aloud. "What are your ordersss, M-Master?"

Keith and I shared a look and then he said, "Lead the way. Let's see this enemy spy for ourselves."

I could name all of my father's top spies. I knew every knight or combatant in his service who had any skill. I had even memorized the features of all the relevant mercenaries the king of Drendil worked with.

None of them were sitting in the guardhouse drinking tea with Sithli.

"Brownie?!" My best friend's name escaped me. "What are you doing here?"

The bard kicked back from the table, laughing. "It's good to see you too, Henrietta! Or should I say *princess*?"

When the woman stood up, she dwarfed everyone in the room by a head. Her father was a half giant—it's where she got her strong build—and her mother was a priestess, which is where she got her angelic voice. Not that being a priestess gave you an angelic voice. Brownie's mother just happened to have one.

Brownie also got her violent brown curly hair streaked in red from her mother. And when she smiled, she lit up the room with her high Charisma score.

Nobody stopped us as we went in for a hug, though Sithli tensed. I had to be careful of the lyre slung over her shoulder, and she had to be careful to not smother me.

I loved her hugs.

After a strong squeeze, she held me at arm's length to look me over.

"You don't look tortured," the bard stated. She eyed Keith behind me. "And you don't look like a sadistic freak bent on destroying our lands."

"What makes you say that?" Keith's grin was vicious and intimidating.

"Your guards politely escorted me here and served me tea and scones."

Sithli looked affronted. "What else would we do? You hadn't done anything yet."

Presumably, Brownie hadn't set off any of the golems, so she was only there for questioning because of her clothing.

"Did you like the scones?" I cut in. Panlith had used my recipe, so even though I hadn't made them myself today, I still wanted to know Brownie's opinion.

"They were delicious," she grinned at me. "Now, am I to be hauled off and thrown in the dungeon, or are we going to grab some more tea and have a visit?"

"I think you would like the dungeon," I said, poking the woman in the arm. "It has plants and a daybed where you can faint dramatically."

Brownie laughed, full bodied. "I do love being dramatic."

I peeked at Keith. "Is it alright if I show Brownie around?"

"That's fine." He gave me a soft smile, so delicate and endearing I almost needed a daybed myself. "I trust you'll have a lot to catch up on. I'll see you at dinner?" He hesitated a fraction of a second then said, "Your friend is welcome to join us, of course."

"Oh! I'm sorry, this is Bronwynn Lyriel. She's a bard, and my best friend." I blushed a bit, embarrassed that my excitement had overcome my manners. "Brownie, this is King Keith Monfort of Nilheim."

"Actually"—Brownie put her hands on her hips and drew back her shoulders magnificently—"You are looking at Minstrel Bronwynn now."

"You leveled up?!" I couldn't help myself and made a very undignified squealing sound.

"Congratulations, Minstrel Bronwynn." Keith walked over and slowly reached out and put a hand on my shoulder. "You may call me King Keith. I hope you enjoy your stay at our castle." He leaned in close and spoke softly in my ear, "I'll be in the office if you need me. We can talk about our . . . *interests* later. I won't keep you." He took a breath and continued, "but I do feel like putting off important conversations won't get us anywhere."

"Alright." Holding hands was heart-wrenching enough, but this was on a whole new level! I felt my ears heat up, and I resisted the urge to hide my face in my hands. "If it's alright, I can introduce Brownie around and then show her to her room. She does have a room, right?"

"There is a spare room attached to your suite . . . or I could find her one on the main floor?" Keith offered.

"If it's all the same to you," Brownie cut in. "I'd rather stay with Henrietta."

"*Oooooh*, a sleepover!" I thought about fitting in time to chat with Keith and settle in Bronwynn. I turned to the minstrel and asked, "Why don't I have the maids give you a full body bath and massage treatment? I could step out then?"

"Or"—Brownie eyed the two of us—"I could wait right here while you two go talk about whatever it is I'm interrupting? We can do all of that together when you're done. You know I don't care about etiquette. It won't kill me to finish my tea with Sithli. We were talking about that one time I played in Oakley while the stage was on fire."

I put my hand on Keith's and asked Brownie, "Are you sure?"

"Of course I am!" My friend plopped herself back down in her seat and slapped the table. "No sense in putting off for tomorrow what you could talk about today . . . Honestly, I forget half the things I put off for tomorrow. Better to just get it sorted out now." Brownie shooed me and the king of the Dark Enchanted Forest toward the door, then turned to the lizard guard and said, "Now, where was I, Sithli? Ah yes! So this young wizard was eating his lunch at the tavern I was performing at, and he'd never heard the story of Drendil's song 'The Tragedy of Magicians.' Can you imagine? Anyway, there I was . . ."

I loved Brownie; she was a riot, but also one of the most understanding and supportive friends anyone could have.

Keith's hand fell away from my shoulder. He opened the door for us, and we slipped out of the room just as Brownie regaled Sithli with the angry wizard's misplaced [Fireball] hitting the little table she had brought onstage to hold her mug.

CHAPTER 74

Assassin Is a Perfectly Respectable Class Choice

Keith

They could have popped into the next available guards' room, but Keith wanted to talk in a nicer setting. It was only a few minutes' walk to cross the castle courtyard and slip into the garden. When they got to the path, Keith offered Ria his hand, and she took it naturally.

This was also where they'd first really gotten to know each other . . . their first date. He stared around at his godmother's plants, and for the first time in a long time, he didn't feel that lonely comfort in the garden. He had new memories to cherish.

"I know it's been a short time since you came here," Keith started, trying to find the words, "but I don't want you to leave, and until yesterday . . . I didn't believe you would actually stay."

Ria looked like she had something to say, but stopped and waited for him to continue. They stood in front of the Venus lily pond, and Keith lifted her hand.

"I like having you here—I *love* having you here." He sighed and looked Ria in the eyes. "And I know you filled out those immigration papers, but it's more than that. I worry that we will crush your father's army, and you'll need to go back to Drendil and take over the throne. I keep thinking about how undefined our relationship is . . . and how I'm *more* than just interested."

"Really?" She was smiling brilliantly up at Keith.

"Really really." He reached out and pushed her hair behind her ear. "I want to kiss your nose when it scrunches up after I tease you. I want to wrap my arms around you and not worry that I'm going too fast." He paused for a breath. "And I want to think that you'll stay here, with me. After your parents' war, and after the Spring Ball, and after you've explored the entire Dark Enchanted Forest."

"Keith?" She reached out and grabbed onto his robes. "Could you lean down here for a second?"

He did as she asked, and she gently pulled him until their foreheads were touching. Henrietta tilted her chin up and kissed him.

"I'm not going anywhere," she said firmly. "I like it here. I *love* it here . . . and as long as you'll have me, then I'll stay."

The words slipped out. "Forever?"

Henrietta chuckled. "Do you want to marry me? Is that what you're asking?"

"Yes. No. Maybe?" Keith sighed; a small smile tugged at his lip. "I was going to ask you . . . later. I actually brought you here to ask you to the Spring Ball. Officially. How about we start there?"

Henrietta returned the smile. "I would love to go to the ball with you. And won't that just be poetic? The Heroine of Justice sharing her first debutant dance with the Dark Lord . . . Brownie will probably write a song."

"I'll have to brush up on my dancing," Keith said. "Speaking of Minstrel Bronwynn . . . you don't think?"

Henrietta shook her head violently, her poofy brown hair falling in her face again. "No, no, no, she's definitely not a spy. Or an assassin. Probably."

Keith pushed her hair back behind her ear and raised an eyebrow at her.

Henrietta shrugged. "Even if she *was* an Assassin, which is a perfectly respectable class choice, she is not my *father's* assassin."

"Then I won't worry. Or, I *will* worry, but I'll wait to see." Keith stood up straight and straightened his collar. Henrietta had pulled it into disarray earlier with her kiss, and he wanted to look respectable for her friend . . . Was he missing another button?

"So, to be clear." Henrietta grabbed his hand this time. "We're going to the Spring Ball together?"

"Yes."

"And we aren't engaged?"

"*Yet*," Keith stressed. "We aren't engaged *yet*."

"So you turned down my romantic proposal standing in front of your man-eating flower garden? Because you want to ask me yourself?" Henrietta was obviously enjoying teasing him. His blushed all the same.

"That's not—You can ask me again at the Spring Ball?" He gave up any pretense at a surprise.

"No, that's fine." Henrietta squeezed his hand gently. "You can propose next time."

He sighed. "Do you think Minstrel Bronwynn is done with her tale?"

"Bronwynn? Never. She can tell stories for hours. We'll have to go save Sithli ourselves. Not that he'll want saving; her storytelling skills are *amazing*." Henrietta and Keith started walking back to the guardhouse.

Keith stopped them in the courtyard. "Why don't you take Minstrel Bronwynn to settle in, and I'll finish up what's left in the office?"

"I'll see you at supper?" She squeezed his hand once more before letting go and taking a step back.

"See you at supper."

They went their separate ways, and Keith hurried to his office. He needed the distraction. That conversation had gone further than he'd thought . . . and better than he'd hoped.

He was settled in, going over ground reports and merchant complaints, when Chloe burst into his office. Everyone kept working, though his castle administrator team nodded politely at the necromancer.

"You're back!" she accused, hands on her hips.

"So it would seem." Keith just looked at her for a second before going back to signing documents.

"Don't you wanna know what happened?!" She leaned forward, golden hair sweeping over the edge of his desk.

Thankfully, it was a large enough desk that she didn't disturb any papers; not as impressive as his worktable in the inner sanctum, but solid and wide.

"You said *yes*, right?" He casually finished scanning the page he was working on—another report from the Drendil border saying all was quiet, though new supplies had arrived for the troops—and stamped it with his royal seal before moving to the next report.

"You're insufferable," Chloe stated, then she gave him a self-satisfied grin. "And I'll have you know that *she* said yes."

Keith kept down a small smile that played across his lips at the reminder of his own princess. When he was composed, he glanced up at Chloe. "Congratulations. When is the big day?"

"That's why I'm here!" Chloe waved a hand over his paperwork. "When is your stupid war going to be over and done with? I want to start planning our wedding *now*."

"You know as well as I that the Drendil army is set to arrive in a week." Keith pushed up his glasses and eyed his frustrated friend. She was a general in the Dark Army and important to the resurrection of his minions, though she probably wished she could just elope. Her and Julia had been a long time coming. Then he had a nervous thought. "Where *are* you having the wedding?"

Please don't say—

"Here, of course!" Chloe's eyes glazed over as she thought of her future wedding. "We'll hand out invites at the Spring Ball! I expect the entire Continental Council to come! There is that field beside Her Eminence Feliwyn that hasn't moved much the last decade. It'll be perfect to host the three hundred guests—"

"*Three hundred?*" Keith choked. He was about to wage a bloody war beside that field. The cleaning alone was going to be a nightmare, not to mention having to get it ready for a royal wedding.

"Of course. Whose wedding do you think this is?" Chloe smiled smugly.

He certainly wouldn't have chosen it for a venue. Honestly, he bet Ria would prefer a destination wedding somewhere exotic. With a dungeon. And interesting new food. Or perhaps he would hold it at the Hollow. The elves weren't holding true to the treaty as it was, and despite his frustration with the clingy duke's daughter, Henrietta would enjoy the company. He would need to plan accordingly to have his own quality time with his very popular wife . . . as much as the thought of locking her up for a week, alone in a tower somewhere, had tempted him.

Jealousy was praised by dragons, and Keith had been raised by one of the best . . . Still, he'd figure it out.

CHAPTER 75

The Dark Enchanted Forest Had Sturdy Porcelain

Henrietta

Bronwynn was still regaling Sithli with her adventurous trip to the Sunshine Coast in Sumbria—the southern tip of the continent, not the northern independent duchy.

During the revolution twenty years ago, Grand Duke Lysander, the level ninety-one Arcane Sorcerer, had fought against General Mathis, the level seventy-two Sage of Aegis, and cut a canyon through the center of the kingdom. The country had literally been split open north to south by magic. Now, North Sumbria was ruled by Duchess Calisto at the northwestern point, the middle became Servalt under their new king and queen, and the south remained Sumbria.

I came in as Brownie explained the importance of a lady's fichu in Sumbria, and how she had uncovered a noble assassin during her royal performance.

"I'm back," I said simply in a moment Brownie stopped for breath.

She tossed me a big smile. "Let me just finish this. You see, the assassin had seats next to the royal box, and as I was performing 'The Traveler's Anthem,' I saw this man switch to a *purple* fichu scarf!"

"Ssstop, he didn't?!" Sithli was on the edge of his seat, gripping his teacup. I feared for the fine porcelain.

"He did!" Brownie laughed. "Sumptuary laws be damned. Not that I blame him—the royal oppression was what started the wars. I noticed three others in the crowd turn theirs to a purple side and had to leap off the stage while in the middle of the second to last verse. It took everything I had to hit those high notes before tackling the assassin and retrieving his poisoned dagger."

The lizardman shook his head. "Who bothersss with poison nowadaysss? It's nothing a potion can't fix."

"The blade was coated in molten ash vane." Brownie shuddered. "So I'm happy they didn't hit anyone."

I whistled low, and Sithli hissed. Molten ash vane stripped flesh from the bones and boiled the blood, killing from the inside and leaving a molten crusty lump of whatever it touched.

The minstrel nodded, finishing her tale. "And that is how I finished the song standing on a subdued rebel in the royal theater."

"Excellent," Sithli said. He released his grip, and I noted that his cup was in good shape. The Dark Enchanted Forest had sturdy porcelain, it seemed.

"I felt for the assassin." Brownie shook her head sadly. "The royals didn't even ask for an encore. No taste."

"Are you sure it wasn't the fact they were almost attacked . . . ?" I broached.

"With that lot?" She shook her head. "They just sat in their box gossiping the entire performance. Not even a thank you for saving them."

Sithli shook his head. "They sssound as bad as Ssservalt."

"At least the royals in Servalt are good people. It's the merchants you have to look out for." Brownie grimaced. "Whereas nobles in Sumbria and Drendil are dense as a . . . Sorry, Henrietta."

"No offense taken." I shrugged. "I'll be the first to admit our court politics are . . . Well, they aren't very nice."

"I ssshould say," Sithli scoffed. "It's a good thing you're here, Princesss. Can't imagine living with a bunch of mage killers."

"I'm glad to be here, Sithli." I turned to Brownie. "And I'm happy *you're* here. Is now a good time to steal you away?"

"A perfect time." Brownie stood up and stretched. She was large and in charge and lit up the room. "As long as I'm free to go?"

She raised an eyebrow at Sithli, but she was obviously teasing. He flicked his tail excitedly. "Of course, Minstrel Bronwynn, if Princesss Henrietta vouchesss for you, then you are welcome . . . You, uh, you wouldn't happen to be putting on any showsss in the Dark Enchanted Forest during your stay?"

"I'll be hitting up the taverns for gigs as soon as I'm settled." Bronwynn had a twinkle in her eyes that I was all too familiar with. "I might be playing at Scowls if my arrest didn't convince the owner to cancel."

"Tadek would never!" Sithli reassured her.

"Come *on*, Brownie." I smiled as I took her arm and physically dragged her away. I knew my friend, and she needed intervention, or she would burst into a private concert for the lizardman right then and there. "You can sing at people later. I want to show you around!"

"I'll let you know!" Brownie shouted at Sithli as she followed me out the room. We exited into the courtyard, and Brownie gave me a cheeky grin. "You've settled in nicely, *Princess*."

"Yes, yes, I know. I should have told you." I felt a little bad, but secrecy came with being the crown princess. I let go of her arm and clasped my hands in front of me in apology. "I'm sorry, Brownie. Still friends?"

"Of course." Brownie wrapped her arm around me in a bear hug and squeezed. My Constitution saved me. The minstrel let go, and then her face took on a conspiring grin. "Also, I *can't* believe you!"

"What?!"

"Don't you *what* me!" Brownie laughed. "I am a Charisma class. I know passion when I see it, and I saw the way the Dark Lord looked at you. You have him eating out of your hands!"

"That's not true," I countered. "He usually eats my food off a plate."

"You're being deliberately obtuse," Brownie teased. "Tell me you're happy here, and they're treating you well."

"I'm happy here," I repeated, "and they're treating me well."

She nodded, adjusting the instrument on her back, and looked excitedly around. "Good. Now show me around this dark enchanted castle and tell me everything!"

I led her into the castle's main entry, where we stopped so she could admire the dark stone interior. The hall had two sweeping grand staircases, one on either side. Going straight forward between the stairs led to the library and the kingdom's bureaucratic offices, including Keith's office and the staff break room. There were two other hallways in the main entrance, one on either of the side walls where the stairs came down. They led to the servants'—the *minions'* quarters and the laundry.

The kitchen was an outbuilding that connected to the castle main hall from a doorway under the staircase on the left. Another outbuilding, a smithy, could be reached from the doorway under the opposite stair to the left.

Upstairs was reserved for Keith and his generals, Feliwyn's and my rooms, and who knew what else. I hadn't gone exploring much. Though if you walked up the stairs and straight down the hallway, you could go across the landing to Keith's inner sanctum; his Dark Magician tower looked very evil from the outside. It looked pretty evil on the inside, too. He even had a giant snake construct that curled up in the rafters where sunny spots from giant skylights illuminated the room.

I linked arms with the minstrel and immediately took her to the one place I loved most.

CHAPTER 76

Luckily, I Am a Patient Dark Lord

Keith

Keith received a report from the mouse golem he had tailing Minstrel Bronwynn that told him she and Henrietta were still baking in the kitchen.

Well, Henrietta was baking. Bronwynn was telling a story about last winter's hunt for the White Stag in Peldeep, and how many people had fallen over from the spiked apple cider.

Fall was his favorite time of the year, and it was so far away. They needed to finish the war, go to the Spring Ball, and then suffer through summer and the Summer Masquerade before the cold, crisp wind heralded cozy blankets and warm tea and scones.

Of course, he had warm tea and scones all year, but there was something magical about autumn and its aesthetic.

Keith sighed and turned back to his reports.

Suddenly, Rufus burst into his office. Unlike the usual suave grace that carried the man, he was in a sheer panic.

"Why didn't you warn me?" he demanded. There were a lot of people bursting into offices these days; Chloe, Rufus, and even himself. Was this what it was going to be like for the foreseeable future?

"About what?" Keith couldn't even *remember* the last time he'd seen his friend looking so out of sorts.

Rufus stood up straighter and tried to compose himself. "Our new *guest*."

"Minstrel Bronwynn?" Keith stamped a sheet of paper and put it in the to-be-filed pile.

"She's a Minstrel now?" Rufus asked, excitedly, then he paused. "Wait, never mind that. What is she doing in the kitchen?"

"Why are you asking me?" Keith countered. "I think it should be obvious enough: Henrietta is baking her some bimbleberry scones."

Keith hoped they saved him some. He would hate to hold a grudge against Ria's oldest friend.

Rufus ran a hand aggressively down his face. "How long is she going to be here?"

"As long as she wants. Or more, as long as Ria wants." Keith raised an eyebrow at his friend. The man had just told him how much effort he went to in order to see famous bardic performances around the continent. Now that they had one of the most renowned minstrels in their castle, he should have expected this. "I should let you know, Minstrel Bronwynn is joining us for dinner."

Rufus made a choking noise and pulled at the collar of his crisp white shirt. "How do I look?"

Keith raised an eyebrow. "Uncomfortable?"

"You're useless," the commander general told his king. "I'm going to go find Chloe."

Keith waved dismissively at his best friend. "You do that. I'm sure she isn't distracted by her new fiancée. If you're worried, why don't you just skip dinner?"

"Are you mad?" Rufus glared.

Keith eyed Rufus. "Not particularly. Though some might wonder how I wouldn't be mad at your insolence. Luckily, I am a patient Dark Lord."

"I'm leaving," Rufus stated. "I'll see you at dinner."

The beastman stalked out on a mission to go find Chloe and do whatever it was they would do in order to prepare him for eating dinner.

Keith didn't know what the fuss was all about; he didn't care what he looked like in front of Ria . . . The Dark Lord glanced down at his own tunic. The top two buttons were broken, creating a V-neck shape as the fabric dangled open. The bottom button was gone, and another button had snapped in half, hanging on by a thread.

Keith stood up. Maybe he *should* change his clothes before dinner.

"It pleases this Rinrin that Your Viciousness has come to me." The ratkin in charge of Keith's wardrobe looked up from darning his socks.

The Dark Lord didn't visit the laundry room very often, but that was where Rinrin was, and he needed her. The room was filled with giant boilers being stirred by her ratkin family and one stone golem. "Do you need more golems?"

He asked because the idea of a ratkin falling into the boiling waters flashed before his eyes, and he immediately started planning improvements for the laundry operation.

"Yes," Rinrin said simply, nodding. "That would do nicely."

He couldn't imagine how much burn salve and potions the castle approved for the kitchen and laundry room; that wasn't the kind of report that passed his desk. Hopefully, he could move a few heat-resistant golems here, and they would save on pain and suffering—and also the kingdom finances.

He wouldn't dream of suggesting the same to Panlith. The thought of burnt toast at every meal for a week made him shudder. He left the kitchens alone, approved most of whatever they requested, and Keith rejoiced in a variety of sweet, sweet pastries. More, now that Henrietta was making him personal treats.

On the topic of Henrietta . . .

"I'm here because of my buttons. Could you fix them for tonight?" Keith plucked at his clothes.

"His Viciousness *wants* Rinrin to repair his buttons?" Rinrin sniffed, a single tear running down her cheek. "I have dreamed of this day! This Rinrin will do so. Gladly."

Keith eyed the moist-eyed ratkin. "Should I come back—"

"No!" The ratkin jumped to her feet. "Take off your clothes *right now*. I will repair them! Toto, bring the new batch of arachne thread!"

One of the ratkins jumped up and ran for the storage closet.

Keith crossed his arms in front of him defensively. He looked around the room at his minions, who had stopped to watch the exchange. "Now, just wait one second, Rinrin. I'm not going to—"

"I'll fix the buttons!" The ratkin stalked closer to the Dark Lord, a gleam in her eye that had nothing to do with tears.

Keith came to dinner with clothing that had been washed, repaired, and ironed. He pulled awkwardly at the done-up collar that hugged his throat, and hoped that it gave him the proper appearance of a Dark Magician King.

By royal decree, no one would ever speak of what had happened in that laundry room.

CHAPTER 77

It Was Terrible.
It Was Heartbreaking

Henrietta

Bronwynn and I enjoyed a lovely afternoon romping around the Dark Enchanted Forest castle.

I hadn't actually spent much time in the village, though I'd heard wonderful things about Scowls. Brownie let me know that she'd been in the middle of securing a performance spot at the tavern when the guards had arrived and escorted her *politely* away for questioning.

If they honored the agreed-upon times, Brownie would be performing for three nights starting tomorrow.

"So let me get this straight," Brownie said. They were walking toward the main dining hall for dinner. "King Keith takes meals with everyone? Every day?"

"Kinda?" I shrugged. "It's mostly us and the generals, and they come and go depending on work. Rufus and Chloe live in the castle, so they're around. The other generals live in their own territories guarding the four borders, and there are a few nobles, but I don't know much of how it works; it's entirely dependent on the territory?"

The elves, the naga, the lizardkin, and the beastfolk all had some form of hierarchy, but it wasn't consistent across the Dark Enchanted Forest.

"So *I'm* having dinner with the Dark Lord and his generals?" Brownie asked, amused.

"And Countess Julia of North Sumbria. She's Chloe's fiancée," I added. "Oh. And me, of course."

"Well, this will be fun."

I agreed. I enjoyed the nights when everyone had dinner together just as much as I enjoyed those warm nights when Keith and I had our dinner privately in the garden. There hadn't been snow since the winter solstice, and beautiful sunny days with a light breeze had come nice and early this year. Every chance I got, I took my meals outside.

We were the last to arrive for dinner. I nodded at everyone and then showed Brownie where the food was laid out. Each dish was separated, and there were serving utensils so we could pick and choose what we wanted.

I was partial to the slow-roasted honey-glazed duck, whipped garlic spuds, and salad. Panlith made a baby green salad tossed with nuts, unigoat cheese, bimbleberries, and rose petals that I could eat for every meal.

"Wow." Brownie took a deep breath, appreciating the smells. She chose a bowl of wild mushroom soup, citron baked fish, and roasted peppers stuffed with candied nuts and creamed unigoat cheese. She leaned in and whispered in my ear, "Can I come over for dinner every night?"

I smiled up at her. "You are always welcome here and I'm sure Keith wouldn't mind, though I'll double-check with him later."

We approached the table. I took my seat right beside Keith, and there was a spot beside me for Bronwynn. Chloe and Julia were talking amongst themselves but shot us a nod. Rufus was sitting across from me and took one look at us before downing an entire glass of wine.

"Greetings, Minstrel Bronwynn," Keith welcomed with a political air. Turning to me, his face loosened into a smile. "Ria, how was your afternoon?"

"Lovely! I—" It was then that I noticed something that stopped me in my tracks. It was terrible. It was heartbreaking. My eyes glued to Keith's tunic and the atrocious button that was sitting against his throat. I coughed, pretending I needed to clear my throat. "I showed Brownie around the castle."

"It's a very nice castle," Bronwynn added.

Keith's pointed ears flushed pink. From the bard's compliment or because I hadn't stopped glaring at his chest, who was to say. I dragged my gaze back to his face and tried to get myself together. Of course he would repair his clothes sometime . . . I shouldn't be so upset at the loss of a perfectly delightful clavicle.

I needed to calm down.

"Brownie is performing at Scowls. Do you wanna go?" I asked.

Rufus made a strange squeaking noise. We all turned to look at him, and he calmly picked up his empty glass and tried to drink. He put it down a second later and smiled thinly. "Don't mind me."

Keith waved at the man. "Minstrel Bronwynn, have you met General Rufus Triever? He's the highest-ranking member of my army, and a lover of music."

Brownie stared at Rufus for a long second. "Actually, you *do* look familiar. Have you been to my show before?"

"I've had the pleasure," Rufus replied, "of seeing your performance at the Peldeep Festival of Lights. What nights are you going to play at Scowls?"

I whispered to Keith while Brownie told Rufus her schedule. "Is something wrong with Rufus?"

Keith took off his glasses and cleaned them using his robe. "What makes you say that?"

"His tail." The appendage was straight up behind him. The longer he spoke with Bronwynn, the more it started to twitch. "And is he *drunk?*"

Rufus himself was stiff as a board. It was impossible to tell if he was flushed under all that fur, but one of his ears drooped. I had a feeling he might just fall over at any second. He leaned forward as he asked Brownie about her song lineup.

He knew the names of all her songs.

Keith chuckled and shook his head. "I don't think he's drunk. Not with his monstrous Constitution. He'd have to down a few barrels at least."

"If you say so . . ."

Brownie laughed. "If *this* is what's for dinner, I'd be *happy* to perform at the castle anytime. If you have any requests, just let me know."

"Truly?" Rufus asked.

"Hey, watch the tail, Rufus!" Chloe chided.

The beastman curled his suddenly violent tail in his lap and held it there, looking sheepish.

Julia laughed. "If there's going to be a performance, then count me in. You rarely make it all the way up to North Sumbria, and I'll have something to talk about at the Spring Ball."

"I thought you'd be talking about our wedding?" Chloe piped in.

"I will. But I am a politician's daughter, and that means I need more than five talking points for every event." Julia shrugged. "So far I'll have the war, our wedding, Dark Magician Keith falling in love with the heroine"—Keith made a choking sound at that—"and a private dinner with the bard herself, Minstrel Bronwynn. I'm one gossip short on spilling the tea, but I'm sure *something* will pop up."

Brownie bowed slightly at Julia. "It has been an honor."

Ria tugged at his sleeve. "Would you like to go together?"

"Tomorrow evening?" Keith nodded his agreement. "How about we let everyone in the castle go early? Scowls could open the patio to accommodate the rush."

Rufus breathed a shallow, "Yes!" under his breath. He was gripping his tail really hard, and I hoped he had a healing potion on him for the bruises he was giving himself.

"And feel free to put in a good word with the duchess"—Brownie winked at Julia—"I'd be happy to do a show for the Spring Ball if there's time."

"My mother would *love* that."

Brownie's eyes swept over everyone at the table and finally landed on me. I'd been enjoying watching the conversation and eating my duck.

I patted my lips clean and gave her a winning smile. "Looks like you'll be playing every evening for the rest of your stay, so we'd better have a fun sleepover tonight. I've never had anything like this before, so we'll make it extra special! I've already asked the lizardkin maids to prepare a relaxing massage, and I've sent up the rest of my baking to snack on while we chat."

"That sounds wonderful." Brownie sighed. The minstrel's eyes swept over everyone at the table and then all of a sudden, her demeanor changed. She stood up, and I felt Keith tense beside me. "Alright, I've seen enough."

There was a strange confusion that settled over the dinner table as everyone stared at Minstrel Bronwynn. She stared back.

"I'm convinced." She looked at me.

I replied, "Convinced of what?"

"That you aren't a bunch of bloodthirsty demons who've captured our princess and plan on destroying Drendil," Brownie said. Julia coughed, laughing into her hand. Chloe shrugged, and Keith relaxed beside me.

Rufus was the first to reply. Hastily at that. "You can be reassured, Minstrel Bronwynn. Henrietta is better off without Drendil, and none of us have the time or care to conquer it."

"He's right, Brownie." I pulled her sleeve gently. "The only thing we've been planning is defense."

"Which is *why*," Brownie stated, "I'm here to tell you that Drendil is launching a surprise attack."

Everyone at the table stood up. Keith demanded, "When?"

"They've already crossed the border."

CHAPTER 78

I Guess There's No Time for a Manicure

Keith

"They are attacking from the east." Bronwynn told everyone at the table.

Keith's thoughts raced, immediately moving armies in his mind's eye. "From Servalt?" he asked, frowning. "The king and I have a treaty."

Bronwynn shrugged. "One of their merchant guilds smuggled a hundred Drendil soldiers on ships they sailed up the coast. Soldiers all with Assassin-class skills. They have already entered the forest, since the automata were thin along the border crossing. They're waiting for Knight Commander Havork to give the signal." She glanced at Henrietta. "They'll be launching a pincer attack as early as tomorrow, after the regular army marches here from the south."

"I guess there's no time for a manicure, then?" Ria joked.

"How do you know this?" Chloe demanded. She stood up and placed one hand on Julia's shoulder for support. "How do we know you're not here to deceive us?"

Before Bronwynn could say anything, Rufus cut in, "Minstrel Bronwynn is speaking the truth."

Nobody argued that. Rufus had an incredibly useful skill that allowed him to discern lies; another reason why he was Keith's right-hand general.

"Does it really matter?" Keith added. "Any one of us could crush the assassins or the army."

"He has a point, love." Julia reached up and squeezed Chloe's hand. "Drendil had Sir Havork and the Heroine of Justice as their only level sixty adventurers. And now Henrietta is on our side."

"We were letting the Dark Army fight because they really wanted to, and we were hoping to keep down the bloodshed with strategic battle plans allowing Drendil time to retrieve the fallen," Ria piped up beside Keith. "Though I'm not sure that'll be possible with a group of assassins."

"The assassins were masquerading as a merchant caravan when they crossed the border. I only came here to check if the rumors were true." Bronwynn shot a look between Ria and Keith, then she sat back down. "And I'm happy I did."

Keith's voice was low when he said, "Thank you, Minstrel Bronwynn, for letting us know."

Chloe let out a huff, but since she was the only one left standing, she promptly sat down as well. She crossed her arms and pouted. "*If* it is as Minstrel Bronwynn reports, then one of us will have to head out to defend the eastern wood."

"Why not the General of the East?" Ria asked. "I thought there were generals for each part of the forest, and Rufus guarding the castle?"

Her question was met with an awkward silence.

"I guess we *could* let Knolith know . . ." Keith mumbled, though he knew it wasn't really a viable option.

"I wouldn't," Chloe said. "He'd never let us hear the end of it."

Rufus tapped the table with his claw. He explained to the princess, "Knolith is almost finished closed-door cultivation of the [Ten Thousand Star Arts] after *finally* finding the [Heavenly Purple Grade Frost Grass]—"

"Whatever *that* means," Chloe grumbled.

"—and expressly requested that he be *left alone* until the summer solstice," Rufus finished. "The lizardkin general is very hot-tempered and would probably freeze the Drendil army into statues and shatter those statues into a pile of shaved ice. They would be *very* difficult to put back together again . . ."

"I mentioned him because an assassin might wake him up as they come through the eastern forests, and the only thing worse than *me* disturbing him would be Drendil disturbing him . . ." Keith rubbed the bridge of his nose, exhausted at the idea of the amount of paperwork that would cause.

"Want me to deal with them?" Henrietta put up her hand. "I have most of the Drendil spies memorized . . . which reminds me, don't you still have some assassins locked up?"

Keith shook his head. He didn't think it was a good idea and tried to dissuade her. "One, are you *sure* you want to face off against a bunch of Assassin-class fighters in a part of the forest you've never been to?"

"That . . . is a good question." Ria *had* faced off against the griffin egg thieves in the east, but that wasn't exactly a *full* tour of the Dark Enchanted Forest's eastern wood. And the class came with a lot of annoying skills.

"And two," Keith continued, "the assassins I captured aren't from Drendil."

"What?"

Keith shrugged. "I don't know where they are from *yet*, but it's not Drendil."

The room turned as one to Minstrel Bronwynn, who was happily sampling a spoonful of mushroom broth. It was her turn to ask, "What? I just boated up with everyone, since the border was closed. Do you think I know *everything*?"

"But *do* you?" Ria asked.

Bronwynn gave her a playfully violent grin. "I know there were forty-seven people of various Assassin based classes, from Rogue to Blood Mage, who were on the ship when I boarded. We picked up another sixty-one between Sumbria and Servalt."

Keith raised an eyebrow as she continued.

"I'd assume the first set were from Peldeep, since that was the port before mine. The rest were Gloria's guild members.

That woman loves to find ways around places like the Dark Enchanted Forest. I wouldn't be surprised if she had an entire collection of assassins leveled up special for each kingdom."

Bronwynn spooned another spoonful of soup and made appreciative noises.

Chloe shot a look at Rufus, and he shrugged. "She's still telling the truth. Or what she believes to be the truth."

"That's a handy skill." Bronwynn admired the beastman, and his tail started wagging gently before Rufus got it under control.

"So then, *who* is going to head off the army traveling up the eastern side?" Chloe demanded.

"I have an idea." Ria put up her hand again. She turned to Keith. "You know, *we* never got a chance to finish our date . . ."

Keith thought it over and couldn't help himself. His lips twitched into a half smile. "A hundred specialized assassins from around the continent *does* sound like an interesting evening."

"You're both crazy." Chloe glared at us. "Come on, Julia, let's go back to b— *upstairs.* I need a relaxing evening if I'm going to be out resurrecting everyone tomorrow."

Julia excused herself and trailed after her riled-up fiancée. Ria said goodnight to Keith and Rufus and dragged Minstrel Bronwynn up to her rooms.

Keith was left listening to Rufus freak out about how amazing Minstrel Bronwynn was, but he was too busy thinking about his date with Henrietta to mind.

He'd have to stay up late to catch up on paperwork and the projects he was tinkering with . . .

CHAPTER 79

I Thought I Was the Weird One!

Henrietta

"Wow, is this really where you live?" Bronwynn spun around my parlor.

The comfy fainting couch with lush pillows and a tea table covered in a pile of cookbooks were set in front of the warmth of a crackling hearth. It was a beautiful spring day, and the freshly cut flowers that covered the room made everything cheerier.

The walls were covered in bookshelves and assorted dark portraits and paraphernalia. My favorite was a collection of crystal mushrooms growing on the fireplace mantel. In the evening, they cast glittering orange-and-white lights on the ceiling as they caught and reflected the fire's glow. The nights were still cold, usually accompanied by rain and the odd windstorm.

Everything was a reminder that I was staying in the rooms of the former queen of the Dark Enchanted Forest, though I liked to think I was making the room my own. Even if I barely used a quarter of the space.

Yes, the place was that big. I had only ever peeked into the adjoining spare room where Brownie would be sleeping, but I figured it was about the size of the minstrel's lodgings back in Drendil.

"It's been my home since I arrived." I kicked off my boots and slipped into a pair of comfy floofpoof-shaped slippers. It was sweet of the maids to leave Brownie a pair of her own; they were wolf shaped.

"I repeat, wow." The minstrel collapsed on the couch. Relief washed over the woman, and she sighed. "Today has been *a day.* One I was *not* expecting to end like this."

"Oh?" I rang a little bell that would let Tulith know I wanted to see her. The lizardkin maid knew my plans for the evening and would be joining us shortly with after-dinner treats, followed by a two-person bubble bath and massage in my bathing room. "You weren't expecting dinner with the Dark Lord and his generals?"

"Ha! No, I was not." Brownie chuckled. "I was hoping to find you well and whole. Worst-case scenario, I'd get you out; best case . . . Actually, this *is* the best case."

"I certainly think so." I joined her, kicking my slippers up on the low tea table. Very improper and unprincesslike; my mother would've had conniptions.

Brownie sat up and gave me a *look*. "Is *everyone* in the Dark Enchanted Forest this nice?"

"Yes! *Finally!* I thought I was the weird one!" Something inside me broke open with all that I'd been holding back. "It's absolutely unrealistic. Everyone, and I mean *everyone*, has access to potions and healers and help whenever they need it. People are treated with kindness, and everyone gets to *be* people, from monsters to humans to mixed races. And no one cares—Alright, I think the elves care? But I haven't been there yet. Oh, but they do have . . . *different* ideas about the undead, and they consider ruthlessness a virtue. Though, come to think of it, so did mother and father . . ."

"Well then, I'm not surprised you decided to stay. And that certainly explains why they seem to like you." Brownie nodded. "I hope the invasion doesn't succeed and you *get* to stay."

All I could do was shrug. "My parents have made it clear they want me dead. Perma-dead. So the only way I'm going home is in a casket."

Our discussion was interrupted by a group of castle maids come to lavish us with tenderness and care. Brownie and I went to bed ready for the next morning.

Of course, we weren't *all* ready for the next morning.

Brownie and I went to the breakfast parlor to grab breakfast while Rufus paced outside. I wondered if he was waiting for someone specifically but decided to pay it no mind. Shortly thereafter, Keith and Rufus entered together.

The Dark Lord had dark bags under his bloodshot eyes and headed straight for the strongest Peldeep Breakfast Tea. I noticed he still had all his accursed buttons.

"Don't look at me like that, Ria," he murmured, taking an appreciative sip of tea. "I don't have [Mana Burn]. I just wake up like this."

"I know that!" I dragged my eyes away from his perfectly collared tunic and waved my hands in front of my face. "I didn't mean to look worried."

"Are they always like this?" Bronwynn asked Rufus as he took a seat across from her. I resisted the urge to kick her under the table.

"Yes." The beastman smiled at Brownie. "How did you sleep?"

She replied, "Wonderfully, thank you. This is one of the best castles I've stayed at. Anytime you want to hire me for a show, I'd be happy to perform for the Dark Horde."

"That reminds me," Keith interjected, "you're still performing at Scowls tonight?"

"Yes, I'll be sad to miss you."

I tilted my head to the side, questioning, "Why would we miss it?"

"Aren't you hunting down assassins?" Bronwynn laughed. "There are a hundred closing in on us from the east, and at least five hundred Drendil soldiers attacking from the south . . ."

Rufus scoffed. "Wait. Are they sending less than a thousand? Maybe the regular army can handle everything . . ."

"I'm sure we can finish things up before dinner," I said, eating the last of my breakfast. Keith was right behind me. I made a fist and cracked my knuckles unbecomingly. "My [Sword Aura] skill should have them hunted down in no time."

"That reminds me." Keith's eyes glazed over as he pulled up his character sheet and notification tab. He concentrated long and hard until I suddenly had a system prompt.

Quest Offered

Hunt down and stop the Assassins who've breached the Eastern
Border. [0/108]
Reward: 1080 EXP

I accepted the quest. Bronwynn was happily eating her food, but Rufus looked like he'd also gotten a prompt. He choked on his tea when he read it, and I had to wonder what quest Keith had sent his way.

It would be rude to ask, so instead I said, "I'm almost ready to head out. Is there anything you need, Keith?"

"I need to stop taking my wings off in weird places," the Dark Lord joked. I blushed a bit. I suppose I *might* hold some responsibility, as I'd forgotten to grab his wings when I'd carried him off to bed. The Pounce Protectorate were going to drop them off as they did their rounds, but that might be a few more days yet.

"A leisurely stroll up the Great Road then? Or a cart pulled by alligator-dogs?" I offered. I thanked my luck that I had never seen a normal horse in the Dark Enchanted Forest. On that note, I should tell Keith about my allergy when we were alone.

I was about to suggest carrying him the whole way when Gimtak materialized in the room with us. A small popping sound and a slight wave of air hit everyone around as the imp suddenly took up space flying over the kitchen table.

"Your Viciousness!" The imp was in a panic. "Your Viciousness, your golems have set off the alarm!"

"Report!" Keith stood up, the full weight of his office suddenly bearing down on us as he *became* the Dark Lord.

"Drendil's army is marching from the south," Gimtak announced. Keith and I shared a look. The early attack was as Brownie had warned. We were not expecting Gimtak to continue, however. "And there's word from Kith Bog, my liege. It's on *fire*."

CHAPTER 80

Desperate Times Call for a Desperate Dark Lord

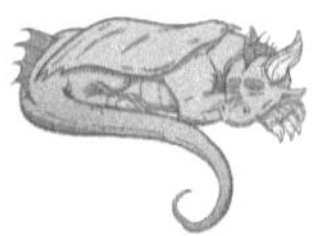

Keith

There were three lines of defense between Gerda's bridge and the castle, and no added difficulty from an early attack. They were ready if someone attacked today, tomorrow, or any day between now and when Keith felt he could disband the units stationed there.

As such, Henrietta and Keith left for the lizardkin village with Sithli, who'd run into the room seconds later in a full panic as news spread around the castle.

It only took them a few minutes to reach Kith Bog thanks to Gimtak's [Portal] skill.

It wasn't something Keith used very often, as the portal was Gimtak shaped and it came up to just above his knees. But desperate times called for a desperate Dark Lord crawling in front of Henrietta. Through the portal. To Kith Bog.

Keith arrived first, appearing beside the bog-beast stables. The golem that usually lived half sunken in the mud and grass there was the one who had set off alarms back at the palace.

It was not where he had left it.

The floating wooden plank streets were too damp to burn properly, but a few houses were ablaze, their thatch roofs alight and smoke billowing. Keith first ensured there were no enemies nearby.

Henrietta appeared next and stood beside him, her gaze sweeping over the village.

Sithli bolted for his home on the other side of the village.

As planned, Gimtak teleported back to the castle. They were expecting a pincer attack from Drendil's army, and Gimtak could keep them updated.

There were a few lizardkin using perks to spray water, and others carrying buckets in a line. Many had sunk into the bog with the golem to protect them and were watching with bright eyes from afar. The golem stood with them, a giant protector for those who needed it.

"My [Sword Aura] says there aren't any enemies nearby," Henrietta told him, grinding her teeth. "We can focus on putting out the fires."

Her [Quick Step] activated, and she was off. As he prepared water-based spells, Henrietta took her sword and cut a wave that arched over a house, putting out most of the flames.

"By the Great Wyrm Who Gifts Water to the World, [Rainfall]." Keith raised both arms and channeled mana into his spell.

[You have attempted to use the High Draconic Spell: **Rainfall**.]
[You have a 72% chance of success with a +2.5% modifier from
Skill: **Magic (Level 5)**.]
[You have succeeded. **Rainfall** duration = 85 minutes]

A dark haze of clouds gathered around his hands and swirled into the air. The sky rumbled with thunder, and a drizzle of rain turned into a sprinkling which turned into sheets. Cheers were muffled by the heavy deluge, but Keith sighed in relief when the fires faded out. They could have been magical flames, which would have been that much worse.

They were lucky that it was spring and the bog was full, heavy with melted winter snow. He still took careful consideration and checked the bottom of the bog over for burgeoning flames. All it took was an ember in the mulch to burn toxic fumes and deep flames.

"By the Great Wyrm Who Knows Each Primal Force, [Sense Elements]."

[You have attempted to use the Low Draconic Spell: **Sense Ele-
ments**. You have succeeded.]

He sighed when he found nothing but earth and wood.

"Thank you, my king. I shall report." A heavily pregnant lizardkin woman walked up to him. She bowed. "Two dayssss ago, our home moved to the eastern sssside of the Great Road."

She pointed behind Keith, where he saw the telltale cobblestone in the distance. His connection to the forest was tied to his Dark Magician King title. Using the [Mind Map] perk, Keith could sense the movement of the Dark Enchanted Forest. It wasn't strong, as he'd rarely cared to cultivate or use the ability.

From what he could sense, the village had moved from just east of Lake Loria, with a path connecting close to Gerda's bridge—where he knew it had been for most of the year—to halfway between the Servalt border and the Nilheim castle.

"Lesss than an hour ago, tensss of flaming arrowsss shot at us from the road," she continued. "We initiated evacuation immediately. No one was killed, though we've lost a quarter of the village'sss infrastructure."

"I see." Keith nodded; he took off his glasses and wiped water from the lens. "Have a full report on my desk tomorrow at the latest."

He resettled his glasses and pulled a bag of five thousand gold pieces from his storage unit. "And use this to replace everything you can. Kith Bog will be exempt from one year's tax, and I should have a hundred able bodies at Kith Bog by week's end."

"Milith!" Sithli ran up to them and wrapped his arms around the pregnant woman. After carefully examining her to see if she was alright, the lizardkin turned to Keith. "Permission to ssstay and help clean up, Your Viciousnesss?"

"Permission granted."

Henrietta rejoined him then. She greeted Milith as well, reassured that the lizardkin was safe.

If Keith recalled correctly, Henrietta had visited Kith Bog that first week after moving into the castle. She had already made friends.

Ria's clothes were soaked, and her fluffy hair lay flat. Her bangs caught water droplets and dripped rain down her cheeks.

"We have to go after the ones who've done this!" his princess said with a passion and anger he'd never seen before.

"We will. Or we'll see them when they reach the castle," he told her.

She shook her head. "I want to find them *before* they reach the castle."

Keith nodded. Gimtak hadn't sent word, so he assumed the band of assassins were still in the forest. "Run or fly?"

"Fly."

Keith regretted leaving behind his construct wings in Gren's Keep. They were being transported to him by the army and would arrive in their own time. In the meantime, he had to fly the old-fashioned way.

He popped a mana potion to recover from the [Rainfall] spell . . . just in case. He could learn from his mistakes.

Keith and Henrietta made their way to the Great Road nearby. It was out of range of Keith's [Rainfall] spell and thus clear of the downpour. He picked up Henrietta and activated his draconic [Flight] spell with no difficulty.

They found the first shoe within minutes. It was sitting beside the road, close to a holly bush. Keith sensed that the holly bush was *extremely* pleased with itself. The Dark Enchanted Forest didn't *like* fire. It was sensitive to the smog, and any controlled burning was managed very delicately by the elves. Keith couldn't imagine it took kindly to invaders lighting its home on fire without permission.

"My quest updated," Ria let him know. "There are four less assassins to defeat."

Keith continued to concentrate on flying. "Too bad; that's four less opportunities to gain experience."

They were almost to the castle when Henrietta let him know that she'd detected enemies. By that point, there were only seventy-five of the original hundred and eight targets.

The more fool they were for traveling in the forest beside the Great Road instead of on its much safer cobblestone path. It was normal, of course, for Rogue types to hide in the bushes . . . but not when the bushes could eat you.

Keith noted the assassins had returned en masse to the Great Road. It'd only taken losing thirty or so people.

Henrietta called out, her voice enhanced by some skill or perk to resound around the forest, "Surrender peacefully, or on my name, Princess Henrietta Doryn of Drendil, I shall *end* thee."

And then things got interesting.

CHAPTER 81

Veralyn's Enchanted Restraint Manacles

Henrietta

[You have attempted to use the Perk **Quick Step**. You have succeeded.]
[You have attempted to use the Perk: **Quick Draw**. You have succeeded.]

I let go of Keith, dropping twenty feet to the earth below. I landed kneeling on one knee between the assassins and the road to the castle.

"It's the target!" a beastman with drooping dog ears and a bushy moustache cried out, pointing at me. "Get her!"

I drew Jacqueline from her sheath in the blink of an eye as I stood. A knife ricocheted off my blade, falling to the side.

[You have attempted to use the Perk: **Force Thrust**. You have succeeded.]

The assassin who'd attacked me was impaled in her right shoulder, and I swung her in the way of four blades that were thrown my way. Two short swords were lunged toward my legs, but I jumped in the air and kicked the assassin off my blade, sending her tumbling through a line of attackers. One arrow nicked my sleeve as I twisted in the air.

[You have attempted to use the Perk: **Multitask**. You have succeeded.]

My mind suddenly had no difficulty compartmentalizing the groups of assassins attacking me. Jacqueline sang in my hand as I let myself go and let my senses keep me on my feet. I had little opportunity to check on Keith, but I wasn't worried about him.

He fought off assassins more often than I did.

My abilities kept me from being overrun and stabbed to death. [Force Thrust] had a pushback effect that I utilized when it was available again, and my Strength stat alone let me knock back anyone caught by my strike.

Every chance I got, I sent assassins flying into the woods. Only one in four came back. Seventy-five became sixty, which became fifty-two and then thirty-nine. At that point, I had to use [Resist Poison], because an acrobatic masked assailant had flipped behind me, diverting my focus.

I could only [Multitask] to defeat attackers I could see. It cost me a split second, granting a window for a poisoned spear to stab into my left leg.

I was used to losing limbs from my earlier dungeon delves, so a mere stab wound was but a painful annoyance. The spearman, a half elf, broke out into a self-satisfied grin that shifted to horror when Jacqueline crit [Void Damage] in his chest.

There wasn't much left of the assassins on that side of the battle . . . Actually, Keith had managed to subdue and chain up the few who remained standing.

He raised an eyebrow my way. "You know, Ria, it's hard to question them if there isn't anything left. It's a lot of extra work putting the pieces back together. It's only good manners to [Revive] them and send them back to . . ." Keith lifted and shook one of the assassins, a partially transformed wolfman. "Who is your guild leader?"

"We'll never say!" The assassin tried to spit on Keith, but the Dark Lord was holding him aloft and simply turned the beastman to his neighbor to take the spittle.

"So I knock you all out and send half of you back to Gloria Welns and the other half to Derek Stannard with a letter demanding an explanation for why they've sent assassins after me and broken our little agreement," Keith told the bunch.

"Jokes on you, we—" a sneering voice jeered from one of the tied-up members before his neighbor silenced him with an elbow to the solar plexus.

"What?" Keith crossed his arms and pressured them with his kingliness aura. I really needed to ask him if it was an actual ability so I could learn the actual name.

"He means that it wouldn't matter because you aren't their target," I guessed. "I am."

Keith dropped the assassin he was holding. The man grunted as he hit the ground next to his fellows. "Still! How are so many assassins getting into my kingdom? I don't see anything that's letting you bypass my golems' spells! You should have activated *something* when you snuck into Nilheim." It was obvious Keith was tired of his well-crafted peace being disturbed. "And why would you light Kith Bog on fire—"

"I mean, it's an easy target," I pointed out. "And on the way."

"—and while being so terribly organized at that," Keith finished, frowning. "Unless . . ."

"Distraction tactic?" I offered. "But why?"

"They wanted more of us out of the castle?" Keith reasoned. "To thin out our defensive ranks?"

"To help the Drendil army or assassins get at me?" I speculated.

"Or both." Keith sighed.

I stared at the assassins, many of which were struggling against their bonds. A few were stealthily trying to pick the locks on their manacles. Keith seemed unconcerned.

"What did you use to catch them?" I asked, intrigued.

"Something they won't be able to break free of: Veralyn's Enchanted Restraint Manacles. They're based off the ones used to hold Sir George during his trials. They are a work of art, if I do say so myself. I couldn't break free with my magic, and I don't think even you could break them with your Strength stat."

I eyed the manacles closer. "I'd love to try! You should lock me in them sometime!"

Keith choked on air.

Just then, backup arrived, a golem three times the size of its master walking out of the woods. It was reptilian in nature, as were many of his larger constructs, but its base shape was humanoid. Behind it, a platoon of some thirty lizardkin and naga soldiers marched or slithered up the road from the direction of the castle.

"Lieutenant Franni Bertand reporting for duty, Your Viciousnesss." A lizardkin woman with purple-tipped scales and short red hair stepped forward. "What are your ordersss?"

Keith tossed a set of keys at the woman. "Gather up those who can be put back together again, wake them up, and send them to the Assassination Embassy in Peldeep. These"—he waved over the awake and alive few—"can go to Gloria Welns in Servalt."

"Is that—" Henrietta started but didn't finish. Keith turned his attention her way, waiting for her to continue. She took a deep breath. "Is that wise? Sending them to Servalt?"

"Servalt does have many problems, corruption being one of them. But Gloria isn't someone who would break a treaty. I'll be sending someone to have a talk with her when this is all said and done. In the meantime, she'll be pleased with my gift." Keith waved at the assassins. "Any she doesn't keep will be used to barter back those who I've sent to Peldeep. And hopefully distract both guilds long enough to keep them out of trouble."

"Yes, Your Viciousnesss. Right away, Your Viciousnesss." Lieutenant Bertand carefully stuck the key in her pocket and turned to her soldiers, barking orders.

Keith faced Henrietta. "I think it's time to see what damage Drendil's army has managed to inflict on our forces."

Ria smiled a slow, sinister smile, adorable on her delightful person. "And if my plan worked."

CHAPTER 82

She'd Magically Befriended All the Minions

Keith

Keith and Henrietta made it back to the castle in good time. They'd expected to find a flurry of activity . . . but instead, they found soldiers kicking their feet outside the walls and milling about on the road.

Everyone stood straighter and tried to appear at the ready when Keith passed by, but all in all, everyone looked bored.

It wasn't much better inside.

"No new reports yet," Rufus told Keith. The beastman general was standing in the castle courtyard cooling his heels.

"No fighting? What's happening with the defense? Drendil should have attacked around the same time I left. Fill me in from there," Keith prompted.

Rufus shook his head. "I meant there isn't anything new to report since you left."

Henrietta broke in. "Then what is the Drendil army doing? Are they just waiting to attack?"

Rufus's response was unexpected. "That's the thing. We don't *know*."

"What do you mean, you don't know?" Keith demanded. "Is everyone dead?"

Rufus shook his head. "No, the front line against Drendil is sitting tight. They've just not actually *seen* Drendil's army. We're all just . . . waiting."

"Give me a second. I should have just done this in the first place." Keith opened up his [Mind Map], showing where his constructs were. He selected a mouse that was supposed to be following the army. It was rubbing its face in a field by Lake Loria, far south of the first line of defense. "Foolish of me to expect any competency from Drendil."

From what he could see, they were in the Dark Enchanted Forest. Just, stopped. All along the road, soldiers dressed in Drendil attire sat or stood. Some were arguing. Some were yelling. Some had already been dragged off and deposited back at the border.

Keith popped out of the mouse golem and back to himself.

"Let's go see what's happening."

Henrietta and Keith drank a few potions, grabbed a snack, and took a bathroom break before they left. Ria came back with a clean outfit. She'd changed into a loose white tunic and dark-green vest, with pants and shin-high black boots. Her hair was pulled back into a poofy bun at the nape of her neck.

"Ready?" Keith asked, reaching out a hand to the princess.

Ria nodded and let Keith pick her up by scooping one arm under her thighs. Her arms wrapped around his neck and plucked at his tunic. "You know, I could get used to flying like this."

Keith swallowed nervously, thankful that his tunic had survived the fight that morning with all his buttons still intact. "I'll see if I can't take us flying sometimes. By the Great Wyrm Who Breathes Air into the Sky, [Flight]."

They rose into the air, traveling south. The high-level spell had taken a good chunk of his mana an hour later when they reached Chloe and Julia at the line of defense closest to the castle.

Henrietta hopped down and went forward to greet the couple while Keith used the opportunity to replenish his mana with a potion.

"I would have expected you to be at the front line?" Ria told Chloe. "To deal with the recovery right away."

The necromancer flicked her long blonde hair behind her. "That's what my new team was trained for. The healers need the experience. If they can't do it themselves, then I'll have to step in, but in the meantime, we'll stay back. I was honestly expecting a message by now . . ."

"Lieutenant Patina is in charge of the first line." Julia chuckled. "That woman can strip the skin from your bones with her voice. She'll have Knight Commander Havork begging for mercy."

"I don't know," Henrietta countered. "I've fought with Sir Havork since I was a child; he's stronger than he looks. He's not as strong as I am, but it's very close. I haven't been able to beat him in a fair fight, even after I passed his level."

"Really?" Chloe raised an eyebrow, but still looked unconcerned. Keith wondered what manner of class could defeat a Void-damage user. Maybe he'd ask Sir Havork. For reasons.

Even if he said no, there wasn't anything stopping one of Keith's constructs from following the human around and learning a thing or two.

"He's much more experienced," Ria explained. "It's like he knows all my moves before I make them. I'm technically faster than he is, but I can barely land a hit. And when I *do*, he usually blocks it with his [Absolute Shield] perk."

Ah, that might have answered his question already. Still, he'd have the general followed back to the border.

"You haven't received a message," Keith interjected, addressing something Chloe had said earlier, "because last we heard, the Drendil army hasn't even *reached* Lieutenant Patina."

"They haven't reached the lake?" Julia frowned. "I know they're a big army, but even that's slow."

"I bet Godmother woke up and ate them," Chloe said. Keith knew she wasn't being serious. If Feliwyn *had* woken up, they'd have seen the smoke from here.

That dragon was *not* a morning person. Even if "morning" was midafternoon on a warm spring day.

"How big?" Ria asked.

"Only about five hundred strong," Keith answered. He'd had someone fill him in on their break. "There are more, but anyone under level fifteen is trailing behind as baggage or already dropped off at the border."

"Or dead," Chloe added. "I bet the forest ate anyone who wandered off. It's not kind to those it sees as an enemy."

Henrietta turned to Keith. "This has come up a lot, and my elf friend Amy mentioned it, but is the *whole forest* just one entity?"

"Yes."

"No."

Keith glared at his necromancer. "The land is entirely under the control of the Hollow Tree. We both know that," he said.

"But there are treants and other plant creatures with free will who are a part of the forest," Chloe argued. "The rivers and lakes aren't controlled, and the Pixie Prim have their own gardens that use spatial magic to keep their flowers free of its influence."

"Yes, but *that bush*"—Keith pointed at an elderberry bush on the side of the road; it wriggled a bit at his attention—"is a part of the whole forest. Every plant and rock is connected to the Hollow Tree." He pointed at the ground below them. "The only thing stopping the Dark Enchanted Forest from ripping the earth out from below our feet and killing us all is courtesy and energy expense."

"My point still stands." Chloe pointed at her own chest. "*I'm* not connected to the Hollow Tree, and *I'm* a part of this kingdom. And just because the ground is listening doesn't mean it's not true."

A stone popped up and leaned against Chloe's shoe. Keith was surprised; the Dark Enchanted Forest wasn't often willing to be a part of the conversation. Chloe was *also* surprised. The woman gave Keith a huge self-satisfied grin.

"See!" She pointed at the stone, which promptly lay flat again. "It agrees! Ha! I *told* you."

Keith rubbed the bridge of his nose out of habit, his glasses lifting askew for a moment. "I think it's time we moved on."

Ria was staring between the bush and the stone, her face deep in thought.

She was still thinking when he flew them to the next line of defense. The middle line was led by a troop of naga. They were bored and distracting themselves by doing practice bouts. Henrietta was welcomed, but despite the many requests, managed to leave without getting pulled into a fight.

When they reached the first line of defense, Patina was waiting to greet them. Keith had the satisfaction of seeing the selkie's jaw drop when he landed with Ria still in his arms.

She got herself together in an instant, standing at attention. "Your Viciousness."

"Lieutenant Patina."

"Henrietta," Henrietta added, introducing herself. "I take it the army still hasn't arrived?"

Patina looked the princess up and down, twice. Then she turned to Keith. "They haven't. But we know where they are. You'll have to see it to believe it."

Keith sighed; he hoped that Henrietta could win over his cousin as fast as she'd magically befriended all the other minions in his army. "Show me."

CHAPTER 83

How Rude

Henrietta

I didn't know what I was expecting to find when we walked south, but Gerda standing on a bridge braiding her long—Wow! I hadn't realized it was *that* long—hair into a collection of plaits on her head was *not* it. She was almost finished, but had a few parted sections left.

I was surprised no one had noticed us as we came into view; I'd certainly noticed them.

"It's a dragon!"

"We've already *said* dragon. It has to be an armordillo."

"Why would you think it's an armordillo? That's the dumbest idea yet."

"It could be a trick. What if it's a specific *kind* of dragon?"

"Well, I don't wanna be sent flying like the last guy, so you'd all better figure it out soon."

Keith was walking right beside me, which meant I heard him quietly murmur, "Fascinating."

It wasn't exactly the same as when I'd answered riddles in the past; this time, magic positively radiated everywhere. Even I could feel it.

On the other side of the bridge, I spied a pop-up canvas shade, its flaps pulled open.

Inside, Sir Havork sat silently listening to the leaders of each division, one hand over his eyes, deep in thought. Knights I'd trained with, adventuring parties I recognized, and mercenaries I'd never met all milled about. The army stretched behind them down the road. Those within view looked tired, injured, or bored.

"We should stop guessing and attack again!" Sir Phineas, one of the stronger Drendil knights, slammed his fist into an open palm. "The beast can't be *that* powerful. She is just bluffing."

"Bluffing?" A mercenary wearing a crossed lace up vest popular in Sumbria scoffed. "She's lasted through two assaults already. Don't you know anything about trolls? We're just lucky she hasn't eaten anyone. We can either solve the riddle or go around."

"You tried that." The high-level adventurer Trevor Malory rubbed his arm. It was a telltale twitch when he was holding himself back from clobbering a self-centered noble. I'd gone dungeon delving enough times with him to know his temperament. He was the leader of the Lancers, a powerful group of adventurers that had settled in Drendil. "Anyone who goes west gets ripped to shreds by treants, dire wolves, and the literal forest. And anyone who goes east"—he waved to emphasize his point—"risks waking Feliwyn. Or getting pulled into the lake and eaten alive by the denizens of evil lurking beneath the waves."

"Poor Sir Tilly."

Keith, Lieutenant Patina, and I were almost at the bridge. Oddly, the Drendil army still hadn't noticed us. I felt a surge of irritation; how badly had army discipline deteriorated in my absence?

"Just tell me the riddle again, and if we can't solve it, I'll launch another attack." Sir Phineas picked up his shield. "We'll start with the arrows this time. On fire, if we have to."

"No." Everyone turned to Sir Havork. He uncovered his eyes and told them, "Fire will only make the forest—"

His words cut off as saw me.

Gerda also noticed our approach. She glanced over her shoulder.

"Hello, Princess." The troll woman picked up her last strand of loose green hair. "Just give me a minute; these ruffians arrived while I was getting ready this morning, and I'm still doing my hair. They should send word if they're going to arrive early."

"How rude," Lieutenant Patina said dryly. I looked at the selkie, and she raised an eyebrow. "*Of the soldiers.*"

"This would have been so much easier if I wasn't in the middle of my morning ablutions." Gerda sighed. "I barely had time to put on my boots and grab my hair ties."

"Gerda's been holding them off for almost two hours," Lieutenant Patina explained, shaking her head.

"What can I say?" Gerda worked her fingers through her braid, twisting the strands. "I'm good at making riddles."

"Henri," Knight Commander Havork called out to me. He strode out of the tent and straight up to Gerda's bridge. "Henri, come here; we need to talk."

"What? Is the princess there?!" Sir Phineas strolled over to the bridge and squinted past me. Could . . . could he not see us?

Keith's hand reached for mine, and I took it, squeezing harder than I should've. He didn't flinch. His voice was soft. "Whatever you want to do, I'll support you."

A metaphorical weight lifted from my shoulders, and I smiled up at him openly. "Thank you."

"Henri."

I looked up at the man who'd practically raised me. Who'd taught me how to fight, how to survive—in more ways than one. I let go of Keith's hand and stepped forward onto the bridge.

"Wait!" Sir Havork and Gerda cried out at the same time. Gerda even dropped her braid, putting out a hand in warning.

It was too late. The force of the bridge magic engulfed me, and I felt it settle.

[You have entered into the Area of Effect Skill: **Troll Magic**.
Answer the Riddle to proceed.]

"What's this?" I looked at Gerda as the woman dropped her braid and slapped herself in the face.

"I've never actually used [Troll Magic] on you before. Most people don't need me to waste the mana," she explained. "And I've activated my highest-tier magic for this. No one can cross the bridge either way until the riddle is solved."

"It only applies if I try to get to the other side though, right?" The pressure felt . . . odd. Like I was walking through water.

Gerda frowned. "You can't cross the bridge without feeling the [Force Effect], and you can't walk off the bridge without activating the attack." Gerda sighed. "Anyone trapped has to answer the riddle correctly or be attacked. And unfortunately . . . I can't deactivate it."

"You have to stand there until someone answers the riddle?!" I asked, eyeing the magic.

"Yep. The first time I tried it, I was stuck for days. I was practicing on a smaller bridge with less foot traffic." Gerda shrugged.

"Days?" Sir Havork sighed.

"Then it'll be fine." I nodded and walked over the bridge. Each step was met with heavier weight as the power of her skill bore against me. By the time I met Gerda at the middle of the bridge, I'd started taking physical damage. My Constitution took the edge off, but it was taking all my Strength just to stand there; a weaker foe would have been sent flying. I imagined that was the point.

I stopped at the edge of the bridge, staring at Sir Havork. He didn't draw his blade . . .

I was hoping that he wouldn't try to kill me, and I was glad to see I was right. Getting this close to him, even trapped in [Troll Magic], could have ended badly if he aimed to end me.

"Sir Havork." I looked up at him, calling him by a familiar title.

His eyes softened. He'd become older in the months I was gone, with more gray hair along the sides of his head. Or maybe I just hadn't realized he was an old man until now.

"I've come to take you home. Your parents—" he began.

"I'm not going."

"Your parents have something important to tell you. They've sent me to bring you back."

I shook my head. "They will only kill me—"

"I guarantee you that is no longer the case."

"—but even if I *wanted* to return, I wouldn't. I'm happy here."

The old knight stared at me for a long time.

Behind him, Sir Phineas confirmed my earlier suspicion when he yelled, "If the princess is here, grab her and let's go! What are you waiting for?"

"Shut up, Phineas." Knight Commander Havork lifted one hand and made a signal for *Stop them*, or as I fondly remembered him joking, *Deal with that annoyance.*

Trevor happily took out the knight with a left hook to the gut, using a fighter skill to get through the man's armor. Phineas hit the ground on his knees, clutching his stomach and wheezing for air. It looked like Trevor had even dealt Surprise Attack bonuses despite warning from the sign.

"It's important," the knight commander continued. "Your parents have something to tell you."

"You can tell me."

"I *can't*." He looked pained. "You have to come home and hear it from them."

"If they have something to say, they can tell me themselves. Have *them* enter the Dark Enchanted Forest."

"No king would endanger himself . . ." He trailed off, his eyes flickering in Keith's direction.

"Then I'm sure I'll see them at Grand Duchess Calisto's Spring Ball, if they have the nerve to show up." I didn't know where the strength to talk back was coming from, but I felt like the entire Dark Enchanted Forest was supporting me.

I repeated, "I'm not going."

CHAPTER 84

What About My Experience Points?

Keith

The ring on Keith's right index finger was warm against his skin, letting him know that it had worked.

There hadn't been enough time to craft anything impressive last night, but his Mechanical Enchanter title wasn't for nothing. And after the dungeon, he was being extra cautious of his own fragility.

So he only took five points of damage from Henrietta's grip instead of twenty-six . . . That didn't seem like much, but with his base hit points at four hundred, every little bit counted.

[**Automaton: Lulu** has completed the Task. **Automaton: Lulu** asks if there is another **Command.** Yes/No]

Similar notifications had been popping up all morning, and each made him smile a small, vicious smile. He mentally selected [No] and turned his attention back to the matter at hand.

He'd watched Henrietta walk into the [Troll Magic], and for a moment . . . just a moment, he'd felt like she was leaving. Walking away. He'd known in his heart that she wouldn't, but his body had almost moved on its own, reaching to drag her back.

Instead, he'd stood aside. Patina had shot him a look like he was pathetic. He'd ignored her.

Ria was telling everyone her choice. She repeated, "I'm not going."

Sir Havork frowned at Ria, and Keith's fingers itched to cast a draconic wind spell to send him flying. Or maybe a lightning strike. His water magic could raise the lake and drown them all . . . but then, he'd have to clean up the mess.

And it would interrupt Henrietta's conversation; she didn't like it when people were rude.

"You'll regret this," Knight Commander Havork told her. Funnily enough, it didn't sound as threatening as it should have. Keith knew the knight was Henrietta's mentor, so their relationship might make it difficult for him to outright kill her . . .

Keith didn't even want to think about what would happen if he ordered his minions to betray each other. For all Chloe and Rufus teased like cats and dogs, they'd probably overthrow him and put him through counseling if he tried.

"I can live with my decision," Ria spoke confidently. "But the *only* thing I would actually regret would be not giving you this."

The knight tensed, but Henrietta simply took a step back and bowed. "Thank you for training me all these years. Goodbye, Sir Havork."

Henrietta turned and walked back to the other side of the bridge. Keith walked up to meet her at the border. She couldn't leave the space without answering the riddle or taking damage, so Keith brought out a high-grade health potion. She just smiled at him and shook her head.

Then she sat down cross-legged on the bridge, facing the enemy. "I'll stay to watch until everyone has gone home."

Sir Havork sighed deeply before looking at Keith. "You'll make sure she's happy?"

"Of course." Keith couldn't help the bit of a sneer in his smile. Henrietta was already happier in *his* kingdom; Keith was sure of that.

The old knight turned on his heel and walked back toward the command tent.

Just then, Patina cut in. "Wait, they aren't *actually* going back, right? What about our battle? What about my *experience points?!*"

A few on the opposing side also started mumbling. Who knew if the Drendil king would pay for a failed invasion. Keith shrugged. "If you want EXP, send everyone to Deep Shoals. We're paying our people to be on standby for the week, anyway; might as well clear out the dungeons."

He needed *so* many crafting materials for his upcoming list of projects. More defense items for his person, a set of matching rings . . . and he needed to reinforce all the furniture.

"You can't be serious?" Patina waved her hand at the large army right in front of them. "You think they'll just pack up and go home? What's to stop them from waiting it out?"

Ria chuckled. "Don't worry, Lieutenant Patina. We've already handled the army. They have to go back today. Tomorrow at the latest."

"What? Why?"

Keith supplied the answer. "Because they're all out of supplies."

Ria put in, "You've already emptied the grain wagon, haven't you?"

Keith smirked. "The grain wagon? My automata have taken everything but the fish jerky. Let them snack on it all the way home."

Sir Havork turned on his heel just before he reached the other leaders. "You've done *what?*"

"I've stolen all your food. And water. If you don't believe me, go and check the wagons. You really shouldn't have been so focused on attacking the bridge troll."

"Trevor! Paxton!" Knight Commander Havork shouted. Two men in the Drendil army jumped. "Go check our supplies. Now."

"How long were they attacking you?" he heard Ria whisper to Gerda.

"They spent five minutes trying to guess, then they attacked for an hour. Then a break to guess again while they sent scouts along the river to see how far the magic went. Those scouts didn't come back." Gerda was delicately arranging her hair into some sort of coif. "They spent the next hour trying to pile mercenaries on to see if sheer force could break through, and stopped to take a break just before you showed up."

Ria nodded. "Plenty of time, then."

Keith was impressed. He interrupted. "How long can you keep this spell going, Miss Gerda?"

"Actually, the spell is enchantment based. Once it's cast, it's cast. It will last until the riddle is answered or the mana runs out—and I had a *lot* of troll magic saved up." The troll shook her head a little to make sure everything was secure. "[Troll Magic] is surprisingly powerful, especially after I captured all of the bridges in the Dark Enchanted Forest."

"*All of the bridges?*" That was news to him. ". . . Does my drawbridge count?"

"Ah! Well . . ." The troll hesitated, telling Keith all he needed to know.

"Your self-report as a part of section 3(f) of the Domain Influence section of your tax forms should have included which bridges you have domain over." Keith crossed his arms. On the other side of the bridge, soldiers were returning at perk-assisted speeds.

Gerda sighed. "That's correct. I haven't reported it because, well, I was worried about the attention. The teleport point at the castle is very useful."

"I'll have my office send you the fine and the appropriate paperwork."

"I get to keep them?" The troll seemed genuinely surprised.

"Maybe not *all* of them, and certainly not my—"

"Oh!" Henrietta interrupted. "That means I don't have to go for an hour-long run to reach your place anymore!"

Keith's mouth snapped shut, and he gave a strained smile. "We'll talk."

"Maybe we should be paying attention to our enemy," Patina reminded everyone. "It looks like they've finished discussing."

Sir Havork was marching back their way with a vengeance.

CHAPTER 85

Let's Hear the Riddle!

Henrietta

I wondered for just a moment if we'd gone too far, taking Drendil's supplies.

I *may* have been a bit angry that they were marching on my new home. I also *might* have gone a touch overboard having fun playing with—I mean, *organizing* the automaton army.

With the majority of their forces stuck in the forest, there was almost nothing stopping Keith's [Construct: Small] automata from overrunning Drendil. He had full control of their economic import and export lines, and was capable of destroying the kingdom from the inside out. I shivered, thinking just how much we—I mean, Drendil had underestimated Nilheim.

I had never realized how protected Drendil was from the rest of the continent. Because it was only accessible by water and the forest, they'd never really focused on their land army. After all, the forest was just "a misbegotten collection of ragtag monsters." The pitiful forces my father had sent into the Dark Enchanted Forest were the outcasts of the bigger, stronger naval fleet.

To be fair, few skilled soldiers could be spared when leviathans, pirates, water drakes, and the odd school of killer tadpoles hit the coastline on a semiregular basis. Which was why I had spent so much time up north in the Depths of Despair Dungeon. Where better to train to protect Drendil than in an ocean-themed tower dungeon?

On the route here, Keith had told me that he'd sent constructs to hide under wagons, in the bushes, and out of sight. I couldn't be sure how much the forest itself had been attacking the scouts, but whosoever it didn't pick off would've been taken care of by his automatons.

"Henri. I'm returning to Drendil as promised. Give us back the supplies," Sir

Havork ordered. He'd come right up to the bridge and crossed his arms, staring down at me.

"I'm afraid I can't do that, Knight Commander." I reverted back to his official title. "You can tell my father thank you for the dowry."

The knight looked stricken, actually taking a full step back. "Wait, you—?"

"I'm joking." I wasn't joking, but I cut him off anyway. "Now pack your army and march home, or I'll be forced to send them home in wagons."

And this time, I'd have the *automata* pull the wagons. I had a Spring Ball to get ready for! What was I going to wear? Rinrin had mentioned dresses a few weeks ago . . . I wondered if Keith would like to wear matching outfits?

Slow down, I told myself. We weren't even engaged yet. *Yet.*

"I did leave you the jerky," Keith reminded him. "And your elementalists should have water. You'll be home in no time."

Havork looked me over, and I could see the moment he gave up written on his face.

"Alright. I was sent to deliver a message to the princess and to fight for her freedom . . . and you've heard the message."

"I have."

"And your freedom?"

"I'm freer than I've ever been," I assured him.

"Then I have fulfilled my duty. Goodbye, Princess."

Knight Commander Havork turned on his heel and activated a perk to be heard over the entire army. "Attention!"

Ranks of soldiers, knights, and adventurers all came to stand on the road in a beautifully timed display of efficiency and discipline. Knight Commander Havork was nothing if not efficient when left to manage on his own. I felt bad to see him go back to Drendil.

"Pack up and prepare to march south!" His voice echoed in the trees, and I had a strange sense that the woods approved. Perhaps it was my [Sword Aura] perceiving the movement of leaves and branches that played like stressful background music, but the entire area went from hostile and violent to calm and unassuming in a breath.

A few of the soldiers whispered, "South?" or, "Already?"

The knight commander looked at his officers and, still projecting, announced, "We are marching home."

Trevor threw an unconscious Phineas over his shoulder; I hadn't seen when the adventurer had fully knocked the knight out. No matter. It was probably in response to Havork's orders to deal with the knight. Trevor and the rest of the Lancers were going to suffer more pushback from the knights after today, but managing the rivalries between factions in Drendil was no longer my task.

Trevor nodded in the general direction of the bridge I was on, and I nodded back. He hollered, "Have a good life, Princess! You deserve it."

I felt touched.

His words also got a rise out of those close by, but no one outright argued as people I'd known in passing all my life gathered their things and settled in to go back. Some whom I'd personally led or adventured with waved in my general direction.

I watched them all go with a bittersweet feeling in my heart.

"Why did it seem like they couldn't see us?" I asked Gerda.

The bridge troll explained. "The [Area of Effect] spell creates a pocket space on the bridge and up the river using dimension magic. I made everything deliberately obfuscated should the Dark Horde roll up behind me. And I especially didn't want them seeing *you* in case they redoubled their efforts. That commander is a strong one, though. He saw right through me."

"He is." I nodded. "His Perception is very high."

Keith waved a hand. "I'm impressed at how fast they're packing up. Do you think we can go home soon? This entire escapade has been an embarrassing farce."

"That depends"—I smiled—"on how long it'll take us to solve the riddle!"

Gerda laughed.

"If you're making sure the Drendil army fully retreats," Lieutenant Patina said. "I'll deal with all of ours who are still expecting a fight."

"I'll let Quinton know you're on your way," Keith replied.

"General Pounce is so busy with the twins, I think I could march everyone past Gren's Keep before he got the message," Patina snarked. "Thank goodness for Mistress Puma."

"'No one checks like Puma Checks,'" Keith, Gerda, and Patina quoted at the same time. I mouthed the saying once so I could join in next time. There was still so much to learn!

Patina headed back up the road.

"I must admit, Miss Gerda," Keith said, "I'm intrigued. Which riddle held off the entire Drendil army for these five hours?"

"Okay," Gerda started. "So this spell has a tiered system which includes the riddle itself and two more hint riddles if you fail. With the amount of time they spent attacking instead of guessing, I only had to give them the riddle and a single hint."

"Hints are for the weak!" I accompanied the statement with a wolfish grin to let them know I was joking. "Let's hear the riddle!"

I got a notification with the riddle as Gerda recited,

> "Its birth is laborious, it can be bought,
> Its flesh is leathery, all over taut,
> It lives as long as elves or fae,
> In time, its name will fade away.
> What am I?"

CHAPTER 86

Miss Gerda Did Not Disappoint

Keith

"Treant?"

"Ancient Tortoise?"

"Wyvern?"

"Wraith?"

"A lizard wizard?"

"Gorgon?"

"Dragon? Ah, we already said that. Drendil did too, didn't they?"

Keith was the one offering the answers, as he was the only person not under the influence of the spell. If Henrietta guessed incorrectly, then she'd be attacked by the magic, and if she guessed correctly, it would break the spell, and it was possible the Drendil army would take the opportunity to turn around and attack.

Miss Gerda shook her head at each guess. When Henrietta had an idea, she spelled the word in the air for Keith, and he asked for her.

Keith scratched his chin. "You said that you gave them a hint? What was the hint?"

"Wait, don't tell us!" Henrietta cried, covering her ears. "Keith!"

"What?" He raised an eyebrow. "I can't imagine a Master class like your knight commander doesn't have points in Intelligence, or at the very least someone at his side who's solely there for their Intelligence stat."

"You have Intelligence eighty-five! No one in the entirety of Drendil has over sixty, and they work in the tax offices, not the army," Ria countered. "Shouldn't you be able to answer this riddle in your sleep?"

"Do you know how many answers I've come up with for this riddle? Seven hundred and ninety-four." Keith could think of even more that fit partially. His mind easily compartmentalized the possible answers for each line of the riddle.

By cross-referencing all creatures with a high risk at birth, a leathery skin, who lived long, and who could be purchased at a market or a guild across the continent . . . there were just too many that fit. His innate skill lay in complex magical formulae, memorizing, placement, and comprehensive deconstruction of mana networks. Not solving children's riddles.

"We should narrow it down with the second riddle, or we'll still be here long past when the army crosses back over the border." Keith tried to say this gently; he knew how much fun a good challenge was. Any other day, he might have relaxed and just stayed here guessing riddles until sunset lit the horizon. But he was itching to get back. "So, Miss Gerda? The second part?"

> "Its birth is laborious, it can be bought,
> Its flesh is leathery, all over taut,
> It lives as long as elves or fae,
> In time, its name will fade away.
>
> You need the light to see it clear,
> But time in sun, its greatest fear.
> It dwells inside and underground,
> Fire burns its body brown."

"Well, that didn't help." Keith was still left with two hundred and forty-five possible answers after processing the new data. "We'll need the next hint."

"Actually," Ria's smile was radiant, and she let out a short laugh. "I think I've got it! Oh, Gerda, that's so clever!"

Keith frowned. "What is it?"

"I can't say." The princess pointed in the direction of the retreating army. Her eyes sparkled as she teased, "And I'm not telling. You wanted the extra hint! Now you can use it to figure out the riddle yourself."

"You know, Princess." Miss Gerda hid a smile behind her hand. "You've had a *lot* more practice with my riddles than His Majesty."

"Still." Ria linked both hands behind her head and craned her neck back to gaze up at me. "It'll be fun."

"Ah, well then. I'll just have to entertain." Keith wanted to bend over and kiss her nose. But he couldn't afford to get stuck in another dimension right now.

He rattled off a few correct answers: phoenix, world serpents, fox spirits, to various undead or dungeon-born monsters. After another half an hour, he sighed. "We need to leave soon if we're to catch Minstrel Bronwynn's show. What's the third clue?"

Miss Gerda recited,

"Its birth is laborious, it can be bought,
Its flesh is leathery, all over taut,
It lives as long as elves or fae,
In time, its name will fade away.

You need the light to see it clear,
But time in sun, its greatest fear.
It dwells inside and underground,
Fire burns its body brown."

Wind tears up words you've never heard,
Earth will scour, mud mark blurred,
Its body alone, can untold feed,
Only water makes it bleed."

Keith slapped himself in the forehead, carefully missing his glasses. "I can't believe I didn't see it immediately. A book."

"That's right." Henrietta stood up and stretched. "It's [A Book]!"

The world distorted as countless mana particles dispelled a dimensional veil over the bridge. It rippled in waves down the river to both sides. The sheer force of the spell left Keith breathless; it was a work of *art*.

"Would you two like to come in for a cup of tea?" Miss Gerda asked. Keith was about to politely refuse; he really needed to monitor the retreating army, but thought better of it. Portal travel was much faster. He sent his automaton Lulu a new task before turning to a bright and cheerful Henrietta and offering his arm. "Shall we?"

"Thank you." She took his arm, and everything was right with the world.

They wandered underneath the bridge to Miss Gerda's portal door. It was artistically ornate with a collection of flowers carved into the arch. He was again surprised by the complex spellcraft the troll had used in creating her home. It had a subtlety and workmanship one didn't often see in her generally brutish and overbearing race.

If he didn't convince her to join up with the Dark Horde, then he would kick himself. This tea was the perfect opportunity to do so . . .

It also portaled Keith and Ria to their home drawbridge.

Even if she didn't want to join his forces, Miss Gerda would be required to start immediate work as bridge maintenance officer and road waterway inspector. That included signing the usual magically enforced contracts for loyalty and vacation days. And he needed to investigate who in the tax department had failed to notice that a single troll now controlled every one of his major bridges.

He couldn't have just *anyone* opening up a portal into his castle without some assurances. If she refused . . . they could cross that bridge when they came to it.

And Keith just knew that Henrietta would be so disappointed if they needed to destroy the bridge troll should she turn out to be a true threat. But for now, he needed to be thinking of a suitable reward for holding off the Drendil army. It was a lot to think of over cheese biscuits and a delectable pumpkin spice cake.

Luckily, Miss Gerda did not disappoint.

CHAPTER 87

A Song About Magical Arson

Henrietta

"Alright, alright! No shoving! I'll be here until St. Veralyn's Day." Minstrel Brownie's voice could be heard over the crowd as if she were standing right beside me and not up on the stage in Scowls. "Who's ready for a rowdy song to start off the evening?"

A cheer of excitement nearly shook the tavern. Most of the furniture, I noted, was enchanted or made from incredibly durable materials. Some of the tables were even reinforced with strips of iron casing. His Royal Viciousness had declared tonight a celebration of Nilheim's "overwhelming victory over the invading forces of Drendil," although everyone I had spoken to was actually disappointed by the lack of experience points.

Keith and I sat in the back of the hall, lounging at a cozy corner table. We were nursing mugs of warm honey and cream, with a foam top and a dash of cinnamon sugar to tie it together. We were also cuddling. It wasn't something I was familiar with, but as of this evening, it was my new favorite thing.

"You don't think she'll play the song about us, do you?" Keith asked, a little nervously. "She said it wasn't ready yet. I don't know if *I'm* ready yet."

"Have you never had a song written about you?" I reached up and plucked at his neatly done-up buttons. They so rudely covered his neck, and I had an unending urge to rip them off.

"Well. There was this one that kept popping up a decade ago in Drendil about how I ate babies . . ." Keith coughed. "But I'm happy to say it didn't get popular."

"*I remember that one!* He'll come for your child so hold them tight. The Dark Lord will feast till your bone's clean white. So lock up your doors and turn off the light!"

Brownie cut me off with the start of her show. Probably a good thing, since Keith had buried his face in his hands. He looked to be in pain.

"I'll start the night with a crowd favorite, 'Tammy's Tavern.'"

Now Tammy was a mean one who would water down the beer,
Her inn was full o fleas and her face a happy sneer,
No matter what you did you couldn't get her to admit,
That the floaties in your drink were spit, and not some barrel grit!
So Jack and I went up the hill to see what could be done,
To rid us all of Tammy's ill before the rising sun.

She smokes like a dragon, poison in the flagon.
And she keeps all the change for a tip!
She won't wash the dishes, or debone the fishes,
She slaps you for giving her lip.
So tonight is the night, friend, we'll give her a fine end,
One long overdue, gather round,
By spell or the sword, if you're in get on board,
We'll burn the place down to the ground!

So off we went together, to share in one last drink,
And Jack he brought his axe and Jill her quill and ink,
But what happened one fateful night I never will live down,
Tammy must o seen through us, she spiked our final round!
Ol' Roger the Rogue was out on the table, and Jack asleep at the bar.
The moaning and groaning, the stomachs unloadin', and Tammy just
laughed from afar.

But Jill, oh Jill, with her ink quill, was a rowdy magical lass,
She danced in the aisle, she danced on the table, she danced on spilled
beer and glass.
And when she fell down
In a heap on the ground,
She hated the grime and the smell,
So she whipped out her book,
That was all that it took,
To activate skill and a spell.

The fireball took to the beer and the wood,
And the clothing of some sorry few,
The cry and the clatter were stopped as the crowd,

Rushed to exit the inn two by two.
Some carried the fallen by head or by tail,
Some carried them over their back.
But none tried to save the old inn or the maid,
As it all burned down in a stack.

The crowd was singing along. For a song about magical arson, it was very popular in taverns around Valaria. It was always amazing to watch Brownie work. Her voice was lyrical but very emphatic, and she could sing like a nightingale or a gritty old sailor at the drop of a hat.

"I still can't believe *that*"—Keith pointed to where a particularly enthusiastic fan was trying to contain himself—"is my Commander General."

Rufus was vibrating with excitement as he sang along with the songs. He knew all the lyrics to every song Brownie sang, including "Minstrel Fine," "Dragon's Wife," and "Ander's Widow." He sang a beautiful harmony to "The Traveler's Tale," and just watching him was as entertaining as watching Brownie.

Though I'd never tell her that.

For some reason, he was trying to hold it in, and besides singing along, he stayed seated. It looked like his claws were gouging holes into the bar with his grip, though his tail gave away his happiness. The proprietor, a male selkie named Vincent, had chastised the general, but everyone knew he would repair the damage.

"Woooooooooooo!" Rufus howled along with everyone else as another song ended.

"I'd like to see him let loose at one of the concerts. I'm more surprised Brownie doesn't recognize him; he's clearly been to her previous shows, and he's very . . . well, big and noticeable?"

Keith let out a soft, "Heh, heh, heh. I just had a thought."

"Yes?"

"What if," Keith surmised, "she's never seen him in his human form?"

"Ohhh. She mostly plays in Drendil and only travels to festivals in other kingdoms a few times a year."

"If you think about it, few, if any, have seen him in his human form. He could come and go without causing too much trouble."

I nodded. Our food arrived, and we enjoyed some fish cakes, stuffed mushrooms, and tossed flowers. There were a lot more varieties of food harvested in the forest. Since arriving, I'd had at least fifteen different kinds of mushrooms, four different tubers, and over a hundred different edible flowers. My favorites so far were the glowing blue stringy mushrooms with little green gills, and the ignia bulb flower that I tapped, and it burst open with motes of pollen sparkling in the air and settling like sweet glitter on the rest of my plate.

"I'm so happy Brownie will be here for St. Veralyn's Day. I'll be sad to see her go, but if she's performing at the Spring Ball she'll need to get there early to prepare. I'll miss her when she's gone."

"We can invite her often," Keith said.

It was a kind offer, and I thanked him. He looked at me for a second and sighed. "You know you can invite her whenever *you* want, right? I'm just saying that *we* could invite her for official things as well."

"Oh." I blushed. Actually, I hadn't realized that.

Keith took a sip of his drink and came away with a bit of foam on his lip. We both laughed.

I was so happy I didn't think of the *other* important event coming up.

CHAPTER 88

If Your Wife Accidentally Kills My Wife, I'm Not Going to Be Happy

Keith

St. Veralyn's Day dawned bright and damp. Morning mist faded as the sun climbed higher in the sky, and everyone in the Dark Enchanted Forest was busy celebrating the holiday with family.

Streets were decorated with tassels, magical lights floated everywhere in greens and pinks in honor of the Green Dragon whose favorite color was rose pink.

Keith normally enjoyed being home at this time. He'd tramped around the Dark Enchanted Forest enough these last few weeks, and his inner sanctum called. He had so many ideas for new constructs, and they would take time to map out. He also had some furniture to reinforce, and he wanted to optimize his wings for two-person flight.

He'd been tinkering since he'd gotten back.

But today, all of that was set aside. Today, he had a beautiful princess to escort.

"They can really go at it when death isn't a concern." Henrietta sat with Keith while they overlooked the castle's royal duels from the second-floor balcony. The courtyard in the castle village had been set up with two rings used for all manner of activities. There had been dancing, plays, magic, skill demos, and now, open dueling for everyone's entertainment. Anyone who wanted satisfaction could compete on tournament days like this to gain attention or seek justice or both.

The sanctioned dueling was relatively new, he was reminded, and had become all the rage across the continent a scant few years ago. He had a newfound appreciation for it, as his meeting with Henrietta had sprung from a misunderstood duel request.

Not that people *needed* to duel out their frustrations. He'd set up a comprehensive system for complaints management as part of the monstrous resources department.

He noticed some of his people looking up at the royal box and adjusted his gaze to stern. Usually, Rufus presided over the festival and the duels, though there had been that one disastrous time Chloe had done it. There'd been so much glitter that she was now banned from organizing any future public events. He'd taken over the duty today so he could show his people his princess. Er, their princess. Their future queen? He felt a blush creeping up his neck.

"It's so handy having a necromancer on staff." Henrietta interrupted his thoughts, looking to where Chloe was reattaching an arm.

"Actually, Chloe isn't usually here. They have to make do with Revive potions. And today she's letting the new healer squad handle the majority of the work."

[Resurrection] brought anyone dead back up at peak condition, but [Revival] just got them back up on their feet. It . . . wasn't ideal.

They both watched with bemusement as Countess Julia suplexed a challenger. Chloe's fiancée was having a marvelous time.

Henrietta bit her lip. "Do you think I . . . ?"

Keith let go of her hand. "I bet you she'd love the challenge."

Henrietta made an excited *squeak* and jumped up. She aimed and leapt over the side of the balcony, landing in the ring next to Julia.

Both women laughed and got into place for the duel.

Henrietta didn't even use Jacqueline, keeping her sheathed, and instead gathering [Sword Aura] around her index and middle finger. Julia seemed a little insulted at first before Chloe leaned over the fence and yelled, "Void-damage sword!" at the paladin. She did a double take and then accepted the arrangement without complaint.

Henrietta used her fingers like a blade, activating her skills as if she wielded a sword. Julia dodged some and took a few hits with a magical shield.

Keith reinforced the shields around the ring. No one wanted to have to [Resurrect] a civilian from the audience; there would be so much paperwork.

"If your wife accidentally kills my wife, I'm not going to be happy," Chloe said, sneaking up on him while he was watching the fight.

"We're not married yet," Keith deadpanned, not letting her get to him this time. "And technically, you're not married yet either."

"You're no fun." Chloe took Henrietta's seat beside him. "Is everything ready?"

"Yes."

"You're not worried?"

"I'm not going to answer that."

"Fair enough." Chloe flinched as Ria sliced Julia's arm, but the paladin used the opportunity to punch the princess in the gut. Ria doubled over, but she was laughing and commending her opponent on a fine hit.

The match devolved into Julia practicing her strikes while Ria dodged and coached her movements. The cheering eventually died down as the audience grew bored, and Keith was forced to call the duel a draw. Both women were sweating, bruised, and bloodied, but each bore a wide grin. They walked out of the ring side-by-side.

Afterward, Keith took *his princess* around and bought them matching bracelets. Hers was a blue closely matching the color of his eyes, and his was a fawn brown that matched her eyes and hair. He gently played with the rope braid around his wrist, thinking about all the enchantments he could fit into it.

The market in the castle courtyard was triple its normal size with the festivities, and people were visiting from all over the kingdom to celebrate. It wasn't as active as previous years, though; he had sent word to all of his nobles and generals recommending that they spend time with their clans this year—he didn't want to host people. Not while there were still all these blasted assassins about.

He had thought that routing their main group would have given them pause, but the attacks had resumed a few days later.

"Tell your master I'm tired of the annoyance. I'm going to begin executing you lot and sending you back as controlled ghoul assassins. We'll see if a constant stream of brainwashed killers with in-depth knowledge of his castle changes his tune," Keith told the young woman who was being dragged off by Vikli and Brithli, two fill-in guards who covered for Chikli and Sithli during the holiday. He ordered, "Give her to Rex."

His giant wolf construct would carry her by her chains all the way to the Drendil border. Rufus didn't want them in the dungeon, so he was deporting them for now. That was going to change right quick.

With perfect timing, Henrietta came back from the ladies' room.

"I'm ready, let's go!" She grabbed his arm, and they finished perusing the last of the shops.

Keith whisked her away to a late dinner, catching Minstrel Bronwynn's last show. As planned, it was ridiculously late by the time they got back to the castle. Instead of seeing her to her rooms, Keith took her to the outlook at the highest point of his inner sanctum. They could see out over everything from up here.

The spring night was chilly, but the sky was clear and full of stars. The moon was high above, and Keith mentally ticked down the seconds while they stargazed.

"Henrietta." He leaned in and kissed her on the cheek.

"Yes?" She covered the spot with her hand.

"Happy birthday."

She tackled him for a real kiss.

CHAPTER 89

Still, Still, and This One Won't Stab You

Henrietta

Last night had been the most wonderful time of my life. I'd gone to bed content, exhausted, out of breath from kissing, and ready to live the rest of my life as an official adult.

The system updated my filed paperwork, and my character sheet changed to Henrietta Doryn of Nilheim. I kicked happily on my bed and rolled around a few times hugging my pillow.

I was officially free to be *me*. And *me* wanted to spend the rest of my life in this Dark Lord's castle baking cinnamon buns and filling tax revenue forms with the odd quest.

I woke up a bit sleepy but ready for the day. Nothing was going to stop me from celebrating my first day as a citizen of the Dark Enchanted Forest with my friends.

At least, that's what I thought.

I stopped by Brownie's door, but I couldn't sense the woman inside. She'd been out later than I with the celebrations, and no doubt grabbed a room at Scowls.

I wandered down to the kitchen . . . and Panlith *wasn't there*. My hands immediately reached for Jacqueline, who was still in my bedroom. The entire kitchen was clean and empty of *anyone*.

Unease came over me. The castle was quiet. *Too* quiet.

I exited the kitchen into the dining area, and no places were set. I told myself that maybe this was a day of rest. Maybe nobody had thought to tell me that in Nilheim, everyone slept in the day after St. Veralyn's Day and just took time off?

Even the servant's quarters were empty. None of the lizardkin maids could be seen. Keith's office was empty, papers neatly stacked, and chairs pushed in.

There was something I was missing, but I didn't want to bother Keith; it was still hours until he normally woke up. I was wandering about when I sensed movement outside.

My feet carried me downstairs and out into the gardens. The corpse roses had bloomed overnight with some new fertilizer to inspire their buds. The entire place blossomed with color.

"*Shhh.*"

I heard a sound further down the path and walked that way. As I turned the corner to the nook where Keith and I usually enjoyed our afternoon tea, I was met with a thunderous shout.

"Happy Birthday, Henrietta!"

Keith, Brownie, Gerda, Rufus, Chloe, Julia, and all of the castle minions were there. Even Lady Amy was present.

Keith came forward and wrapped his arms around me. "Happy birthday, love." He handed me a kerchief to wipe my eyes.

I smiled through the tears. "Thank you, everyone."

There was breakfast and a private concert from Bronwynn as she regaled everyone with funny stories about my days dressed up as a maid running around the city. The entire affair lasted until noon, when everyone had to get back to work.

I took Brownie and Lady Amy to the drawbridge with Gerda, who scolded me saying she was *not* a teleportation hub, but for just this one time she would make an exception because it was my birthday.

The four of us ended up spending an outrageous amount of time having tea and scones. Lunch became afternoon snack, and only when everything was cleaned up did Gerda let us all out at our respective bridges. We dropped off Amy first.

"I'm going to be busy until the Spring Ball." The bridge troll told me as we waited for Gerda's perk to cool down. There were still a few minutes until she could connect to the castle drawbridge. "I'm getting my dress made in Peldeep and then I'll be travelling straight to North Sumbria."

"You're going to the Spring Ball?" I was happy she was going, but usually, only the powerful, the eligible, and the important were sent invitations. And you *needed* an invite. Even I would have been turned away at the door without one.

"I wouldn't miss it for the world," Gerda assured me.

I hesitated to ask, unless it was considered rude, but Brownie had no compunction. "How'd *you* get an invite?"

"I have my ways." Gerda winked, but she didn't elaborate. Come to think of it . . . hadn't Julia owed Gerda a favor to cross her bridge?"

"I'm going to be performing," Bronwynn stated proudly, "So that means we'll *all* be there."

"Except Amy," I added. The poor elf girl still had to fight for time off, and there was no way she'd make it to the ball and back. I wondered if she received an invite; I wondered if her father would even let her *know* if she'd received an invite. Maybe I would audit the Hollow this year and find out . . .

"It's going to be something. Until next we meet, Princess." Gerda reached out and magicked the door open to a familiar moat. The edge of the water was very narrow, and I had to hold on to the doorway to not fall directly into the water.

As I left the bridge, the troll called after me, "Have a wonderful birthday!"

And I did.

It was my day off, so I wandered back to my rooms to do some light reading. When I arrived, however, I was met with a team of ratkin.

"This Rinrin greets Her Viciousness." The ratkin came forward and motioned me to come in. The title made me blush, but I let it slide. It was my birthday after all, and I could give myself a small gift.

"Rinrin." I nodded. "What's all this?"

"The arachne have sent the cloth you like, Mistress." Rinrin waved forward a pair of primly dressed ratkin assistants, each holding a bolt of shimmering fabric in a color somewhere between dark blue and purple. "Just in time, too. We are fortunate that the weather has been so sunny and warm. Yes-yes, this will do nicely."

Rinrin had taken over tailoring my clothes up to this point, turning the previous Queen of the Dark Enchanted Forest's wardrobe into the current fashion for me to use. I'd only given her a general idea on my Spring Ball gown and apparently, she wasn't fixing up an old piece but making me a new one! Some of the pieces were already cut out based on my previous measurements. There were . . . a *lot* of pieces.

"Oh, Rinrin, this is too much!"

"Tsk," went the ratkin. "Rinrin has only just begun. Now come stand here. Still! Still, and this one won't stab you."

She had silk pins clenched between her fingers in one hand, and a pair of long, sharp scissors in the other. I gulped. "Alright. Just let me change out of my shoes . . ."

My pair of beautiful low-heel calf-high boots were presented before me, black and embroidered all over with roses of silver and blue threads. The young ratkin bobbed a quick bow, "Here, quick-quick, Princess."

I accepted my fate and put on the boots, then stood perfectly still as the group ran around pinning and trimming fabric all over me. I wasn't pricked even once.

After all was said and done, I collapsed into bed smiling.

Happy Birthday to me.

CHAPTER 90

That Wasn't Becoming of a Dark Lord

Keith

This is your newest Potts's Cast.

Mount Vemund is going to have a high drop rate for porous clay this week; those skilled in pottery and sculpting terracotta earthenware can find chunks falling off the mountain in Martin's Grotto.

Sumbria might be making a last-minute appearance at the Spring Ball. Countess Peregrine Fern just lost her fiancé to pirates. The young Lord Geoffrey was a terror, so I congratulate the woman on dodging that bullet, erm, arrow. Countess Peregrine can take over for Julia, who is no longer on the market.

Speaking of the ball, this caster has it on the best authority that Lavender the Lizard Wizard will be pouring drinks and putting on a magic show. Anyone hoping to meet the legend will have to wait in line.

There is a 140% crit rate when using spear attacks in the Depths of Despair Dungeon this month, so get out there and start farming EXP!

Knight Commander Bastian of Peldeep won a bolt of pink silk from the St. Veralyn's Day Crafting Competition with his 108 hand-sewn toys, including dolls, balls, stuffed animals, and play food. He donated all of the toys to orphans. I don't know about the rest of you good gentles, but I'm excited to see what the knight commander does with all that pink silk.

**There will be a stampede of capybara next week, as they'll
be disturbed from their home by poachers. The capybara
are friendly creatures and will need to be rounded up and
returned to their natural habitat. There is going to be a short-
age of carrots in Sumbria next month unless something is
done.
This is Madame Potts's Cast,
Until next time, dear listeners.**

Keith read the report and sighed. Things were finally settling down after the war—if anyone could even call it a war—and his mind was on paperwork and proposals.

Chloe was in full dragon-bride mode, sending in requests for more and more ridiculous decorations. Keith was nervous about having the wedding so close to an actual dragon, but on second thought, Feliwyn would probably enjoy the idea of sleeping through a royal wedding.

He'd have to discuss things with Grand Duchess Calisto during the Spring Ball, or after the ball if she was too busy. He also wanted to create some new golems for the laundry room. He was doodling designs on a notepad at his desk when Gimtak flew in.

"Your Viciousness, another delivery for the princess." The imp whipped out a sealed letter and flapped it about.

Keith sighed, recognizing the seal. "Toss it with the rest."

Gimtak nodded, flying over to a small basket on the floor by the window. In it were all of the letters from the king and queen of Drendil. They were exhausting to read, and he'd run out of any desire to look at the things, let alone waste the mana required to light them on fire.

And he really shouldn't burn them without reading first. So he'd been putting them in a basket and contemplating making one of his minions sort them out as a punishment . . . but then, said minion would be reading Henrietta's mail, and that wouldn't do.

"My liege, perhaps you could ask the princess?" Gimtak offered, eyeing the pile.

"But I told her I'd handle it," Keith argued. "She doesn't wish to receive any mail."

"She's a grown woman," Chloe said, having walked in unannounced while the pair were still wondering what to do with the basket. "If it'll make it easier, *she* can light them on fire."

Keith felt a small smile tug at his lip, imagining her doing just that. "I'll bring it up. What can I do for you, Chloe?"

"I'm just saying goodbye," the necromancer informed him. She had her long blonde hair in two braids and was wearing comfortable sky-blue riding clothes.

"We're off to help mother-in-law set up the Spring Ball and start writing the wedding invitations. So much to do, so little time."

Keith mumbled, "You can say that again."

She let Keith know the plans for the healers in her absence, and Keith was glad to see her off. The wedding plans were worse than the war plans, especially since Henrietta had actually *liked* war planning. When Chloe had offered to include Ria in the wedding plans, the princess had shriveled up like a pile of expired adhesive that looked like it would shatter if you so much as poked it.

She was happy to talk about the wedding cake, and then she bravely ran away.

Speaking of running away, Keith glanced at the clock. It was time for his mandated break.

He played about in his workroom for a while until he had a working design for a construct limb that could be outfitted to a small ratkin. It would protect them from boiling water. He'd considered a full golem, but he had no idea what techniques were required to wash laundry. And in no universe would he just assume that the task was easy.

Instead, he focused on creating tools for the ratkin to use that would help them finish their tasks safe and secure.

When he stumbled into his room that night, tired but pleased with his work, he was met with a terrifying sight.

Rinrin stood in his chambers, a measuring stick in one hand and a long pair of glistening scissors in the other. Her eyes gleamed with an intensity that made him physically take a step back.

Too late. A ratkin closed the bedroom door just behind him.

"This Rinrin needs to fit your outfit for the ball, Master." The scissors snapped twice as the royal seamstress walked slowly toward him. Keith tried to compose himself as every fiber of his being screamed to run away.

That wasn't becoming of a Dark Lord, though, so he simply accepted his fate.

The ratkin smiled. "Now, stand very, very still, Your Viciousness. So Rinrin doesn't cut you."

CHAPTER 91

It's Functional!

Henrietta

I stared at our luggage with wonder. It was like we were going off to war instead of a ball. Our things were loaded into a wagon pulled by an alligator dog lead by Sithli. It was almost *overflowing* with trunks and suitcases and boxes.

Couldn't everything fit into a magic storage pouch?

We weren't going to be traveling in the wagon, of course. The king of the Dark Enchanted Forest had his own ornate magical carriage, arching silver swirls like fire on an inky body so black it shined. I lifted up a hand, and a distorted reflection copied me in the sheen of the paneling. Instead of a living horse, a black brass construct horse named Fifi tossed her head and stamped the earth impatiently. Steam poured from her nostrils, and her eyes glowed with magical fire.

Keith walked up to me as I was admiring the work of art before me.

"I made Fifi back in my dark past," Keith admitted. "When I enjoyed riding across the forest in full splendor and showing off for my soon-to-be subjects."

I made appreciative noises at the construct, who accepted my admiration with a swish of her mane.

"But this"—Keith reached around me and opened one door to the carriage— "was my mother's. She built it herself, I'm told, when *she* was a young girl."

"Thank you." I accepted his hand and climbed inside. Everything was inky-black soft leather with silver buttons. The seating was plush, and there was space for two on either side. "It's beautiful."

"And even better," Keith sat down beside me, our legs touching. He reached over me and hooked his finger through a small loop, pulling up a little table that settled over my lap. He enthusiastically proclaimed, "It's functional!"

I couldn't help myself; I laughed. "I do like things that are beautiful *and* functional."

My eyes fell on his lips, and I was tempted to attack him right there in the carriage. I held myself back—there was time for kissing later. "Do we have everything? How long is the trip by dark enchanted carriage? Who's coming with us?"

"Hold on, let me answer your questions one at a time." It was Keith's turn to laugh. "Sithli and Lilith are coming, and we'll have one night's rest at the border inn before we arrive at Grand Duchess Calisto's estate tomorrow morning. Everything has been double-checked, from clothing"—he shuddered almost imperceptibly—"to antidotes. You have Jacqueline and your enchanted jewelry. I have enough mana potions stored to keep me through an entire *day* of [Mana Burn]."

"Which you won't *need*, because you'll be extra careful," I reminded him.

"And I'll tell you if it happens anyway. You can [Resurrect] me if needed," Keith said. "Just like you'll tell *me* if something bothers *you*."

I lifted up the table and slipped it back in its slot beside my seat so I could reach out a hand, rubbing it over the spot on his arm that I'd cut with Jacqueline. "Wait, antidotes! I didn't pack the ones you gave me already."

"No matter. I've filled my own storage ring, and I have a gift for you." Keith pulled out a small black ring etched with Venus lilies. He slipped it on my right-hand ring finger. "Here's a Revive potion, a Resurrect potion, Sleep antidote, a Paralysis potion, and a Paralysis antidote. There are also antidotes for Venus lily, shroomdoom, greendeath, corpsewilt, dandyvine, Plittsmouth scorch, dragonsbane, waurg, and belladonna.

"If you get hit by molten ash vane, pour health potions directly on your skin. There just needs to be enough of your body left to [Resurrect] later. You can cut off a limb for me to work—"

"Keith, I'll be fine! I'm more worried about *you*." I reached up to his face and ran my hand over the short beard on his chin. "I can take a hit or ten; you're a much softer target."

"I'll have you know that no assassins or poisons have breached my shields since"—Keith stared pointedly at Jacqueline—"long before you."

"Then as long as we are prepared, that's half the battle." I blushed, rubbing the handle of my sword.

"Of course." Keith shrugged. "There's nothing saying the assassins in Madame Potts's Cast are after *us*. Everyone at the Spring Ball is a powerful figure and subject to a few enemies."

I didn't believe that, he didn't believe that, but I nodded anyway. "We'll just take healthy precautions. After Madame Potts's prediction, the perpetrators might change their mode of assault anyway."

"There's one more thing . . ." Keith rubbed his neck nervously and held up a small button. "I've made this for you . . ."

I took the plain circle of polished brass and examined it on my palm. It felt slightly warm to the touch. "What is it?"

"It's a tracking construct. It'll allow me to find you with my [Mind Map]. But I don't think you should accept it."

"Why not?"

"My [Mind Map] provides a magical map of anywhere my constructs or I have ever been, and tracks both myself and my constructs on it. If you're carrying this . . . I'd essentially be following you around on a private mini map, spying on your every move and knowing where you are at all times. It's simply *not acceptable behavior* from a gentleman, and I don't think you need to be monitored; you're more than capable of looking after yourself." He reached out to take it back but I moved it out of his reach

"You're right; I'll be fine without it. But I'll keep it *for now*." It was a violation of privacy and respect, but it was also a guaranteed Dark Magician King swooping in to save me if something went horribly wrong. I was only sad that I didn't have a way to track him. Just for this, of course! Not all the time . . .

A knock on the door of the carriage drew our attention. Sithli's voice came from outside the door. "We're ready to go, Your Viciousnesss."

"Then let us be off," Keith ordered. "We'll have lunch at Thistlecrick; I've heard that Derilla Vane's come out of his diapause slumber."

"As you wish, my liege." Sithli walked back to the wagon and hopped on, signaling the carriage train to start moving. Fifi whinnied like a real horse, though the sound echoed eerily long.

We set forth at a quick pace.

The carriage had more than just a worktable; the seats reclined as well! I'd never been so comfortable in my life as I lay on the makeshift daybed with Keith, chatting about anything and nothing as we sped toward the naga mountain in the north. I was vigilant, but no one attacked us en route.

Apparently, the footpath I'd taken at the first turnoff toward Thistlecrick was *not* the official road. Granted, the road liked to wander up and down the north facing Great Road at the whims of the Dark Enchanted Forest, so I had no way of knowing.

Elder Clarissa of Clan Lamia was waiting for us at the entrance to the city. She had Marik beside her on the right, and Terra on the left. The other families had sent representatives, but none of the younger crowd I'd met the last time.

I'd have to take the time to memorize the major nobles of the forest. Eventually.

But not today.

Elder Clarissa slithered forward and bowed to us after we exited the carriage. "Your Viciousness, Princess, our master awaits you in the Great Hall."

"Well met," Keith told the woman, taking my hand and sliding it through his. "Lead the way."

CHAPTER 92

He Won't Kill Us While We're Visiting

Keith

The first time Keith had met Derilla Vane, he'd escaped the not-so-careful watch of his godmother while she lounged in a hot spring.

He'd been five, and sitting around scratching scales for a few hours was *not* his idea of fun, so he'd wandered off into the caves to hunt frogs.

Instead of frogs, he'd been met by eyes, many, many eyes.

Unbeknownst to all, the arachne had settled in the mountains, silently spreading their webs through the deep caves beside Thistlecrick. In his meandering, Keith had found one of the caves and a young arachne boy. Derilla's two regular-sized and six smaller emerald eyes peeked out from inky black hair as he paused in the middle of practicing web spinning. He stared at the strange, demi child that had entered his cavern.

The two had stood there, taking each other's measure, before launching into battle.

The boys fought to a stalemate, fang versus magic, spinner versus shield. They eventually swore an oath to let the other go free, if for no other reason than they'd both grown bored waiting for the other to fall.

The two had spent the rest of the afternoon catching frogs, until Derilla's elders had found them. There had been a great commotion, but the arachne elders permitted Keith to live because killing him would have made Derilla an Oath Breaker.

They'd let him go, and on that day the Dark Enchanted Forest discovered a new race of monsters in their midst.

Feliwyn had *not* been pleased, but the dragon eventually accepted the arachne into her domain after they'd promised her fifty bolts of spider silk per year.

Feliwyn very much liked pretty things.

Shortly after that, Chloe and Rufus had been picked up and tasked with keeping him alive until he was old enough to fight off assassins and arachne and worse.

Derilla Vane had grown up strong enough to claim the title of General of the North. Keith probably should have informed Henrietta about Derilla's race, but he was used to her unfazed appearance to all things evil.

Including himself.

"Oh my," Ria breathed. "It's a *spider*."

"*He*," Keith chastised, squeezing her hand. "*He* is a spider."

"I am, and I always have been." A deep chuckle sounded throughout the hall.

Elder Clarissa, having finished escorting them, politely excused herself.

The General of the North was of average height for the intelligent races, and his head came up to just below Keith's chin. He had jet black hair, cut short and swept back with winged sides, and his eyes shone the same green as in his youth. He wore a fine white spider silk tunic, fastened around his waist with a brown leather belt. Below the belt was his spider body. As far as Keith understood, the carapace held the arachne's intestines, sex organs, and thread spinners, while the upper anthropoid torso held the heart, lungs, kidneys, and other important organs required to keep his fleshy bits functioning.

"Hello, my friend." Keith reached out and locked forearms with the arachne.

Derilla flashed Keith a sharp-toothed grin, his spider chelicarae fangs protruding out of the sides of his mouth and curving inward. "Well met. And who is *this* tasty morsel?"

"Someone who could wrestle you into submission faster than my godmother," Keith mused. Instead of replying herself, Ria looked distractedly off in the distance. Her notification tab must have reacted. "Henrietta, Derilla. Derilla, Henrietta.

Hearing her name, Ria recovered herself. "It's nice to meet you."

The princess crept forward and offered her hand. Derilla, with his usual predatory grace, scooped it up and bowed low for a kiss. His poisonous fangs mere inches from her flesh.

"Charmed," the arachne said; he held Ria's hand longer than was polite, and she frowned, snapping it back.

"I thought you said that you'd tell me if you were uncomfortable?" Keith teased. There were still moments when she revealed that she came from another culture.

"Be nice." Derilla moved back, giving Ria space. "I am pretty terrifying by human standards."

"I'm not afraid!" Ria countered, her eyes glinting with a fierce intent. "I'm just wondering why my [Sword Aura] is flagging you as an enemy who wants to kill us?"

Derilla threw back his head and laughed. "Because I *am*."

Keith felt a headache coming on.

Henrietta's hand went to her sword, but Derilla only laughed again. "I will not attack you *here*, Princess. You're under my hospitality."

"Then why?"

"I might ask *you* why you have your class skills active while in my home?" Derilla crossed his arms.

She shrugged. "I used it en route and never bothered to deactivate it. And assassins are everywhere these days. Though I wasn't expecting the notification to warn me about *you*, General Vane." She stared pointedly at the arachne.

"He wants to be king of the Dark Enchanted Forest," Keith explained. "He hasn't figured out how to kill me or rule without needing to take a nap in the cold. Oh, and I'm just *more powerful* and *better at fighting* than he is."

"For now." Derilla gripped a fist and pointed a finger at Keith. "I may rest in the winter, but you have stagnated while I grow stronger. As you tinker with toys, I train in darkness. I will drink your blood and feast upon your corpse until Chloe wrestles it from my [Mana Drain Web]."

"He's also fun at parties," Keith deadpanned. That particular perk had been an inconvenience the last time they'd fought. "And keeps his hospitality. He won't kill us while we're visiting, but every few years, he challenges me for the kingdom."

"Can just *anyone* challenge you for the kingdom?" Ria let go of the hilt of her blade and turned big eyes on Keith.

"Technically?" Keith shrugged.

At the same time Derilla said, "No."

"Anyone from Nilheim may challenge me." Keith pushed up his glasses. "During the winter solstice."

"It's most inconvenient." Derilla Vane sighed, then waved the two of them over to the veranda door. "I am at a disadvantage. But the higher my level, the easier it is to ignore my physiological needs like torpor."

Keith took Henrietta's arm again and escorted her outside. A light rain had rolled in, dripping off the curved roof overhang above them. A merry fire flickered in a brazier, providing enough warmth that the cool air wasn't uncomfortable. There was a short table with cushions laid out around it, and Keith let Ria take a seat first before he plopped down beside her.

"What level *are* you now?"

Derilla smiled, revealing all his sharp, pointy fangs. "Seventy-one."

Henrietta started and stared at their host over her shoulder. Keith raised an eyebrow.

"Congratulations." He took off his glasses to wipe them as they fogged up from the cool damp. "I suppose we'll be seeing you at the castle again this solstice?"

"Count on it."

Keith enjoyed the misty afternoon aesthetic and settled in for some moon-shaped floofpoof egg cakes and lotus tea.

He had his mouth full of the dessert when Ria asked, "Will I be fighting beside you this winter . . . or do I get to compete?"

CHAPTER 93

Miss Hammerwinkle's Axe-Throwing Tea Party

Henrietta

I thought it was a reasonable question, so I was surprised when Keith started choking on his pastry.

Derilla just stared at me for a moment before bursting into deep-throated laughter. "I see the rumors are true, then?"

I shrugged. Keith had rejected my proposal, so this was going to be on him.

"You *could* compete." The Dark Lord composed himself and shot her a soft half smile. "Do you *want* to compete to become queen of the Dark Enchanted Forest?"

"One way or the other." I flashed Keith a sly look.

"Good to note that I have some decent competition this year." Derilla refilled my small teacup. "Maybe we can have a friendly bout beforehand?"

Keith voiced, "I wouldn't—"

"I'd love to."

My Dark Lord face-palmed and turned to his friend. "Your funeral."

"I'm obviously a higher level." Derilla waved off Keith's concerns. "It'll be a fun match."

"Why do you assume I'll win?" It was too bad Keith had choked on his pastry because *wow*, this was delightful.

Keith stared pointedly at Jacqueline, whom I'd brought with me to the table. I shrugged. It wasn't as though I'd wake her up for a simple spar. I'd suffer the consequences if I did. And critical hits weren't easily won when fighting a trained opponent. I didn't say *that* aloud. No sense revealing my strengths or weaknesses to a man—er, arachne who wanted to kill us.

I sized Derilla up as I considered my experiences with arachne. I'd fought a nest before, in the Dungeon Valley Crest. The monsters had an uncanny skill with traps and enjoyed eating their prey alive. They were one of the biggest reasons I liked to solo the dungeon. Even though I'd only seen midlevel arachne, they had a way of spreading [Panic] or [Fear] effects from their specialized [Intimidation Aura] skill. It was a work of art.

Deadly art.

"Should we fight after lunch?" I rolled my shoulders, actually eager for the chance to spar. I had a lot of frustrations to work out these days. Julia hadn't quite been at the level to give me a real challenge.

Derilla looked out over the mountains, the spring rain a dull drone. Layered soft-gray clouds let in light while showering the hot springs below with countless droplets. It was a beautiful afternoon, but admittedly very wet.

"I have only just awoken." Derilla offered me a polite excuse. "We may take to the plateau and test each other's skills when you are free after the ball."

"When next we meet." I nodded.

We settled into comfortable silence, finished our snacks, and then bid Derilla Vane and Thistlecrick a polite farewell. A small part of me was sad that I didn't get to visit with the naga I'd met earlier, but I would see them again soon. After all, traveling about Nilheim was my greatest joy—after kissing the Dark Lord of Nilheim, of course.

My [Sword Aura] proved a useful skill while journeying, and we only passed one person who showed up as a threat between the hot springs and the border. Lilith handled it so Keith and I could relax and enjoy the ride.

Though Keith excused himself shortly after we set off to get some last-minute work done.

"Can I help with anything?" I asked, eyeing the pile of documents on his lap.

He looked up at me over his glasses. "You are helping."

"How so?"

He took a deep breath through his nose and resettled himself. "You're *here*. But if you want to divide and conquer these 'talking points for the various kingdoms of Valaria,' I won't stop you."

He pulled out a stack as thick as my arm. "Here. These are the reports on Baldorin's economic struggles. With the trade guild feuds, assassinations, failed feuds, deaths, births, royal affairs, and artistic cultural scandals of the last few years . . . On second thought, maybe you should read *all of these*. You're a royal too. I should've thought about preparing you—"

"It's alright." I didn't want him kicking himself over this, especially when I did have *some* etiquette beaten into me already. "We have time, and we can help each other at the ball. Pass me the first pile."

That's how I spent the rest of our trip reading about dwarven royal feuds. I was reading with fascination about a unigoat that had ruined Ms. Hammerwinkle's axe-throwing tea party when we reached the edge of the forest.

The trees continued, but we'd *definitely* left the Dark Enchanted Forest.

I could *feel* it. Something was gone. Something small and comforting; something magical, a sense of being watched . . . I'd grown used to the playful sentience that filled the woods.

And now, we were riding down into the city that sat on the North Sumbrian side of the border: Holly Hill. The town sprawled over a pair of forested hills. Houses nestled between trees, and the entire place was a plethora of magical wonders. North Sumbria was best known as the birthplace of Archwizard Jeffrey. Jeffrey, who mass created wonders such as the Crystal Cast Network and street lamps and teleporter pads. Though the pads were only found in North Sumbria, and no one really knew how they worked.

Taking them apart destroyed the internal spell script, and even simple tinkering with the plate deactivated it permanently. A few were lost before everyone gave up. Better to try again when another magical engineer reached a level high enough to stop destroying national transport artifacts.

Even in this small town, hours from the duchy capital, the entire place was vibrant with magical *things*. There were construct carts that picked people up and delivered them across town, baby strollers for mothers to load up and push children around with ease, and pocket watches that always told the right time without needing to be wound. It was in everything big and small, and it was marvelous.

Keith must love visiting. I glanced his way; his legs were crossed, and he was slumped forward reading documents.

Usually, as I understood it, Rufus attended these kinds of events as a representative. I'd only gone a few times myself, mostly to events in Peldeep, but as a minor, there was little I could assist with. My parents used the opportunity as a way to get me access to local dungeons.

We pulled up at the Waddling Wombat Inn at sunset, and despite doing little to nothing except sitting, I was ready for bed.

Of course, Fate had other plans.

CHAPTER 94

What's a Little Duel Between Royal Neighbors?

Keith

When Keith escorted Henrietta into the Waddling Wombat, he was *not* expecting to run into the most exhausting excuse for an elf in all the known kingdoms.

But here they were.

"If it isn't the *Dark* Lord of the *Dark* Enchanted Forest in his *dark* carriage right when it's about to get *dark* outside." Crown Prince Deryl of Sumbria snidely remarked. He had a few overly-dressed-for-travel attendants who stayed back from the exchange. Deryl himself wore an obscene amount of lace for someone on the road.

Keith resisted the urge to rub his temples. "Your Highness. Good to see you; I'm surprised to see you *here*, though. I wasn't aware that the Sumbrian royals were issued any invites to this year's festivities?"

Or any other year, for that matter. North Sumbria had a long memory, and the grand duchess held a very deep hatred for those who were at fault for her husband's final death.

"I forget your kingdom is so *behind* on the news. To think you don't even listen to Madame Potts's Casts? Tsk." The elf flicked his chin up in distain and struck a pose. "I am, of course, escorting the lovely Lady Peregrine Fern to the Spring Ball this year."

The woman was nowhere to be seen. Lucky her.

"I see." Keith nodded. He leaned down and whispered in Henrietta's ear, "I'm sorry about this . . ." before putting on his most politically empty smile and saying, "Crown Prince Deryl, may I introduce you to Princess Henrietta Doryn of *Nilheim*?"

The elf did a double take, then frowned at Ria. Keith wished that he could've excused the princess to their rooms while he finished with the prince. But it was important to notify everyone—especially this particularly annoying gossipy offspring of his peers—that Henrietta would not be attending the Spring Ball without backing.

"Princess Henrietta?" Prince Deryl eyed her up and down. "You? I feel sorry for the marquess. No wonder my parents never invited you to our royal gala."

Keith had run into the insufferable boy a few times, but he'd never felt the inclination to punch him in the face until this very moment.

"Actually, they have. I refused to attend." Henrietta shrugged. "If you are an example of what I missed, then I haven't missed much." A huge smile broke out across Keith's face as his princess continued. "Now, if you'll excuse us, we shall retire for the evening."

"Good night, Your Highness." Keith followed her lead and walked around the shocked elf.

Deryl's cheeks burned red as he spun to call after them, "You may have shamed Drendil and made your bed with *monsters*, but soon—"

A large palm came down heavily on the elf's shoulder. A fully armored knight stood in the doorway with an eclectic group of adventurers behind him. "You'd be wise to stop now, Prince Deryl. The Dark Enchanted Forest has many friends."

"That's *Crown Prince* to you, Knight Commander," the elf retorted but looked visibly subdued.

"Have a good evening, *Crown Prince*." Knight Commander Bastian of Peldeep let go of Prince Deryl and strode past him. Some of the knight commander's people nodded politely at the prince as they walked past the elf. The crown prince made an angry chuffing sound and stormed off. He had a few retainers himself, who excused themselves to run after him.

"Greetings, Knight Commander." Keith clasped arms with the giant of a man. "It's good to see you again."

"Likewise. Let's check in, and perhaps I'll see you at dinner?" He let go of Keith's arm.

Henrietta declared, "That would be lovely. I'm famished. We haven't eaten anything since lunch!"

Knight Commander Bastian chuckled and waved for them to go first. The elderly lady at the front desk looked slightly frazzled, probably from dealing with the Sumbrian royal. She welcomed everyone nonetheless and issued room keys with efficiency and skill. After Keith rented two rooms, one for himself and Sithli and the other for Lilith and Henrietta, he sent his minions to go and prepare the rooms upstairs.

"I'm overjoyed that Prince Look-At-Me Sumbria hasn't come back down," Henrietta mumbled as they claimed empty seats in the first-floor tavern. She took her travel cloak and threw it over a chair at the larger empty table beside them, saving it for the Peldeep group.

"Thank you for forgiving me, throwing you to the wolves like that." Keith passed her an enchanted chalkboard with the menu, and then filled her glass with water from a jug stuffed with water, lemon, and cranberries.

"Think nothing of it. It was refreshing being able to join in on the conversation. Good thing Bastian arrived, or I might've challenged the Sumbrian crown prince to a duel." Ria's smile turned menacing. "We are in North Sumbria, after all, and what's a little duel between royal neighbors?"

Keith immediately pushed down a niggling curiosity at how familiar his princess was with Peldeep that she called the knight commander by his first name. He glanced over the menu himself while replying, "We can ask the grand duchess about duels when we see her tomorrow. I'm interested in how they became so popular."

"Good idea." Henrietta looked over Keith's shoulder and waved. "Speaking of Peldeep, here they are! Bastian, over here! We saved you a table."

The knight commander had taken off his helmet. He had harsh features, short, tousled silver hair, and piercing purple eyes. A small smile teased the corner of his mouth as he greeted them. "Thank you."

"Thank *you*," the princess replied.

"Well met, Bastian." Keith put down his menu and reached out a hand to cover Henrietta's. He recognized most of Bastian's companions, famous adventurers all, including the young androgynous boy disguised as a squire. Keith nodded at the lad. "And of course, it's a pleasure to see you again, Your Majesty."

CHAPTER 95

Their Royal Highness of Peldeep

Henrietta

Magical whirls of red and gold flashed as a seemingly young squire turned into Their Royal Highness Rowen of Peldeep.

As they were of no particular gender, Rowen was neither a king nor a queen, enjoying instead the ambiguity of other titles such as Their Royal Highness, Their Majesty, or even Their Rulership.

When I'd visited Peldeep in the past, I'd been impressed by the festive culture they inspired. Their lands were full of brevity, with a light hint of cleverness. *To be sly is to be wise, but to be true is to be happy*, as the saying went. And that saying was the embodiment of Their Royal Highness of Peldeep.

"Oh, Monfort," the smiling royal laughed. They'd taken on a beastkin's form, with added fox ears and a bushy tail. Elaborate robes with beautiful peony prints fell softly about them, and their long straight hair was a mix of black and red. They leaned back in their seat. "You always see right through me. Care to tell this one how you do it?"

Keith shrugged, telling a half-truth. "I have Intelligence eighty-five and a head on my shoulders. Bastian brought along three members of the royal guard *and* a child to the Spring Ball? He's not a babysitter . . . and I can't see you missing the most interesting event of the year, what with all the hints from Madame Potts."

"That woman is a delight." Their Highness glanced down at the menu. I noticed they'd been given a jug full of lemon and cucumber and fresh mint, and briefly wondered what determined which water jug went to which tables. The group quietly waited and watched Their Royal Highness reading enthusiastically, and I caught Bastian hiding a small sigh.

Rowen put down the menu and their eyes snapped up to *me*. "Greetings to you, Princess. And congratulations on your new . . . *home*."

There were many words they might have said, but home was a good choice. I smiled. "Thank you, Your Majesty."

"None of that!" The ruler of Peldeep waved a hand, and suddenly, there was a young woman in standard adventuring attire sitting where they'd just been. "Call me Rowen."

"Are you intending to go in disguise for the whole trip, Rowen? Or just until you reach the palace?" Keith inquired. His fingers ran along the top of my hand, and I shivered.

Rowen waved at the waiter to come take everyone's orders. A wise waiter who, upon noting the magical displays and titles being bandied about earlier, had taken to serving our tables exclusively.

"Ladies first." Rowen waved a hand expansively. "I'll have the lamb shank with mushroom gravy. It sounds *divine*."

"I'll have the lamb quay-sa . . ." My tongue tripped on the unfamiliar word. Whatever it was, the description sounded delicious.

The waiter asked, "The quesadilla, miss?"

"Yes! That one, please." Flat bread pan-fried together with meat and cheese and spices sounded exactly like what I needed.

The waiter nodded, finished taking everyone's orders, and then walked back to the kitchen. Keith had chosen a simple potato leek soup with garlic toast, and Bastian a boar cutlet on spuds.

I didn't want to speak over the ruler of Peldeep, but it had been a while since I'd seen Bastian and was wondering how we could catch up. Back when he was just a knight, he'd been assigned to the group that went dungeon delving with me. It'd been almost two years since I'd last seen him.

Bastian noticed my stare. His eyes wandered to the hand held by Keith and back again. He raised one eyebrow.

I blushed, recognizing the question. Almost imperceptibly, I nodded my head to show that yes, I was *in fact* courting the Dark Lord of Nilheim. And wonder of wonders, he was courting me back!

Bastian relaxed a trifle, returning his gaze to his ruler . . . I knew in my heart of hearts that Rowen was a married and happy Their Royal Highness; a parent with children older than myself . . . but it was hard to handle them flirting with *my* Dark Lord.

"Of course, if you're interested in joining our court for a moon viewing next month, there would be ample room for you." It was the light tease in their voice that turned my stomach. And if I was not mistaken, they'd altered their new form to emphasize certain . . . *features*.

"My apologies, Your Majesty," Keith politely refused. "But I'll be in the middle of wedding plans, and it will be hard to get away."

One of Their Highness's guards choked on their lemon water. Bastian frowned at the man, and he stuttered as everyone's attention focused on him. "My apologies. I didn't realize Your Viciousness was engaged?"

Keith shrugged and shared a quick look with me before saying, "I'm not. My necromancer, Chloe Watercress, is marrying Julia von Slyke."

"Calisto's heir. I'd heard." Rowen laughed. "Did the grand duchess poach one of the most powerful women in your army?"

"Actually," Keith grinned, "*I* poached *her* heir. Julia announced that she's officially moving to the Dark Enchanted Forest."

Their Royal Highness blinked. "That would mean . . ."

"Julia's *brother* will inherit the duchy." Keith let go of my hand and took a sip of his own water.

As far as I knew, Grand Duchess Calisto had two children, Julia von Slyke and Julian von Slyke. No one knew why, or at least *I* didn't know why, but he'd gone north after his father's death. He'd been little more than a young boy at the time. Few had met him over the years, and rumors had spread like wildfire in his absence.

There was a silence around the table, finally broken by Rowen. "Well. Things will be more interesting at this Spring Ball than I thought . . . Does Calisto know?"

"She knows Julia and Chloe are getting married," Keith said. "I don't actually know what else she knows other than that."

The ruler of Peldeep chuckled. "A most interesting ball indeed."

CHAPTER 96

Being a Dark Magician King Was Hard, but Dating the Heroine of Justice Was Harder

Keith

After Keith shared his news that Julia was moving to the Dark Enchanted Forest, everyone became lost in their own thoughts. Dinner arrived, and it was excellent. Henrietta kept throwing looks at Knight Commander Bastian like she wanted to say something, and Keith's curiosity won over his jealousy.

Just as everyone finished and headed up to bed, Keith called Their Royal Highness to chat outside, distracting the old fox long enough for Henrietta to get the chance to speak quietly to the knight.

Keith leaned up against his carriage, breathing warmth into his hands. "Rowen, I met one of your children in my kingdom. She seems to be getting along just fine."

Rowen's fox ears perked. "Ah, my darling Penelope. How *is* she doing?"

"Singing up a storm and befriending a lizard wizard, last I visited." Out of the corner of his eye, Keith was pleased to see that his plan had worked; Ria was busy whispering to Bastian. It wasn't that he *wanted* her to go off chatting with other men . . . but she was a grown woman with friends of her own. If she wanted to talk to one of them, he needed to figure out his own problems.

Keith missed what Their Royal Highness had just said, but it was something about babies. He simply replied, "I wouldn't know," hoping it was the right choice.

Rowen tapped their chin twice. "Then maybe I'll swing by on the way back home. Is she still at that beastfolk village?"

"As far as I know." He wouldn't have normally shared the happy couple's location, even with her parents, as he didn't know their circumstances. But if the old fox already knew, there wasn't much sense hiding it.

"Thank you. Have a good night, we'll see you at the ball." Their Royal Highness lead their retainers, Bastian included, upstairs.

Henrietta rejoined Keith and gripped his arm. "Thank you."

"Did you have a nice chat?" Keith didn't bother resisting the urge anymore; he leaned down and sniffed her hair. The smell of warm spices with a hint of caramel sugar filled his nose.

Ria leaned in and rubbed her face on his arm. "Mm-hmm."

Keith waited, arching an eyebrow.

Ria explained, "Madame Potts made his life very uncomfortable. The man isn't very social at the best of times, let alone after being called out as one of the continent's most desirable . . . Come to think of it, why weren't *you* included in that list?"

"Good question. Maybe I'm too old? This also isn't my debut; I had my coming out at sixteen, and I had *no* intention of suddenly getting married at the time." Keith and Henrietta walked up to the top floor and separated, facing their rooms. "And any hopeful partners or *stalkers* were easily dealt with accordingly."

"Oh?"

"Rufus is a very good second in command. His capacity to sniff out drugs, potions, spies, and hidden assailants is exceptional."

Henrietta shuddered. "I couldn't imagine being the target of unwanted attention like that."

"It's not pleasant, and it might play a part in why I'm still single."

"Aside from being the Evil Overlord, Dark Magician King of Nilheim, Vicious Ruler of the Dark Enchanted Forest?"

"Says the Crown Princess and Heroine of Justice. Who, I understand, is *also* unwed."

"Not for lack of trying," Henrietta mumbled. She looked between Keith and her bedroom door. "Let's talk more tomorrow?"

"Of course. Good night, Princess Henrietta."

Her voice was full of lighthearted teasing as she returned, "Good night, Dark Magician King Keith."

Keith stared at her door for a moment after it closed. He briefly considered sweeping in and ordering Lilith to bunk with Sithli for the night.

Briefly.

Their Royal Highness was long gone by the time Keith rolled out of bed. Sithli was already out preparing the wagons, so Keith had the room to himself. His morning ablutions were rudimentary while traveling, kept to the minimal brush-hair-and-teeth-and-shave-face routine. He missed his usual morning bubble bath and servanted ministrations.

He'd done far too much traveling this year, and he still had more coming. He sighed. Being a Dark Magician King was hard, but dating the Heroine of Justice was harder.

It was well worth it, though.

Henrietta was awake and happy to see him when he wandered downstairs for breakfast. Her poofy brown hair and soft brown eyes looked the same, but there was something different about her. He tried to figure out what it was, and Lilith coughed from behind the princess, motioning to her lips.

They were lightly colored with a soft pink. He stared. It had been a very long time since he'd kissed those lips. At *least* a day.

There was something wrong with him. He gathered himself and complimented Ria over breakfast. She laughed off his words, but he could tell she enjoyed his praise.

"I'm trying to move from dungeon war paint to debutant war paint," she joked.

Keith laughed. "I can't wait to see you in your finest. Rinrin assures me that we will be a sight to behold, with matching outfits no less." He pushed down the unease that resurfaced every time he thought of that disastrous fitting. It was getting easier.

All too soon, they were alone in the carriage again, heading toward Grand Duchess Calisto's palace. There was a lot more reading for Ria than himself, as he'd finished the last of his required reviews before bed. It was her turn to be immersed in interkingdom gossip while he relaxed and kept an eye out for assassins.

They didn't meet any, but it was distraction enough to keep him occupied and not thinking of his princess sitting very close beside him in a carriage on a makeshift bed.

He had made sure there was ample light, sheer curtains, and an open atmosphere in the carriage. Henrietta didn't seem to mind the enclosed space, and he wondered if it was because it wasn't a cold dark room, or if she was just pushing down her anxiety.

Either way, he planned extra stops along their journey, and he kept up a steady [Cantrips: Dancing Lights] perk. Consideration wasn't hard, just time consuming. It was also why he'd put Rufus on guard duty for Henrietta's friend.

It was barely midday when they arrived at Grand Duchess Calisto's palace. It had only *felt* like an eternity.

CHAPTER 97

Decorum be Damned

Henrietta

I'd been to the Sumbrian Royal Palace, the Emerald Palace of Peldeep, the Servalt Castle of Ashes, and the Capital Castle in Drendil, the last of which I'd grown up in. My trips to the Baldorin Council had not granted access to the royal suites, but since they were carved into the mountain, it wasn't something you could look at from the outside and admire.

I'd seen the wonders of the Dark Enchanted Forest and beheld marvels that could only be found in the twisted environs of dungeons.

And yet, Grand Duchess Calisto's palace was still *breathtaking*. Spires of ornate shimmering teal and coral pink reached into the sky, all at different heights. Great archways of floating crystal bridges connected the buildings, catching the light and scattering it into rainbows that lanced to the earth far below. The entire palace was enclosed by delicate white peaked metal fencing that I didn't need [Sword Aura] to tell was magically enhanced. Mana rippled in the air, thick enough to tickle the senses.

Our carriage entered through the open front gates, in line with three others that had arrived around the same time. The entry led to a one-way road that circled around a shimmering fountain to the front doors of the biggest and tallest tower, a pure-white edifice that stretched up at least twenty floors.

The palace doors opened, and attendants exited to create a welcoming path leading up to the entrance. A statuesque woman descended the short stair and walked with grace toward the first carriage. She wore a soft flowing dress made of tan-colored arachne silk. It accentuated her night-sky black skin and long loose dark-red hair. Streaks of gray and gentle crow's eyes betrayed her age and her trials in life.

Grand Duchess Calisto personally welcomed her guests as they exited their carriages. We were third in line, and my heart fluttered with growing anticipation.

I recognized the first to arrive as Duke Wyldon of Servalt, a scholarly young man who was high up in administration, and nephew to the queen of Servalt. He was diligent and strict, following the rules of the law with a hard hand. He exited his carriage alone, and politely greeted Her Grace before being guided inside by an attendant.

The following carriage held an elderly couple who dismounted painfully slowly. The woman kissed Calisto on both cheeks in greeting, then they ambled in after their own guide.

Finally, we arrived at the front. Sithli hopped down and opened the door to the carriage, and I realized I was sitting closest to the door. Decorum be damned, I stepped down first, offering my hand up to the Dark Lord. He laughed and reached out to take it.

Grand Duchess Calisto managed to suppress a half smile that played on the corner of her lips. Her voice was rich and cultured as she spoke. "Greetings, King Monfort and Princess Henrietta. I hope your travels were calm and quiet."

Keith smiled regally. "Thank you, Your Grace. It was a pleasant trip."

"It is wonderful to finally meet you, Your Grace." I wound my hands around Keith's arm. "I'm honored to receive your invitation. Your home is beautiful, and I cannot imagine anywhere else more perfect for my debut."

The duchess dropped a bit of her formality, and her smile softened. "You are well met, my dear. If you have time today to join me for afternoon tea, I would love to have you. I'm sure we have much to talk about."

There was nothing I wanted more than to have tea with one of the most influential and powerful women on the continent.

"I would love to, Your Grace."

The duchess eyed Keith. "I apologize for stealing your partner, Monfort. It's but a small affair to introduce the newly eligible young men and women to each other. And to ease them into things."

"Think nothing of it. I will enjoy your hospitality in other ways. Might I perchance beg leave to peruse your library?" Keith asked.

The duchess smiled. "Of course you may. And if there's time, I'd love your opinion on some of the new magical tools I'm designing."

"Absolutely," Keith announced eagerly. He didn't bother hiding his interest and used his free hand to push up his glasses. "I'm fascinated with your new 'moving rooms,' the ones that travel up and down your palace, among other things I noticed since we crossed the border."

"Yes, the magical 'elevators' were a challenge to complete, but they've made traveling around the palace so much easier. I look forward to your critical eye on how their mechanisms might be improved."

It would be unfortunate that Keith couldn't join us for tea, but I was happy that he would have something even more exciting for him to do in the meantime.

Keith visibly composed himself and brought up the other matter we needed to discuss during our visit. "And, of course, I look forward to hosting Your Grace this summer at my own castle."

"Not if I convince them to move the wedding," the woman threatened. "We can discuss things before you leave, but where are my manners; I've left you standing here for far too long. Please, follow Daj. He shall guide the two of you to your suite."

Keith and I stared in shocked silence at the smug grand duchess as we both realized what she'd said.

CHAPTER 98

I Ask for Decorum and Restraint

Keith

Keith wondered why it seemed like every single person in the entire world was trying his patience.

Not that he was surprised, mind. He'd visited this palace before and knew what was to come. This was probably revenge for his necromancer cavorting with her unwed daughter for the past six months. The woman was a brilliant leader . . . whose sole joy in life outside of magical crafting was teasing the youth and matchmaking. This was why he only attended one of her events every year. Chloe could take the rest.

He realized with a pang of guilt that his *princess* had probably been blindsided.

Said princess was standing perplexed. "Our suite?"

The duchess simply raised an eyebrow. "I've given you two a private suite in the east wing, far from any . . . unpleasantness that might occur from *other* visiting royals."

Ria's voice was similar to one of his automatons. "With multiple bed*rooms*, though?"

"Of *course*; you're not married *yet*," the duchess replied, scandalized. She stared pointedly at Keith. "So I ask for decorum and restraint." She then turned an equally pointed stare at Henrietta. "That goes for you too, Princess."

Keith felt embarrassment inflame his cheeks as it hadn't since he was a boy, his hand caught in Feliwyn's hoard looking for high-level spell books he wasn't ready for. "I think you are mistaken, Your Grace."

She turned back to him, stately and poised, but Keith gave as good as he got. "Unlike *some* unnamed royal heirs, we are more than capable of controlling our wanton ardor."

"Keith!" Henrietta, who was still in shock that the most graceful and innovative mind on the continent was a veritable tease, gasped.

"What?" Keith shrugged.

The duchess nodded, sharing the joke with a warm smile. "I can't imagine what royal house would allow such impropriety. Surely you can't mean such scandals are occurring in your own castle? Truly, Nilheim is the den of iniquity they all claim."

"Jealous rumors. You will see for yourself when you come for the wedding," Keith said, getting in another jab.

"Unless I convince them to move the wedding." Her light smile and tone was ruined by the determined glint in her eye. "Now, if you would please excuse me, it appears that I must see to my next guest." The duchess made a delicate shooing motion with her hand. "Our weather foreteller has called for light showers this afternoon, so take your time settling in. Let Daj know if you wish to dine with us or in your rooms tonight."

"Thank you, Your Grace," Keith replied, and they followed the attendant into the palace. Daj was a very long-eared and lithe man, so brown he could be mistaken for markleberry spread.

Conveniently, they entered just in time to miss Crown Prince Deryl yelling at his valet for being slow-witted.

Keith almost wished he could stay and listen to how Calisto handled the boy. Instead, he enjoyed the wonder on Henrietta's face as they made their way through the crystal palace, slowing down to explain what he knew of the building and its artefacts. "The entire palace was constructed by the late Grand Duke Lysander as a wedding gift for Her Grace," Keith explained. "The previous estate was burned down by the prince of Sumbria during their courtship."

"I can't imagine coming home to a burned down castle," Henrietta said, angry on their behalf. "The history of Sumbria is depressing, even more so as I get to know the legends from that time."

"Your Highnesses." Daj bowed. "We've arrived at the elevator. We ask that you refrain from any magical workings or combat while in transport, or we may upset the construct and fall to our death. Thank you."

Ria tensed beside him. His eyes swept the small room, bright and welcoming and made out of the same shimmering opaque magical crystal aesthetic that the rest of the palace was crafted from. It would be a tight fit for the three of them. Keith slipped her hand into his and gave it a slight squeeze.

She hesitated but lightly squeezed back.

"Which floor are we on?" Keith asked Daj. He'd never been in the eastern tower, but all of the palace operated the same way.

"The fifth floor, Your Viciousness."

"Then if it's all the same to you, I'll take the stairs." He smiled down at his princess, explaining, "The alcoves in each staircase have historical artifacts and abandoned magical tools that Her Grace left half finished. You wouldn't mind accompanying me on a tour, would you, Henrietta?"

The look she gave him almost made his knees go weak. A smile bloomed across her face, and he ignored the fact that Ria simultaneously looked like she wanted to kiss him or burst into tears. Or both. "I'd love to."

"As you will." Daj bowed and closed the doors into the magical transport. He gestured for them to follow and led them to a sweeping stair that spiraled around the inside of the outer wall. One side of the stair had tall, peaked windows that looked out over the trees, interspersed with cut alcoves full of wonders.

"I've read a number of books on Calisto's unfinished works. This"—Keith waved at one ornate round dome the size of a garden sundial, with divots and an elaborate carved enchantment on one side—"was meant to send messages across the kingdom. The System has a number of perks which allow us to speak with our party members at great distances, or even send written messages between the notification interface. She was trying to recreate that."

"What stopped her?" Henrietta examined the device. They had passed by self-moving armored sentinels who could only wave (not very useful against intruders), swords that always glowed in the light (but not in the dark), and a machine that blew hot or cold air (but only if you blew on it first).

Magical enchantments were finicky, as Keith knew, and perfecting new ones resulted in many leftover rejects. He hadn't had the chance to see these ones in person before.

They took a while to ascend, partly because he spent so much time examining the tools.

Which meant that by the time they arrived at their suite, Lilith and Sithli had already unpacked. They had a shared bathroom, lounge, and work desk, with two bedrooms. Lilith and Sithli would stay in the servants' quarters on the same floor.

After some debate, Keith and Henrietta decided to eat dinner together that night in their lounge. Tomorrow would be a light afternoon tea with the debutants, several hours to prepare, and then the Spring Ball.

He fondly remembered the year Rufus, Chloe, and himself were first invited. It had been a Winter Ball, and they'd arrived late due to snow on the roads. Rufus had been so stressed that he'd thrown up. Chloe had drunk too much of the spiked cider and accidentally [Raised] the roast unigoat . . .

He just wished he could attend the afternoon affair with Henrietta tomorrow. He trusted Duchess Calisto, but he was still worried.

Before Daj left, Keith had asked to be informed when the Drendil royal couple arrived . . . and there was still no word even after they retired for the night.

CHAPTER 99

You're Not Just Any Debutante; You're Our Debutante

Henrietta

Lilith pulled at the peach-colored lace trim on my shoulders and smoothed down the matching day dress I'd chosen for the afternoon tea.

My senses were sharp enough that I could *feel* Keith pacing in the lounge. He'd been nervous all morning, even waking up early to go with me while I did some morning training.

I allowed the hovering because he was pretty, even if his accursed clothing was fixed to look prim and proper. I didn't know how to bring up how much I missed his disheveled look, like he'd just rolled out of bed . . . Maybe I could do something about it after we were married.

"Lilith, you don't have to fuss. I'm not looking to catch anyone's eye at this tea party." I waved off the lizardwoman, who had finished with my dress and gone back to playing with my hair. Again.

"But Princesss," Lilith argued, using a pin to secure a stray wisp into place. "You're not *just* any debutante; you're *our* debutante."

The sentiment hit me harder than I could have expected. I whispered, "Thank you," and let her finish fussing over me.

My hair had been twisted into strands framing my face, starting at my forehead and ending in a bun at the nape of my neck, and then tucked all over with small white pearls. My makeup was light, with just a touch of color on my lips, a thin line of coal on my eyelids, and a brush of glitter around the eyes.

I was as ready as I'd ever be. I opened the door to indeed find Keith pacing. His gaze traveled over me, and I loved the way his entire demeanor softened. He stopped when his eyes landed on my hands.

"I'm not allowed to bring Jacqueline to the tea party," I explained, raising the sword I was holding. "So I was wondering if you would watch her while I'm away? She will probably be fine, but if I get into trouble, she might . . . act out."

Keith tentatively took the sword, wincing a bit. "Act out how?"

"She won't attack you." Probably. "She'll just get upset and go looking for me."

The first time I'd been sent to the punishment room after I'd bonded with Jacqueline . . . well, she'd reacted poorly to my initial upset. It had taken a year to repair the damage she'd inflicted on the castle trying to get to me. I had to figure out other ways to sneak out after that.

"She'll be a reliable alarm to let you know if I'm in danger," I finished.

Keith gripped the sword firmly. "Then I'll take her with me on a walk . . . If she suddenly tries to find you, it'll cause less damage to the palace."

It was my turn to wince. I would *hate* to face Grand Duchess Calisto if *my* sword blew out one of *her* walls. Better to lock me in a dark room and throw away the key.

Who am I kidding, I'd face a thousand disappointments before choosing to suffer that again.

Maybe I should stop joking about it, even in my own mind. I sighed.

"I'd also like you to hold on to *this*." I shoved a ring at him.

When Keith took hold of the small black ring, it magically resized itself to fit on his smallest finger. "Isn't this . . . ?"

"I think you need +2 Constitution more than I do." I reached out and wrapped his fingers around my grandfather's ring, securing it in his palm.

I wasn't the one who couldn't take a hit.

"I thought this was an heirloom piece?" Keith asked.

"We've already broken up the set. My father has the +4 Dexterity necklace, and my mother has the other earring; it grants +4 Perception. There's a bracelet in my sock drawer at home that gives +2 Strength. I hate wearing it because it gets in the way while swinging a sword."

I rubbed the ring etched all over with lilies that Keith had gifted me. "Besides, now we're fair. Unless . . . you won't accept the ring, as you've already rejected my proposal?"

"You know that's not fair." Keith slipped the ring on awkwardly as he juggled the sword at the same time. Afterward, he slipped Jacqueline through his belt, dangling her so she was held up by her handles hooked on his belt alone.

I laughed. "Let me."

He lifted both his arms, and I stepped under them, focusing on tying the sheath properly to his belt.

Keith took a deep breath and tensed. When I was done, I looked into his eyes. Slowly, he leaned forward, but instead of kissing me, he pressed his face into my shoulder and the curve of my neck. "I plan to accept all of your gifts," he murmured, his breath hot against my nape.

I shivered. Maybe I was teasing him too much. I reached up and ran my fingers through his hair. His horn was on the opposite side of his head, and it didn't poke me. I grew bolder and actually touched it, running my hands over the hard surface. Keith's lips parted and he muffled a moan into my shoulder.

"Princesss." Lilith coughed from the entry. "It really is time to go to the tea party now. We don't want to be late."

Keith took a deep breath and stood straighter. "Thank you, Lilith. This is your day, Ria, and you can't be late. The tea party is held in the gardens, so it's a bit of a walk. May I escort you, Princess Henrietta?" He offered his arm.

I took it. "It would be my pleasure, Dark Lord Keith."

We walked down the stairs and into the castle proper, where many other young nobles had gathered. Just before we joined them, Keith leaned down and whispered, "One last thing? Try not to get upset on my—on Nilheim's behalf."

"What does that mean?"

"You keep forgetting that I'm the *Dark Lord*."

He let go of my arm as an attendant welcomed me to the throng of clamoring youth.

There were a few last stragglers, and then an announcement that we were welcome to follow the staff.

Suddenly, Duke Wyldon of Servalt was beside me and offering his arm. "Shall we?"

CHAPTER 100

It Pleases Me That You're Not Dead, Monfort

Keith

Keith rubbed Jacqueline's hilt as he watched Henrietta leave with someone else. He had to admit that as much as a sword got in the way, it was comforting to carry around.

Especially a sword that specialized in killing *him*.

He wandered the castle aimlessly, and eventually found his way outside to a courtyard with benches and a fountain.

He wasn't alone.

"Greetings, Your Highness." Keith nodded at a young woman reading a slip of paper on a bench at the fountain. She looked up, shocked, and then grinned at him playfully.

"Monfort. What brings you to the garden? I thought you'd bury yourself in the library while you waited." Rowen waved the paper in their hands and said, "But perfect timing. I'm sure you've been distracted with the princess all morning, and probably didn't get the *news*?"

Keith quirked an eyebrow but didn't disagree. He had no idea what the fox was talking about. "What is it?"

Rowen handed over the page, and in neat scrawl, it read:

A surprise Cast today, with interesting news!
I have been fortunate enough to change the future a few times.
As such, many of my predictions are out of date before I have
the chance to give them.
I hope this is one of them, and it is no longer valid . . . but just
in case, I'll let you all know anyway!
At the stroke of midnight, please don't stand beside the green

**oak tapestry. And if you like your green oak tapestry, maybe
move it?**
**In other news! I have it on the best authority that Chancellor
Fernley in Peldeep is smuggling a group of blue pandas and
should be stopped. Those bundles of fluff can be found under
Gorge Turpin Bridge.**
**Finally, if your assassin never made it home last night, you can
start your searching at the guild in Peldeep or Servalt. Maybe
next time don't attack an Enchanted Forest that can kill you
all by itself?**
This is Madame Potts, signing out.

I read the paper at a glance and handed it back to Their Highness.

"The pandas?"

Rowen scoffed. "They were rounded up within the hour, of course. We take Madame Potts very seriously ever since she saved my life last year at the Festival of Lights."

"I can imagine." Keith felt a bit guilty, having never much listened to Potts until Henrietta had showed up. It didn't seem important unless it was directly about the Dark Enchanted Forest. Plus, he didn't really trust foretellers. "What is the point in showing me this?"

"There's a green oak tapestry in the Grand Hall. Where we're going to have the Spring Ball tonight." Rowen rolled up the page and ate it, their mouth opening into a giant toothy maw and closing again as if nothing happened.

"Is it *still* there?" Keith chuckled. He could only imagine how busy the palace already was without having to relocate a wall tapestry.

Their Highness's smile turned vicious. "You think this is funny, but you didn't almost *bath* in molten ash vane magicked to look like regular bath water. I would have died a very painful and permanent death if Bastian hadn't burst into the Forbidden Palace after hearing the Cast. Smart boy."

The Forbidden Palace was home to the Peldeep ruler and their consort. It was separated from the main Emerald Palace, and it was punishable by *permadeath* to intrude on the grounds. Keith's estimation of Bastian went up considerably.

Keith countered, "I assure you I take it most seriously. If you recall, Henrietta was actually supposed to slaughter my entire army and then kill me in my own inner sanctum."

Rowen was silent for a moment. The fact that without Madame Potts neither of them would be here today left a deep impression on the pair.

"It pleases me that you're not dead, Monfort."

"The feeling is mutual, Your Majesty."

Keith decided that was enough pleasantries and asked, "Can I expect you for Chloe and Julia's wedding?"

Anyone who had arrived by today had received their invite to the wedding with their lunch. Keith and Henrietta had gotten theirs in person. Chloe had popped by at breakfast to personally hand them over.

"The Peldeep royal family will attend in some capacity or another. That's who the letter is addressed to, anyway," Rowen answered. "Inconsiderate. It's like they don't want me to come. Now, when have I ever caused mischief at a wedding?"

Keith opened his mouth to say he was there when Their Highness had pretended to be the bride or groom at no less than three such affairs, but he thought better of it.

Rowen sighed. "All these young faces; I'm getting too old for this. Maybe it's time to abdicate."

"I can't imagine. What would you do with all that free time?" Keith ran his hand over Jacqueline. No response, so he fiddled with the ties.

"Sleep?" Rowen shrugged. Suddenly, their guise melted away, and an older-looking man with long red hair and a moustache stood up from the bench. He wore pants and a vest with pink accents. "Travel? Play with my grandchildren?"

Keith offered, "You could come to *my* wedding when it happens. I'll officially invite you, Their Royal Highness Rowen of Peldeep. Ruler to Ruler. No 'Royal Family of Peldeep' nonsense."

"Then I'll attend." Rowen reached out and put a hand on Keith's shoulder. "Congratulations."

"Don't congratulate me just yet. I still have to ask the princess."

Their Royal Highness looked taken aback, then they threw their head back and roared with laughter.

"I turned her down already, so we'll see if she forgives me." Keith smiled, content in the knowledge that Henrietta *would* say yes. Probably.

Rowen was still chuckling as they patted Keith's shoulder a second time. "I knew there was a reason I liked you, Monfort."

"I thought it was because I can see through your disguises?"

"Not just that." They shook their head and let go, crossing their arms in front of their chest. "Though now that you mention it, I *still* don't know how you do that!"

Keith sniffed. "I'm just an excellent judge of character."

Their Royal Highness eyed the Dark Lord. "It's not a skill? Or a perk? You'd tell me if there was a perk that could bypass my illusions?"

"There *are* perks that can bypass your illusions. And skills and spells. But I didn't use them. I just happen—" Keith stopped as the ruler of Peldeep whipped his head in the direction of the tea party and frowned. "Oh, that's not good."

Keith felt a thrumming at his side.

CHAPTER 101

Wait! I Haven't Been Tortured!

Henrietta

I'd met Duke Wyldon a few times in the Servalt Court. Once when I was visiting as a delegate for the queen's birthday luncheon, and a second time when he'd been accompanying his king to sign a trade tax revision on the treaty between Drendil and Servalt.

Both times he'd been firm and professional and distant, so I was surprised when he stepped forward to be my partner for the luncheon. I allowed it, given our previous relationship, and the fact that I didn't want to be the only young lady unescorted; all around us, young men and women were pairing off.

"It is a lovely day, Duke Wyldon." I smiled, falling into the habitual etiquette ingrained into me at my mother's knee. Namely, a bland face with a fake smile.

"It's not raining, which I admit is a nice change." The young man, perhaps twenty-one, glanced at the sky warily.

"Is there a lot of rain in Servalt these days?"

The gardens we walked out into with the rest of the group were beautiful. There were a variety of spring flowers I couldn't name, their multicolored hues a clear sign of careful magical crossbreeding. White fluffy clouds moved over the sky, but there was ample sunshine. I inhaled deeply through my nose; the air was warm and smelled like spring.

The duke nodded. "It's been windy and wet and miserable for weeks back home . . . Princess, I actually had a question for you—"

"Welcome to my afternoon tea, everyone! Please take your seats."

Before he could say more, our hostess greeted us and waved us to take our seats at a long table set for ten on each side and Grand Duchess Calisto at the head. If this were more official, each spot would have nameplates with the seats laid out by rank. Instead, we all just sat with our partners in order of arrival.

I was sitting in the fourth seat from Duchess Calisto on her right. Duke Wyldon sat one closer. I'd never met the two girls between myself and the head table, but I would guess they were from North Sumbria, as they had beautiful hazelnut black skin. They also wore the straight soft fabric fashion of the duchy and had escorted each other.

Bastian sat further down and across from me, escorting a Sumbrian girl. She had a white fichu tied in a bow at her breast and her long pink hair in a half ponytail. She was a timid thing, tiny, with big eyes and a delicate nature.

"Thank you all for joining us today," the Grand Duchess announced. "We will have refreshments shortly. I encourage you to use this time to get to know your peers."

At that, the duchess excused herself and walked over to what looked like her head butler. He was dressed in similar attire to the rest of the castle staff, except he had four bands sewn to his arm and a tie.

"Are you Duke Wyldon of Servalt?" one of the girls asked my escort. They must have been all of sixteen at my guess.

He sat straight and nodded. "I am, and this is Princess Henrietta Doryn of Drendil."

"Nilheim."

Everyone table turned to stare at me.

"What?" Duke Wyldon also stared at me.

It wasn't polite to correct my date or to introduce myself . . . but neither was not answering while everyone just stared at me. "It's Princess Henrietta Doryn of *Nilheim*."

The pair immediately across from me, a dwarfess and a human, exchanged worried looks. The duke frowned. "Is that why the Dark Lord let you come here? You've been tortured into immigrating—"

"Wait, I haven't been tortured!" I protested. "And I was allowed to come because I received an invite." She paused. "Alright, I also got the Dark Lord's permission to attend, but that was back when I was his prisoner and . . . I'm not telling this right."

I couldn't help it; I face-palmed. When I looked up from my hands, everyone was still staring.

"You're not in Nilheim anymore, Princess," the duke declared. "And you shall never have to step foot in that terrible place again. Even if I have to marry you myself! We will find a way."

He was very noble, but also very mistaken.

"No, no, I'm very happy in the Dark Enchanted Forest. I promise!" No one seemed to believe me, so I tried to explain. "I love baking in the kitchen, and going to the dungeon with Rufus, and having tea in the man-eating flower garden."

The human across from me, a young man dressed in clothing from the empire further north, fainted. His dwarfess partner caught his head and leaned him gently on the table. Her fake smile never faltered.

She was an excellent table partner.

The two girls from North Sumbria were giggling, and the other nobles whispered among themselves.

"They have you working as a servant and keep you in the dungeon?" Duke Wyldon was aghast; he slammed the table and stood, drawing even more attention as grand duchess looked our way. "It's worse than the rumors. I will lodge a formal complaint with Nilheim. Do not worry, Princess, I will—"

I panicked. Duke Wyldon was still speaking when I grabbed his shirt and *pulled*. It wasn't enough to tear the piece of clothing from his body—I had training in restraint—but I pulled hard enough that he hit the chair with a *whomp*.

I could feel Jacqueline's gentle response to my panic and I tried to calm my nerves as best I could. She shifted and then went back to sleep.

"Listen to me," I yelled. "I'm happy in Nilheim. I signed the paperwork myself. And I'm already seeing someone!"

One North Sumbrian girl asked, "Is it General Rufus? What I wouldn't give to get invited to his dungeon."

"Tabitha Hughs!" the other North Sumbrian gasped. "I'll tell your mother you said that!"

"Cousin Julia married into Nilheim, or will shortly," Tabitha countered. "I can too."

"My daughter is marrying Necromancer Chloe from the Dark Enchanted Forest." Duchess Calisto rejoined us, smiling down on her nieces. Presumably her nieces, as they called Julia *cousin*. I would go with that. "You should have all received her invitation this morning."

"Grand Duchess," Duke Wyldon of Servalt turned to our hostess, and in front of everyone declared, "Princess Henrietta is in grave danger, and I fear she's under a mind spell as well. Can you help us?"

I couldn't help it; I face-palmed a second time.

CHAPTER 102

Some People Have No Respect

Keith

Keith was held back by Their Royal Highness Rowen as he made to fly into the air toward the tea party.

"You can't," Rowen stressed, placing a firm hand on Keith's shoulder. Unlike the jovial pat from earlier, this was a viselike grip that kept him rooted. "Her Grace is there, and we can't interfere. Henrietta is safe; she's just a little embarrassed."

Knowing that Ria was safe helped settle him. "How do you know?"

The fox grinned. "I'll tell you if you tell me how you always know it's me?"

Keith shook off the hand and considered.

"Your eyes," Keith lied. "They're always like a fox no matter your form."

"And you are an evil tyrant who tortures your prisoner in the dungeon and makes her cook and clean for you." Rowen laughed.

"What?"

"You lied and I played a trick."

"How much of your trick was lies?" Keith asked, glancing again in the direction of the tea party. He felt relief when he realized that Jacqueline had fallen back to sleep.

"Very little." Their Royal Highness looked behind Keith and sighed deeply. "But now we have other problems."

"Hello, Dark Lord, Your Highness," Crown Prince Deryl sneered as he joined them in the gardens.

Keith immediately regretted not flying off and ruining the tea party.

"Crown Prince Deryl." Rowen inclined their head ever so slightly.

Keith did no such thing. "What brings you outside today?"

The prince's eyes darted in the direction of the tea party. "I just wanted to make sure no caused a disturbance. It wouldn't do if our delicate flower of Sumbria was harassed by one of your ilk."

Rowen choked on air. "I hope you do not treat all of your trading partners this way, young prince. Or there won't be any left by the time you ascend."

Prince Deryl flushed with anger and growled out, "King Rowen, was that a threat?"

"No. This is." Rowen's magic swirled around their body. A great show, but as Keith knew, unnecessary. When everything settled, a giant fox with seven tails took up a significant portion of the garden as it loomed over them. The sheer force that rolled off the fox left Prince Deryl on the ground, shaking in terror. "If you do not change your ways, boy, then no one will find your bones when your own people tear you limb from limb and leave you for the dogs."

It was too much for Prince Deryl, who scurried to his feet and ran for the palace door, tripping in the process. He was blubbering about telling his father as he ran back inside and out of sight.

"Was that truly necessary?" Keith asked, crossing his arms. "He'll be king one day, and we'll both suffer."

"If he becomes king, we'll suffer nonetheless." There was a *pop*, and a middle-aged noblewoman stood where the fox had been. "Really, calling this beautiful face 'King.' He has no taste."

"You would have chastised him even if he'd called you queen," Keith pointed out.

"True." Rowen nodded, adjusting their blue summer dress all covered in flowers. "Some people have no respect."

"Alright, who scared Crown Prince Deryl? He's gone and messed himself."

The two rulers turned to the entrance to find an exasperated Countess Julia von Slyke. She wore her usual full-plate paladin armor. And she looked angry.

Rowen's voice dripped honey as they said, "Julia! Congratulations on your wedding. Your wife is sure to make a beautiful bride."

"Thank you?" Julia gave Keith a confused glance.

"Their Royal Highness of Peldeep and I were discussing your engagement earlier," Keith explained.

"Ah, and was that before or after you used an offensive skill on one of our guests?" Julia crossed her arms.

Rowen gave up the pretense. "I assure you; I did not use any skills. I merely bared my teeth at the boy. I can't imagine why a simple smile would leave him so distraught. I guess I'd better go make some formal declaration of apology." They shared a toothy smile with Keith, fangs showing. "Just another reason to abdicate."

"And you, Your Viciousness?" Julia turned on Keith. "You didn't attack the prince?"

"I did not. Though in Their Royal Highness's defense, the prince crassly mis-titled them."

Julia flinched. "Foolish. But it does not excuse their own poor behavior."

"Spoken like a true paladin," Rowen said, approaching the woman with a light hip swagger. They fluttered their eyelashes at Julia. "Care to show me where I can meet with Grand Duchess Calisto after the tea party? I'd like to make the appropriate reparations for being such a rude guest."

"Your Highness, are you not going to apologize to the guest you accosted?" Julia questioned, but Keith noticed a smile tugging at her lips.

Rowen placed a hand delicately on their bosom. "Of course I will. Eventually. And through the proper channels."

Keith knew they would find some way to turn the apology into a subtle insult, if it even made it to the prince. "I think I'll make my way back to the main hall and wait for Henrietta there. Have fun apologizing, Your Highness."

"I will." The fox took Julia's arm and walked back inside ahead of the Dark Lord.

Keith didn't mind; he hadn't sensed anything from Jacqueline since that first light thrum. He would meet Henrietta in the hall, and they would go back upstairs and get ready for the ball. And he'd finally get to see her in her matching dress.

Despite unwelcome attendees out to murder him, the evening was looking to be very promising. Very promising indeed.

CHAPTER 103

Without Nefarious Intent

Henrietta

"Your Grace, I have it on the best authority that Princess Henrietta Doryn of Nilheim is not under a curse, a spell, or the effects of a potion," Grand Duchess Calisto told Duke Wyldon tartly. "Now, refreshments have arrived, so I will ask you to take your seat."

Wyldon looked like he was going to argue, but facing Duchess Calisto's polite and firm smile, he deflated.

It was an interesting sight to see on the strict man.

I smiled at our hostess. "Thank you, Your Grace."

"And you, Princess, I will thank you to control your outbursts. It is unbecoming of a lady. Chloe has assured me that your courtship with the Dark Lord is above board and without nefarious intent." The duchess addressed the rest of the table, "Now that everyone has had a chance to introduce themselves, we can discuss the plans for tonight!"

I felt bad for the four of my fellows who hadn't had a chance to introduce themselves because of me. One glared my way, and I tried to apologize with my eyes. The woman huffed and stuck up her nose. She was a striking redhead with cherry-colored lips and a pale complexion. The other three just looked nervous.

The duchess instructed, "Now, each of you should have an escort tonight. If anything changes that, tell me *immediately*. Otherwise, you will gather in the main hall to enter the ballroom after the dinner bell, so make sure you have an early meal. If you are too nervous to eat anything, do not worry, as there will be simple fair later in the evening. You will all enter as you are announced and gather in the center of the floor to start the first dance."

"Your Grace." The red-haired woman who'd glared at me held out a closed fan to get her attention. "Could you honor us with advice on how to navigate your specific Spring Ball successfully? It seems some of us are lacking in proper etiquette training."

Duke Wyldon flinched beside me. He fiddled with his glasses, and I was reminded of Keith.

The grand duchess raised a single eyebrow. "Lady Cassandra Cress, I do not like your tone. Some here are not blessed to have parents, let alone etiquette lessons on how North Sumbria hosts a debut. At least one among us was only recently freed from a five-year sleep spell. This does not mean they are lacking, they are simply learning."

Lady Cassandra flicked open her fan to cover her embarrassed frown.

"Still, as you asked so kindly," the duchess continued, "I will share some useful tips."

There was an excited murmur around the table.

The duchess cleared her throat. "It is important to have an escort, but it never hurts to have a backup if yours is suddenly cursed or indisposed. Frog princes aren't usually a good catch as it is; they were usually cursed for a reason."

She picked up the glass on her table and tapped the side. A light *ting* sounded. "As a helpful tool, we use glade crystal for our glassware. If you remember the sound of your glass when you put it down, you will know if anyone has poisoned your glass when you return to it."

Duchess Calisto's lesson continued, covering the basics from how to hold a fan so that an admirer from Peldeep knew you were interested, to how long a fainting spell should last; it was ideal to count three hundred seconds, no more or less, before showing signs of waking up. She even did a review of the dances and their steps, using the opportunity to tell everyone that Minstrel Bronwynn herself would be singing accompaniment for the evening.

It was a very informative afternoon.

"Princess, please tilt your head back further. I'd like to add a bit more crushed seashell around your eyes." Lilith took a poofy brush and dabbed the outside of my eyes with glittering powder. I had no idea where everything for this evening had come from. I'd never purchased rouge in my life. Or seashell powder. Or eyeliner. Or sparkles.

Lilith even dusted sparkling powder over Keith's black construct button that I had hung on a silver chain about my neck.

I'd had a final dress fitting with Rinrin, so I shouldn't have been surprised when I looked at myself in the mirror. My soft brown features traditionally faded into the background, but it was hard to fade anywhere when every part of me sparkled.

My dress had short, tufted sleeves, a corset-style bodice, and skirts that came down to my calves. They were longer in the back. Even my black boots had silver threading. They were perfect to move around it, with just enough of a heel to support me while I was dancing and still functional for the expected fight.

It was impolite to wear weapons, but I couldn't resist bringing the silver boot needle that I'd purchased from Frolin. And I convinced Lilith to use the hair tie dangling lock picks to secure my hair under the intricate braided bun. They looked like any of the other decorative silver pins in my hair.

I was tempted for the umpteenth time to keep Jacqueline under my full skirt . . . But no. It was Grand Duchess Calisto's palace. She was infamous for her events and their safety. This was the most anticipated debut of the season, and coming in armed would have been the height of bad manners.

I left Jacqueline on my bed.

Keith was waiting for me, dressed in a matching purple-blue silk coat with silver thread embroidery. He wore pants, a vest and decorative jacket, and a long-sleeved shirt.

I felt underdressed next to him, with my delicate fabric and bare arms. I suddenly understood why Sumbrian women liked fichu.

"You look wonderful," I told Keith, who was busy staring at me.

"As do you." He offered his hand, and I took it.

I teased him when he checked to make sure that the storage ring was still on my pinkie finger. Then I checked that he was still wearing my +2 Constitution ring. We were as ready as we'd ever be.

Walking down the stairs, Keith said, "Ria?"

I squeezed his arm lightly so as not to break it. "Yes, Keith?"

We could hear the crowd below. In just one more bend, we'd be there. Keith slowed and leaned down to kiss me on the forehead. He took a deep breath through his nose before pulling back to say, "I love you. Please don't die tonight."

I laughed. "I should say the same to you. And please don't murder my parents at the Spring Ball? I am embarrassed to call them my relatives already, but causing a scene on top of that would be mortifying."

". . . I'll try."

CHAPTER 104

What's Your Dexterity?

Keith

They'd made it downstairs with no fuss, arriving near enough of the door to the hall that they found their place in line quite easily. "Dark Magician King, Keith Monfort of Nilheim, and Princess Henrietta Doryn of Nilheim," an attendant announced as they entered the hall. It was decorated with spring flowers, pastel colors, and magical lights that floated overhead.

Keith led Henrietta to their place in the center of the hall, preparing for the first dance. Over her shoulder, he spied the king and queen of Drendil, looking furious. The king bit his finger, and the queen glared daggers at him over her fan. They stood amidst nobility from Drendil and Servalt, and the king turned to speak with a clean-shaven, middle-aged man all dressed in green.

Keith and Henrietta had a while to wait as all twenty or so debuts were announced, and Keith decided his time would be better spent watching Henrietta instead of her awful parents.

"What was your Dexterity again?" he asked out of the corner of his mouth. They were meant to be on display and poised, ready to start with the music.

"Twenty-two," Ria murmured. "What's yours?"

"Forty-two."

". . . I guess our first dance won't be that bad. I was kicking myself that we didn't practice." Ria glanced around the hall. "Not that I was worried; I've activated my [Etiquette] skill."

"That's a useful skill."

"Forty percent bonus rate to critical success in dancing, dining, and discourse."

"Do you use it often?" Keith wondered, recalling how many times he'd been affected by their conversations; confused, intrigued, or amused.

"Yes, but it's just a reminder for socially acceptable boundaries. I ignore it when I'm not surrounded by nobles," Ria explained.

"And since you came to the Dark Enchanted Forest?"

"Being able to tell when I was making the lizardkin uncomfortable that first week really helped."

A flute sounded throughout the hall, signaling the dancers. Keith lifted his hand facing her, and Ria gently pressed her palm against his. Her hand was smaller, calloused, with blue nail polish that matched both of their outfits.

That hand could crush his bones in a second, but that never stopped him from wanting to hold it.

Light string music from a lute accompanied the flute, and they dipped into a reverence, each bowing or curtsying respectfully. Rising from the bow, Keith cupped her palm, and swept his free hand to Ria's lower back. A drum beat joined in, slow and steady.

And then they *danced*.

They moved across the floor, indifferent to the blatant stares from the crowd. Keith let the music guide them as he drowned in the attentions of the woman in his arms. Ria was smiling up at him, oblivious to anything but their first dance.

Then she whispered, "I'm sorry."

The words drew Keith out of his revery. He spun her, skirts brushing his legs as she went, then pulled her back into his arms. "Is that more punishment time in the dungeon I hear?"

She let out a laugh and leaned in closer, letting him hold her tighter than was proper. Neither cared. "We're going to have to face them after this, won't we? My parents."

"We could just kill them?" The joke was in poor taste. He made it anyway. "They would make lovely corpse roses."

"Keith?!" Henrietta missed a step, but his hold on her hand—and her own Dexterity—saved her. She completed a graceful dip and they were together again.

"Yes?" He feigned innocence, smoothly guiding her out until they were arm's length apart, connected only by her hand in his. As the music came to an end, Keith spun Henrietta into his arms. They came together and stopped just as the last notes of the flute trailed off.

"I love you too."

It was only then that Keith realized. In all the planning and preparation and panic over the evening . . . he'd slipped and confessed. In the stairwell, of all places.

It hadn't been the most romantic place to say "I love you" for the first time. He wanted to kick himself, but instead, he just smiled down at his princess. Knowing she felt the same way was exhilarating and humbling.

How did this even happen? One minute he'd been challenged to a fight to the death by some girl with a big sword who smelled like scones, and the next he was dancing the night away and getting ready to propose.

Cheering resounded about the hall in honor of the completion of the first debut dance. Keith offered his hand and escorted her off the dance floor—in the opposite direction of her parents.

He wanted a drink in hand before he faced the king and queen of Drendil. Not to imbibe, but to keep his hands busy so as not to summon flames and light them on fire.

Henrietta loved it when he lit things on fire.

Alright, she loved flying through the air while he lit a dungeon on fire. He would get in trouble from multiple sources if he lit someone on fire in the ballroom. Grand Duchess Calisto would give him that disapproving look. She was a menace, and a neighbor worthy of respect. Better to shatter a glass.

Chloe was standing beside the drinks table with Julia and the grand duchess. They toasted Ria and congratulated her on her first dance.

Keith watched over the princess as she accepted a glass of sparkling cider from Julia. His gaze swept the room, taking in all the important and unimportant attendees of the evening.

Minstrel Bronwynn had stepped onto the dais, joining the musicians to sing accompaniment for the rest of the evening..

Gerda, the bridge troll, leaned against the wall like one of those wallflowers Feliwyn wrote about in her lurid romance novels. She wore a form fitting purple evening gown that let her blend into the crowd of noble's seamlessly. How had she gotten an invitation?

Their Royal Highness was poised as an elderly man and chatting up a pair of debutantes. Keith was too far away to smell the telltale perfume favored by the fox, but he couldn't imagine any other ruler on the Valarian continent who would wear violent-pink arachne silk robes in such an . . . ostentatious manner.

It had been a good idea to come this way, Keith thought. Henrietta would be surrounded by her friends when her parents finally caught up with them.

Which was, unfortunately, right now.

I Will Never Marry You

Henrietta

"Henri!"

I couldn't help it; I flinched. Something in Mother's voice did that. Maybe it was the way she stressed the *EE* sound longer than necessary. I put my polite smile back on and turned to greet my parents.

"Mother." I curtsied. "Father."

I didn't officially greet Knight Commander Havork where he stood behind my parents, but our eyes met. His face was impassive.

Keith reached a protective arm around me, settling his hand on my back and giving me extra support. "Good evening, King Simon, Queen Thalia."

"Do not speak to me, Monfort," my father snarled. "I've had enough. We're here to bring Henrietta home, and there's nothing you can do here to stop us. Get over here, Henri."

King Simon gestured for me to stand beside him, but I didn't move. "I apologize, Father, but I won't be going with you."

"You dare!" Queen Thalia snapped her fan with a force that usually signaled an unfortunate evening of discipline for me... Honestly, I needed to stop glossing over the unpleasantness; it signaled physical and emotional abuse. "Henri, come here *this instant*."

Out of the corner of my eye, I saw Julia grab Chloe and hold her back. Our conversation had drawn other people's attention as well. Bastian stepped forward, frowning, the Sumbrian noblewoman still on his arm. Lady Cress sneered, laughing at the commotion we were causing.

Grand Duchess Calisto arrived, drawn by the commotion, and stepped up beside us. "Excuse me, Your Majesty. Henrietta is a guest at my ball, and as an adult, she is free to make her own choices."

Queen Thalia laughed. "My child will obey or suffer the consequences. She'll *want* to join us, as we have something very important to tell her. We are her elders, and she will respect our age and wisdom."

My father waved at someone in the crowd. "We have good news, Henri. If you hadn't failed so utterly to complete the simple task you were assigned, we wouldn't have had this wonderful opportunity."

A man with lanky features stepped forward. He was wearing a green suit of straight trousers and an overly long waistcoat. If I had to guess, I'd say he was in his forties, but it was hard to tell with his clean-shaven, sharp features. He looked me over with an appraising eye, taking longer to assess my hips and feet. I almost regretted my ankle-length dress, but the boots would be perfect for kicking him in the—

"Princess Henrietta," his voice dripped honey, with a stickier undertone, as he bent at the waist.

I thought he was giving a customary bow, but his arm snaked out and caught my hand. Startled, I almost attacked on reflex. As it was, I did not break his fingers. Though when he dragged my hand to his face and planted a wet kiss on my palm, I wished I had.

"Let us introduce Marquess Chadwick Dorset," Father announced.

When the marquess didn't let go of my hand and instead breathed heavily on my skin, I snatched my hand back firmly. As was expected, the man couldn't compete with my strength. I'd never met him before, but something about the name sounded familiar—

"He's your fiancé, dear," Queen Thalia told me.

My mind froze. A wash of Keith's royal intent burst out behind me, hitting my parents and the marquess. He controlled it well; no one else close by batted an eyelash.

"No," I breathed the word, then, stronger, I repeated, "No. I refuse."

"It's not up to you, Henri," Mother said slyly, casting a side-eye at Keith, my parents' titles countering his own. "We drew up the contracts while you were still a minor. Any chance you had to argue was lost when you *didn't come home*."

"She isn't a minor now," Keith spoke over my shoulder, hard and angry. "You have no power over her."

"She has been promised by magical contract to me, Your Viciousness." The marquess was sweating, failing to resist Keith's title effect as he was driven to one knee. Despite this, his voice rang loud and clear. "Attack me all you want; there's *nothing* you can do about it."

A murmur arose among the crowd. I cursed. It was unfortunate that we were so close to the refreshments table.

I stuck up my hand to get people's attention. "I could kill you?"

"And I could feed your body to the sirens of Lake Loria. Or use your flesh to feed my roses," Keith told the man matter-of-factly, as if he were speaking of no more than the weather.

The marquess laughed a sickening giggle that made my skin crawl. "Destroy me, and you will only show the world how untrustworthy the Dark Enchanted Forest truly is, and it would still do nothing. The girl is promised to the Marquess Dorset—whoever that happens to be. If I fall, others will simply take my place."

"I could exterminate your entire line. It would be effortless, like squishing bugs."

My parents just stood there, looking for all the world as if everything was falling into place. My stomach dropped out from under me. There was something else going on here.

"Monfort," the grand duchess whispered to Keith behind me, "while I understand, I need to ask you to move elsewhere if you are going to be threatening my other guests."

"If Your Grace would allow us—" Keith's voice was drowned out by my parents.

"There are other ladies vying for the position. This is an opportunity you will not squander." my father told me. "It would be a shame if you became a second wife. Or a concubine."

Queen Thalia tsked. "Just another way to embarrass us."

"I refuse!" The words were ripped from my chest as a part of me rebelled against my parents. There were too many people fighting over my future, and I wasn't going to sit back and take it anymore. Jacqueline stirred on the bed upstairs, and it was all I could do to prevent her from cutting a line clean toward me.

I took a deep breath and stated, "I will never marry you, Marquess Dorset. Not ever."

"Oh, really?" The marquess managed to climb back to his feet when Keith paid mind to the duchess and drew in his kingly aura. The man patted his clothes a few times. "If you're so inclined, Princess, then I would be happy to give you an option to withdraw your suit."

That wasn't what I'd been expecting to hear. "Really?"

He nodded, smiling a too-wide smile that made me unconsciously lean back into Keith's chest.

"That is"—the marquess held out his hand—"if you'd allow me just one dance to try and change your mind."

CHAPTER 106

Please Don't Destroy My Palace

Keith

Keith wrapped his free arm around Henrietta protectively. His other hand still held a full glass of champagne. The stem was only slightly cracked.

"You can forget asking—"

"To be clear"—Henrietta tilted her head and observed the marquess—"if I dance one dance with you, then you will honor your word and annul any magical contracts between us?"

The marquess placed a hand on his heart. "Princess, if you give me one dance, I will try to convince you to marry me. If you still refuse, I will issue terms. But"—he stared at Keith, looming over her—"I will do so as respectable adults who speak for themselves. Away from your captor."

"I'm not—"

"He's not—"

The marquess cut off both Keith and Henrietta as he replied, "Do we have a deal or not?"

Keith wanted so desperately for Henrietta to say no. There were a million ways to break a magical contract if one knew the terms. There were always loopholes. Of course, they had no idea what those terms were, and he doubted the king and queen of Drendil had been foolish enough to bring the contract here, where he could easily steal it.

Though, knowing them . . .

"I'll do it," Henrietta replied.

Keith winced, feeling her pull away from him. "Are you sure? It's probably a trap."

Henrietta smiled up at Keith. She gently placed a hand on his cheek. "If it's a trap, then I'll just have to punch my way out. I really don't want to summon

Jacqueline if I don't have to—the repairs would be substantial unless I use her official summon, and that takes up a ridiculous amount of mana."

"I heard that." Grand Duchess Calisto came forward and stood beside me. "Please don't destroy my palace. Though"—the older woman eyed the marquess—"from all my years of experience, I might as well start preparing the bill now."

"You can't be serious?!" Chloe nearly yelled.

Keith's resisted the urge to light the man on fire as Henrietta accepted Marquess Chadwick's hand and walked back toward the dance floor. His princess and the marquess were just in time to start a slower song. Instrumental music filled the room and the two started a leisurely pavane perfect for a shared conversation.

Something didn't feel right.

"I told you, Monfort." King Simon stared after Henrietta and the marquess and then back at the Dark Lord. "I would have the last laugh."

Keith couldn't remember him ever saying that, but then again, Keith had stopped bothering to read letters from Drendil.

He regretted that now.

"King Simon," Keith ground out, watching Marquess Dorset say something that obviously upset Henrietta. Keith felt his blood boil in his veins, but he schooled his features. He looked down on Henrietta's parents and said, "If anything happens to my princess, I will not rest until the perpetrators have suffered all the injustices they have wrought upon your Heroine of Justice."

"Do you hear this, Duchess Calisto?" Queen Thalia snapped her fan shut. "Threats! At your Spring Ball. I demand that you ask the Dark Lord to leave. He is a menace and a danger to us all!"

The grand duchess replied with all of the grace and poise of her station. "Queen Thalia, that is only a threat to the wicked. I cannot imagine that you or your husband have ever treated Henrietta with anything but the love of a parent."

Henrietta's mother turned red with fury, and her father choked. King Simon was the first to recover. "Of course, Your Grace; we have given everything to raise our child."

"And can you imagine? This is how she repays us." Queen Thalia used her closed fan to point at Keith from his head to his feet. "By joining the forces of evil! She is a shame upon the family. Her only option now is to secure a good match."

Keith couldn't listen to this any longer. He downed the glass of cider in his hands, ready to go out and get Henrietta back with his own two hands.

Suddenly, there was a scream from close by, followed by shouts "P-P-Poison! Help! She's been poisoned!"

Keith's head whipped in the direction of the person shouting. Rage filled his chest; he knew this had to be part of Drendil's trap.

He was there in mere moments. Bastian, the knight commander of Peldeep, leaned over the body of a young woman choking on the floor. Her fingernails were turning green, and white foam flecked her lips. It was Countess Peregrine Fern of Sumbria. Keith stopped and opened his [Mind Map]. Henrietta was standing in the hallway outside the ballroom. He had time. Wuarg poison started mild, but within a minute, the countess would be in a world of suffering.

"Tip her head back and hold her shoulders down." He ordered. With practiced ease, Keith pulled the prepared antidote from his ring and knelt beside them. Bastian did as asked, and Keith unceremoniously dumped the vial into her mouth.

It was over in seconds.

She coughed and spluttered now, but in a few moments, her skin would slowly lose its purple sheen.

Keith stood back up, storing the empty vial back in his storage ring. "She'll be fine. I—"

He was interrupted by an excited cheer from the circle of onlookers.. Keith ignored them and tried to move towards the dance floor, but was hampered by the crowding sycophants. All he could make out was a sea of frills and flounce.

And according to his map, Princess Henrietta had left and was halfway across the palace.

CHAPTER 107

You Are Annoyingly Sharp for a Princess

Henrietta

A Few Minutes Earlier

"Thank you for accepting my request, Princess."

The marquess held my hand in his sweaty palm. There was a ring on his index finger that showed the insignia of his household: a magpie in flight.

"Just tell me how I can break the engagement papers and I'll be on my way," I said, allowing him to pull me onto the dance floor. I took my place across from him, along with the twenty-odd other couples who were lined up there.

"Soon, my pet." Chadwick let go of my hand just long enough to dip into an overly dramatic reverence. A new song started, with a simple lute and drum playing a sedate pavane. The steps were simple; perfect for holding polite conversations with your partner.

I had no intention of being polite. I smiled at him and curtsied half a beat late.

"If you call me *pet* a second time, I am going to walk back to the Dark Lord and let *him* handle this affair." I chastised myself for the threat. I needed to keep things pleasant until I learned more about the magical contract. If this didn't work out, I'm sure Keith would figure out something. Hopefully without bloodshed.

The marquess laughed. "Feisty. No need to worry, my dear. I'm harmless."

"I'm not."

Chadwick raised an eyebrow. We were then at the front of the line of the dancers and separated to do a figure eight with the two couples beside us.

I spied Keith on my way around. It was hard to make him out through the crowd, but it helped that he hadn't moved from the spot where I'd left him. He was struggling through a conversation with my parents.

Honestly, I felt worse for leaving Keith with them than I did for walking into this obvious trap. The marquess was underestimating me.

"We're dancing," I pointed out once we came together again. "As bargained. Now, speak; what do you want for dissolving the contract?"

"All in good time, Princess. You haven't heard my suit yet," he reminded me. "A deal is a deal."

We executed a slow turn, stepping apart before coming together again. I gritted through my teeth, attempting to be civil, "Go on, then."

He leaned in conspiratorially, but I kept myself at arm's length.

"When you marry me," he began, "I shall bring you back to my estate, and you will live the life you deserve. I know how you've been raised and I can offer you pleasure untold. You'll never have to lift a finger. Please me, and I promise you an heir, jewels, and slav—*servants*—to wait upon you hand and foot . . . "

Every word he said churned my stomach and left me with a feeling of deeper disgust for this man, and he wasn't even done.

"However, if I find you do not satisfy me, then I will have no need to keep you. I'm sure one of my men would love a royal wife."

Chadwick looked like he was enjoying himself immensely. Maybe I needed to slip and accidentally break his fingers . . . No, I needed information first.

The music took a turn, but the marquess spun us out to the edge of the dance floor. We were steps from one of the exits, but still standing in the light of the hall.

"You are disgusting," I said bluntly. "I will never marry you, so what happens when I say no?"

"It is exactly as I offered; I give you the terms, and a way out."

"You didn't answer my question." I repeated. "What happens when I say no? I'd like to know the term before agreeing to them, please."

The marquess tsked. "You are annoyingly sharp for a princess. The terms are simple. Should the magical contract signed by the king and queen of Drendil on behalf of their daughter, the eligible Princess Henrietta, not be fulfilled, the following terms will come into force. The kingdom of Drendil shall owe me five thousand gold coins, and the Princess Henrietta will forfeit ten thousand experience points. Additionally, Drendil shall grant me five hundred cattle, three hundred acres of land, and the title of a count of Drendil."

He squeezed my hand. "What say you, Princess Henrietta Doryn? Will you honor the contract and agree to be my wife?"

[**Marquess Chadwick Dorset** wishes to confirm the Terms of the
Marriage Agreement between the Kingdom of Drendil and the
Marquess Dorset. Do you accept Marriage to the Marquess Dorset?
If you select Yes, you will gain the temporary Title: Fiancée.
Yes/No.]

I didn't trust the man as far as I could throw him. I expanded the terms and activated [Quick Read] to review the document. It was a standard political marriage agreement that had been signed by her parents in promissory. She was still required to acknowledge the agreement before any title would come into effect, and had one year from the time of the contract creation to fulfill the terms. Otherwise, the contact would be terminated without reparation.

The contract had an exit clause . . . but I didn't want to wait around with this over my head for a year.

Everything he had said was true, including the part where if one contracted party were to kill another, they would be subject to the [Bond Breaker] title for one years' time. But there was an extra clause he had *not* mentioned. If a party member rejected the agreement early, they would also suffer the [Bond Breaker] title for the remaining duration of the contract.

If I didn't know better, I would have been tempted to just say [No] and suffer the rebuff. It just reduced a person's highest stat to ten.

But I *did* know better. This entire thing was a trap, and I was embarrassed for anyone who even thought it was going to work.

I looked down at the marquess, who's satisfied smirk started to waver when I just smiled at him.

"Well?" He demanded, squeezing my hands harder than was polite. Not that it bothered me much.

"I would like to thank you for the dance, marquess." I told him. "But I don't think you will be hearing what you want to hear from me today."

There was always another choice. And I chose to not select [Yes] *or* [No]. I could present my case before the council on the morrow and try to convince them that the contract should be null and void.

Now, if only my parents or the marquess did something stupid to help my case.

"I am sorry that it had to be this way." The marquess paused our dance right beside the stage. I barely felt the blade cut into my finger where the marquess's ring stabbed me. My [Resist Poison] perk was high, and I felt it working, but whatever hit me was strong enough to knock out a wyvern.

[You have been **Paralyzed**. Time until effect wears off 00:02:00]

I had several Paralysis antidotes in my storage ring. Unfortunately, it was hard to give myself a Paralysis antidote when I was already paralyzed . . . still, two minutes wasn't so long.

The marquess tsked. "That should have lasted an hour. Ridiculous. I'll need to speed up the timetable." He made a motion with his hands above his head.

It must have been a signal, because an instant later a scream resounded around the hall.

The marquess wrapped an arm around my waist, lifting my stiff body and walking to the side of the stage. His words faked concern. "There, there, darling, let's get you to a fainting couch."

I decided it was time to poke my sleeping sword, who stirred. I debated just summoning her outright then and there . . . it was hard to hold a sword when you were paralyzed. I could wait and do it wherever we ended up when the paralysis wore off. In all my experiences being kidnapped as a princess, this one was the most ridiculous. If I wasn't worried about Keith getting trapped talking to my parents all night, I would have been excited to see how they were going to get me out of the palace.

I know how *I* would have done it.

We were through the musician's entrance in seconds, where two men were waiting. One, wearing the clothing of a North Sumbrian attendant, activated a Rogue perk. All of my jewelry and valuables flew into his hand. His fist closed around my rings, earrings, and button necklace—and then he vanished with nearly everything I owned.

All except the storage ring Keith had gifted me, which had resisted the man's attack.

[You have been **Paralyzed**. Time until effect wears off 00:01:17]

"Hurry up and throw her with the others!" The marquess shoved me off to a strong-looking young man in musician's clothing holding a set of manacles. With his hands free, Chadwick pulled out a scroll and cast, "Activate: [Lesser Portal Door]."

That was actually a good idea, and I commended his decisions. Though that particular spell wouldn't get us far enough to actually leave the palace itself, it could get us away from prying eyes. *Well done marquess.* Then I registered the other thing Chadwick had said. *What others?* My mind raced and something I should have noticed much sooner clicked into place. I raged.

[You have been **Paralyzed**. Time until effect wears off 00:00:46]

I stopped imagining what it would be like to punch the marquess in the face as a familiar set of manacles clicked over my wrists and carried me through the portal, leaving the marquess behind us.

I sent a silent apology to Keith. It was going to take a little more time to clean this up than I thought.

CHAPTER 108

Where Is Henrietta?

Keith

Keith reminded himself that everything was going to be alright. He might have repeated it in his mind three times already, but it bore repeating.

Henrietta was someone he respected, including her choice to get kidnapped. He assumed it *was* a choice; even *he* would be hard-pressed to move her if she said no.

Chloe had come up behind him, ready to [Resurrect], but only as a last resort. She never would have offered if it wasn't for Grand Duchess Calisto's backing. Some nobles were . . . *picky* about resurrection. Unless it happened in a dungeon, many kingdoms in Valaria ruled that the second a person died, they were barred from inheriting. They were allowed to stay alive, but for all intents and purposes, they were legally dead.

He thought it foolish; how *else* was anyone supposed to rule for a hundred years as an undead horror?

Honestly, what idiot poisoned someone at the most popular gathering of high-level magic users on the continent anyway? When *everyone* with half a brain was ready for a poisoning? On second thought, there was a good possibility that all these milling nobles didn't even have half a brain between them. He tried to push through, and a young princess with a tiara and a gown covered in far too many ruffles put her hand on his arm.

"Oh, thank you, Dark Magician King. We were so scared! How did you know what to do?!" Her eyes sparkled, and her cheeks were flushed. Several other young ladies pressed against him.

He didn't have time nor care for explanations. Keith settled on the easiest solution: he released his royal aura from Dark Magician King and used a perk for added measure.

[You have activated the Perk: **Intimidate**. This has a cone-shaped
Area of Effect. Targets affected by the Perk have the temporary
condition **Fear**.]

"*Move.*"

The group surrounding him flinched back, overcome by his attack. Those strong
enough to resist were also smart enough to choose to step aside of their own accord.

When an Arcane Sage commonly referred to as the *Dark Lord* told you to
move, you *moved.*

Keith stalked off, barely hearing Chloe explain. "Her fingernails were turning
green, she had pale spots on her neck with white foam on her lips, and it didn't kill
her outright—that's wuarg poison. Keith gave her the antidote, so she'll recover.
Worst case, she would have died after all of her organs failed, and then I'd have
[Revived] her. It's not a nice way to go, though, so I don't recommend it."

"Monfort." Duchess Calisto was beside him as he reached the spot on the
dance floor he'd last seen Henrietta. "What is happening?"

Henrietta was on the move, very quickly, and heading *not* toward their suite.
In fact, she was going in the complete opposite direction. "Henrietta is missing.
You might want to find her before her sword destroys—That's right, Jacqueline!"

Keith *didn't* know if the construct had been compromised. He could chase
after it throughout the entire palace, or he could follow the sword. He raised an
arm and recited the shortcut to a mid-tier spell, "[Haste]."

Mana wrapped around his legs and body. Keith nodded at the grand duchess,
and then he was running. He wanted to be there for Ria if she needed him, so he
rushed upstairs to their suite of rooms.

He was calculating the inevitable bill when she destroyed a wing of the palace
dealing with whatever was happening.

Lilith, carefully cleaning and packing a pile of beauty products, was startled
as Keith burst in. "Your Viciousness!"

Jacqueline Tiamat la Fleur lay undisturbed on Ria's bed. Keith stood there,
panic worming its way through the pit of his stomach as he picked up the blade.
It was restful in his grasp, which meant Ria *probably* wasn't in danger. She had
chosen to walk out of the ballroom without him.

No . . . No . . . Trust. Take a deep breath.

He would go back to following the construct. Maybe they had a means to
coerce her.

"Lilith," he ordered, "your mistress is missing. Inform the palace staff, block
the exits as best you can, and for all the gods"—he picked up Jacqueline—"don't
stand near any green tapestries."

He was off again as the final word left his mouth.

*   *   *

Grand Duchess Calisto worked fast, and by the time Keith had reached downstairs, attendants in organized groups were already being dispatched to search the palace grounds. The Spring Ball celebration continued in the ballroom, music echoing around him.

Jacqueline remained undisturbed at his side.

"King Keith!"

Unexpectedly, Gerda ran up to him wearing her flowing purple gown and holding an axe. With her free hand, she pointed at one of the staircases on his left that led exactly to where the construct was guiding him. "I lost Henrietta here, but then I saw the king and queen of Drendil running that way. Actually *running*. Their rooms are on the fourth floor."

He eyed the troll. She was Henrietta's friend, and a powerful magic user in her own right; she could handle herself. They would divide and conquer. "I will *speak* to the king and queen. You find Marquess Dorset's room and see if she's there."

Gerda nodded and hurried away. Keith launched himself into action, running. When he reached the stairwell, he took the stairs two at a time.

The fourth floor had three suites, and one of the doors was open. Keith approached the opening slowly.

Two voices were arguing inside.

"Why isn't he here yet?" King Simon whined. "Does he know how *hard* it was to get here this fast? I had to *jog*!"

"Inconsiderate, is what it is," Queen Thalia replied. "I don't know *what* our idiot child sees in that *monster*. But now that we have her heirlooms back, we have no need—"

"And where *is* Henrietta?" Keith asked, startling the pair when he stepped into the doorway. The construct button showed up in this room on his [Mind Map], despite Ria being obviously absent. Queen Thalia was in the process of putting on a familiar earring, her fan placed on the low table in front of her.

He resisted the urge to simply kill them now. Chloe could find out everything she needed from her undead—and wouldn't that be just deserts for the royal couple.

"Wouldn't you like to know." Queen Thalia was the first to compose herself.

King Simon stood in between Keith and his wife. He stamped his boot onto the beautiful rug, leaving ugly scuff marks. He drew himself up and said, "Henri is *ours*. I don't know what brainwashing you've done, but it stops *now*, Monfort."

"*Henrietta* is a person. She belongs to no one but herself." Keith walked forward until he loomed over the despicable excuse for a father. "And *you* lost any right—"

A flash of light flared around Keith, and he threw up his arms, chanting his quickest defensive spell, "[Shield]."

Unfortunately, he wasn't hit by an attack.

CHAPTER 109

It'll Be Alright

Henrietta

We came out into a small room in presumably the servants' quarters, and I felt the first waves of portal sickness overtake me. That was one nice thing about being paralyzed—I didn't have to worry about emptying my stomach from the nausea . . .

It was also really hard to focus while being carted around like a sack of flour. I tried calling out to Jacqueline, but nothing happened, so then I tried reading my notifications tab.

[**Veralyn's Enchanted Restraint Manacles**: A modified version of the restraints designed for St. George's Trials. Prevents access to all nonpassive Titles, Skills, Perks, Bonded, and Equipped Items. All Attribute stats capped at 15.]

If I'd had the ability to groan, I would have. Veralyn's Enchanted Restraint Manacles were *really* hard to break. And they came with the highest debuffs any item could carry.

I wasn't too worried, though; I'd spent a lot of time adventuring. It was just a matter of finding someone with a sword I could *borrow*.

Oftentimes, I cursed that one's character sheet skills were not useful if I didn't think to activate them. This was an occasion I was happy that the two were separate. I had the muscle memory and practical skills of a level sixty-eight swordswoman, even if I couldn't execute a system [Force Thrust].

I moved on to examine my character sheet.

Name:	Henrietta Doryn of Nilheim
Occupation:	Crown Princess
Level:	68
Experience Points:	318/17000
Hit Points:	159/225 (1809)
Mana Points:	170/225 (1139)
Bonded Item:	[Unavailable: Veralyn's Enchanted Restraint Manacles]
Class:	[Unavailable; Veralyn's Enchanted Restraint Manacles]

Titles:

[Human] 0, [Noble] 10, [Prince] 20, [Crown Prince] 30, [Warrior] 40, [Aura Knight] 50, [Sword Master] 60

Special Effect:

Veralyn's Enchanted Restraint Manacles

Attributes:

Strength:	15	**Intelligence:**	15
Dexterity:	15	**Perception:**	15
Constitution:	15	**Charisma:**	15

Skills:

[Unavailable: Veralyn's Enchanted Restraint Manacles]

I had a pitiful amount of health and mana. As I was reading, they brought me into a room where I was unceremoniously dumped next to two other people tied up with magical ropes and sitting on the floor: a kitchen boy and *Brownie*. I tried to call out to her, but I was still paralyzed.

[You have been **Paralyzed**. Time until effect wears off 00:00:34]

"A famous minstrel, a blackfog spy, and a crown princess." Marquess Dorset looked down on us and let out an unpleasant giggle. "I always find the perfect souvenirs when I travel."

"People are *not* souvenirs." Brownie looked up, glaring. She was weeping quietly, her entire demeanor broken.

I couldn't imagine what they'd done to make such a strong, confident woman cry . . . and I decided then and there that the marquess would pay for whatever cruelty he had—

"And I'm not much of a minstrel," Brownie choked, *"without an instrument."*

"You should have thought of that before you broke your lute over my servant's back," Chadwick chastised. The man wearing musician's clothing glowered at the bard, rubbing the back of his neck. The marquess continued, "I'll buy you a new lute. Or whoever buys *you* will buy you a new lute."

"I play the lyre harp!"

"I do not care," the marquess retorted.

Alright, more things were falling into place! Marquess Dorset was a *slave trader*. I finally remembered why his name felt so familiar! Madame Potts had mentioned him in one of her foretellings.

The Marquess Dorset is the slave trader you're looking for . . . Something, something about orphanages.

Why was he standing here and not in prison?

[You have been **Paralyzed**. Time until effect wears off 00:00:06]

Only six more seconds! I needed a plan better than just "hit the marquess in the face with my manacles." As much as that sounded satisfying. I relaxed and took a deep breath as I regained the ability to use my limbs. I sat up and inched toward Brownie.

"You won't get away with this." I started strong with a very cliché line, hoping that would get his attention. It didn't.

"I already have." Chadwick threw another scroll. "It's time we departed. Activate: [Portal Door]."

Those one-time-use lesser portal doors cost a pretty penny. I could only imagine what a midlevel scroll cost. The marquess had his servant, who I realized was the flautist for the orchestra, haul each of us through the portal. The kitchen boy, who was apparently a spy, was sent through first, then a still crying Brownie, and lastly myself. I didn't bother fighting, since they'd already sent Brownie through before I could do anything about it.

I fell to my knees on the other side and dry heaved; that portal was definitely worse than Gimtak's skill. My head spun and my gut wrenched, and I had to wait for the queasy sensation to calm down.

I raised my head in time to watch the portal close . . . without the marquess. I was on the floor at the foot of a bed. There was a window ahead of me, and I could just barely make out the towers from Duchess Calisto's palace over the treetops in the distance. It was still early in the evening, and sunset was a few hours yet.

The flautist downed some type of recovery potion. "That's all of us."

"About time you made it," a woman's voice drawled. I looked up to see a brunette woman in fine leathers wearing brass knuckles. Another slave trader, most likely. I struggled up onto my arms and knees, feeling a little less ill by the second. I sat up and slipped my hand across my boot, palming a silver needle.

I could do this.

"I didn't see *you* doing the carrying," the flautist snapped. He looked past me. "I'm impressed our knight protector got here so quickly. You didn't need to worry so much—we wouldn't hurt the merchandise."

"All the same," a familiar voice spoke behind me, and I spun around to face him. "I'll take the princess. The wagons are ready out back."

Knight Commander Havork reached down and helped Brownie to her feet, gentle but firm. He pushed the bard toward the brunette with brass knuckles. Brownie tried to clock the woman over the head with her bound fists, but the brunette caught her fist easily and towed my friend outside.

The kitchen lad was still recovering from his portal sickness, and unfortunately, couldn't hold in his dinner.

"Why do I always get the messy ones?" the flautist grumbled. He reached down and grabbed the boy by his tunic, dragging him to the door. He stopped in the doorway and waited for us. "Come on, then."

Havork eyed me cautiously.

"I can't believe you're doing this," I accused, gripping the needle hard enough it pricked me. "You're not seriously going to help slavers? *I thought you had honor!*"

My old mentor flinched but just said, "This will go easier for you if you don't resist."

Nothing, *nothing* could have convinced me that Havork would be working with slave traders . . . except seeing him here in person. It was a complete betrayal of everything I knew about the man.

Which meant I hesitated to outright stab him in the face until I got some answers.

Havork bent down and scooped me into his arms. He grunted and seemed to struggle lifting me.

"What now?" I asked, waiting for my time to strike. I only had Strength fifteen, but I was close enough for a surprise attack.

I wished I had my sword, but what use would that do. I probably couldn't use Jacqueline properly even *if* I could summon her. Stupid manacles.

"We all go for a nice carriage ride to the Servalt border and meet the marquess in Colwood," he explained. We followed the others out into a hallway that ended in a set of stairs and a door to outside.

Havork stopped at the bottom of the stairs. What was effectively a wooden box masquerading as a "carriage" waited for us. There were men and women stationed around the carriage, loading cargo or keeping watch. I thought I counted nine or ten all told but wasn't sure.

Brownie was nowhere to be seen, so I assumed she was already in the box. The flautist was chasing after the kitchen boy, who had attempted an escape. There was a scuffle, and the boy was tackled to the ground while everyone else just watched.

Some of the group laughed.

Others continued their tasks.

"You know I can't go in that carriage," I told Havork. If he took one step toward it, I was going to attack him. "*You* know I can't. Please don't make me."

I tensed, but he made no move.

I tried to maintain my image, speaking matter-of-factly . . . but I felt my voice break at the end. I would fight with my little silver boot needle until they knocked me unconscious before anyone convinced *me* to get into *that small, dark box.*

The knight commander grimaced. He glanced at the slave traders, distracted with the runaway spy boy.

He whispered quietly, "It won't be for very long."

"I'll barely last one hundred seconds before I do something stupid," I told him. Even now, I *wanted* to trust him. To believe in the Havork I knew and respected. I'd forgotten what it meant to love a parent, but he was the closest thing I'd ever had to a real father.

His face was unreadable, and I tensed.

"Did you know I'm actually quite good at riddles?" he said suddenly.

"What?"

To our side, the kitchen boy pulled out a knife from *somewhere.* Good for him!

I looked up and raised a questioning eyebrow at the knight commander.

He sighed and said something I was *not* expecting.

"If you want to know why it'll be alright, I'll give you the answer. It's *a book.*"

CHAPTER 110

Physical Torture Would Have Been Preferable

Keith

With his basic shield already active, Keith wasted no time manipulating mana to cast a higher-level spell. "By the Undaunted Scales That Guard the Wary Wyrm, [Dragon Shield]."

[You have attempted to use the High Draconic Spell: **Dragon Shield**. You have succeeded. Mana Cost: 450 Mana. Durability: 1000HP.]

Only after he was suitably wrapped in two bubbles of protective power did Keith turn his attention to his new surroundings.

He was alone in a dungeon cell, inside a bright-pink bubble that pulsed ominously. Gods only knew *which* dungeon cell; that bright light must have been a teleportation trap. Simple enough to deal with. He activated [Mind Map].

A map formed in his mind's eye. His constructs were usually bright lights upon it to tell him where they were. Several years ago, he'd sent out a small army of tiny constructs to march as far as possible in order to fill up his [Mind Map]. As a result, he had most of the major roads and cities unlocked, though some of North Sumbria and a small portion of the Dark Enchanted Forest were still grayed out.

That was the downside of ruling a country with constantly shifting sentient geography that liked to keep some of its secrets.

This time, however, the *entire map* was grayed out. He didn't have a map at all.

Hmm, a pocket dimension seemed likely. He would need to confirm it through a series of tests, the first of which would be to see if he could use abilities that influenced outside the sphere, since his abilities were still functioning inside it.

[You have attempted to use the Perk: **Remote Access** on
Automaton: Delilah. You have failed.]

He opened his notifications tab to see if he was under an effect. Nothing showed in the pop-up window.

"Ah, that idiot did something right for a change," a voice drew Keith out of his contemplation.

Marquess Dorset was standing just outside his dungeon cell.

Anger, frustration, and a touch of fear burned in Keith's chest. "*Where is she?*"

"The princess, my *wife*, is on her way home," the marquess said, frowning. "She is no longer your concern. I know you thought to have Drendil by marrying that drab excuse of a—"

There was a commotion as King Simon and Queen Thalia entered the dungeon, complaining vehemently. They came into view being led by a servant in Servalt colors. Keith watched and waited; intelligence would come first, and lighting the marquess on fire would have to come second.

"Dorset! You wretch, what is the meaning of this? We were enjoying a celebratory wine!" King Simon demanded.

Queen Thalia screeched at their escort, "This is not the *proper* way to escort a queen! Don't you know *anything*? Look what you've done to my dress pleats!"

The servant ignored them. "Everything is going as planned."

"And the knight commander?"

The servant smiled. "He's with the rest of the team bringing your new toys. The poor bloke hasn't suspected a thing."

Assuming they were talking about Havork, Keith seriously doubted that. If Henrietta was to be believed, the man always suspected something. It was his job.

"Excellent." The marquess laughed.

"What is your plan, Dorset?" King Simon seethed. As much as the man was a cruel and incompetent leader, he was not fully the fool. "If you don't return quickly, everyone is going to assume you kidnapped Henrietta. You were the last one seen with her."

"But will they?" The marquess snorted. "While I'm waiting patiently in my room, the king and queen of Drendil, their knight commander, *and* the princess are all missing."

"You . . ." King Simon's face contorted with rage. He took one step toward Dorset, only to be met with force as the marquess shoved the king backward into the open cell behind him. His servant pushed the queen in, and the marquess slammed the door shut in their faces. They howled in outrage.

Dorset's face contorted into a sinister grin as his Rogue servant presented him with everything of value the royal couple had been wearing, as well as a few other recognizable pieces. "Excellent." The marquess inspected each—including a small button. Keith sucked in a deep breath at the sight.

"I am telling you this now, Dorset." Keith glared daggers, and his mana fluctuated dangerously. "If you hurt even a single hair on Henrietta's head, you won't have any bones left to [Raise]."

Chadwick pocketed the valuables. "Oh, Monfort. You have other things to worry about. With the Dark Lord missing too, who won't suspect you of foul play? I will have the throne, courtesy of the Drendil regalia *and* the princess, and the pleasure of watching you die. You all just sit tight and wait for me to come back."

The marquess pulled a scroll from inside his vest and dropped it to the floor.

Dorset opened an incredibly rare high-class magical [Portal: Gate] that could cross kingdoms. He stepped on top, and the light engulfed him, leaving behind the servant to watch them.

He was a level eighty-three *Arcane Sage*; there weren't many magical things that could contain him for long. Now, if only he weren't being tortured from the moment Dorset left, things might have gone easier.

It wasn't physical torture, sadly.

In fact, physical torture would have been preferable to what he was actually suffering: being trapped in a cell beside his soon-to-be in-laws *and their incessant whining*.

Keith got to experimenting.

It was hard, but he let the vitriol and anger go in one ear and out the other. The servant watched on, but he had long ago plugged his ears.

Keith tried activating a few other perks. [Identify], he got nothing. [Ventriloquism], he couldn't connect at all to his constructs. He moved to [Sense Motive] and [Sense Enemy], and that gave him further clues.

He couldn't [Sense Enemy] the servant right in front of him.

With a bit of mana manipulation, Keith attempted to examine the pink bubble. The second his power touched the barrier, that part of his mana disappeared. Actually, worse than that, the mana just *ceased to be*.

He hissed. Keith didn't think it was *purely* Void based, as that would have made it impossible to see through . . . but whatever title, skill, perk or spell this was . . . it was *laced* with Void.

The mastermind behind this was *very* thorough. Keith didn't think Marquess Dorset was high enough in level, or ostentatious enough to construct something as profound or pink as this Void pocket dimension.

He was struck by a horrible thought. *Their Royal Highness?* No, surely not.

Keith tried to keep his spells going while he tested his perks and analyzed the bubble—and blocked out his neighbors. And as he worked, he did his best to ignore the small distracting feeling that he'd forgotten something . . .

What happened to Gerda?

CHAPTER 111

An Emotional Support Brownie

Henrietta

The kitchen-boy-who-was-actually-a-spy dropped his knife when he hit the ground chest first, the flautist-who-was-actually-a-slave-trader kneeing him in the lower back. The boy switched to screaming for help. He *was* dressed as a palace worker, and if anyone who wasn't working for the marquess had been around to hear, then he might've had a chance.

The screaming ended quickly when his captor pulled a bottle and emptied it out onto the boy.

The boy slumped over, asleep from the potion. I looked between the carriage and Knight Commander Havork.

"A hundred seconds," I repeated myself. If he'd known the answer to Gerda's riddle all along, then he'd already helped me once before. I was willing to give him one chance.

The knight nodded back almost imperceptibly. Louder, he called out to the flautist, "Are you almost done? It's past time we leave."

"I don't see you helping to make it faster!" The man lifted the boy by his shirt again and dragged him to the carriage. He ripped open the door, revealing a quiet and calm Bronwynn sitting on a bench against one wall. The boy was thrown haphazardly inside, and then the slave trader waved us forward.

Every part of me screamed to *not get into the box* . . . but I let Havork put me through the open door. He took a step back and was replaced in the doorway by the flautist. I resisted the urge to stab him in the face with my boot needle. Instead, I sat beside Brownie and leaned into her for emotional support. She wrapped an arm around me.

She'd always told me she loved her nickname because she was sweet, dark, and a little nutty. Her sense of humor *did* cause more than a few delicate souls to flinch. As someone who had a sweet tooth, I liked the idea of an emotional support Brownie.

"Now, don't make a fuss," the flautist threatened. "Or you'll end up like *him*. And don't bother screaming—the carriage is spelled for sound."

Then the door closed.

The light blinked out in the well-sealed carriage. It was great for transporting things so people couldn't see what was inside . . . or outside. I closed my eyes against the darkness.

One . . .

Nothing happened in one second. And though it felt like an eternity to go from one second to two seconds, it wasn't very long at all.

Two . . .

I felt the familiar, overwhelming terror seize my limbs, clawing at my senses and making my breath catch.

Five . . .

My heart raced. The pit of my stomach clenched until I tasted bile. I held it in, but the nausea swimming in my throat and pressing against my chin threatened to push me over. I lifted my fists and awkwardly pushed the one not holding the needle against my lips. The orichalcum metal of the manacles cut into my wrist.

Ten . . .

Why did ten seconds *take so long?* I leaned harder into Brownie. Somewhere far away, but right beside me, I heard a soft, "It'll be alright."

Twenty . . .

Someone climbed onto the carriage seat outside, rocking everything slightly.

I wanted to slide to the floor. I wanted to press my back against something and curl my knees into my chest. I wanted to cry out against the all-encompassing dark.

Thirty . . .

The carriage jolted and rumbled as we began to move.

I wouldn't even make it. I didn't *need* to make it. I had a weapon . . . and Revival potions worked if they were administered within eight hours of death. They would probably stop within the next eight hours and check on us.

Thirty-one . . .

A single tear burned my left cheek. I put my hands back down. I opened my mouth to do something. Scream? Ask for a song? Yes, I could ask Brownie for a song to distract me—

Brownie pulled away from me suddenly. Her absence almost undid me then and there.

"Brownie?" I called weakly.

Thirty-two . . .

Don't stop counting. I can't stop counting.

My manacles were lifted and fumbled with. Brownie swore under her breath.

Thirty-three . . .

It was *useless*. I'd already tried to break Veralyn's Enchanted Restraint Manacles with Strength, and two entire groups of Assassin-class guild members hadn't been able to pick the locks. It's why I hadn't bothered with the set in my hair.

Thirty-four . . .

Click.

My wrists were free and light. A weight metaphorically lifted off my shoulders as I felt my character sheet reinstate my stats. More importantly, my bond with Jacqueline became active again. I felt her sudden awakening.

Hmm . . . sweet? What have they done to you? How DARE they?!

I activated a title ability I rarely bothered using, since Jacqueline was more than capable of reaching me on her own. It cost a lot of mana, but nothing was going to stop me from *getting out of this box.*

[Do you wish to Summon your Bonded Sword: Jacqueline Tiamat
la Fleur?
Mana Cost: 10 x Miles = 580 Mana. Yes/No]

I hit Yes. Power swirled around my right hand, and my *wonderful* sword settled there.

Jacqueline's voice calmed me. *I am here now. We can cut them all. Just let me slice out their guts for what they have done. Bathe in their blood and drink in their death. The sunlight is close, just swing me.*

Just let it go, my darling. Swing the blade, and I will cut you free.

Brownie whispered, "Ria?"

With just enough control left to *not* kill my best friend, I whispered, "Stay to my right. I'm getting out. I need out *now.*"

The sharp tip of my sword pierced right through the wood of the ceiling and stuck out the top of the carriage, letting in splinters of dim light.

I activated [Bludgeoning Cut]. Jacqueline swung in an arc through the roof and down the wall. When I ended the cut below the wagon, I felt a portion of the framework give. I opened my eyes to the light, and I saw Brownie had pulled the spy boy out of harm's way.

The carriage shook violently as it started to sag, and there were screams outside. I started to fall forward, but my Dexterity saved me.

"Are you good in a fight?" I asked as I lifted Jacqueline back into position.

"I can help," Brownie assured me.

"Lift your arms; I'll be gentle."

Brownie closed her eyes and looked away as I sliced through the regular rope with my magical sword.

The carriage came to a messy halt as we prepared for battle.

CHAPTER 112

A Higher Intelligence Means Nothing If You Can't Use It

Keith

The more time he spent analyzing the pink dome, the more Keith was certain of two things:

One, it *was* in fact a pocket dimension laced with [Void Damage].

Two, Henrietta had the patience of a saint. He was surprised she hadn't acquired the title while growing up. Anyone who suffered the king and queen of Drendil as parents and walked away a decent person *had* to qualify for sainthood. Doubly so, as she'd somehow resisted the urge to stab them into oblivion with her [Void Damage] sword.

He'd tried to draw Jacqueline from her sheath and cut through the bubble—as a Void artifact herself, the sword could probably interact with it—but he'd been unable to touch her handle without getting stung with bouts of sword intent. He got the message that she was not willing, and he wasn't going to fight with a sword.

A sword that suddenly vanished from his hip.

It happened so suddenly, from one moment to the next, that he didn't even see it happen. He blinked, then smiled wolfishly. He adjusted himself to ensure nobody else would notice the missing sword, and felt an invisible weight fall from his shoulders; if Ria had her sword, nothing could stop her.

"Monfort, have you figured out how to get us all out of here yet?" King Simon's words pierced through Keith's moment of relief, and he marveled at the sheer audacity of that statement.

"How about I ask *you* a question," Keith ground through clenched teeth. "Where is Henrietta?"

"Who cares?" the king snapped back. "When we don't even know where *we* are!"

"This never would have happened if *you* hadn't sent Havork to escort Henri," Queen Thalia screeched at her husband. Keith flinched. So did her husband.

"You can't blame *me*." King Simon tsked. "*You* were the one whose skill promised Marquess Dorset was telling the truth and trustworthy."

"Why, I never!" The queen huffed.

"You did, actually." The king frowned. "Now I see where Henri gets her lack of wits. A higher Intelligence means *nothing* if you can't use it."

There wasn't much else Keith could do at this point, so he released the lesser [Shield] spell. He massaged an ever-growing headache.

Keith continued trying other perks and spells. Ever one to learn from his mistakes, he took out a mana potion at some point and restored his mana.

Ria would kill him if he died here from his own folly.

Their guard frowned at him but didn't make a move to stop him, so Keith kept his mana full. He continued recasting [Dragon Shield] and drinking mana potions while he kept poking at the barrier.

Hours dragged on; at least two, he was sure. The marquess returned, stepping into place outside Keith's cell.

Keith crossed his arms, ready to cast a second spell if needed, while reactivating [Multitask].

"Dorset!" King Simon walked over to the bars and clanged his cuffs loudly on the metal. "Let us out of here *this instant* or our knight commander will hunt you down and *end you*."

He sounded very confident. Then again, his knight commander *was* a level sixty paladin.

The marquess just raised an eyebrow. "Havork is sworn to obey the king and queen of Drendil, not *you*," Dorset retorted. "Who do you think *that* will be when you're dead?"

"I'm too pretty to die." Queen Thalia burst into tears.

"I assure you, that is not the case." The marquess pulled out a vial.

Keith pointed out the obvious to stall for time. "You can't kill the king and queen of Drendil and expect the council to accept you ascending to the throne? You'll have the King Killer title."

"Ah." The marquess smiled at Keith. "But *I* didn't kill them. *You did*."

"Are you offering to give me the chance?" Keith turned a thoughtful look on the king and queen. He *had* been daydreaming about that very thing.

They shrank back from their cell wall.

"That *would* make things easier."

Keith sighed. "As much as I'd love to, I'll let you do your own dirty work. I'm interested to see how you'll manage this."

"Can we talk this over?" King Simon cut in, but the fight was leaving him. Keith could tell. He had backed down from the cell door, going to stand beside his wife. "It's not too late to let us go and go back to working together."

"I'd like to see you try to get one past Witch Agatha." Queen Thalia stopped sobbing to glare at their captor. "That woman can sniff out the truth like a dog. A most unbecoming ability, but I'll allow it if it means *you'll pay for what you've done*." She waved at her legs. "Just look what you've done to my dress! This is embroidered with arachne silk, you uncultured, pathetic beast!"

Watching the marquess suffer what Keith had suffered almost made the past few hours worth it.

"Bring in the slave," Dorset snapped, and the servant left. He came back with an unconscious Lieutenant Franni Bertand slung over his shoulder. She looked much the worse for wear, but was still breathing.

"Oh, great!" Queen Thalia moaned. "Another monster."

King Simon eyed the lizardkin and took a slight step behind his wife, putting her between him and Franni.

Keith frowned. The last time he'd seen the lieutenant, he'd sent her to the border with a lot of assassins trussed up with Veralyn's Enchanted Restraint Manacles, one of which Franni was *wearing*. He didn't like the implications of what that meant . . . but it explained a lot.

The man handed the marquess a high-level antidote, and Chadwick uncorked it, downing the contents. The servant showed off another Rogue ability when he pulled a glass container holding a small poofy black mushroom with ominous swirling blue mist from out of nowhere.

"A shroomdoom," Keith remarked. "I see you came prepared. You're planning to frame me through a servant?" He knew of a dozen ways that could go wrong, but he wasn't about to tell his *enemy* that. The mushroom was a very deadly fungi that when disturbed, exploded highly poisonous spores. He had prepared his own shroomdoom antidote, as well as one for Henrietta, and pulled it out of his storage ring now. It didn't hurt to not take chances with his magical prison.

"Correct." The marquess smirked.

"Wait!" Simon cried. "You can't do this, or you'll break the magical contract."

"Actually, you'll be happy to know that I'm not the one who's hired this man. I'm just here to *watch*."

The servant, who'd presumably already downed his own antidote, smiled as he put the shroomdoom on the floor in front of the royal's cell.

"How much are they paying you. Whatever it is, I'll pay you double—triple!" Queen Thalia wheedled, a hint of fear in her eyes.

The man ignored them, stood up, and tossed the lizardkin onto the shroomdoom. Great billowing plumes of spores filled the room, their glowing blue dots almost beautiful.

"See?" the marquess gloated at the king and queen's unfortunate ending. "My plans are going perfectly."

Keith let the man think that as he hooked a thumb through his belt and calmly waited for his princess in shining armor to come and rescue him.

CHAPTER 113

Could I Fight While Flying If I Rode Keith from Behind?

Henrietta

[You have been affected by the Perk: **Strength of Sound**. +2 Strength for 10 minutes.]
[You have been affected by the Perk: **Inspire**. Your abilities cost 10% less for 10 minutes.]
[You have been affected by the Skill: **Idol**. When acting in the best interests of Minstrel Bronwynn, Health regeneration is 5% faster for 20 minutes.]

I was as ready as I'd ever be.

Destroy them, I heard my sword sing. *They will perish in agony!*

She was always a little *extra* when she was awake. I concentrated elsewhere.

"FORMATION!" the flautist's voice called outside, instructing our enemies. "GODS CURSE YOU, JACK, GET YOUR WHIP AND GET BACK INTO FORMATION!"

I edged close to the hole I'd sliced into the carriage to look outside. Which meant I was in position when a face peeked through. The brunette woman smiled maliciously. "Put the sword down, Princess, and I'll leave your pretty face unscarred."

I didn't deign to reply and just raised the point of my blade. She dodged as her smile grew wider. "Good choice. [Blazing Fist]."

Her hands burst into flames, and she swung with one brass-knuckled fist on fire. I swung Jacqueline up in a block, and my vision flashed white from the roaring flames. Jacqueline protested and flared [Intent], cutting the woman's hand.

"Ah!" the brunette screamed.

In her moment of distraction, I dropped to the floor and swept her feet out from under her, sending her toppling back outside the carriage.

"Stay here," I told Brownie.

"But I'll miss all the fun . . ." I heard her grumble as I jumped outside and landed in the open, surrounded by enemies. Sunset was an hour away, and hints of red painted across the sky.

I wondered idly how long this was going to take without perks; it was easier to get information out of people if they weren't a puddle.

I took in my surroundings as I dodged an arrow to the face. The carriage had collapsed off the side of the road, and there were five guards surrounding me. Their horses were being managed by another two, who were trying to move their bucking charges out of the way. The flautist was standing on the carriage seat, yelling orders.

Maybe if we were loud enough, Keith would fly by and see the commotion. I imagined flying back home happily snuggled in my Dark Lord's embrace. Could I fight while flying if I rode Keith from behind? Piggybacking, maybe? I was joking to myself, but I really hoped he was out looking for me. And that he was unhurt.

I needed to get out of here to find out.

The brunette slave trader sat up off the dirt. "Ow! My hand, you wretch!"

"Sorry," the words slipped out of me at the same time as I followed through with Jacqueline, and she dropped like a sack of potatoes.

Then all chaos broke loose.

Another arrow whizzed past my face. A poisoned throwing knife missed my arm. A spear *thunked* into the carriage beside me. My body danced, and I lashed out with Jacqueline as the guards all worked together to subdue me.

A chubby blue-haired man charged in and swung at me with an axe, his [Felling Blow] perk missing my nose by inches as I rolled to the left. His blade sunk deep into the front wheel of the carriage behind me, and he cursed as he tried to pull it out. I got his legs as I swept past, and he fell to the ground.

Three [Rapid Fire] arrows entered my senses, and I blocked the first two, but the third nicked my thigh, introducing poison into my leg. I grabbed the throwing knife from earlier and tossed it back, scratching one of the archers. My [Resist Poison] perk activated, and the poison burned away. The archer wasn't so lucky.

Knight Commander Havork remained on his horse, hand on his sheathed sword, and a sad look on his face. I ducked another arrow and a [Water Ball], then ran the archer through.

"You *idiots!*" the flautist, who was still on the carriage seat, screamed at the two with the horses. "Leave them and get in here!"

Three down, six to go. The guy with a whip sported an amazing pencil moustache . . . On closer inspection, I wondered if he'd actually *penciled* it on. The swirls weren't straight.

He lashed out with flair, and while I was parrying a blow from a halfling woman holding a sword as big as Jacqueline, he managed to loop his whip around my ankle. Its barbs cut into the leather of my nice boots as he attempted to pull my foot out from under me.

It was admirable that he thought he could trip me, but that was never going to happen. I kicked, and he was sent off his feet. Then I rapidly spun to the side as a blonde-haired woman in a cute halter top, skirt, and tights missed me with her [Slash]. I wasn't so polite.

Another one down.

I barely registered the flautist in the background yell out, "*You!* Knight! Stop her!"

As I rolled, I swung Jacqueline wide one-handed; a risky move, but it *did* cut the tip off the spiked whip as moustache man was picking himself up from the fall.

One of the horse handlers hit me with a throwing star as I stood. It did little to no damage, but it pinched. I bit the star and pulled it out of my shoulder, dropping it to the side. My [Resist Poison] perk activated again.

Knight Commander Havork stayed on his horse and just shook his head. "I'm afraid I was not tasked with keeping your guards safe, merely escorting the princess."

"One chance to run away!" I told the remaining guards, reassured by the knight's inaction.

No one paid me any mind, and the moustache man attacked me with his whip again. I charged him at full speed, ducking under the strike and following the whip back. I watched his confidence turn to worry as I got within arm's reach. He jumped back, activating a skill that sent him elegantly leaping across the field.

Two pouches sailed through the air from the side, aimed at my legs. I bent my knees and, despite the biting pain in my nicked thigh, backflipped out of the way. The tiny packets exploded in a plume of red smoke that made my eyes tingle even at a distance. I landed beside the horse handler who'd thrown them.

His defense lacked refinement, and I went right through him to get to the next handler, a man with both arms transformed into giant badger paws; a shifter.

The flautist was screaming something again, but this time, I was entirely focused on not dying and missed it.

The halfling with the outsize sword [Charged], which meant she'd be at me in seconds.

I only needed seconds.

The shifter swiped his badger paws at my throat, and everything slowed as I moved my head to the side and activated [Death Parry]. A claw caught my ear. Jacqueline came up, and my sword met the halfling's as she struck. The blades slid down each other, and I flicked my wrist just enough to open a path. The halfling's blade cut into the shifter instead of her intended target.

"You'll pay for this." The halfling pulled free her blade and resumed her stance.

"Or," I offered, placing the carriage to my back, "I just pay you now to go away?"

"Don't listen to her," the flautist yelled, "and you can have the shares of the fallen."

"No deal, Princess." The halfling grinned. "I'll get paid *plenty* by the marquess."

I was tired of going easy . . . and in my peripheral [Sword Aura], I saw the whipper running back into the fray.

I missed a sentient Dark Enchanted Forest who took care of stragglers. I wanted to go *home*.

The halfling swung at me, and a whip cracked beside my head, but I dodged each blow and tried to attack back. I positioned the moustache man and the halfling in line with each other.

I executed my [Aura Blade], swinging Jacqueline in an arc and sending energy slashing across the landscape. The halfling went down for good, and the whipper just barely managed to survive. I took a deep breath and readied myself for another attack. Our eyes locked . . . and he promptly ran away.

"That's it." The flautist hopped down from the carriage and took a step along the side of its ruined frame toward us. "If you want something done *right*, you have to do it—"

A heavy set of Veralyn's Enchanted Restraint Manacles came down on his head as he walked past the hole in the carriage.

The man shook from the force of the blow, dazed.

"That's for my beloved Suzette!" Brownie announced, brandishing my manacles threateningly from the hole. Then she jumped down and applied her entire weight on an elbow to the man's forehead.

He dropped like a stone.

CHAPTER 114

Molten Ash Vane

Keith

"So, what now?" Keith asked the marquess after his future in-laws were taken care of. "You drag me to the council and put on your little show?"

The marquess laughed. "Wouldn't you like that. No, no. I'm just waiting for a *special* delivery. I'm patient. It'll take a few days for my bride to reach home, so I'm in no rush."

"I wonder," Keith said. "Did she say yes?"

"Not *yet*." The marquess looked like someone had offered him a tray of cinnamon buns. "But that's half the fun."

"Good luck with that." Keith gleefully imagined Ria picking up the man and throwing him out a window. The Rogue servant stripped the Veralyn's Enchanted Restraint Manacles off of Franni, and he opened the cell to the royals to toss in the lizardkin, not bothering to lock it behind her. Then he gathered up the squished and sad-looking shroomdoom and carefully put it back into the glass container.

"So," Keith asked, curious if his own theory was correct. "how did you get your hands on my lieutenant?"

The marquess laughed. "They were easy targets for the Servalt Assassin's Guild. Once they dropped off their prisoners, they had let down their guard. They came with such fun toys too."

"I don't believe you. Lady Gloria would never attack someone returning fallen members to her," Keith pointed out. The woman might have been an assassin, but she had a code all unto herself.

"Welns was a terrible guild leader," the servant spoke, drawing my attention to the man. He was medium build and looked nondescript with brown hair and brown eyes. Easily forgettable and easily the perfect face for a rogue.

"Don't give away too much," Chadwick chided, though his self-satisfied grin belayed any real bite to the order.

Keith frowned. His treaty wasn't with Gloria Welns, but with the actual Assassin's Guild . . . Still, if there was a new leader, maybe they had found a way around it. This was going to be a lot of paperwork and some legwork when he returned home. With his princess, whenever she deigned to rescue him.

More work for Rufus when Keith got back, he decided. The beastman deserved a challenge, and crushing the new boss of their neighboring Assassin's Guild into polite submission sounded like just the thing.

He was meditating on the best course of action when the sound of footsteps drew his attention to a man with cat ears and scruffy whiskers standing in the dungeon entrance. "Manny, I've got the goods—Ah, good, you are here, marquess."

The catkin shoved a clear bottle of red liquid with flecks of black swirling inside at the servant.

Molten ash vane.

"Good job. I'll dispose of Their Royal Pains from Drendil." Manny the servant swished the liquid around in the bottle, catching the dim light of the dungeon. "And you can say last you saw, the lizardkin offed them. If they bother asking you at all."

"Just because they have me under house arrest doesn't mean they won't ask me under truth spell all manner of annoying questions." The marquess scoffed. "I'd rather have a plan on top of a plan. And even if they *don't* ask me at the council meeting tomorrow, they're bound to come around asking questions once it's discovered that I'm actually married to the princess."

The servant smiled a vicious smile. "I might even have enough to get rid of the lizardkin while I'm at it. The more the merrier."

"Wait until we've turned away," the marquess ordered, grabbing the catkin and facing the wall. "The last anyone saw of Simon and Thalia has to be the lizardkin killing them."

Just then, the wall exploded.

CHAPTER 115

What a Disgrace to the Arts

Henrietta
Earlier

"Bronwynn, that was amazing!" I chose that moment to pop a mana potion *and* a health potion.

"Thank you." Brownie swung the manacles around deftly then threw them on the ground. She gave the flautist a scathing look. "I can't believe I went with him on a water break. He played so nicely, too. What a disgrace to the arts! I should get his flute and stick it up hi—"

There was a cough, and I turned to face the only other person left. Knight Commander Havork smiled sadly from his horse. My breath caught in my throat, and I found myself lost again.

"I don't understand," I whispered.

I didn't understand *why*. Why hadn't he just freed me himself? Why had he worked with the slave traders? Why had he just *sat there*?

"*I* don't need to understand. Thank you for the keys. Speaking of which . . ." Brownie squatted and started rummaging through the flautist's clothes. She pulled out a pouch and two rolled-up scrolls. "Loot!"

Brownie saw that I was just standing there, staring at my mentor, and headed for the carriage. "How about I just go get the boy while you talk?"

"I'm sorry Henri—*Henrietta*." Havork swung off his horse and faced me. Slowly, he approached and lowered to one knee. With intent, he drew his sword and stabbed it into the earth. I flinched. That was *not* the way to treat a blade.

He drew a deep breath. "It may have been my duty to train you . . . but from the first step you took on the field, I have watched you. I have seen you face trials and tribulations and walk away head held high. I know how hard you struggled to do what was right, even when you fought against the darkness and your own fears. And as I breathe, you have grown into a strong, worthy, and benevolent ruler; more worthy than any other in Drendil. I am proud to have walked with you, and I am proud to have called you my princess."

He smiled up at me, and a fierce determination filled his voice. "Which is why I have no regrets breaking my sworn oath to my king, for what use is wielding a blade for a man I do not respect? I decided that day at the bridge that I would no longer be a puppet in childish games." He let go of the sword and bowed low, touching one fist to the ground. "I will accept whatever punishment you wish to bestow, for as an Oath Breaker, I have nothing left to lose."

I stared at the knight with wide eyes.

Oath Breaker. A paladin's oath to their god or to their liege was the *foundation* of their power. It was far worse than a Bond Breaker title, and it reduced *all* stats to ten. When Havork had taken my side at the bridge, he'd broken his oath, and he'd done it for *me*.

He didn't free me today because he *couldn't*. With his Oath Breaker debuff, he was essentially powerless. At that point, it was better for *me* if he just waited on the sidelines.

I stepped forward and hugged him without permission. He stiffened, looking up at me with surprise. Jokingly, I asked, "As for punishment . . . have you ever visited the Dark Lord's dungeon?"

Brownie stole—*borrowed* the slave traders' horses and rode back to Grand Duchess Calisto's palace while I ran a safe distance ahead to avoid any reaction to the beast.

We'd decided that Havork would remain at the scene, and I would send him a cleanup crew. The kitchen boy had woken up while I was downing a mana potion from my ring, and I didn't bother to stop him as he immediately made his escape into the night.

A spy in North Sumbria wasn't *my* problem, though I would politely inform the duchess and let her sort out her staff.

It took almost an hour for the horse to make it back.

We let the city gate guards know about the defeated slavers before heading straight for the palace.

Grand Duchess Calisto was there to meet us at the same place I'd rolled in with Keith that first day. She must have heard from the city guard. Sunset was just falling, and the shadows only accentuated the bright lights and festive sounds coming from the ballroom.

"Princess, I'm so glad to see you're safe." The grand duchess swept forward to greet me, taking my hands into hers. "We were all so worried when you disappeared."

She led us inside after reassuring me that her people were en route to pick up Havork.

"I'm sorry for taking you away from the party because of a few slave traders," I apologized.

"And *I'm* sorry that you were kidnapped and enslaved at *my* party," the duchess said dryly.

We were brought to a beautiful office, ornate and classically styled. There was a grand desk with a small seating area in front of it. A couch and some chairs were pulled up around a small table that had hot tea and some snacks. Including a cut up cinnamon bun. I took a seat on the couch and waited for Keith to join us. Brownie and Calisto chose to sit in the chairs.

I took an appreciative sip of rosehip tea and picked up a stick, skewering a bite-sized piece of the gooey soft treat. "Can I just say, whoever it is that's been sharing North Sumbrian food with the rest of us is *my* hero? I'd love to meet them before we go home."

Brownie made appreciative noises, and I set aside a bun for Keith. I hoped he'd get here soon.

"I'd *also* like to meet them." Duchess Calisto grimaced. "And then, I would shake them silly and *fine* them for all the problems they've caused me."

"Wait, what?" I put down my teacup.

"It's just as I said." The duchess frowned at the cinnamon bun on my stick. "Someone has been spreading all of these amazing foods across the continent, and I don't know if it's on purpose, but everyone assumes it started here. I've been dealing with famous chefs and cooks, entitled royals, and even adventuring parties coming to North Sumbria looking for the origins of it all."

Brownie leaned forward and took a second piece. "I'm not surprised. Ramen is probably my favorite thing to eat after my own mother's rhubarb crumble."

"And that doesn't take into account the *dueling*, which was barely used before someone started talking about it all across Valaria!" Our hostess rubbed her temple delicately, reminding me of Keith. "Now, everybody and their human is running around dueling. Not to mention everyone accrediting us with fashion, hairstyles, and more! 'It's all the rage in North Sumbria' my *left foot!*"

As the entire picture fell into place, I marveled. "With your duchy being our continent's center of the arts, it's *easy* to assume these things originated here . . . but why?"

"The gods only know." The duchess sighed.

As I thought about duels, my mind wandered back to Keith. "I'm sorry for changing the topic so suddenly, but after the marquess kidnapped me, I haven't had a chance to reconnect with Keith. You've summoned him, yes—"

"The marquess? He's still upstairs under guard and hasn't moved all evening." Duchess Calisto frowned. "We thought you'd been taken by *your parents*."

"What? Why?!" I stood up. *If* Marquess Dorset was upstairs, then I had a bone to pick with him. With the council meeting tomorrow, it was almost worth the Bond Breaker title. That reminded me; at some point, I would need to request an audience.

They would also need to know that I was going to marry Keith Monfort, Dark Magician King of Nilheim—and no one was going to stop me.

"Because they went missing shortly after you did . . ." The duchess hesitated. "And so did King Keith. The last I heard, he confronted them in their rooms and hasn't been seen since—"

A knock on the door made everyone turn. A familiar face met mine—Gerda the Bridge Troll.

She was panting as she gasped out, "I know where the Dark Lord is."

CHAPTER 116

The Guard Wasn't Turned into Paste

Keith

"Keith!"

"I'm here," Keith replied. The dust from the collapsed wall still obfuscated most of the room, but it was settling fast. Through the haze he saw Henrietta in full glory and wielding Jacqueline with both hands, climbing awkwardly over the stone rubble that was once a wall. The catkin groaned, but no other movement could be seen from the ground, and Ria squatted to hit the man's head with the pummel of her sword.

Manny was struggling to his feet, coughing. When he had breath, he yelled, "INTRUD—" before Ria also cut him off.

The Heroine of Justice punched him in the face. To everyone's surprise, the guard wasn't turned into paste but simply stumbled back. The bottle in his hands sailed through the air and shattered on a wall. The wall began to sizzle and spit as it melted away wherever the liquid touched. Keith flinched.

Henrietta's face contorted into disgust as she recognized the molten ash vane.

"Now, what were you going to use *that* for?" she asked aloud, eyeing the melted wall and the man. Then she paused to read something on her character sheet and visibly paled. "Oh no!"

"Wait up, Henrietta!" Gerda appeared in the hole in the wall and clambered over the debris in her evening gown. Her own sword hung from a belt she'd found to wrap around over her dress.

Keith noted with amusement the tiny scrap of green fabric sticking out of the rubble beside the bridge troll. The wall opened into a stone hallway that looked like a gallery, each side lined with portraits . . . and a green wall tapestry.

"Ria," Keith said his princess's name gently.

Henrietta's head whipped up in his direction, and her face broke out into a wide grin. "Keith!"

Manny tried to stand up again, but before Keith could warn Ria, Gerda finished the job. She knocked him out and got to work shackling the man with his own set of Veralyn's Enchanted Restraint Manacles.

"I'm so happy you're safe." Ria unclipped a large metal ring with two keys on it from Manny's belt.

"The feeling is mutual." He smiled at her while she attempted to unlock his cell. Unfortunately, neither fit.

"No worries." She tossed the keys away without a thought. Ria reached around to the bun at the back of her neck and dug out a lockpick. "I came prepared!"

"I love you," Keith said, because he couldn't say anything else.

"The feeling is mutual," she teased, repeating back to him what he'd just said.

"The marquess probably has the key," he said, pointing at the rubble.

She sighed. "I'm not much at picking locks, anyway. I'll go unearth the idiot."

"Pass over the picks." Gerda walked up and put out her hand. "I'll start just in case we can't find the key."

Ria managed to pull out the very dead marquess around the same time the bridge troll picked the lock.

"This bubble's a Void pocket dimension." Keith held up a hand to hold Ria back when she rushed toward him. "You can't touch it, and I haven't figured out how to get out yet. Dimension magic isn't really my specialty."

Ria and Gerda stood there for a moment, both studying the pink dome.

"Let's wake up Marquess Dorset and get some answers. But first, [Harvest Kill]." The entire set of Drendil's royal jewelry set, the construct button, a rough map of North Sumbria, a pair of keys, a spare pair of Veralyn's Enchanted Restraint Manacles, and a shiny rock all fell into her hands. "Loot!"

She pocketed everything and then pulled out her one Revive potion, opened it, and poured it into the man's mouth.

His body glowed slightly. Unfortunately, [Revive] didn't heal injuries like [Resurrect], and the marquess still sported a terrible sword wound from where Jacqueline had burst through the wall.

Chadwick sputtered. "What—Argh! How dare—"

Ria didn't wait for the man to recover himself. She snapped her fingers in front of his face twice to get his attention. "How do we get Keith out of the trap?"

"I'm not a *mage*." Chadwick scoffed, summoning a health potion from somewhere and downing it. "How would *I* know?"

"He really is useless," Gerda said.

"You will rue the day—"

Ria didn't let him finish speaking a second time, this time shoving a scrap of tattered green tapestry into his mouth. She walked back to Keith's cell while Gerda tied up the marquess.

"What if I hit it *with* [Void Damage]? Does [Void Damage] work on [Void Damage]?" Henrietta leaned closer to inspect the dome through the bars.

Keith nodded at her sword. "I would be more worried that the [Void Damage] would void the dimension itself. I'd rather not think about what that would do with me still inside."

"I'm going to lock up the bad guys while we brainstorm," Gerda said. "In case one of them has any tricks."

"Good idea, Gerda." Ria nodded.

Keith felt a knot form in the pit of his stomach. "The keys on the ground are to the cell beside me . . . I should tell you now, your parents are in there."

Henrietta glanced over at the cell, seeing the three bodies lying there. "Oh no . . ."

"Ria." Keith didn't know how his princess was going to react, and he was furious that he couldn't give her a reassuring hug right then and there.

"Lieutenant Franni!" Ria continued, looking devastated. "What happened?"

Gerda opened the door and dragged the three victims out.

Ria pulled out her Resurrect potion and poured it down Franni's throat without hesitation. The lizardkin came to quickly and with much better grace than the marquess had. Then again, a Resurrection potion was a better option that left her in the peak of health.

Franni was on her feet and asking for orders in very quick succession.

Henrietta nodded. "For now, Franni, there's backup coming just behind us. Could you wait outside and show them where we are? We can catch up after this."

"Right away, Princesss!"

"Speaking of catching up. What happened?" Keith inquired, knowing that he'd ask again for every last detail when they were safe. And after he'd had a calming bubbly bath. The entire affair was too much, and he was ready to be done with it all. Adventures were for adventurers and heroes—like his princess. He was supposed to stay home and greet her triumphant return with a warm castle and a cup of tea in the man-eating flower garden. "And how did he capture you in the first place?"

"I figured that we could ask the Continental Council tomorrow to cancel the contract, and when he poisoned me, it was going to be a perfect exhibit to our case! That was . . . until they shackled me with Veralyn's Enchanted Restraint Manacles. Havork slipped us the key to the manacles so I could get free and summon Jacqueline. I defeated all of the slave traders except Jacques the whipper, who escaped." She quickly corrected herself, "Oh, and the one Brownie hit on the head."

"I see." And he did see. She was brilliant as ever.

"Then, we made it back to Grand Duchess Calisto's and found out you were missing."

Keith sighed. "I was tricked into a trap by your *parents*. I am utterly ashamed."

"And *then*," Henrietta continued after taking a breath, "it turned out that Gerda went to Marquess Dorset's room at the start of the night, and he was meeting with a runner. She tracked the runner all over the city as they did errands and then the whole way here."

"The catkin?"

"Yes," Gerda replied, locking the cell door with their three prisoners inside. She walked up to start a full inspection of the pink trap encasing him.

"Yes," Ria said at the same time. She continued. "We followed the trail here. It took a few hours to get here from Grand Duchess Calisto's."

"Really?" That piqued his interest. Henrietta could go a long way in one hour. "Where are we?"

"Almost to the Servalt border, in a small place called Colwood."

"And you say Gerda *tracked* the catkin?" Keith frowned. "How did she do that? He was *quick*."

"I don't know the whole of it, mind." Henrietta shrugged. "But Gerda got ahead of him to the bridge just outside the city then hit him with a 'You have three days to find the answer to my riddle or I'll eat you' riddle. He laughed at her and kept running."

"Foolish man." Gerda shook her head. "It's like he'd never met a bridge troll before."

"Many haven't." Keith chuckled. "Still, he should have known better than to leave something like that hanging. Those tales always end in tragedy."

"I don't think you'd actually eat him," Henrietta corrected.

"I appreciate your faith in me," the bridge troll joked. "It's not a perk I use often. Tracking people for three days and waiting around so I can pop out whenever they next reach a bridge is a lot of work."

"Sounds fun, actually." Keith smiled. "Maybe not now—I'm far too busy ruling a Dark Enchanted Forest and wooing the Heroine of Justice to play those kinds of pranks. But it would have been perfect in my younger days."

"Speaking of ruling the Dark Enchanted Forest." Henrietta pretended to pout. "You didn't propose in front of the entirety of Valaria's well-to-do like you promised. Does that mean I have to wait until the Summer Masquerade?"

"I barely lasted *this* long; I won't make it three more months." Keith wanted to kiss her so badly, but there was still permadeath blocking his path. That was a thought. "Actually . . . what if I just died? I would probably leave a piece behind, and you would have plenty of time to get me to Chloe, even if the pocket dimension collapses—"

"Let's not, just in case." Ria shot him a serious expression and refused outright. "I'll run back to get someone else who knows anything about dimension magic."

Gerda scoffed. "I'm right here, you know. Dimensional-troll-magic user, *right here.*"

The two stared at her.

Gerda sighed. "Just step back and let me take a look."

CHAPTER 117

Cheat with Bridges

Henrietta

[Bond Breaker]
[As per Section 7 of the Marriage Agreement between the Kingdom of Drendil and the Marquess Dorset:
Confirmation of Agreement is required before the Terms of Agreement come into effect. Should Princess Henrietta or the King or the Queen of Drendil reject the marriage, she will be found in breach of the Contract and suffer the following:
Special Title: Bond Breaker
Revert Highest Stat to Base 10
-100 Reputation with Servalt
Special Title: Bond Breaker will remain in effect until Henrietta Doryn fulfills the Terms of the Contract or until the Terms are no longer Binding.]

Gerda examined every inch of pink bubble, slowly and carefully, and I was impressed at how comfortable she was doing so in a formfitting dress.

The troll was wearing a stunning mermaid-cut evening gown in a soft violet that complimented her green complexion. And heels.

This was why I wore boots. In case I needed to fight off slave traders and rescue the king of the Dark Enchanted Forest from a dank, cold dungeon.

I smiled at my friend. "Can you free my would-be husband from his eternal pocket dimension?"

"Chadwick outdid himself with this one . . ." Gerda whistled.

"If there's anything I can do, Miss Gerda, just let me know. Though I hesitate to withdraw my own wards—they aren't protecting me from the [Void Damage], but there may still be other traps," Keith said. He looked exhausted, his hair all rumpled.

All of his buttons were still done up, though. Pity.

"Hmm, that shouldn't be necessary." Gerda circled what she could of the bubble. I remained quiet so as not to disturb her work. Finally, she sighed. "It looks like a trap space with added [Void Damage]."

Keith offered, "If it helps, I was portaled here and found myself already inside the bubble."

"They portaled you into the trap." Gerda kicked a stone from the destroyed wall. It hit the pink bubble and was consumed by the Void. "That means it's an enchantment. It's maintained by its own mana, and we could potentially just attack it until there isn't any mana left to sustain it."

"I don't know if that will work," Keith said. "I have a perk that lets me connect to my enchantments and resupply them with mana from a distance."

"Beg pardon, Your Viciousness." Gerda lifted one eyebrow at the Dark Lord. "But you are a level eighty *Arcane Sage*. This was cast by someone under level sixty."

"Still." Keith shrugged. "That doesn't stop the dimension from collapsing on me and Voiding me out of existence."

Gerda put her hands on her hips. "Which one of us is the expert in dimensional magic?"

"You can't expect me to believe that you're an *expert* in one of the most difficult forms of magic just because your class lets you make portals! You just cheat with bridges."

The two of them began arguing back and forth.

I contemplated throwing rocks at the spell until it popped, then something Gerda had said piqued my interest. "Wait, Gerda, how do you know the caster is under level sixty?"

"Because my [Pocket Dimension] skill only lets me analyze things of equal to or lesser—"

The troll cut herself off, and it looked like she had an idea. "Anyone got a waterskin?"

Keith twiddled his fingers. "I can make as much water as you need in here, not that it'll help."

"I do." I pulled out one from my storage and handed it over.

"Now, no one say anything, or the dungeon might explode. I hate [Mana Burn], and this is more complex than I'm used to."

We both readily agreed and let the woman do her work in peace. Gerda walked up to the bubble and began using the broken pieces of the wall to build a small arch in front of it. We watched in confusion as she worked, only realizing what we were looking at when she was almost done.

"It's a bridge!" I cried.

"*CHEATING WITH BRIDGES!*" Keith announced indignantly.

"Shut it!" Gerda uncorked the pouch and laid it down so a trickle of running water snaked beneath the "bridge."

> "In Between the light Unseen,
> Void and Space all mixed in place,
> By Water's gift, [Dimension Rift]."

Gerda gathered her magic all around her, and I could see wisps of aquamarine power floating into a formation. The water beneath the bridge flowed toward the bubble but rose on strings of mana as it touched the outer surface of the dome. The droplets, reinforced with magic, bobbed into a spell pattern in the air as if they were dancing raindrops.

Slowly, ever so slowly, the water became a gently spinning circle that wound around the pink bubble, enveloping it within the trail of droplets.

"I'm going to try and take control of the dimension. I'm a bridge troll. This is my bridge. That is my *space*." The waterskin was out of water, but more water manifested itself. Gerda instructed, "When I say so, take your sword and stab the bubble to destabilize it."

More and more water rose from beneath the bridge to join the initial formation.

I pulled my sword from her sheath and prepared to execute a sword perk. Jacqueline was wary of the bubble, and of her own volition, released a sheen of [Void Intent] that rippled along her blade.

The water was now whirling in a streaming tornado of white, far more than could have possibly fit within the waterskin. Power crackled within it, and I could just barely make out the pink of the bubble.

"Now!"

I focused my all into my sword. "[Force Thrust]."

Jacqueline hit the wall of water and smashed through it to the bubble. Sparkles of black and pink and silver and green erupted from the area around the sword in a blast of mana. My sword sung. She laughed. She screamed. Jacqueline's [Void Intent] consumed the dimension walls as it was in turn consumed by flecks of Void.

My hands burned, and I struggled to keep them steady against the swirling tide. It took everything I had to keep Jacqueline pressed against the sphere. With my Bond Breaker title, Strength ten just wasn't going to cut it. Or pierce it.

I wasn't going to make it.

I gritted my teeth. *NO!* My grip tightened, and I pushed forward, my scream rising to meet Jacqueline's. I wasn't anywhere near as strong as before, but I didn't need to be *strong*. I just needed to be strong *enough*.

I'm so proud of you, sweet. Jacqueline Tiamat la Fleur let out a final burst of [Void Intent], helping break through the pink dome.

The entire thing shattered.

CHAPTER 118

His Greed for Cuddles

Keith

Keith watched as thousands of tiny pink mana particles rained [Void Damage] down on his defense. His high-tier [Dragon Shield] was eaten away by the shattered bits of Void, with only a few shards passing through to land on him.

[You have taken 18 Void-based Damage. HP 382/400]

Keith didn't wait; he rushed forward and caught Henrietta in an embrace. And then they were kissing.

She felt amazing in his arms. He eventually broke the kiss and buried his face in his princess's fluffy brown hair, breathing in her cinnamon spice and sugary scent. There was still so much to do before the night was over, but it could all wait until they were done.

So what if Gerda was there to watch them hug it out. Let her.

When they broke apart, they found half a dozen royal guards standing around them. Gerda lay sprawled out on the floor, exhausted from the major magical working.

"I brought them as requesssted." Lieutenant Franni stood to attention.

"Alright, everyone," Keith started, then glanced at the hole in the wall. "This *is* everyone?"

"Yesss, Your Viciousnesss," Franni stated. "With about twenty of Grand Duchesss Calisto's best adventurersss."

"Then they can help us cart everyone back to the palace. I'm sure the council will be very interested to know about an interkingdom ring of slave traders." Keith squeezed Ria's hand in support, knowing that her parent's would be punished with the group.

"That everyone *already knew about*," Gerda snapped. "Madame Potts cast about them months ago!"

"Then I think it's about time we head back."

After rounding up everyone, it was well past midnight.

It was dark outside, but a full moon illuminated the overgrown and poorly managed estate. The entire place was in need of repair, and probably purchased recently for nefarious intents.

The only one worse for wear on their side was Gerda, who simply needed time and a mana potion.

He owed the bridge troll, and would reward her handsomely for her assistance. And after that? He needed her magically audited *yesterday*. He needed *all* his kingdom's trolls audited yesterday! How had he never been warned about them in his lessons?!

Keith wanted a nap. Badly. Right now. But it would have to wait. They had a three-hour ride ahead of them.

And another problem to solve. Henrietta would never last riding a horse the whole way back.

"I guess there is nothing for it." Keith smiled. "I'll just have to carry you."

"Do you have enough mana left?" Her concern didn't stop her from reaching her arms around him and letting him pick her up in a princess hold.

"I'll summon Fifi to meet us halfway." He reached out to the construct then and there, pleased to note the willingness he felt from his dark mare. He wasn't surprised—Henrietta had a way of befriending all of the beasts of the Dark Enchanted Forest. He hugged the princess closer, until her head rested comfortably on his shoulder.

After tonight, he didn't want to be separated from her side for even a second, and traveling with the Heroine of Justice gently snoring in his arms was a perfect way to keep *him* awake.

There was so much to think about. And plan. Three hours was more than enough time to get it done . . . and to satisfy his greed for cuddles.

Chloe and Julia met them at the city gates three hours later, escorting them back to the palace. Mostly because Chloe was too impatient to politely wait for them in the parlor. Usually, only the watch and the bakers would be up this early, but Duchess Calisto's palace was vibrant with life. Hostlers prepared transport for any of the previous night's visitors hoping to get back home early, and many a man-at-arms hustled to load carriages with luggage. That wasn't even counting those in North Sumbrian colors. The grand duchess had hired many attendants to be ever ready for her guests, especially during the festivities.

Everyone watched wide-eyed as they rode onto the palace grounds. They were an interesting sight, to be sure.

At the front, the Dark Lord held the Heroine of Justice, who was snoring, in his arms. They were accompanied by the Paladin of Light, Countess Julia von Slyke, and her fiancée, Necromancer Chloe Watercress. Next, two dozen of the duchess's royal guard rode with a bridge troll. And everyone was still dressed in their finest.

Third, Chadwick, a Servalt marquess not worth mentioning, and his attendants were tied together in pairs and riding a few heavily guarded horses. The marquess had woken up partway through their trip and had tried to escape. It hadn't gone well for him.

And of course, the king and queen of Drendil were there. But they were thrown over a saddlebag like luggage and hardly worth mentioning.

And finally, Lieutenant Franni took up the rear.

Everyone had gone quiet, watching them ride up. Keith didn't want to wake Ria, so he activated his powerful [Flight] spell to get down and gently princess-carried her inside. The grand duchess met them halfway up the stairs.

"You've made it back! And all in one piece; how splendid." Calisto noted her attendants carrying in the sacks full of royals and made a disapproving tsk. "Or, at least, everyone important made it back in one piece. Shall we go in? It's *cold*."

"Before we do," Keith said quietly, conscious of his sleeping princess. "Can I confirm how many of the council are still in residence?"

He would make sure that as many as possible would be there for his morning audience, if he had to unpack their carriages himself.

"All of the ones who attended the Spring Ball are still here," Calisto assured him. "We decided to add tonight's events to the meeting. Head off any wars, rally the forces for a continental search and rescue, so on and so forth. Luckily, you rescued yourselves. I have it on good authority from the council that there would have been much lording-it-over-thou from whomever helped *you* specifically. Not to mention requests and favors."

Keith shivered, imagining just what kind of *favors* Their Royal Highness Rowen of Peldeep would demand if they'd managed to rescue him.

"Before you go," Duchess Calisto waved at their baggage. "What am I doing with *those?*"

"We'll raise King Simon and Queen Thalia when the council meets," Keith replied. "The marquess is tied to a horse outside. He's good with portals and is subordinate to someone very powerful, so be sure to keep him locked up safe."

"I see." Calisto shared a nod with Keith before bidding them all a polite good morning.

Keith went and took his princess to bed.

CHAPTER 119

Screw Propriety:
I Need Portable Tea

Henrietta

I woke up stiff and sore and still tired, with a pair of long arms wrapped around my waist. Keith breathed deeply into my hair, and when I pulled away to look at him, he mumbled a rough, "Good morning."

This . . . wasn't what I had expected to wake up to, but I wouldn't complain. We were both fully clothed, and cuddling him in bed beat cuddling him on a horse.

"Good morning." I ran my fingers through his messy morning hair. Black locks had bunched around his horn, as they were wont to do, and I carefully detangled them.

His eyes were closed against the soft light that seeped into my room through the curtains. It made him look like some kind of black-horned seraph. I smiled as I leaned forward and kissed him on the nose.

That got his attention; blue eyes opened and stared at me fondly. "None of that, or I'll—Well, whatever we do, it'll have to be after a *bath*."

I dragged my eyes down his body and gasped. "Oh no! The sheets!"

Fighting a bunch of slave traders, blasting through a dungeon wall, breaking a magical dimension, and riding cross-country for hours on end was *not* the way to stay pristine or clean.

My stunning blue-purple dress was torn, muddy, burned in places, and caked with so much dust and grime that I had no doubt that the servants were going to need magic or a burn pit for the bedding. Someone had taken off my boots, at least.

"I'm sorry. I was so tired, I just barely got us to bed," Keith said, sheepish. "[Cleanse]."

That *helped* . . . but I was still a mess.

"I'm surprised my dress held up so well." I admired the silky, beautiful fabric. Then I glared at Keith's clothes. He'd taken off everything but his pants and tunic. His buttons glared back at perfect eye level, mocking me with their thereness.

Keith chuckled. "Arachne silk. Stronger than any ordinary thread, and more durable."

"Hmph." I sat up quickly, throwing off our blankets and hopping out of bed. "I'm going to clean up!"

Keith rolled onto his back and threw his arm over his eyes. "I'll be up in a bit."

In the common area, Lilith was pacing nervously; not her usual professional maid demeanor. She stopped when she saw me and hurried over, tears in her eyes. "Mistresss! I'm so glad you're alright!"

"I'll be better after a *bath*." I plucked at my dress. "And fresh clothes."

The lizardkin gave me an intense stare, taking in my disheveled, rough appearance. "Leave it to me, Princesss."

A few minutes later, I was lounging in an enormous porcelain tub with rose petals adorning the crystal waters. It smelled of lavender and bliss.

It was a lovely half-hour soak, with foot rubs. Not long enough to feel fully rejuvenated, but enough time to feel alive again. I donned a respectable day gown, soft and clingy and pale pink.

Keith met me in a new set of dark robes over a fresh linen shirt with three buttons at the neck. He must have found his own bath or used more magic to get clean.

He was carrying a plate of breakfast, and I fell in love with him all over again.

"I love you," I told him, grabbing an onion-and-cheese scone slice lathered in melted butter off the plate. It was warm and buttery and rich. I almost cried, it tasted so good.

"And I you." He leaned down and pressed a kiss to my forehead. "Now, let's go tell everybody else. Sithli let me know the council is in session as we speak. Shall we?"

"With pleasure." I finished off the scone.

He set aside his platter and picked up two large mugs of fresh hot tea, handing one to me. "Here, we can drink these on the way. Screw propriety: I need portable tea."

I laughed; after last night, I was desperately in need of caffeine myself. They'd prepared my favorite elderberry and nettle tea, and the scent of it was almost as relaxing as the tub. I took a sip and felt my entire body infused with the warmth of the hot beverage.

Arm in arm, teas in hand, we made our way downstairs. Daj, the polite attendant who'd shown us our rooms, was waiting to lead us to a large round atrium near the middle of the palace grounds. The ceiling was domed glass, and there was foliage decorating the walls, along with beautiful hothouse flowers.

A half-moon table had been set up in the middle, and many of the most power-ful and influential people in Valaria sat around it. I recognized Their Royal High-ness of Peldeep, Grand Duchess Calisto, Necromancer Chloe, Duke Wyldon of Servalt, the Grand Pontiff of Sumbria, Wizard Lorthar from Hemlock Hill, and Agatha, the Witch of Winter's End. There were a few others, I had not met yet.

To join, one needed to be over level sixty and have influence over the conti-nent—*or* represent a country, as Chloe and Wyldon were doing.

Knight Commander Havork had not taken his place at Drendil's seat. He stood uncomfortably off to the side, arms crossed and somber. No one had bothered to restrain him, though he was obviously being brought forward with charges.

"Welcome." Grand Duchess Calisto motioned me and Keith to stand before the council. "We have been waiting."

Keith and I shared a look, and he stepped forward first.

"Grand Council, I have come before you today to issue a formal complaint against Servalt, and request sanctions against Drendil for their part in kidnap-ping and trafficking."

There was a quiet mumble and a few shared looks among the council. Keith watched Duke Wyldon of Servalt, but the man did not refute. He even nodded for Keith to continue.

"Marquess Dorset of Servalt, a known offender, kidnapped and enslaved at least four people last evening," Keith began.

"We have dealt with Marquess Dorset already," Duchess Calisto informed us. "So you may speak your piece, but know that a [Truth] spell has verified his side of the story."

Keith acknowledged her grace and continued. "I was portaled to a trap pocket dimension, and only freed by Princess Henrietta hours later."

"Is this when Simon and Thalia fell?" Witch Agatha demanded. "Do you claim that you had nothing to do with it when you were found in the cell next to their bodies? Chadwick may have been tried with trafficking, but *you* stand accused of the murder of Drendil's king and queen."

"That"—Keith pushed up his glasses with a practiced move—"is because Marquess Dorset set up to frame me for their deaths. He was the one responsible, however. You may use [Truth] magic on me if you do not believe me."

All turned to Wizard Lorthar, who sighed and lifted a finger to cast a spell. "[Detect Lie]."

Gray magic swirled into a ball in his hand.

"Repeat that last part," the wizard ordered, and Keith obliged, explaining the shroomdoom, and the royals' untimely demise. The gray orb remained unchanged. Lorthar faced the council. "He speaks the truth."

Witch Agatha harrumphed. "You returned them too late to be revived, you know. How do you explain that?"

Keith spread his hands, innocently. "We had a trying evening, Witch Agatha. It was not our responsibility to repair the damage done by Servalt. I am not the ruler of North Sumbria, nor the victims' liege lord."

Witch Agatha turned piercing eyes on me. "What of you? Are *you* not responsible for this either?"

I stepped forward to stand beside Keith. "It is true that I did nothing to aid the king and queen of Drendil. But I am no longer a citizen of Drendil. Even *if* the council does not recognize my immigration to Nilheim, I would still be found not guilty of treason."

"Why is that, Princess?" Lorthar cut in, intrigued. He still held the truth-telling gray orb, confirming everything said. Witch Agatha short the wizard a glare but turned back to hear my answer.

"In Drendil, they do not legally recognize revival outside of the dungeons. And for all intents and purposes, legally, Simon and Thalia were no longer the king and queen when I arrived." Speaking my parents' names—without title, even—was a strange feeling. I ignored my discomfort as I continued.

"I would also like to make an official statement on what happened last night. As my parents were the ones who sold me to Marquess Dorset, they too were tricked by him. When I found Keith, slave traders working for the marquess were in the process of trying to pour molten ash vane on my mother and father."

The council all reacted to the mention of the poison. Grand Duchess Calisto turned to her neighbor in concern and whispered, "That is five times this year I've heard about molten ash vane popping up."

"I would also point out"—Keith waved at Chloe—"that just because the time for resurrection has passed, it does not mean they are gone forever. *If* the council agrees to my demands for justice, I would offer to [Raise] King Simon and Queen Thalia. They could live on, though stripped of their Royal title. We could also use this time to have them officially abdicate the throne."

"To *whom*?" Witch Agatha frowned. "The princess? She's not without a hand in this. How do we know it wasn't *her* idea all along? Working with Nilheim to overthrow Drendil, as King Simon and Queen Thalia always feared?"

I resisted the urge to violently reject the proposal, simply saying, "Please no. I gave up my right to inherit ages ago. I have a cousin; he can have it!"

Witch Agatha scoffed. "We all know that your cousin Francis is an incompetent louse."

"Agatha!" the Grand Pontiff spoke for the first time, his giant, bushy eyebrows raising. Not enough to see his eyes, though, so he wasn't truly scandalized. "We do not insult the misfortunate . . . Grand Duke Francis may have chosen

Intelligence as a dump stat, but he is still a person whom we as the council represent."

"Fine, yes, that wasn't *kind of me.* You know, the Witch of Winter's End, 'Oh, She of the Frozen Heart,' and 'The Cruel Sorceress of Ice,'" she mocked with a note of scorn. "Regardless of what you all think of me, what I said still stands. The boy is *not* fit to rule, and his son is too young."

Keith held up his hand and spoke, "What about a regent?"

CHAPTER 120

Witnessed!

Keith

Keith's words made everyone pause to consider.

Henrietta jumped on the chance. "A regent who could be trusted! There's one honorable enough, renowned for his valor and strength still living in Drendil. I'm sure between Knight Commander Havork and Aunt Beatrice, they could run the place just fine. Until Crown Prince Nathaniel comes of age?"

The princess took the opportunity to throw the entire mess at her mentor.

Keith was so proud.

Before anyone else could speak, Knight Commander Havork stepped forward and bowed deeply. "I cannot, for I am not worthy. After serving King Simon and Queen Thalia for so many years, I would beg the council leave to repent." He took a deep breath. "My oath to serve had become my undoing . . . and I have no regrets with my new title." He smiled sadly at Ria. "My only regret is not betraying my oath sooner."

"He speaks the truth," Wizard Lorthar stated, lifting his hand holding the gray orb. "And I'm beginning to question how Drendil has survived this long. *Who* doesn't want *power*? The crown princess and even its knight commander reject the throne. What's wrong with the place? How has Nilheim not overrun it ages ago?"

"There's nothing wrong with Drendil." Havork stood straighter. "Only with those who were in power for far too long."

"Isn't Knight Commander Havork here to be punished for his involvement in this debacle?" Their Royal Highness of Peldeep smiled a sly smile. "What better punishment than to serve as regent? The one thing he does not wish to do?"

"But I am an Oath Breaker," Havork protested. "I am unworthy, and I have lost my powers."

"There are ways to have your title removed," Keith put in dryly. "This is *the Valarian Council*. They have the power. Princess Henrietta was also going to request the council to review her Bond Breaker title."

"I'm sure we would all be happy to cancel your marriage contract when we get back, Princess," Wizard Lorthar stated. "But you knowingly killed the marquess. Title revisions are a serious matter! Not to mention that Chadwick, Simon, and Thalia have lost their titles already just by being dead."

"It is unprecedented to change more than one per meeting—" the Grand Pontiff started.

Their Royal Highness cut the old man off. "Point of order, it's not. In the weeks after the Sumbrian Civil War, we had to strip no less than seventy-four titles. That was before you stepped up as the new Grand Pontiff. I had the pleasure of stripping your predecessor of her title, actually."

"The point," Witch Agatha argued, "is that it's a lot of *work*."

"I don't have to get my title stripped," Henrietta offered, "if it'll be easier. My parents can be dethroned, and with Sir Havork made regent, I can just go on some quest or other to break it. Or just wait out the year."

Wizard Lorthar nodded sagely—or rather, *wizardly*, since he wasn't over level eighty or a Sage. "A quest. Good, good. That's the usual way of things. I approve."

"All in favor?" Duchess Calisto raised a hand.

"Wait!" Keith didn't believe what he was hearing. He grabbed Ria by the shoulders and searched her eyes. All he found was resolute conviction. He disagreed. "I don't *want* to go on a quest. I want to go home to our castle in the Dark Enchanted Forest and get married and live Happily Ever After."

Henrietta laughed and hugged him. But it wasn't her usual, about-to-destroy him, bone-crushing grasp. It was a gentle, firm touch that made him want to go and do terrible, unspeakable things to the marquess.

"Did you just ask me to marry you?" she asked, repeating her words from that time in front of the corpse roses.

Keith smiled down at his princess. Loudly, so that all in the atrium could hear, he spoke.

"Heroine of Justice, Henrietta Doryn of Nilheim." Keith bent down on one knee and pulled out an ornate spiral ring with enchanted sapphires that he'd personally made just for this moment. The largest sapphire in the center, a darker blue then the rest, he'd even managed to enchant with a +3 Constitution modifier.

He reached out and took her left hand, slipping the ring into place.

"From that first day you walked into my inner sanctum and didn't kill me, my life has been turned upside down. I've never told you"—Keith squeezed her hand—"but I was already suffering from [Mana Burn] at that time. One hit, and you could have gone home victorious."

"Really?" Ria asked, nervous and excited. "I would have won?"

Keith nodded. "Instead, I had the pleasure of spending time with you. Getting to *know* you. And falling in love with you."

"I love you too, Dark Magician King Keith." Ria's bright smile belied the tears in her eyes.

Keith reached up and tucked a brown lock behind her ear. "I want to spend the rest of my life with you. I want to drink tea in our man-eating flower garden and eat bimbleberry scones and file reports together in our office. I want to go on dungeon delves together. I can't imagine life without you anymore. Ria, will you marry me?"

"Yes!" She said, and then actually took the time to select the option on her notification tab.

Keith stood up to embrace her, and Henrietta grabbed Keith's collar with all of her Strength to pull him down for a kiss. Their Highness Rowen jumped to his feet, applauding. "Witnessed!"

Which was exactly when Keith's shirt ripped open, violently flinging buttons across the room.

CHAPTER 121

Your Line Ends with Me

Henrietta

[Requirement for the Marriage Agreement between the Kingdom
of Drendil and the Marquess Dorset: the eligible Princess Henrietta, is no longer valid.
Special Title: Bond Breaker is no longer Binding. Title lost.]

My Strength stat returned to its rightful level just as I kissed Keith. The contract had been made invalid when a member of the Valarian Council approved my marriage while I was still promised to another, and my long-time desire to rip open Keith's shirt had finally been fulfilled.

I wasn't expecting either, but I didn't complain. Instead, I kissed Keith passionately and with renewed fervor. We stood there in what felt like a timeless moment, clasped in the other's embrace. I was pretty sure my left foot lifted off the floor.

"Ahem-hm-hmm," Grand Duchess Calisto coughed when things went on longer than expected. "Congratulations, Princess Henrietta, Dark Lord Keith."

A few council members were glaring at Their Royal Highness for going forward with the motion before an official vote . . . but the ruler didn't seem to mind and accepted their ire with grace. I could only imagine the amount of paperwork they would be forced to fill out for helping us, and I smiled a thank you. They winked back.

"Now that that's settled"—the Duchess waved a hand at Chloe, sitting a few seats down the table—"I move that we finalize the matter with Drendil and then give the responsibility of cleaning up this mess to the new ruler. Any questions before the motion?"

No one said anything.

"All in favor of accepting Knight Commander Havork Everrond as Regent? Select [Yes/No]."

The council were all in agreement save a few who chose not to vote. Chloe was among those who'd abstained, due to a conflict of interest.

"As the hostess of this meeting, I will moderate the will of the council. This concludes the agenda." Grand Duchess Calisto thanked the members as they all stood and left. Duke Wyldon bowed, a small apology for the trouble I'd faced at the hands of his countryman.

Their Royal Highness Rowen winked at us as they walked by. "Remember, Keith, a *personal* invite!"

Regent Havork just stood there, looking shell-shocked. I held Keith's hand in mine but used my free hand to reach out and pat the old man on his shoulder. He slowly turned to stare at me, still processing what had just happened.

"Could you do me a favor?" I asked him, handing over the entire Drendil heirloom royal set. There were entire parts of the castle that could not be opened without the set, including sections of the royal suite. It wasn't exactly good of me to take parts of the ceremonial set when my parents sent me off to die . . . but I didn't regret my first moment of rebellion.

Havork took the pieces and nodded creakily. "What would you have me do?"

"Could you approve my cousin Francis's divorce?"

"Your cousin wants a divorce?"

"No, but his wife petitioned the courts last year. No idea how he captured her, but it would be lovely if you could free her and maybe grant her justice?" I sighed. "It was going to be the first thing *I* did if I ever became queen."

"Then it shall be done."

The grand duchess and Necromancer Chloe joined us, coming around to the front of the half-moon table. Calisto waved toward a door on the opposite side of the atrium from where the council had exited. "If you two are done, shall we visit Simon and Thalia?"

Chloe saddled up beside Keith as we all followed the duchess. "Rufus is going to have a field day with your proposal. 'When you didn't kill me' indeed."

She shook her head, her long golden hair catching the light. "At least Julia brought me somewhere *romantic*. Points for high drama and maximum formality, I guess. Godmother would be proud. It was very *you*."

"Chloe," Keith replied, "do you think Rufus will say yes when I ask him to be my best man?"

Keith laughed as a look of anger and utter betrayal warred across the young woman's face.

"You wouldn't! I'm obviously your right hand," she proclaimed with proud hauteur.

"You could be one of my bridesmaids?" I offered.

Chloe put a hand on her chest, further offended. "Not even the maid of honor? See if I get you anything fancy." She flounced ahead of us, then turned around and stuck out her tongue.

Havork trailed behind as we all followed Calisto into the side room containing my parents. They'd each been set on top of a prepared pair of small beds.

"What happened to Chadwick?' I asked, curious.

"He was charged long before you arrived. Duke Wyldon of Servalt is cooperating, and they've seized all of his assets. Chadwick is being imprisoned in the Baldorin mines. I owe you a set of Veralyn's Enchanted Restraint Manacles, as we portaled him away with yours still on him."

"That's not necessary." Keith's reply was quick and final. He could give up a pair knowing they were being put to good use. And he could always make more.

Everyone in the room turned to Regent Havork, to see what he would decide. He squared his shoulders and announced, "[Raise] them."

The duchess waved at her future daughter-in-law. "Necromancer Chloe, if you would do the honors?"

"My *pleasure.*" Chloe rubbed her hands menacingly before throwing her arms out, twiddling her fingers. "This will only give them a *chance,* though. As long as we are all aware? Depending on their willpower and desire, my [Raise] skill will assign them with an appropriately leveled Undead status."

"So they might come back as a wraith? Or a lich?" I asked.

Keith raised an eyebrow. His voice dripped with contempt as he said, "I strongly doubt that. I have my doubts that they'll have enough willpower to come back at all."

"What are you going to do with them?" the duchess asked. "As your undead, you'll control them. I doubt anyone on the council failed to notice that little trick in your request."

"I don't know . . ." I murmured. "But . . . I don't want to see them. Not for a long while, at least."

"Nilheim law will require us to release them as soon as possible," Keith answered. "Though they will still count as prisoners of the kingdom. I believe Henrietta wanted her parents to experience what it meant to be a *monster.* I was thinking they could spend some time in the army doing grunt work. Or they could always spend the next decade in the dungeons leveling up. They made a child do it, so I'm *sure* they have *no* qualms completing the same tasks *themselves.*"

"You could always send them back to Drendil," the grand duchess opined. "Let them taste what they built."

Keith and I shared *the look.* I'd been told married couples could speak with their eyes, and I was pleased to see that it worked for fiancés, too.

"That sounds like a wonderful plan, thank you," I agreed.

"Alright, I'm ready." Chloe closed her eyes as she concentrated. "Soil of the Earth that Connects the Flesh. Way of the Wind that Breathes Life in the Storm. Fire in the Soul, Hosted after Death. Blood that Binds, Return and Take New Form. [Raise]."

Glowing green mana pulsed from her fingertips and settled over my father. Chloe immediately repeated the spell, and the glow covered my mother as well. It was an anticlimactic way to lose everything; Drendil law was quite unforgiving to the undead. Mother would hate that.

We waited.

Simon Doryn of Drendil awoke first, moaning, his body shifting slightly. Soon after, Thalia sat up and stretched as if she were waking from a simple nap. Or rather, her *soul* sat up, leaving her body behind. When mother opened her eyes, they were black pits set in a spectral face, her "skin" now looking more like transparent white cloth than anything else. Her mouth hung open unnaturally wide, and her body wore the dress she'd died in, though now it was pure white and filled with ragged holes. My father grunted and sat up next, disoriented as he looked around. His eyes were yellow instead of white, and his skin had lost all its vibrancy. His gaze fell on me, and he immediately snarled.

The sound was as inhuman as he was. I'd gotten so used to the high-level undead in the castle that I was momentarily shaken. My father coughed and managed a broken, "Hen-ri! T-Traitor!"

"I should have known better than to expect anything else." Keith looked on in disgust. Not at how they looked, I presumed, as he was used to such things. He confirmed my thoughts by saying, "Though it doesn't surprise me that Thalia had more backbone than Simon. A basic zombie and ghost. Not good for much more than cemetery guard duty. Typical."

"What have you done?" my mother screeched, and I flinched from the pitch. She looked down at her patchy body in horror. "What am I *wearing?!*"

"Simon and Thalia Doryn of Drendil." Duchess Calisto drew their attention. "It is by order of the Valarian Council your fate was given to your people, and by the grace of those you have wronged, you have been permitted to live the rest of your natural life. For consorting with criminals, trafficking, and *so much more,* you will be returned to Drendil with Regent Havork and supervised until such a time as he feels you are ready to make a fresh start."

"What?!" My father glared at Havork. He was the first to get used to his new state, standing beside the bed to face the regent. "You! You betrayed us!"

"You betrayed your kingdom and your people," Havork replied with no remorse. "And you betrayed your own daughter."

"She cavorts with *monsters!*" Thalia declared, casting hate-filled eyes my way. "*Ooooh!* How will I ever match *anything* with this skin tone!"

My rebuke lodged in my throat.

Keith frowned, finally speaking to the pair. "I wouldn't throw stones. You are now what you have always discriminated against."

"What?!" Father demanded, looking down at himself. He still wore his fine button-up suit, though it showed all the signs of what had transpired.

"A *monster*." Keith grimaced. "Weak ones, at that. Though I hesitated to say it, as I believe you've both proven more monstrous than *any* of my own minions."

I gripped Keith's arm. He covered my hand with his own. I took a deep breath.

"Mother, Father."

Mother looked at me then pointedly away; she hadn't accepted things yet. Father already had that look in his eyes when he was searching for something to criticize.

"This is the last we will ever speak, so know this: I am disappointed to call you my parents," I told them. "You are *forbidden* from entering the Dark Enchanted Forest. I hope you live long lives, knowing that your line ends with *me*, for I am disowning you. Goodbye."

I pulled Keith's arm, and we both walked out.

The intangible weight of a lifetime of expectations and worry and grief slowly fell from my shoulders. No more *running away*. No more assassins in my sock drawer—though I'd still ask Keith to check every night before bed.

I was finally, truly, *free*.

I dragged my fiancé off to celebrate.

CHAPTER 122

There's No Help for It

Keith

Keith had a headache, and that headache's name was Chloe Watercress.

"WHAT DO YOU MEAN YOU'RE ELOPING?" She reached out and gripped Julia's arm for strength.

Grand Duchess Calisto had invited Henrietta and Keith to join Julia and Chloe and herself for dinner that evening, and everyone was talking about their plans moving forward.

"We just thought it would be easier on everyone if we quietly—" Henrietta began.

Chloe shot to her feet. "Easier? EASIER? When were you thinking of eloping?"

Keith, who was the most interested in forgoing a big wedding, answered, "June? Their Royal Highness was invited, so they could be our witness. We would be in Peldeep in time for the Sunstone Festival."

"That's in less than a month!" Chloe looked at her fiancée. "They can't do this. *I* can't do this."

"It'll be alright, love," Julia reassured her with a half smile. "I believe in you."

"There's no help for it!" Chloe placed the back of her hand gently to her forehead. "It'll have to be a dual wedding."

"What?!" Julia and Keith and Henrietta all shouted.

Chloe threw up her hands dramatically. "What else are we going to do? The king of the Dark Enchanted Forest *can't just elope*."

"But sharing our big day . . ." That was the first time Keith had ever seen the paladin pout. "Isn't there another way?"

Grand Duchess Calisto, who had remained silent until this point, coughed gently. The woman slowly smiled and raised a single eyebrow.

"Fine! You win!" Chloe threw up her hands. "You were right, Julia."

"I am?" Julia said, confused. Then she saw the pleased-as-punch look on her mother's face, and something clicked. "Wait—"

"I can't believe this. I can't believe you've talked me into this!" The necromancer turned and waged a finger at the Dark Lord, who had absolutely no idea what she was talking about. "Lake Loria is ready. It'll be *fine*. We can issue invites in person for . . . one month?"

Keith looked at Ria, who was suddenly blushing.

The necromancer started muttering about cake and wandered toward the doorway, everyone watching her leave.

"What's in one month?" Keith couldn't help himself and asked Julia. The woman was glaring at her mother.

Grand Duchess Calisto was the one who answered, looking pleased. "Your wedding, of course."

"The flowers aren't here! They were supposed to be here an *hour* ago. What are we going to *do*? Who do I have to murder to get a corpse rose around here? *Keith!*"

Keith walked up, dressed in his imposing Dark Lord's robes. His collar was a little rumpled and was hanging open.

Rufus walked up with a flattering array of Venus lily blooms to place on the small tables decorating the clearing. He passed a single corpse rose to Keith.

"I knew there was a reason you were my best man!" Chloe stated, delicately pining the peonies in place.

Keith teased, "I thought he was *my* best man."

"I asked him *first*," Chloe snapped. "Also, *I am your best man.* You are only *getting* a best man because I let you have *my* wedding, so it's only fair!"

Despite adamant arguing on his part, Chloe was determined to throw them a wedding, come rain or shine. And she had invited *everyone*. In exchange, the Grand Duchess of North Sumbria was going to host Chloe and Julia's wedding . . . and as Keith understood it, the wedding was going to be *exorbitant*. She would have a three-day celebration and then finish it with the Summer Masquerade.

They had arranged today's wedding around Her Eminence Feliwyn, who still lay napping beside Lake Loria. The ceremony would take place near the belly of the curled-up dragon. The aisle stretched between *hundreds* of people from all around Valaria, many who were in the process of taking their seats.

It was almost time for them to process.

They got into position, and Chloe walked Keith up the aisle.

Rufus escorted Bronwynn, and Chikli escorted Lilith just behind. Julia's brother was supposed to be in the wedding party, but a monster surge in the north had prevented him from attending, much to his mother's frustrations.

Calisto had *not* been pleased, but he was expected to come to Julia's wedding during Summer Masquerade or there would be *words*. The duchess and her daughter were seated in the front row.

Gimtak kept popping back and forth from the Dark Enchanted Forest castle to be sure that everything was fine after they had all abandoned work for the day.

Their Royal Highness Rowen of Peldeep was the officiant chosen by the council to approve the proceedings, and they were in fine form. A stately gentleman wearing all pink arachne silk.

Lady Amy cried into the arm of a young Lamia woman to her left, then she straightened, then she sniffed, then she burst into tears again and turned toward the guest to her right. Derilla Vane looked at the elf with confused, restrained violence as she blew her nose in his direction. Keith watched his arachne friend choose to offer her a new handkerchief instead of just eating her, for which the Dark Lord was grateful.

Keith wasn't looking forward to the inevitable spar Ria would have with Derilla before he returned to the mountains . . . but maybe it would give Keith a show of the arachne's new abilities before their own fight that winter.

Baby griffins flew overhead with aid from the Pixie Prim, dropping flower petals on everyone. They were an unexpected addition as well, and finding perches for their parents had been a fun last-minute [Crafting] on his part.

Bronwynn strummed her new lyre harp and began to pluck a delicate tune.

Keith hadn't visited Feliwyn in all these years, and he had argued holding the ceremony here. At that moment, he was glad they did so, as even a napping godmother at his wedding felt somehow *right*.

He leaned down to whisper, "Good job, Chloe."

She squeezed his arm hard. Not as hard as Henrietta, of course, but enough to show that she appreciated the compliment. They reached the front and took their positions before the napping dragon.

The music changed slightly, and Havork was there, escorting Henrietta up the aisle. She was beautiful, like always. Sweet and soft and lovely. Her dress had a corset-roped bodice and pleated skirts that fell to the knee on her right side but cascaded in waves down the floor over her left leg. She wore knee-high white leather boots. Keith swallowed thickly.

His princess, now his queen.

His *wife*.

CHAPTER 123

Happily Ever After

Henrietta

The reception was in full swing, and I was appreciating *my husband* from a distance as we both greeted guests.

The fact that Keith had let me rip out all of the buttons in his shirts the day we arrived home from North Sumbria reminded me why I loved him so much.

Not just because his clavicle was incredibly attractive, but that helped.

It was wonderful living with a person who celebrated all the things I loved. It was wonderful celebrating all the things *he* loved, even if that meant staying away from the inner sanctum for three days while he worked on interesting magical constructs.

I was distracted thinking about *my husband* when Sithli and Milith approached.

"Princesss." Sithli was beaming and holding a small bundle that was making adorable hissing noises. "May we introduce you to our first offspring? Her name is Ettalith."

"Henrietta doesn't really follow lizardkin naming conventionsss," Milith explained. "But we shortened it. As a thank you for sssaving our village from assassins."

"I did almost nothing," I protested, looking down at the tiny lizardkin babe. "She's beautiful, Milith."

"Thank you!" Sithli answered, pride written all over his face.

"Now we shall be off and let you get back to your big day." Milith dragged her husband away.

Chloe chose that moment to let me know it was time to cut the cake, so I grabbed Jacqueline and wandered over to find *my husband*.

"Rufus, I think you should just ask her out." Keith was standing beside Rufus as they drank from glasses full of bimbleberry cider. "Or better yet, ask her to marry you."

I came into the conversation at a most interesting moment. "Ask who?"

"My commander general is lusting after a certain *bard*." Keith wrapped his arms around me, and I leaned into his embrace.

"I don't know what you are talking about." Rufus crossed his arms defensively. "And *I* think you need a session in the dungeon if you think I'm doing *any* of that."

"Oh, *really*?" I took the opportunity to tease the beastman. "How long has this been going on?"

Rufus was following Minstrel Bronwynn around with his eyes and ears. As much as he might have wanted to defend his case, he was doing a bad job.

"Probably since the first time he saw her play." Keith laughed. He told Rufus, "I've known you since you were a *pup*. You can't tell me you don't like the bard."

Rufus gave Keith an exasperated sigh. "She's *Minstrel Bronwynn*. Of *course* I like her."

"Is *this* why you are still single?" Keith mused. "Because it sounds like this is why you are still single."

"*My king*." Rufus grabbed a glass for himself and downed the entire thing in a single gulp. "My queen. Congratulations on your wedding. I will excuse myself so you can continue to receive your other subjects' blessings."

"You can run away now," Keith told his friend, "but you better tell her before your quest, or it'll be too late."

Rufus waved off Keith's advice and walked off toward the seats closest to Minstrel Bronwynn.

"When is he going on the quest?" I asked *my husband*.

"He's already on it," Keith let me know. "He's just taking time off for today. As with every important quest, he's been tackling the paperwork first. After that, he'll be away for a while."

Someone from Nilheim needed to go investigate the merchants from Servalt who were operating in the Dark Enchanted Forest, and Chloe was planning her wedding. Keith also mentioned something about getting justice on the beastman for a silly prank . . . but he wasn't forthcoming with the details.

So I was in charge of keeping Keith alive and well while Rufus went on his own adventure. Luckily, it was easy to watch someone when you shared a room with them . . . and Keith had thought ahead and reinforced all the furniture in his suite . . .

Though my lounge had needed to be replaced last week, since he hadn't finished enchanting all of *my* furniture yet.

"I've been sent to let you know that it's time to cut the cake." I lifted Jacqueline, still sheathed, in my hands. Keith's eyes softened.

"I don't understand," he said, "what that has to do with Jacqueline."

My cheeks burned as I asked what I'd been thinking. "Well, she's feeling a little left out." Keith looked at where a huge, five-level round cake tower covered in frosted flowers and fresh bimbleberries sat on a table, surrounded by hungry guests. "And I was wondering . . . do you think we could use Jacqueline to cut the cake?"

He eyed the blade dubiously. "Will she [Void Damage] the cake?"

"Of course not." I vigorously shook my head, poofy hair falling loose. "That would be *rude*."

"Then, by all means." Keith reached out and pushed a bang behind my ear. "Let's go cut the cake with your kingdom-destroying, Void-artifact sword. Will there be tea with the cake?"

"Of course!" I assured him. "I picked out the brew myself, *and* I baked the cake. They were practically the only thing Chloe let me do."

The necromancer in question called to us from across the field. She was waving us over. It seemed I'd taken too long to summon Keith, and we were needed.

I smiled up at my husband. "Keith. I love you."

"I love you too, Ria."

The Heroine of Justice held the Dark Lord's hand, and they went off to drink tea and eat cake and live Happily Ever After.

The End.

Even More Dungeons, Dragons, and Debutantes

A notification tab blinked.

[Quest Complete: Survive Season One of Dungeon Delves and Debutantes]
Welcome to the World of Valaria, an Open-World Battle Otome RPG for the ages.
100% Scenarios Completed
100% Map Explored
90% Hidden Treasures Found
76% Characters Found
In Season One, our Heroine worked hard to kill the Dark Overlord and defeat his minions. After overcoming her traumatic past with the help of her love interests, she finally picked a partner for Duchess Calisto's Spring Ball . . . but is she ready to take the next step?

[Quest Update: Survive Season Two of Dungeon Delves and Debutantes]
Welcome to the World of Valaria, an Open-World Battle Otome RPG for the ages.
Season Two features three new ikemen love interests, new dungeons, accessories to Servalt and Sumbria, and new crafting material. But beware the threats of revenge, for a new power rises. And our Heroine will have even more at stake than she bargained for.
0% Scenarios Completed
37% Map Explored
1% Hidden Treasures Found
43% Characters Found

Come back to your favorite characters with even more Dungeons,
Dragons, and Debutantes!

Luckily, Henrietta was starting her own new adventure completely different from the original. She deserved happiness.

As for the rest . . . Well, between magic, foresight, and the treasures, it *should* be enough.

Sigh.

Cheering.

"Which tea would you like with your slice of cake?"

About the Author

Mystic Neptune was born and raised on an island surrounded by temperate rain-forests, lakes, mountains, and endless ocean. She started writing books when she was twelve, and by the age of fourteen she'd written her first novel. It was about an elven space princess whose evil stepmother messed up her trans-dimensional portal trip to university and sent her to a war-torn restricted universe instead. It was very cheesy, and the ultimately-nine-book series was lost forever on the family PC (Windows 95, anyone?) that died a very final death the summer she was sixteen.

By then, Mystic was living with her very sick single mother and her little brother, and working nights to help pay the bills. There was a little time to read during her school breaks, but not for much else—and no money to replace the home computer. So she filled notebooks with the beginnings of stories and eventually got a laptop in college. Around that time, she also met the love of her life, who read just as much as she did, and they got married shortly after a terrible accident befell her . . .

One day when Mystic was walking to the mall, an iron fence from a construction site fell on her. She suffered from amnesia so bad that she had to relearn English and re-meet all her friends and family. She even walked past her mother in the street and didn't recognize her. But it's OK! She got better!

Once she could read again, Mystic got into isekai because she was tired of picking up books only to remember she'd already finished them. Isekai was new at the time, so she didn't need to worry that her silly memory would come back halfway through a story and spoil the ending. Mystic enjoys reading light novels, webnovels, LitRPG, gamelit, and fantasy. She also loves middle grade and YA books. Her favorite authors/heroes are Patricia C. Wrede, Tamora Pierce, and Diana Wynne Jones.

In Mystic's spare time, she writes and does edit-swap date nights with her husband, Jolly Jupiter. O he of famed dwarven comedy! She also runs after her daughter, Phoebe Vaara. Phoebe is named after Saturn's moon, and Vaara means Danger in Finnish and Stranger in Greek. Phoebe is a rockstar social diva toddler who hikes mountains and has more friends than both her parents combined, so it fits.

Mystic is probably writing right now.

DISCOVER
STORIES UNBOUND

PodiumAudio.com

www.ingramcontent.com/pod-product-compliance
Lightning Source LLC
Chambersburg PA
CBHW030920120726
47906CB00002B/419